Otis

CORAL CANYON COWBOYS

LIZ ISAACSON

ISBN-13: 978-1-63876-119-8

1

Otis Young pulled up to the address his truck had navigated him to, already admiring the house. It looked as good in real life as it had on a computer screen, and he knew in that moment that he'd be purchasing this home.

"Look, baby," he said to his daughter who rode in the back seat. "It has a tire swing in the tree."

"Can I swing on it, Daddy?"

"Sure," he said without thinking too hard about it. He'd done all of his heavy thinking in the recording studio that day. The executives from the label would be here next week, and Otis wished he'd made this move already.

"We have to wait for Dave," he said, putting his truck in park. "Plus, there's still a lot of snow in the yard, and you're not wearin' your boots." Moving in the winter would be terrible, and Otis once again blamed Mother

Nature and the whole state of Wyoming for why he still lived in the rental close to the center of Coral Canyon.

This house sat on the northern boundary of the town, in a cute neighborhood—the last one before the highway became faster and only apple orchards separated Dog Valley from Coral Canyon. If he bought this home, he'd only be fifteen minutes from his brother's ranch, fifteen minutes from his ex-wife's house, and fifteen minutes from Joey's school.

It was perfect, and he almost didn't care what the inside looked like. He'd seen the inside of Tex's farmhouse—the house where he and all the Young boys had grown up, Otis included—when he'd first bought it. He and his son had ripped everything out and remodeled and renovated.

Otis could do the same thing to this house should it need it. The location was what he needed, because Lauren, his ex-wife, wasn't well and wasn't getting any better. He didn't have the greatest relationship with her—they weren't Mav and Portia—but they'd sat down over the holiday break and decided that Joey should come live with Otis full-time.

He wasn't touring with his country music band right now. He was living in town anyway, still tweaking and perfecting the music he and his brothers would start recording next week, when the producers from their record label showed up.

He'd been driving Joey to school since last fall, picking

her up, and taking care of her anyway. At this point, she barely slept at her momma's anymore, and Otis didn't like dropping her off there. He had a much bigger support network, and his parents or his brothers had no problem stepping in and helping with his seven-year-old.

"What do you want to do for your birthday, Roo?" he asked her as they waited for Dave to show up. "Let me guess: A cake shaped like a book. No, a rainbow." He grinned at her in the rearview mirror, her fair face lit from within.

His precious daughter would be eight in a couple of weeks, and Otis hadn't heard Lauren say one thing about it. He wasn't going to bother her with it. He'd get all the presents, the cake, the balloons, everything, and make sure Joey had an amazing birthday.

"Can we still go roller skating?"

He'd forgotten about that, but he said, "Yeah, of course."

"Can I invite Mya and Timmy and Eleki?"

"Yes," Otis said, starting to feel like he'd jumped into the lake up the canyon a bit, and the water was freezing and dragging him under by his sopping wet clothes.

"That's what I want to do," she said. "All the cousins can come, of course. And the uncles."

He grinned as he looked out the window. "Of course," he murmured. He'd already gotten over a dozen texts that morning, all from Joey's uncles. They each wanted to know the moment he bought a house, which one it was, and when he could move in. They weren't being nosy. Otis liked to call it *supportive*, and when he got tired of answering their texts and questions, he withdrew from them a little.

Everyone did it; he just happened to be the quietest about it. It helped that he didn't have all the eyes on him the way Tex did. As he thought of his oldest brother, he remembered Tex's wife had also texted him, and Otis hadn't responded.

He picked up his phone and quickly sent a message back to Abby, telling her he was currently waiting at the first house, and yes, it looked nice. She worked at the library in town, and she didn't always have access to her phone, especially if she was in a meeting.

He sighed and rested his head against the cold window, his thoughts going somewhere they shouldn't.

Beck's Books.

The quaint bookshop on Main Street, stuck between the post office and one of Otis's favorite barbecue joints, Bam Bam's. So *of course* he had to go by there often. Joey liked to read, and Otis wanted his daughter to be happy. Not only that, but he had things to mail all the time, and his hankering for brisket could keep him up at night until he satisfied his cravings.

The real craving was another taste of Georgia's lips. She'd called him into her office once, late last summer, and she'd demanded he pretend to be her boyfriend and kiss her. Then *she'd* kissed *him*, and wow, Otis had not minded that one bit.

It was pretend, he told himself for probably the eight hundredth time in the past six months. It obviously hadn't meant anything to Georgia, who'd never called him again for help with her ex, and who'd started for-real dating someone else very soon after that.

Movement in his rearview mirror caught his eye, and Otis said, "Here we go, Roo. He's here." He unbuckled and got out of his truck, opening the back door to help his daughter down.

Dave apologized for being a few minutes late, they shook hands, and Dave led Otis up the cleared driveway to the house. The sun shone today, glinting off the snow in the yard. "The driveway is heated," he said. "As is the front sidewalk. It's nice for small storms, and it helps with the bigger ones too."

Otis looked at the decorative stone in the driveway and leading up to the front door. It wasn't regular cement, and it felt too uppity to him. Was he the type of man who owned a house with a heated driveway?

Dave went on about the double-wide oak doors, the reclaimed barn wood shutters, and how the pillars were original to a historic home that had unfortunately burned beyond saving about five years ago.

Otis didn't care about any of that, so he said nothing. He wanted somewhere that felt safe to him. Somewhere Joey could have her friends over, she could keep practicing the piano, she could have a little book nook with a bean bag so she could curl up and read while he worked on his song-writing. Or whatever.

Dave unlocked the house with a code, and he opened the door. He didn't lead the way in. He smiled at Otis and said, "You two go on in. Look around. Gather your questions. We'll talk in a few minutes."

Otis hadn't been expecting that. When he'd searched for rentals last summer, the landlords always hovered only twelve inches away, anxious to assure him that everything worked properly and what didn't would be fixed or wasn't their fault.

He peered into the house, took Joey's hand in his, and went up the single step into the foyer. Yes, this house had a legit foyer. It wasn't one of those huge sprawling mansions on the southeast side of Coral Canyon, but this house dripped with wealth.

Not in square feet. Not even in land, as the lot was only a half-acre. That was enough for Joey to set up a tent in the backyard during the summer and to roller skate around the front driveway—well, she could do that year-round, what with that heating system beneath it.

The house boasted four bedrooms and four baths, and Otis knew instantly that it had been designed by someone with an eye to use every space as wisely as possible. An office led left off the foyer, and he could see his collection of guitars there. His piano. All his sheet music. To the right from the foyer waited a small mudroom, with shelves and lockers for boots, hats, gloves, and backpacks. No one did that off a front entrance, but Otis loved it. He didn't want messy, muddy boots just left on the tile to rot, and he hated picking up all of Joey's things from where she happened to drop them after school.

From where he stood, he could see into a family room large enough to hold a couch and love seat, television, and a rocking chair. The kitchen sat behind that, with a long, long island where he could probably feed all of his nieces and nephews. A dining room table stood right in front of him, and he could see out the back door, which slid open into the back yard.

A sense Otis could only describe as *home* washed over him, making him warm from head to toe in less than a breath. It felt like God had taken a blanket straight from the dryer and wrapped it around his shoulders, whispering, *You're home, Otis. You're home, and I'm right here with you.*

He turned around and opened the front door again. "I'll take it," he said to a very surprised Dave.

"Really?" the real estate agent asked.

"If I pay cash, will they skip the appraisal?" he asked, meeting the man's shocked blue eyes. "And if they do, and I pay cash, when can I move in?"

Otis circled the block again, wondering why so many dang people needed to use the post office in the middle of the afternoon on a Thursday. He just wanted to dip into the bookstore and get Joey a gift.

For real.

He wasn't even going to see Georgia Beck. He hadn't the last five or six times he'd casually stopped by for some light reading for his daughter, and he couldn't expect this time to be different.

Georgia knew and was real friendly with Abby, but Otis hadn't seen her out at the ranch at all. Abby hardly talked about her friends with him or any of the other brothers, but Otis's heart pounded hard as he saw a car backing out of a spot only a few yards in front of him.

He flipped on his blinker and waited for the woman to back out and vacate her space. Then he quickly pulled into it, thrilled with how close to Beck's Books he'd gotten. He wasn't right in front of it, but a quick glance to the right showed a new window display since the last time he'd been here. He wondered if Georgia or her assistant did those as he picked up his phone, then his wallet, and then pressed the button to turn off his truck.

He still didn't get out, something strange keeping him in his seat. A woman came out of the shop, a brown paper bag in her hand with the embossed double B on it Otis has seen lots of times, usually on his own bag of books he'd bought.

Most people on the street right now seemed to be

frequenting the post office, and after another couple of breaths, Otis felt like his legs would support him enough to walk. And walk he did, right up onto the curb, down the street a bit, and through the door of the bookshop.

The bell dinged, a high-pitched sound that echoed through the shop. No one came to greet him, as they had in the past. The shop waited in silence, and Otis froze, his footsteps suddenly too loud.

"Be right there," someone called, and his heart jackhammered through his ribs as it tried to flee his body.

That was Georgia's voice.

He suddenly couldn't get his to work, and Otis reminded himself that he'd been out with women before. This wasn't even a date, and he scoffed at himself as he stepped over to the bestsellers shelf as if he cared about any of the titles there.

He had, in fact, forgotten why he'd come in here at all. His mind fuzzed, and then he remembered Joey. Of course. Joey. He wanted to get her the new limited-edition collection of the Animal Hunters books she loved so much.

Rounding the bookshelf, the kids' section came into view. In that moment, a terrific crash filled the air at the shop, startling Otis enough to kick his pulse into high gear. "Hello?" he called, now striding with purpose toward the back of the shop where he knew a hallway waited.

It came into view, but no one responded to him. "Georgia?" he called this time, and again, got no answer.

He hurried down the hall and looked in her office. She wasn't there. Another foot or two down, another doorway on his right showed him a huge storage room, with bookshelves around the outside of it, and standing down the middle.

The scent of paper and cardboard hung heavily in the air, and Joey would love that. She'd stand here and say, "Can you smell it, Daddy? It smells like adventure." She wasn't one who loved to go hiking, skiing, or fishing. She preferred her outdoor experiences to come from the books she read, and Otis had long ago given up trying to get her to go play outside. Instead, he hung a hammock in the yard and let her read outside.

"Georgia," he called, knowing he'd heard her voice.

A moan sounded somewhere, and Otis spun back toward the hall, the sound clearly coming from behind him. "*O—tiiis.*"

"Where are you?" he called. "Georgia? Where are you?" He dodged back over to her office, but she wasn't there. His panic picked up speed, like a runaway train, and that was when he noticed the spilled books and toppled cart beside her desk.

Yes, this place was a mess, but Georgia would never leave books on the floor. He ran toward her desk, her legs coming into view. "Georgia!" He knelt beside her, the sight of her passed out, her eyes closed and her head bent at an odd angle against the wall haunting and terrible.

"Georgia," he said, pressing his palm to her stomach. "Wake up, honey. It's Otis Young, and I'm right here."

Her eyelids fluttered, and Otis's hope took flight. "That's right. Wake up."

Georgia opened her eyes, but they didn't focus on him right away. She blinked, her eyebrows drawing down into a V. Then those gorgeous blue-green eyes that had been teasing and taunting him for weeks locked onto his.

"Otis?" she asked.

2

Georgia Beck had no idea how she'd gotten on the floor. Her head sent a throb of pain through her skull to the spot right between her eyes, and she groaned.

"You fainted," Otis Young said, and she had no idea how the man kept getting himself into her office. Her lips tingled, betraying her, at his presence. Sure, she'd seen him around town. At church. Once from a few aisles over at the grocery store. Driving around with his brothers.

"I fainted?"

"Yeah," he said. "Best that I can reckon, at least. I heard this terrible crash, and I called but no one answered."

Georgia sat up—or she tried. Her body didn't feel like it currently had any operating muscles, and Otis thankfully put his hand on her back and helped her sit all the way up. "There you go," he said. "You okay?"

The care and compassion in his voice rang loudly in her ears. James had never spoken to her like that. His stern tone and set-in-his-ways routines were just two of the reasons Georgia had broken up with him before Christmas.

She did miss him.

No, she told herself as she reached up to touch the back of her head. *You miss being with someone. Not him.*

Yes, she went to lunch with her friends. She worked hard here at the bookshop, and she currently had her assistant living with her. Harper had fallen on some hard times with her own significant other, and she'd lost her condo in the break-up. Georgia could admit she really liked going home when she didn't have to walk into a silent house, darkness, and her scowling cat staring at her from atop the refrigerator.

"Georgia?" Otis asked, and her brain sharpened. She looked at him, and the world stopped. It didn't matter that she'd fainted for some unknown reason. Or that her back ached in a whole new way that didn't come from hauling cases of books from the storage room to the showroom. Or that her stomach grumbled at her for something to eat.

Only Otis existed, with those black-as-coal eyes, that jaw that almost took on an angle, and the scent of his strength and power. He smelled like wood smoke and safety, and Georgia wanted to curl into his warmth.

She remembered kissing this man in vivid detail, right down to what he tasted like. How could she not? Their fake kiss was still the very best one of her life, and she shivered as her eyes broke the connection with his only to land on that mouth.

"Hey," he said tenderly, gathering her into those arms so easily, like he did it every single day of his life. She wished, and oh, she wished mightily. "It's okay. You're shaking."

She did tremble for another moment, and then she stilled. "I don't know what happened," she murmured. "I was standing here, going through the books on the cart. I'm redoing one of the display shelves out front."

"Mm hm." Otis didn't release her, and Georgia had no idea how her arm had gotten up and around his, her hand resting lightly on his shoulder. All she knew was that she liked touching him.

"I thought—*I'm hungry. I should get lunch.* And then...I don't know. My stomach sort of swooped a little. I yelled to someone, I think? Someone came in the shop?" She pulled away from him slightly, her eyes now searching his.

"You called to me," he whispered, his throat working hard as he swallowed, almost like he had a ball of sand he was trying to get down. "Then I heard the crash a few seconds later."

She nodded, because that sounded right. "I got sweaty in like, an instant. I thought—*I should sit down.* Then I remembered I had a customer, and...well, that's all I remember."

"You fainted," he said again. "I came running, but I couldn't find you for a few seconds."

"How long do you think I was out?"

"A minute?" he guessed. "I looked in here, but you were behind the desk. So I ducked over to the storage room, but you weren't there either. Then you...." He cleared his throat and looked away.

Georgia needed to stand up. Her hip couldn't keep getting twisted this way. She groaned, and Otis put both arms around her and, with the help of him and the desk, Georgia got to her feet. She kept both palms pressed into it, and Otis did not remove his hand from her back.

"Okay?"

"Yeah," she said, the kink in her hip working itself out. "Thanks." She sighed, her head still a little light.

"You haven't had lunch?"

"No," she said, looking at him again. "What time is it?"

"Honey, it's almost time for me to go pick up my daughter from school. It's after two-thirty." Only concern existed in his eyes, and a love-hate battle started within Georgia. She loved that he was concerned for her, but at the same time, she hated people fussing over her.

"You okay?" he asked, stepping back and dropping his hand.

"Yes," she said with a nod.

"Is lunch here?" he asked.

She shook her head. "I was just going to go down the street and get whatever sounded good."

"What sounds good?" He pulled out his phone as if he could make all of her favorite dishes appear with a few texts. Knowing him, he probably could.

You don't know him, she told herself. One kiss did not make them friends. Or dating. Or anything. In truth, she knew very little about Otis Young, other than he was Otis Young, a talented singer-song writer who'd grown up here in Coral Canyon, the same way she had.

He was three or four years younger than her, and she pressed her eyes closed in an attempt to get her brain to stop regurgitating the information she knew about this man.

"Yeah," Otis said. "I'll call the school. Thanks, Luke." The sound of his voice brought Georgia back to the present.

She opened her eyes and looked at him. "I think I need to go home." If he suggested he take her to the hospital, she'd claw his eyes out. She wasn't going to go there. Never, ever again was she going to go to the hospital.

"Yes, you do," he said with the flicker of a smile. "But first, you're going to sit right down here on the floor." He eased her back to the ground without waiting for her consent. "I'm going to go get some food for you, and you're going to call me if anything goes awry. Anything at all."

He crouched in front of her, his eyes set on Very Serious. "Where's your phone?"

"Uh, the desk?" Georgia reached up and brushed her errant curls off her forehead.

"Got it," he said after twisting and reaching up to her desk. "I'm going to put my number in it, and you're going to hold it with my contact info on the screen. You're going to call me if you feel faint or sick or anything at all." He tapped and swiped as he did it, and a moment later, Georgia held a great prize in her hand.

Her phone with his number in it.

He put his fingers under her chin and lifted her face up toward his. "Tell me I'm okay to go."

"You're okay to go," she said, her brain fog clearing even further. "Really, Otis, I'm okay."

"I'm going to get you some food," he said. "There's a bottle of water right here. You sip on that."

She started to get up as she said, "I can get—" but Otis put his heavy hand on her shoulder.

"Georgia," he said, those eyes not playing games with her now. The fire in them did lick through her, bringing excitement and danger. Oh, how she needed some of both of those things. "If you get up, I'm taking you to the hospital, not going to get something to eat. You choose."

She glared at him. "I'm not going to the hospital."

"Then will you please sit right there and wait for me to get back? I'll be incredibly fast, and I'm already on the screen. All you have to do is tap." He nodded to the phone, and sure enough, it was on, with his name sitting there, his number underneath it. All she had to do was touch the green phone icon, and she'd call him.

"Okay," she said.

"Thank you." He leaned down and pressed a kiss to her forehead, sending a shockwave of sparks and heat down to her toes. "I'll be right back." He straightened, nodded once, and strode out of her office.

Georgia watched him go, marveling at how quickly her afternoon had changed from a mundane one where she redid the display shelves for the fiftieth time that year—and it wasn't even the second week of January—and contemplated closing the shop early, to sitting in her office waiting for Otis Young to bring back a late lunch.

She sighed and leaned her head back against the wall. A twinge of pain scampered down her neck, and Georgia reached up with her free hand and began to probe her skull. She'd fainted and fallen. She had to have a goose-egg somewhere.

After searching every centimeter of her scalp, she still hadn't found anything. No blood. No bumps. "A miracle," she whispered. It was also a miracle that she hadn't been in the shop alone when she'd fainted. If she had, who knew how long she'd have laid there, cold and alone and injured?

She didn't want to think about that.

Her phone rang, startling her, and she glanced at it. Abby's name sat there, and tears jumped to Georgia's eyes. She swiped on the call and said, "Hey, Abs."

"Where are you?" she demanded. "Are you okay? I can be there in ten minutes." She sounded like she was running, and Georgia suspected she was on her way to her office to get her car keys.

"I'm in my office, Abs," she said. "I'm okay." She closed her eyes, the warm touch of air from the furnace brushing her skin. "How did you know I was hurt?"

"Otis called me," she said, her voice slowing with each word. "Are you sure you're okay?"

"Otis went to get food," she said. "I just need to eat. I haven't...."

"You didn't eat again," Abby stated, not asking. "Georgia."

"I know," Georgia said, annoyed with herself and not needing a lecture. "Listen, Abby." She lifted her head and opened her eyes as she looked toward the open office doorway. "Do you believe in...I don't know. Fate? Kismet?"

"What do you mean?" Abby was no longer rushing, which meant she wouldn't come to the shop. She would most definitely be at Georgia's house tonight, probably with a lot of food. She'd even section it off into individual lunch-sized portions, each in their own container, so Georgia had no excuse not to eat on time.

"I mean...I have to tell you something."

"Okay."

"So Otis was in the shop today, right?"

"Yeah, Tex said he stopped to get a book for Joey's birthday."

Georgia nodded, though Abby couldn't see her. "Remember that mystery cowboy I kissed last fall? The one who helped me get CJ out of my life for good?"

"Yes," Abby said, and then she sucked in a horribly loud breath. "Georgia, tell me that wasn't Otis Young."

Georgia shrugged one shoulder, her voice weak and mouse-like as she said, "It was Otis Young."

"By the Dewey Decimal System," Abby said, her voice shocked and full of air. "Georgia. Why didn't you tell me?"

"Because," Georgia said. "Then you'd start swearing in Librarian language instead of helping me figure out what to do."

Abby remained silent for a moment, and Georgia didn't like that. A silent Abby meant a thinking Abby, and Georgia didn't need her thinking too hard about this. "Why do you need to figure out what to do?"

"Because," Georgia whispered. "I liked kissing him, okay? I *liked* it. I like *him*. But then I start dating this other guy—who was a total idiot and so not right for me—and then months later. *Months*, Abs, I pass out and who's there? Who's the *only* person in my shop?"

"I'm back," Otis said, and Georgia looked up at him, her eyes wide and every organ in her body storming at her to hang up and hang up now.

"Otis," she said at the same time she lowered the phone, answering him and her own question.

"Georgia!" Abby cried. "Don't you dare hang up on—"

Her voice cut off as Georgia ended the call.

Otis looked at it and then her as he came closer. "Everything all right?" He got down on the floor and parked himself right next to her, his shoulder touching hers and everything.

"Yes," she whispered.

He nodded to the phone, which still showed who she'd been talking to for the past four minutes and thirteen seconds. "Talkin' to Abby, I see." He handed her a warm plastic container that smelled like heaven in mashed potato form.

She didn't have to say yes. The evidence stared them both in the face.

"I called her," Otis said. "To make sure you didn't have any food allergies." He popped the top on his barbecue container, the spicy scent of Bam Bam's signature sauce joining the party on the floor in her office.

"Ah." Georgia nodded. "Makes sense."

"You didn't tell her about us...you know. Kissing last year. Did you?" He looked at her, something scared in his expression.

"No," she said, her stomach heavy though she hadn't eaten since last night. He nodded and went back to his food, but she had to tell him. Abby could be relentless, and now that she knew the mystery cowboy was Otis.... Georgia didn't want him walking into a war zone out at that ranch where he recorded music with his brother, Abby's husband.

"I didn't tell her about that until just now."

Otis made a slight squeaking noise and yanked his attention back to her. "Why would you do that *now*?"

"Because," Georgia said, emotions streaming through her like kite tails caught in a strong wind. She stirred her pulled pork into her potatoes and lifted a bite. She wouldn't take it until the words inside her mouth made room for the food. She offered Otis a tiny smile that fled as soon as it touched her lips.

He searched her face, alarm and resignation mingling there. Georgia drew from his strength and reminded herself that just because she'd fainted didn't mean she was weak. "I told her now, because once we start dating, she'll find out anyway."

Otis blinked at her rapidly. "We're gonna start dating?" She wasn't sure if he was intrigued or horrified.

Georgia shrugged that same single shoulder she had while on the phone with Abby. "Maybe," she said. "If you play your cards right." With all the words—flirty words too, which made Georgia smile internally—out of her mouth, she could finally take a bite of her lunch.

Otis remained quiet for several long seconds while they both ate. Then he said, "I'm pretty good at cards. The best out of anyone in the band." He looked at her, and she looked at him, and this time, there was no doubt in her mind that his eyes fired desire and attraction at her.

"Great," she said. "Let's see what happens then."

3

Otis didn't like the welcome wagon sitting on his brother's front porch. He frowned at Abby and Bryce, wondering how long they'd been conspiring to ambush him. "At least a couple of days," he muttered to himself.

Georgia had passed out two afternoons ago, and Otis hadn't been out to Tex's since. He'd stayed with her that afternoon, followed her home, made sure she got inside all right, and then awkwardly backed his way out of her front door. She had two dogs and two cats who came to greet him. Well, one of the cats had stayed on top of the fridge, glaring at him like he was the reason the world was so cold in Wyoming in January. He would not want to meet that cat down a dark alley. No sirree.

Just like he didn't want to get out of his truck and talk to Abby or Bryce.

He'd spent yesterday talking to his realtor as they went back and forth on the house, when he could get the cash to purchase it, and how to expedite the process. He had gone by the bookshop just before he had to pick up Joey from school, but Georgia hadn't been there.

He'd dropped off a check for a hefty down payment to get paperwork started that morning, and he expected to be able to move the first week of February. Not quite thirty days, but he and Joey would still be in the rental for her birthday. He'd told her last night, and since the only thing that would upset Joey was the extinction of rainbows and unicorns, she'd chirped, "It's fine, Daddy. We're goin' roller skating anyway."

He'd then had to call the roller rink to find out how to do a birthday party there, and that had eaten away a couple of hours this morning too. Otis struggled to breathe under the weight of full-time fatherhood. He had no idea how to pull off a little girl's birthday party, but he'd die before he disappointed Joey.

"Daddy," she drawled at him from the passenger seat. "Why are we just sittin' here? Aunt Abby is waving at us to come in."

He blinked and looked left. Sure enough, Abby looked like she was bringing in a freight plane, and Otis reached to unbuckle his belt. "Go on," he said to Joey. "I'm going to head out to the studio."

Tex had built a recording studio in his backyard. He'd bought the family ranch where they'd all grown up, and the studio looked like a big, white barn about a hundred yards behind the house. He'd put in a sidewalk, and it had been shoveled and snow-free all winter.

As Joey slid from the truck, Otis plucked his phone from the cup holder and sent Abby a text. *I'm not answering any questions about Georgia.*

He wasn't either. He hadn't asked her out. She hadn't called or texted him, so technically, he didn't even have her number. She had his. That was all.

The ball sat in her court, and Otis honestly didn't know if she'd pick it up and start bouncing it or not. A sigh leaked from his mouth. He hated this part of the dating game. He always felt like the last cowboy chosen, and he only got picked because the teams were uneven, and no one could play if he didn't have a date.

His last girlfriend had ghosted him when they were supposed to have lunch together. *Ghosted* him, like he wasn't even worth talking to. His chest squeezed tight, tighter, and Otis took a deep breath to try to get it to expand properly.

The feelings of unworthiness, of being so inferior to literally everyone else in his life, of thinking something was inherently wrong with him, flooded over him. He tried to swim against the tide, but anyone who's ever been caught in the waves would know how futile his efforts were.

He simply let them wash over him, and they confirmed why Georgia hadn't called or texted yet. She wasn't really interested. He was a convenience. Just someone who was in the right place at the right time for a kiss. It hadn't meant anything to her, and Otis's lips betrayed him by tingling.

He reached up and wiped his mouth as Abby responded. *You think avoiding me will help?*

Holding Abby Ingalls back was like trying to rope the sun and pocket it without getting burned. He looked back to the house, and she stood there, frowning first at her phone and then him. He rolled his eyes, his head, his shoulders, and got out of the truck.

He held up one hand. "I'm not seeing her. We're not dating. It was one stupid kiss from six months ago."

Abby cocked one hip and shoved her hands in her coat pockets. She said nothing as he continued down the side-walk toward her. Their eyes never left one another. "She's my best friend," Abby finally said.

"You say that with such warning in your voice," Otis said. It was his turn to frown. "I'm not going to hurt her." He started to go by her, because it was too dang cold to have this conversation outside. At least Bryce had taken Joey into the house, so he didn't have to do this in front of either of them.

"Otis." She put one hand against his chest, preventing him from moving past her. "You don't know who you are."

"I know exactly who I am," he shot back. His emotions spiraled, and dang it all, his eyes stung. He would not cry.

Not in front of his sister-in-law. He knew her well enough, but she didn't get to know everything.

He wanted to say more, but he didn't trust his voice. Thankfully, Abby never held her opinions back, and she said, "Georgia falls really hard and really fast, Otis. You have to be careful with her."

Otis rolled his eyes again. "Let's recap, okay?" Praise the heavens, his voice came out normal. "*She* pulled me into her office and kissed me. I didn't do it. Then, she never called me about it. We literally never spoke again until two days ago."

Abby took her glaring up a notch, but Otis pressed on. "Then, she passes out in her office, and I was just there again. Tryin' to help. I gave her my number so I could go get food and she could call if she needed anything. Has she used it?"

His sister-in-law's tough demeanor started to crumble.

"Nope," he said. "I don't actually *have* her number, Abby. I stopped by the shop to talk to her yesterday, but she wasn't there. I'm not sure what else you think I should do." He went around her and up the steps, pure humiliation pouring through him. So fragile and tipsy were his emotions that he couldn't stop himself from saying, "Don't worry, okay? She won't fall for me, Abby. No one does."

He wanted to suck the words back in the moment they left his mouth. They were true, but he didn't need Abby's pity. He didn't want her fretting over him, and he certainly didn't want her talking to Tex about him.

The front door opened as he gained the porch, and Tex stood there. His taller, wiser, more talented older brother. Living in Tex's shadow had annoyed Otis for the first two decades of his life. The past fifteen years hadn't been so bad, though, and so Otis wouldn't blurt out something else embarrassing, he strode right into his brother's arms and clapped him on the back.

"Howdy, brother," he said.

"I was just comin' to see what was taking you so long." Tex grinned at him as he stepped back. "Abs? What are you doing out here?" Tex went around Otis and down the steps. "Why aren't you at work?"

Otis knew why, and he glared at Abby at the bottom of the steps. She glared on back, then broke their connection as she looked at her husband. He didn't wait around to hear what she said to Tex. He went inside and closed the door, because he could distinctly hear his mother's voice yelling in his mind that they couldn't afford to heat the outdoors.

That memory caused a smile to touch his mouth, the first one in the past couple of days. Joey sat at the dining room table with Corrine, Luke's daughter, a coloring book spread open in front of the pair of them. Luke's four-year-old would be five in March, and she'd start kindergarten this fall. Luke parented Corrine full-time now too, as his ex-wife had gone to Calgary to visit her parents, then called to say she wasn't coming back for a while.

"Seen Trace?" Otis asked, and Bryce looked up from

his phone. He sat on the couch in the living room, and it took a moment for his eyes to deglaze.

"He's not here yet," Bryce said.

Otis eased himself onto the couch opposite of Bryce. "Who are you talking to?"

Bryce sat up as if he was in trouble. His dark brown eyes glinted with mischief. Otis loved talking to his nephew about the girls in high school, or music, or anything really. He knew how to connect to this almost-adult, male. His daughter?

Otis glanced over to her, knowing she needed something more than he could give her. She needed a mother. He swallowed, remembering he needed to call Lauren before they went into the recording studio. Then, all devices and phones got switched off, and all the kids knew they had to call three times to get something to ring, and they should only do so in an emergency. Like, fire or broken bone emergency.

Abby was here, and Bryce wouldn't be sitting in on the sessions until the last song, probably three or four months from now. As this was their sixth studio album, Otis knew the drill by now. He knew he'd be fighting with Luke every step of the way, and he knew Trace would change the freaking melodies on at least four songs. He probably already had and hadn't said anything yet.

He knew Tex would butcher the lyrics for the first week, and then something would switch in his head, and he'd have everything memorized.

Otis also told himself everything was different this time, so not to expect anything. They'd never recorded outside of the studio in Nashville. They'd never had their kids with them. They'd never been constrained to someone else's schedule, or when the bell rang, or needing to feed someone dinner.

Tex was married now, with a senior in high school. He had more on his mind than normal. *Yeah,* Otis thought. *So he'll butcher the lyrics for two or three weeks until they settle.*

"There's this girl in my government class," Bryce said, and Otis focused on his nephew. He grinned from ear to ear, and Otis basked in the happiness of it. He couldn't stop himself from smiling too, that was how brightly Bryce shone. "Her name is Mindy, and I think I'm going to ask her to Sweethearts."

"Already?" Otis asked. "Isn't that near Valentine's Day?"

Bryce looked at his phone. "Yeah." He smiled at the device. "Do you think I could go this afternoon?" He looked over to the girls at the table. "Or do I need to be here?"

The front door opened, and Tex came inside, Abby right behind him, and Trace and his son, Harry, following them. Harry was eleven, going on twelve this winter, and he wore the same cowboy hat as his father. He didn't speak much, the same way Trace didn't. In all things outward, they were practically twins.

Harry did have a slightly more refined look to him, but in Otis's opinion, that only made him more handsome. He'd break a lot of hearts, Harry would. His mother was a fashion model, now living overseas, so Trace had just purchased a piece of land out here on this eastern side of town to build a house for him and his son.

It wouldn't be done for months yet—nine or ten, if Otis remembered right—as construction in the frozen tundra was slow or nonexistent.

"Better ask Abby," Otis said, getting to his feet. "Is Luke out in the studio already?" Irritation sang through him even as Bryce nodded. Of course Luke was already out in the studio. He liked to pretend he was more serious about the music than the rest of them.

"Dad," Bryce said, getting to his feet. "I want to go with Greg and Hawke to ask girls to Sweethearts." He flicked a glance at Abby, who stood at Tex's side. "Do you guys need me here, or can I go?"

"You can go," Abby said as Tex asked, "Who are you asking?" His eyes narrowed and he held up one hand. "It better not be that Mindy girl. I didn't like those texts she sent you last week."

"Dad," Bryce said with plenty of frustration in his tone. "They were innocent. She wasn't sending nude—" He cut off and looked over to Joey and Corrine. "It was flirting."

"It was *not* flirting." Tex gave his son a dark look. Otis hadn't seen the texts, but he wouldn't be surprised at them. Bryce was almost as tall as Tex. Almost as wide. Definitely as talented—or more—and extremely good-looking. He hadn't had any trouble moving to a new town and a new school for his senior year. He'd been out with probably a dozen girls in the past four or five months since school had started, and he was wildly popular.

Otis swallowed back the bitterness on his tongue. He couldn't be jealous of his eighteen-year-old nephew.

And yet, he was.

His ego already bruised, he turned away from the conversation and walked into the kitchen, where Trace had gone. He leaned down and pressed a kiss to the top of Joey's head. "I'm headed out back, Roo. You listen to anyone older than you. Be nice. Be good. I'll be in soon."

"Okay, Daddy." She smiled up at him, and Otis met Trace's eye. He said something to Harry, the boy nodded, and the two of them headed for the back door.

Outside again, Otis shoved his hands in his pockets and went down the steps first. The quiet stillness out here and the way the snow made everything muted only served to amplify Trace's voice when he said, "I heard you're dating Georgia Beck. How's that going?"

4

Georgia lowered the blinds on the windows at the front of the bookshop. Then the ones on the door. She twisted the lock there, a sigh pulling through her body. The store closed early on Fridays, because no one counted perusing books as date night. She dusted the shelves and turned off lights as she moved from front to back, finally ending up in her office.

Always her office. Sometimes she thought she should put a cot in here and just call it home. She had a bathroom; she could get food right next door. She wouldn't have her pets here, and she'd have to find a place to shower, but otherwise, she could do it.

Tonight, she didn't linger in the office the way she did some evenings. She didn't have a date tonight, and her pulse skipped a beat. She was actually surprised Otis hadn't asked her out yet. He'd said he was good at cards, but his silence the past two days proved otherwise.

She shouldered her purse and checked her back pocket for her phone. It rang when she touched it, and that startled her. It felt almost like the universe had known she needed someone to call her right then, just as a reminder that someone knew she was alive.

Maybe it's Otis, she thought. *Looking for a last-minute dinner date.*

Her smile stretched across her face before she could get her device out of her pocket. Her hopes soared thousands of feet into the air in only a moment, and that only made the crash as fast and as hard when she saw Abby's name on the screen and not Otis's.

She swallowed against the sudden lump in her throat and swiped on the call. "Hey, Abby," she said, her tone slightly pinched.

"Is it true that Otis Young does not have your number?"

"You can't even start with hello?" Georgia griped at her. Sudden understanding bloomed inside her though. "No, he doesn't have my number." She'd never called him after he'd put his number in her phone. She hadn't texted him.

He didn't have her number.

She pulled in a shaky breath, hoping Abby didn't hear that. Fruitless hope. Abby heard everything.

"Georgia," she said, and she wasn't disappointed or

condescending. "If you want him to ask you out, you have to text him first. Or call him, so he has your number." She spoke as if Georgia were one of her misbehaving Bookmobile children, which Georgia supposed she deserved.

"I...I just didn't think of it." She'd gotten a new shipment of books the day after she'd fainted, and she and Harley had spent all day cataloging them, pricing them, and putting them out if they had room. "I got a new kitten last night."

"Georgia," Abby said, and she *was* judging her this time. "You don't have time to take care of a kitten."

Georgia went over to the box where she kept the tiny black and white thing. "It's fine," she said as she picked it up. "Even Ruby likes him. Wouldn't leave his side."

"Ruby would help a serial killer hide the bodies," Abby said dryly. Georgia burst out laughing, and Abby joined in with her giggles.

"Fine," Georgia said, still laughing. "Then Onyx liked him."

"Oh, now you're just lying," Abby said. "Onyx only likes two living creatures. You, and Obsidian."

Georgia pictured the pair of gray-and-white cat brothers she owned: Onyx and Obsidian. They tolerated the constant stream of rescues Georgia brought home, as well as the two permanent dogs, Ruby and Isla.

"You're wrong," she said. "Onyx doesn't like me." He only liked Obsidian, and he wasn't the one who came to curl into Georgia's lap at night. He was either playing

Houdini and hiding, or perched on the highest object he could find and glaring down at whoever dared to enter the house.

"Come over for dinner tonight," Abby said. "Tex said they'll be done recording about seven, and Wade and Cheryl are bringing a whole mess of pizza."

Georgia wanted to say yes. Abby had gotten married about three weeks ago, and nothing had changed in their friendship. She didn't go out to the east side of town, where Abby's ranch sat, often. Abby usually came to town and they went out to eat, or she plopped down on Georgia's couch and talked and talked and talked.

She hesitated, though. "I'd have to bring the kitten," she hedged. "And I'm doing that princess reading party in the morning. I have to be here really early."

"You need help setting up for that, right?" Abby asked. "I was planning to come, but...."

Georgia shouldered her way out of the building and waited for the door behind her to click closed. She tested the handle and found it locked. Satisfied, she turned to put the kitten—whom she'd named Buttons—in the backseat of her SUV. "But what?" she prompted.

"I think you should ask Otis," Abby said, plenty of bite to her words. "You should come out here for dinner tonight and make sure he has your number. Do your flirting magic, and get him and his big muscles to come help you set up in the morning."

Horror washed through Georgia. Instant fire licked up

her throat. "I didn't ask for your dating advice," she said. "And I do *not* have any flirting magic." Her two previous interactions with Otis had been her demanding he kiss her and pretend to be her boyfriend and then fainting in her own bookshop. How were either of those even remotely flirtatious? Or magical?

She shook her head as Abby started arguing with her. Behind the wheel, she started the car and got the heater blowing. "...just saying, you need to at least text him. He can't make the next move if he doesn't have your number."

Georgia backed out of the stall. "Why do you want me to date him?"

"Uh, because he's perfect for you?" Abby hissed. "You were the one who said you liked kissing him. That you liked him. I'm just doing what you wanted me to do—helping you figure out what to do."

Georgia had asked for that help. Her irritation and defenses started to soften, just like butter in the microwave. She drove out of the parking lot, thinking while Abby remained silent. That alone meant something, and Georgia finally said, "I have to get home and feed everyone first."

"It's barely after five," Abby said, her tone light but Georgia knew she scented victory. "We'll probably eat around seven. If you come, you can bring a cake or something. I know you don't like to show up empty-handed."

"Yeah, okay," Georgia said. She didn't feel like arguing, and even more so, she didn't want to eat alone again tonight. "I'm bringing the kitten."

"Otis likes the raspberry white chocolate cake from Kneaders." Abby sounded absolutely gleeful. "Talk later." The call ended, and Georgia huffed into the dark silence inside her vehicle.

She scoffed, and then vowed, "I am not showing up with a raspberry white chocolate cake from Kneaders. Not for Otis." She nodded like that was that, and then she pressed a little harder on the gas pedal so she could get home faster. She needed to feed all the animals, yes. She'd have to tell Harley her plans for that evening. Then, she needed to spend a bit of time getting ready and making sure she looked absolutely stunning tonight. Once Otis had her number, perhaps he'd call, and they could go out.

Yes, she definitely needed a few minutes to go through her closet and find the perfect pair of jeans to wear that evening. After all, she didn't want Otis to forget about her, and she had the perfect pair of black skinny jeans that should get her stuck in his mind.

A few minutes after seven, Georgia pulled into the driveway next door to where Abby now lived. It was her brother's driveway—and used to be Abby's. But the farmhouse drive next door was full of trucks and Abby's SUV, leaving no room for Georgia's.

Nerves fired through her body, and she looked at the two boxes riding shotgun. One held a raspberry white chocolate cake from Kneaders—not for Otis. It happened to be one of Georgia's favorite treats, and she figured if she lost the courage to take it in, she'd at least have breakfast, lunch, and dinner for the weekend ahead.

Buttons mewed in the box beside the cake, and Georgia reached over to soothe him. "It's okay," she said, not looking at the kitten. She kept her eyes fastened to the bright lights spilling from the windows of the farmhouse next door. No one moved about in the chilly darkness, which meant they'd all probably gone inside already. Wade and Cheryl—who'd gotten married the same day as Tex and Abby—had gone next door. The cowboys in the band had come in from the studio.

The house would be full of noise. Laughter. Children. Life. Love. So pretty much the opposite of Georgia's quiet country home and dull evenings. She wasn't sure she fit here, to be honest.

Her phone lit up in the car, catching her attention. Abby had texted. Instead of reading what was sure to be a lecture about either being late or sitting out in her car, Georgia heaved a sigh and started gathering everything she needed to take inside.

The distinct feeling that she was crashing a party moved through her as she stacked Buttons in his box on top of the cake. Her phone sat in her pocket, and her keys did too. She was ready.

Tex had proposed to Abby with a banner that was fifty-two steps long. That was how far it was from her back door to his, and Georgia somehow found the courage to start the journey. She didn't go to the back door, but down the front sidewalk to the main entrance instead. She also didn't have to knock or ring the doorbell—she wasn't sure how she would've anyway.

Abby pulled open the door and stood framed in all that light, love, and energy Georgia had imagined. It pulsed from the farmhouse, and it smelled and tasted and felt better than Georgia had even imagined.

Her best friend grinned at her and hurried forward to help with the boxes. "Oh, he is so cute." She pretended not to like Georgia's soft spot for animals, but Abby was just as bad. She'd even fostered a dog or two over the years until Georgia could take them back or get them with a family.

Her eyes flicked down to the cake. "You brought a cake." Abby looked at Georgia again, her smile twice as wide. "How wonderful. It'll go great with the pizza and salad."

"Abby," Georgia said, not committed to taking a step inside yet. "Promise me you'll let me do this my way."

Abby's smile slipped. She visibly swallowed. "Of course, Georgia."

"He's inside, right?"

"Yes."

"We don't need you playing matchmaker," Georgia said. "Promise me."

"I promise." And when Abby promised something, she kept it.

So Georgia nodded, smiled, and tucked her now-wavy hair behind her ear. "All right. Now, if this cake isn't the most magical and most flirtatious thing ever, I'm blaming you." She giggled with Abby and followed her inside, the vibrant life of the Young family swallowing her right up as she closed the door behind her.

She turned and met Otis's gaze first. It was like someone had put a tractor beam on her and then him, and she felt pulled to him in a way she'd never experienced before. He sat at the table with his daughter and another little girl, and he got to his feet. He paused. He glanced into the kitchen as several people erupted into laughter.

Then he returned his gaze to her and started walking in her direction. He was gorgeous and confident, his head held high. It bore a creamy cowboy hat well, and he hadn't shaved that morning. Probably not yesterday morning either, judging by the amount of dark scruff on his face. Mm, she liked that and wondered how that would feel against her fingers, her face.

He wore the classic cowboy boots, jeans, black belt, and a black and white checkered shirt, tucked in right above the silver belt buckle. He was a cowboy god. Pure perfection. Mouth-watering. Georgia had many adjectives for the man now standing in front of her.

"I didn't know you were coming," he said, his voice making music in her ears.

She looked away from him with difficulty, trying to find something to seize onto. She didn't want to make a scene, and he'd come straight at her. The laughter and noise dialed down and then went silent. Georgia knew then that everyone here knew about the kiss from last fall, and that she'd fainted and flirted with Otis about dating him. She didn't know what else they knew, or who he confided in.

Unsettled, her eyes landed on the cake box. She looked up again, right into those dark, dreamy, dangerous yes. "Yeah," she said, digging deep to a well of strength she hadn't used yet. "I heard you liked this cake, so since you haven't called or anything, I thought I'd bring it to you and make sure you had my number."

5

"Otis," Daddy said behind him, and Otis wanted to swat away the distraction like an errant fly. Couldn't Daddy see he was talking to Georgia? She'd offered him her number, and Otis wanted it more than anything in the world.

"We're going to say a prayer, son." Daddy touched Otis's arm, and he flinched. He looked at his father, who cut a glance to Georgia.

"Right." Otis turned around and fell back to her side. He took the cake from her so she didn't have to hold it during the prayer and then swept his cowboy hat from his head. Across the room—blast Tex and Bryce for having a big, wide doorway that led into the kitchen—he met Tex's eyes. They smiled and encouraged from clear over there, and Otis wanted to turn around and walk out. He'd take his cake with him, thank you very much.

"Lord," Tex finally said, dropping his own chin as his eyes drifted closed. "We thank Thee for this bounty of friends, family, and loved ones who've come to the farm tonight. We're grateful for good food and good conversation. We're grateful for a good session in the studio today. Please bless our kids to be patient with us, and bless us to be the kind of parents they need."

Otis tensed, because he'd been praying for that same blessing for weeks and months now. He loved Joey with his whole heart. He did. He was trying to be the father she needed. He simply wasn't sure if he was accomplishing it or not.

Tex continued with the family prayer, but Otis had started one of his own about his daughter. He didn't want to do anything to jeopardize her mental, emotional, or physical health, and she'd already been through a big change with the move a week or so ago. She hadn't only been taken from Lauren, but her grandmother in Dog Valley too.

Otis still hadn't spoken to either his ex-wife or her mother that day, and guilt tripped through him as "Amen," chorused through the house. He immediately moved away from Georgia. Going straight to her as if they'd been connected by a chain had been a mistake. It had drawn too much attention and probably told her way too much about how he felt about her.

He couldn't quantify those feelings. He had no name

for them at present. He only knew he'd been thinking about her a lot since that kiss, and even more since Wednesday when she'd passed out. He took the cake into the kitchen, which thankfully bustled with activity again as pizza boxes got opened and Cheryl set a huge bowl of tossed salad on the table.

"Eat anywhere," Tex yelled. "The basement is open too."

Otis found a spot way down at the end of the counter, clear back by the steps that went down to the basement, for his cake. He set it down and flipped open the top flap on the box. The scent of sugar, chocolate, and raspberries hit him squarely in the face, and everything tight and tense relaxed.

He loved this cake.

He realized in that moment that he'd left Georgia to the wolves, and he turned to see where she'd gone. She stood next to Abby and Mama, the three of them chatting. She wore a smile, and she kept tucking her hair behind her ear. She'd curled it more than he'd seen before, or perhaps she had naturally curly hair and he didn't know it.

He wanted to, and he quickly found a knife, cut two pieces of cake, and put them on a couple of paper plates. He stabbed a plastic fork into each one and strode toward the women. "Cake?" He offered a piece to Georgia, whose eyes widened. He gave her a smile. "Mama? Cake? Abby?"

"Thank you, dear," Mama said as she took her cake. She returned his girn. "I love dessert before dinner."

"Daddy, can I have cake too?" Joey asked.

Otis looked down at her and booped her nose. "Of course, Roo. Just a sec." He still held one plate of cake. "Abby? Georgia?"

Abby took the cake and gave it to Georgia as she said, "I want one too, Otis. Thanks."

He nodded and went back down the lengthy counter. He cut two more pieces of cake, one smaller than the other for his daughter, and went to deliver those too. He found most everyone else had loaded their plates with pizza, and he skated his gaze past Tex so he wouldn't have to reveal anything to his brother.

He got his own piece of cake, and when he turned to find Georgia this time, she stood only a couple of paces from him. "Abby said we could eat in the basement," she said. "She said it was this way."

Otis swallowed and looked past her. The table was full, and a few people stood crowded around the peninsula island. "It looks full up here," he agreed. He wasn't aware of anyone going behind him and downstairs, and he almost wondered if they needed a chaperone. The last thing he wanted was everyone gossiping about him, and literally everyone in the family had gathered here tonight.

Mav and Dani and their kids. Morris, Luke, Trace, even Mama and Daddy. Wade and Cheryl, and he took up a lot of room in his wheelchair. Franny, Tex's german shepherd, ran around looking for handouts, and Otis couldn't find a place for him and Georgia among the chaos.

"She said she took my kitten down there," Georgia said. "I need to feed him a little, so...I think I'm going to go that way." She looked right and tipped forward to peer around the corner. "It's just right there?"

"Yes," Otis said, finally getting his voice to work. "I'll come down with you. Do you want pizza and salad?"

She brought those pretty eyes back to his. "Yes, please."

"I'll be two shakes behind you."

She only held the plate of cake in her hand, and she put her other one on his bicep. "Thanks, Otis."

He watched her go, completely mesmerized by her in that peachy-pink blouse and those midnight-black jeans that looked painted onto her body. His mouth turned dry at her curves, and he yanked his attention back to getting food so he wouldn't allow himself to think too hard about inappropriate things.

Loaded with two plates of pizza, salad, and garlic bread, as well as his plate of cake, he went down the steps too. His boots made thunking noises, but he couldn't help that. Georgia sat on the loveseat, the coffee table pulled right up in front of her. The box with her little black kitten sat almost against her left foot, which bore an ankle boot with shiny buckles.

He looked at the couch, but it was too far away. So he

stepped around the table to claim the other spot on the loveseat. He set down her food with, "Pizza and salad for you, my princess."

She looked up at him and grinned. "Princess?"

Otis did his best to calm his nerves as he put down his food and then took a seat on the loveseat. It was too soft, and he sank into it too far. He heaved himself back out and onto the edge of it, the way Georgia sat. He met her eyes again. "I think you look absolutely amazing tonight," he said. "Joey would say like a princess." He gave a short laugh that sounded too nervous. "Sorry if you didn't like it."

"It's…." She looked at her cake, which was half gone. "It's okay." She forked up another bite. "I'm having a princess reading party in the morning at the bookshop. Joey should come."

"Are you sure you have space?" Otis asked. "And how did I miss that? She loves everything sparkly, purple, pink, princess, rainbow, and unicorn." He chuckled again, and this time it sounded normal. "And reading. A princess party at the bookstore is like, made for her."

Georgia took her bite of cake, and Otis really, really wanted to taste the frosting against those lips. He told himself he would not. He wouldn't kiss her again until it was real. Very, very real. He wasn't sure his heart could take it otherwise.

"I have space for her," she said. "If you'll come help

me set up." She wore a flirty sparkle in her eyes now, and he realized he'd played right into her hand.

Otis tipped his head back and laughed. "Well played, Miss Beck," he said amidst the chuckles. "Well played."

"Well, one of us needs to start playing," she quipped. "You said you were the best at cards, but I don't know." Her voice moved up in pitch on the last few words. "I haven't seen anything to suggest your dating game is all that good."

"I don't have your number," he said.

"You know where I work—and where I live."

Otis blinked at her. "I came by the shop yesterday. Harley said you were out getting lunch." He cocked his head as if to say, *So there*. When she didn't throw something back at him, he added, "I didn't think stopping by your house seemed wise. A little stalkerish maybe, and well, I have to take care of Joey all the time now, so I can't be goin' to jail for hanging around a pretty woman's house."

She trilled out a laugh that made his blood turn hot, and he smiled at her. Then he dusted his hands together, though he hadn't taken a single bite of anything yet. He tugged his phone out of his back pocket and looked at the dark screen. Then her. Then the phone.

"I guess I'm just waiting for the woman holding all the cards to throw me a bone."

"Hey," she said. "I brought you a cake."

He held up his silent device. "And yet, I still don't have a way to communicate with you unless you want to drive out here every night." He grinned, feeling like a whole new version of himself. One who could flirt and have fun, grin and get the girl.

Georgia made a deliberate move to put down her fork. She reached into the kitten box to extract her phone—no way she could get even the slimmest of devices into any pocket on those jeans—and tapped, swiped, and *tappity-tap-tapped.*

A moment after she stopped, his phone zinged and buzzed, and while he knew it was her, he still looked. She'd said, *Here's my number, cowboy. I like the steak and eggs at The Branding Iron.*

He chuckled, shook his head, and tucked his phone away.

"What?" she asked. "You're not going to respond?"

He picked up a piece of pizza and took a big bite of the all-meat concoction. He shook his head as he chewed, just enjoying this blitzing, tingling feeling moving through him. Georgia had to like him, right? To come out here with the cake, in those jeans, her hair all curled?

"It's best to have a reservation at The Iron on the weekends," she said, plenty of haughtiness in her tone.

He swallowed and wiped his mouth. "Honey," he said. "I'm not going to take you exactly where you want on the first date."

She blinked at him, clearly surprised. "Why not?"

He grinned and shook his head again. "The game's not fun if you know how it ends." He took another bite of pizza and gave her what he hoped was an insanely flirtatious look.

It seemed to work, because her face flushed, and she used the meowing kitten as a distraction for several seconds. Before she could say something else, Otis asked, "Are you free for dinner tomorrow night?"

"Yes," she practically whispered. "After seven. The shop is open until six on Saturdays." Their eyes met, and Otis could see himself leaning in for a kiss. Easily. She'd give it to him too, and a sense of satisfaction he hadn't felt since leaving Florida last year filled him.

He needed someone to like him for him, and in that moment, it felt like Georgia Beck did.

"I'll pick you up at your place at seven, then," he said.

"Where are we going?" she asked.

"It's a surprise." He gave her another look, this time out of the corner of his eye, and she giggled.

"Fine, Mister Young," she said, flirting back with him. "We'll play your way—but." She nudged his knee with hers. "Don't be upset if I'm not dressed right."

"Georgia," he said in all seriousness. "You're always dressed right." Then he stuffed his mouth with more pizza, so he wouldn't say anything else too embarrassing.

A moment later, more footsteps came thundering

down the steps, along with children's voices. Harry, Boston, and Joey entered the living room, and his daughter skipped over to him. "Daddy, can we play the hedgehog game?" She perched on his knee and put her arms around his neck.

He held her around the waist and grinned at her. "Sure thing, Kangaroo. Did you finish eating? This is dinner."

"I'm done," she said, which meant she hadn't eaten more than two bites. She got off his lap and went to play video games with her cousins.

Otis watched them for a moment, and then leaned his head toward Georgia's. "She lives with me now," he said quietly. "Her momma's been sick."

"I'm sorry," she said just as quietly. "Flu?"

"We don't actually know yet," Otis said, shaking his head. "It's not the flu. It's been going on for months now." His concern must've come through in his voice, because Georgia put her hand on his knee.

He looked at it as her touch burned through his jeans and into his skin. He looked at her again, and she gave him a small smile, then pulled her hand back.

He quickly reached out and took it as it retreated, then lifted her hand to his lips. "I'm navigating a lot of new ground right now. Just bought a house yesterday."

Her blue-green eyes shone and shimmered like the Caribbean water under pure sunshine. "Wow, Otis. That's great."

"Yeah." He released her hand and picked up his pizza again. "So, what's the story with the kitten?" He nodded to it and then watched her for her reaction. She barely flinched. "You and animals? Tell me all about that."

6

Georgia woke to a cat alarm the next morning. She hadn't bothered to set a real alarm since she'd adopted Onyx and Obsidian. If she was five seconds late getting their breakfast, she had a mouthful of fur in her mouth, and then plenty of "playful" scratches on her neck.

"All right," she said crossly, pushing one of the gray cats off her chest. "I can't breathe." She glared at Obsidian, who gave her a feline look right on back. "You're overweight," she told the cat. "You can wait a few minutes."

She sat up and grabbed her phone to check the time as she remembered she had an event at Beck's Books that morning. Only six-ten. She had plenty of time, so she padded into the kitchen and got the animals their breakfast. While they noshed, she stepped into the shower, her thoughts revolving around Otis Young.

She couldn't believe the turn the past few days had taken. A week ago, she had not been on this path at all. Sure, Otis had existed in the back of her mind, usually when she ate a TV dinner in front of her latest binge-worthy streaming series. But actually entertaining the thought of calling him, texting him, or somehow inserting herself into his life?

Nope. Nowhere was that on the horizon. As she swept mascara onto her eyelashes, she murmured, "Maybe God gave you guys a little shove."

Maybe He had. Georgia still didn't know for certain why she'd passed out. She knew she hadn't eaten, and she knew that was a reason someone could have low blood sugar, and then lose blood pressure, and then consciousness.

She took longer than normal to get ready, but she reasoned she'd have done that anyway. After all, she had a big event at her bookshop today, and she always put forth her best foot when it came to patrons and the public.

She had to if she wanted to stay in business, and she did. The first few years for Beck's Books had been somewhat of a struggle. Then she'd started thinking more like a library, and they had a lot of events for children. Adults too, and Georgia had started planning ways to get more people through the door—and not always to buy a book.

She sold local artists' wares too, and people came for those. She sold a variety of paper goods and shipping supplies—and being right next to the post office on Main Street had brought her a lot of business in that avenue.

Her events added to her bottom line, and she gave herself a smile as she finally fluffed her hair for the last time.

"Ready?" Harley said behind her, and Georgia met her eye in the mirror.

She kept her smile on her face as she turned. "Don't you look so cute?" Harley was twelve years younger than Georgia, and she still had the glow of of someone who hadn't hit twenty-five yet.

She struck a pose, and with her stylish polka-dot skirt and ruffled and puffed-sleeve black blouse, she reminded Georgia of her younger sister.

Tears instantly came to her eyes, despite the happiness flowing through her and the grin still stuck to her face. She stepped into Harley and hugged her. "Thank you for all you do for Beck's Books." She couldn't really hide the emotion in her voice, but Harley simply embraced her back.

"I love working there," she said. "Besides, you're helping me out by letting me live here. Of course I'm going to do whatever I can to help you." She stepped away and brushed her hands down Georgia's arms. "You look fabulous too." Her eyes drifted down Georgia's sky-blue slacks and back to her geometric patterned blouse, also in a variety of shades of blue. "Anything to do with that cowboy you stayed out past curfew to see last night?"

Georgia tipped her head back and tossed a laugh toward the ceiling. "I was home by ten," she said, still giggling.

"And that's about an hour past your bedtime." Harley cocked her right eyebrow, clearly wanting more details.

Georgia didn't kiss and tell, and besides, there hadn't been any kissing. At least not on the lips. The inside of her wrist suddenly burned, as if it now had a touch-memory of Otis's mouth there.

She rubbed it absently. "He's going to meet us at the shop soon. Let's get loaded up."

Harley nodded and led the way out of the Georgia's bedroom. They already had all the supplies and samples packed neatly into boxes, and they each went back and forth, outside and inside, a few times to get everything in vehicles.

They each had to drive, so Georgia set off for the shop alone. She drove through Brewster's, wondering what kind of coffee Otis liked. Since it was Saturday morning, the line stretched around the building, which meant she had time to text him and ask.

Where are you? he sent back.

Brewsters.

Sweet. I love the Honey Mama there. Joey would love you forever if you got her the Small Squirrel. I never let her get it, and I usually go after I drop her at school.

He sent a smiley face emoji with the text, and Georgia found herself grinning like a fool at the fact that he had the names of the coffees and hot chocolates at Brewsters memorized.

You got it, she sent back to him. Then she gazed out the windshield at the blue sky in front of her, inching forward when she could.

Armed with coffee, she finally arrived at the shop and pulled into her spot behind the building. Harley had beaten her, and the back door stood propped open. Georgia got out and took the drinks into her office, only the sound of the furnace pumping to greet her.

"Harley?" she called just a round of laughter came from the front of the shop. Georgia went that way, recognizing the lower timbre of Otis's voice. Her heart pumped out a ton of extra beats, causing her to press her palm against her chest, as if gearing up to recite the Pledge.

She couldn't see him yet, but the man formed in her mind's eye easily. Tall, dark, handsome, charming, talented, devoted to his family.

He was playing with a very good hand, and she wondered what had happened between him and his ex-wife, or why he hadn't remarried in the years since their split.

She went around the main bookcase that separated the check-out desk from the rest of the store and found him standing with Harley and his daughter, one hand tucked casually into a sexy pair of blue jeans that looked like they had paint splattered on them.

He wore a dark brown leather jacket today, with a hint

of a bright blue shirt peeking through along his throat and down the zipper, which sat open.

Georgia could not breathe. Literally could not. He'd filled the shop with something wonderful and woodsy—his very presence—and with that cream-colored cowboy hat perched so perfectly on his head, and that belt buckle glinting at her from his waist, her knees actually went weak.

"Morning," he said easily, now coming toward her. "Harley said you have boxes in your car too." He gave her a smile full of white teeth and happiness to see her. At least she hoped that was why his smile felt so warm and his eyes danced so merrily.

He paused in front of her and swept his lips along her cheek. "Out back?"

"Yes," she said, finally thawing from his touch. How he moved and talked and interacted with her so effortlessly—and in front of his daughter too—baffled her. She must not affect him as strongly as he did her. That was all.

It was a sobering thought, and she swallowed against the emotion rising through her throat.

Otis had started to walk toward the office and the back door, and Georgia threw a look to Harley before following him.

She caught him quickly and said, "Thanks for coming early."

"You brought coffee," he said, making the turn into her office. "I can smell it in here." He flashed her a smile before picking up her to-go cup and handing it to her. Then he grabbed his and raised it in a silent toast to her.

She did the same, not knowing what else to do, and they both sipped. Otis smacked his lips together and made a big show of going, "Ahh, yes. That is good," which made Georgia laugh.

He joined his voice to hers, and she sure did like the sound of their two tones together. She turned shy, ducked her head, and tucked her hair behind her ear.

His hand came up and retraced the path hers had just taken. "Do I make you nervous?" he asked.

Georgia's chest sunk, and her mind screamed, *Yes, of course you do.*

Her pride would not allow her to say such a thing. "No," she said instead. "Why?"

"You tuck your hair a lot," he said, doing it for her again. Sparks ran down her neck and across her shoulder. "I thought it might be a sign of nerves."

"Maybe it is," she said, vowing not to reveal anything else. "What do you do when you're nervous?" Surely the man got nervous. He performed in front of thousands of people.

Fans, she told herself. Fans were people who already loved something or someone. Maybe he didn't get nervous.

He chuckled and ducked his head, concealing his face with that sexy cowboy hat. "I'm a pacer," he said, raising his eyes back to hers without lifting his head all the way.

Talk about cowboy adorable.

"I mutter the lyrics I'm sure I'm going to forget. My fingers won't hold still, so I'm usually playing some imaginary piano or guitar." His grin widened as his head came up.

She stayed in the moment, though she smiled with him. "That's before a concert, though," she said. "What about if you're just nervous for a princess party at a bookshop?"

He took a step closer to her, his coffee-less hand dropping to her waist. "Same thing," he said. "Except this morning, I rehearsed all these flirty things I was going to say to you when I saw you." He grinned again and stepped back. "I've already forgotten all of them now." He took another drink of his coffee, this time without the show of deliciousness.

"So *I* make *you* nervous." Georgia cocked her hip, hoping he got all the flirtatiousness she she'd just flung at him.

"Oh, definitely," he said evenly, no smile in sight now. He took another sip of his coffee. "I'm better when I'm doing something, so let's go get your stuff. Then maybe I'll be able to think of all the witty things I was going to say." He gave her a sexy smile and nodded her toward her own office door.

Georgia turned and went in front of him, adding an extra swing to her hips as she did. She didn't mind if the man she dated held more control than her, but she did want to know she affected him somehow. There had to be a spark—and there were plenty between her and Otis—and this tiny fear that she'd somehow mess up and lose him, which would be the worst possible outcome in her life.

She did feel like that, and as Otis growled behind her, his hand landing on her waist again, she knew she affected...somehow.

He pressed in close behind her and whispered, "You look amazing today," in her ear.

She shivered, even though she didn't want him to know, and pressed her cheek to his for a flash of time. "Thank you," she said, and then she got her feet moving toward the gaping door and the cold air coming inside. She certainly needed to cool down right now, and she tugged her keys from her pocket to pop the back of her SUV.

Otis joined her at the tailgate, and she looked at him instead of reaching for a box of supplies. "No hint about where we're going tonight? I want to make sure I'm properly dressed."

He swallowed and said, "You could wear what you have on right now." His eyes dripped down the length of her body before rebounding back to hers. "And be fine."

Georgia rolled her eyes to let him know she didn't like that answer. She reached for a box and handed it to him. She kept her hand on top of the box, so he wouldn't walk away quite yet.

"One thing about me, Otis," she said. "I don't want 'fine.' I want spectacular." She raised her eyebrows as final punctuation to what she'd really said—*I want to know where we're going so I can dress well enough to make you growl again*—and then reached for her own box.

She left him staring at her at the back of her SUV, satisfied she'd made her point.

One, she liked him.

Two, she had expectations for their dates, and he better bring his A-game.

Three, and maybe this hadn't been communicated, because Georgia hadn't quite thought this far ahead, if he played his cards right, they could be forever.

And oh, how Georgia wanted forever with the right man for her. Excitement shot through her as Otis's cologne neared inside the shop, because if he was the right man for her, she'd finally get her happily-ever-after with a handsome cowboy, something she'd been dreaming about for several long years.

7

Otis needed to get off his bed and start getting ready for his date. Down the hall in the kitchen, Joey made toast and sang to herself, something that made him smile.

Nothing made him happier than his daughter. Until he closed his eyes and saw the gorgeous Georgia Beck strutting out of her office, that sexy sway to her hips.

He needed this woman in his life, and he'd known it since he'd kissed her last fall. He honestly wasn't sure how he'd survived the months between that event and the past few days. It seemed impossible.

He grinned as his phone vibrated on his chest, and he picked it up again. Since leaving Georgia at the bookstore after the princess event near lunchtime, he'd been texting her all of the things he'd been too nervous to say to her in person.

She flirted on back with him, and it provided him with some of the confidence he'd been lacking lately. He felt strong around her, and even if she hadn't admitted it, he did make her nervous. Still, she held her own against him, and he liked that as much as the soft feminine touch she had with kids, books, and...him.

She'd sent a picture of herself wearing a black maxi dress, with layer upon layer of fabric covering her from shoulder to floor. *This?* she'd asked.

He chuckled to himself, his fingers flying across the keyboard. They'd been playing a fun game about where he was taking her to dinner in just over an hour, and she'd started sending pictures of herself in different outfits, and he'd said he'd give her hints until she landed on the right one. She'd started in the same outfit she'd worn to the event that morning, and while he sure had liked it, it said *professional* more than *first date with this guy I really like.*

He really hoped that was the message she was trying to say with her clothes, as Georgia seemed to say a lot without using words. She had at least four different looks he'd identified, and she had a way of yelling with those perfectly plucked and sculpted eyebrows.

When she'd handed him that box...he'd known in that instant that he'd be telling her where they were going to dinner. That she didn't want a surprise, and if she didn't get her way, this might be the only date he got to take her on.

He re-read his message and sent it. *It's real nice*, he'd

said. *Too much fabric though. That looks like something you wear to church, not to a nice dinner and a concert... with dancing.*

His phone rang, and he swiped it on and tapped the speakerphone button. Georgia had called him three times that afternoon already. "Go for Otis," he said.

"Oh, my word," she said, her voice holding the amount of dryness of the Sahara. "Do *not* answer the phone like that when I call you."

He burst out laughing, and it felt so, so good. "Would you prefer, 'hey, sweetheart'?" he asked.

"It's preferrable to 'Go for Otis,' yes," she said.

"Noted."

"Dinner, concert, and dancing?"

"Yes, ma'am." He grinned up at the ceiling, also noting that she didn't correct him on the *ma'am* this time. She had during the first phone call. "You need a shorter skirt."

"Yes," she said almost absently. "One does when they're going to the Swing Ranch Show."

Otis wasn't surprised Georgia had solved the riddle of where he was taking her that evening. "I mean, the email didn't say that," he said. "But I did watch a video on their website, and no one was wearin' a skirt that went all the way to the floor."

"Mm."

Otis pushed himself up onto his elbows as the scent of something burning reached his nose. "You don't sound excited about the Swing Ranch." He got off the bed and started for the kitchen. "Roo?"

"It's fine," his daughter yelled.

"What's wrong?" Georgia asked.

"Smells like something's burning." Otis entered the kitchen. "Give me a sec." He scanned the old kitchen in the house he rented, and Joey stood at the sink, the faucet pouring water down into it.

"Roo," he said as he approached.

"There was a paper towel too close to the burner," she said, glancing up at him with fear in her eyes. He looked down at the singed, soaking wet paper towel. "I grabbed it and got it out."

He put his arm around her and squeezed her tight. "You were makin' toast, baby. Not eggs."

"I've done it before," she said defensively. "Grandma Echo lets me make scrambled eggs all the time, Daddy." She almost spoke down to him, like he was the stupid one for being concerned his seven-year-old had just used the stove unsupervised.

"I'm not Grandma Echo," he said sternly. "If you wanted to cook, you should've come to get me." He stared at Joey, and her slight shoulders slumped.

"Yes, sir," she mumbled.

He backed up and took a seat at the dining room table. "Go on, then." He lifted his phone back to his ear. "Sorry, Georgia. Just tryin' to make sure we don't burn down this house."

"It's fine," she said. "I *am* excited about the Swing Ranch."

"We don't need to lie to each other," he said, suddenly feeling like he'd made a mistake with this first date.

"Would you believe me if I said I was worried about your dancing ability?"

"I can dance just fine," he said.

"I'm positive of that," she said. "I meant, I'm worried I'll look like a fool *because* you're such a great dancer."

Otis ducked his head as if that would keep his voice low enough that his daughter wouldn't hear him. "Georgia, honey, you couldn't look a fool even if you tried."

She sighed and said, "Wow, Otis. That was a really great line. Is that one you practiced this morning?"

He laughed lightly. "I just came up with it a moment ago, actually."

She giggled too, and said, "Okay, I'm hanging up. I think I have the perfect thing."

"All right," he drawled.

"You send me what you're wearing too," she said. "I haven't gotten a single picture, and you said you'd send me one."

"I haven't gotten dressed yet."

"Hurry up, Otis," she said.

"Why?" he asked, glancing over to the clock on the stove. Joey stood on a stool, stirring her eggs very carefully. He smiled at her back. "I don't have to leave here for another forty minutes."

"I'll be ready in twenty," she said, plenty of coyness in her tone. "If you want to come early, we could...well, I can't wait to see you."

Otis grinned like a fool. "See you soon, sweetheart."

Half an hour later, Otis knocked on Mav's door and opened it at the same time. "Howdy-ho," he called into the house. "We're here." The easiest and best place to bring Joey for babysitting was Mav's, especially on the weekend.

He had his daughter every weekend, and his wife had a boy the same age as Joey. The three of them—Boston, Beth, and Joey—got along really well, and it was hardly any work for Mav and Dani to have her with them.

Tonight, Joey wore a backpack as she came into the house with him, as she was going to spend the night here at Mav's. Otis wasn't planning to be out all night, but by the time the dinner-dancing-show finished and he could get back to his daughter, she'd be asleep. He'd meet up with Mav and Dani at church in the morning and collect Joey then.

After that, he planned to take her up to Lauren's for the day, and he'd probably text Georgia with a new game they could flirt back and forth over.

Mav came out of the kitchen, wiping his hands on a

towel. "Hey," he said, his gaze moving from Otis to Joey. "They're downstairs, Roo."

"Thanks, Uncle Mav." Joey opened the door that led into the basement and skipped her way toward her cousins.

That left Otis with Mav, and his brother perched on the back of the couch. He said nothing, and that only increased Otis's apprehension.

"How's Dani?" Otis rocked back onto his heels and dug his hands into his jacket pockets.

"Good," Mav said. "Tired. Getting real big." He grinned like he'd just given the performance of his life. "But good." His wife was due with their first baby together in just a couple of months. A boy for the pair of them, and Otis was real happy for Mav.

He nodded and smiled. "That's great. Thanks for taking Joey tonight."

"Anytime." Mav got back to his feet. "She's so easy. Did you get the tickets?"

"Yes." Otis followed him into the kitchen. Dani sat on a barstool at the counter, and she looked over from the notebook where she wrote. "Otis." She got to her feet to hug him, and Otis did smile as he wrapped her in his arms. In a lot of ways, Mav and Dani had shown him—and several other of the Young men—what he'd been missing in his life.

With so many new changes swirling around him, Otis found comfort and safety with Dani and Mav. They were rock solid and kind, and Otis needed both in his life right now.

"You're lookin' good," he said as they parted.

Dani put one hand on her belly and gave him a dry look. "Don't tell lies, Otis," she said.

"I'm not," he said, glancing over to Mav. "I think it's a beautiful thing, carrying a baby." He gave her a warm smile, and Otis remembered the feeling of becoming a father. He'd wanted his baby so badly, and while Joey hadn't fixed all that was broken between him and Lauren, he loved her endlessly and always had.

"I'll be happy when I can see my toes again," Dani said, sliding back onto the barstool.

Otis exchanged another look with Mav. "Okay, well, I better get goin'. Thanks again. I'll see you in the morning."

"Have fun," Mav said. He lifted the dish towel in a wave.

Otis nodded and left, half glad and half confused that neither Mav nor Dani had asked him anything about Georgia. Trace had wanted to know how they'd met, and Abby seemed to have endless inquiries about everything from what they talked about to what color of shirt Otis was planning to wear.

Several minutes later, he pulled up to Georgia's cute little brick house on a quiet street. The front yard held a lot of snow, just like all of her neighbors. All of Wyoming.

Her driveway and sidewalk were clear, with a single car that wasn't hers parked in front of the garage.

He went up the walk and the steps to the porch, which a bright light illuminated when it sensed his movement. He knocked; a dog started barking; he swallowed and stepped back.

He told himself not to pace, and he stilled his plucking fingers by putting them in his pockets once more. It seemed to take an eon for Georgia to open the door, and when she did, Otis froze.

She was the most stunning woman he'd ever met wearing a dark red dress that fell to her knees. Up top, the dress hugged her curves and upper arms, then flared at the waist. She wore a pair of black heels, and she looked to the side and picked up a glamourous, glitzy black clutch that bore gems sparkling.

She looked back at him, and he had so many compliments to pay her. Instead of using his voice, he lifted both of his hands to his face and mimed taking a picture. She grinned like the Cheshire Cat, and he knew he'd given her the perfect reaction.

"I need this picture on my phone," he said edging a little closer to her. Something about this woman made him so handsy, and he told himself not to touch her. He'd told himself the same thing in her office earlier that day, and he'd failed then. He'd told himself not to touch her while they ate pizza in Tex's basement. Another fail.

He knew he was going to fail again tonight.

"You got a lot of pictures already," she said. She appraised him, her head moving up and down as she took in his jeans, boots, and leather jacket. "Hmm." Her blue-green eyes shot desire and infernos at him. "I suppose this will do."

He spread his arms and turned in a circle. "I sent you this exact picture."

"It's almost what you wore this morning," she pointed out.

"No." He faced her again. "Those jeans were these trendy things Blaze sent me. These are real cowboy country music star jeans." He pushed down his belt on the left side. "See? Wyatt Walker edition."

Georgia looked at the label and then back into his eyes. "Wyatt Walker is a rodeo guy," she said. "Not a country music star." She rolled her eyes and started to come out onto the porch. He should've backed up. He should've said his shirt tonight was red, white, and blue—with the crimson almost an exact match to that in her dress. He should've said they didn't have to leave right then, because she'd told him to come early, and he had.

Instead, he held very still and let Georgia step into his personal space. She put her clutch against his chest as he took her into his arms. They swayed right there in the haloed darkness and the cold night.

"Mm," she said again. One hand slipped inside his jacket, and a miniature earthquake moved through his muscles. "I think this will do nicely."

"You like my shirt?" he asked.

"Yes, I do." She looked up at him, and he could see she liked so much more than that.

"Is red your favorite color?" he asked.

"Actually, it's blue," she said. "You?"

"I'm gonna go with blue too."

She played with his collar, and he swallowed with how close she was. "Which do you like better? Cats or dogs?"

"Dogs." He smiled at her, knowing her answer would be cats. "Favorite food?"

"Oh, I already told you that." Georgia laid her head against his chest, and Otis breathed in deeply and then out as he held her there. "Steak and eggs," he murmured. "We'll go there next time, okay?"

"Okay," she said. She stepped back, and she looked a little sleepy when she gazed up at him. "I already know you eat dessert before dinner, so since you're so early, do you want to come inside and have a treat?"

"Boy, do I ever," he said, his mind blitzing around from option to option for what she might have in store for him in the sugar department.

She turned and went inside, and Otis wasted no time in following her.

8

Georgia hadn't been out to the Swing Ranch Show in years. The moment the lights came into view, she knew it had been far too long as excitement bubbled through her bloodstream. "How did you get tickets to this?" she asked. "I know they book out way in advance."

Otis sat in half shadows as he drove, and she still couldn't get the sight of him licking his ice cream stick clean from her mind. She'd kissed him before, but it had been a while and not real. A girl could certainly dream about what it would be like to kiss Otis Young in an absolutely real relationship, and Georgia's adrenaline spiked for at least the fourth time in the past hour.

"I know a couple of people in town," he said evasively.

Georgia wasn't sure if that answer annoyed her or not. She supposed he'd called in a favor to impress her, and that shouldn't bother her. If she had clout and celebrity, wouldn't she use it?

"If you had to drink one thing for the rest of your life, what would it be?" she asked, continuing the game they'd started at her house.

"The rest of my whole life?" He shifted in his seat. "I better say water just to be safe."

"Boring," she shot at him. She smiled too, glad when he did too.

"Like when you said your favorite thing to do was read?"

She liked that he gave some of her sassiness back to her. "Yes," she said, tossing her curls over her shoulder. "Like that."

Otis gave a light chuckle, made another turn, and they arrived. Parking attendants waved to them with lit sticks in their hands, guiding them to where to park.

"I'll come around," Otis said, and Georgia stayed right where she was so he could open her door. He tugged on the bottom of his jacket as he rounded the hood, and some of Georgia's nerves vibrated too.

This was different than driving out to a private house in Coral Canyon. Everyone would see them here. Together. The word that she'd started dating Otis Young would be common knowledge by sundown tomorrow, and Georgia told herself it was okay. She didn't have anything to hide.

Otis opened her door and offered his hand. She

placed hers in it, twisted, and dropped to the ground. "Thank you," she murmured. He closed the door and retook her hand, and they walked quickly toward the huge, red barn where the events would take place this evening.

Georgia tasted a touch of magic in the air. It twinkled in the tea lights in the trees and the smiles of the women checking people in. It lingered in the music playing through the speakers, and while it was really cold tonight, the magic made it seem warmer.

That magic streamed from Otis, and Georgia wanted to stay as close to him as she could.

They got seated at a table for two, which was rare for the Swing Ranch Show. Most people sat at community tables, and they'd all have to get up and go through the buffet line to get their food.

At this table, Otis and Georgia would be served. She picked at her fingernails for a moment, the question she'd been building toward on the front of her tongue now. "So," she said, finally looking at Otis. "Why didn't you and your ex-wife work out?"

Otis blinked and looked over to the salt and pepper shakers on the edge of the table. He reached for them and put them in the middle, right in front of the two of them. "It's complicated," he said. "Have you ever been married?"

"No," she said.

He nodded and switched the salt with the pepper. "You know how there are some things that people just say go together?" His eyes met hers for a moment. "Salt and pepper. Peanut butter and jelly."

"Glitter and unicorns." Her voice caught on itself, and that brought Otis's eyes back to hers.

"Yeah." He smiled, but it wasn't a blinding one, nor one filled with joy. This smile felt almost sad, full of understanding and kindness. She liked it as much as the toothy one Otis had given her before.

"Like that." He took a big breath. "Lauren and I were like that. Everyone thought we were so good together. You hear that enough, and you start to think it's true." He pushed the pepper away from the saltshaker. "But sometimes, you can have one without the other and it's okay. Sometimes it's better."

Georgia nodded, keeping up with him. "You didn't love her?"

"No," Otis said. "I didn't. I thought I did. I thought because we were good friends and everyone said we belonged together, that well, I guess I thought that was love."

A man arrived at their table and plunked down two thick glasses of water. "Should only be a few minutes now, folks," he said. "No allergies here?" He looked from Georgia to Otis and back.

She shook her head as Otis said, "No, sir. No allergies."

The waiter nodded and moved on to the next table. Georgia thought that might be the end of her serious conversation with Otis, but he asked, "Have you ever been in love, Georgia?"

"Once," scraped out of her throat. She reached for her water and took a big gulp. "But there's familial love. Brotherly love. Surely you understand that."

"I do, yeah." He nodded, pushing the salt back together with the pepper. "It's different, though." He leaned back in his chair and folded his arms. "I was young. I didn't know what I felt or didn't feel. My hindsight vision is a lot better than what I saw at the time."

Georgia nodded.

"We were married for a couple of years," he said. "We had Joey, even though we both knew things weren't right between us." He paused, and Georgia simply waited. "I don't think either of us knew exactly what it was. We tried counseling. The band was doing really well, and I'm sure that didn't help, because I was gone a lot. Living in another city. Recording there. Then tours." He sighed again. "Eventually, I realized I'd never really loved her. I think she knew the same thing, and we split up."

"She lives around here?"

"Dog Valley," Otis said. "She's got some health issues she's still figuring out, so Joey moved in with me just after Christmas." He leaned forward and unwrapped his straw. He stuck it in his water and took a long draw, apparently done.

He looked at her again. "What about you? Who were you in love with?"

Georgia wanted to wave her hand and swat away his question. He'd answered hers, and her pulse raced as she opened her mouth.

"His name was Cameron Lund," she said. "We dated my last year of college in Jackson." Now that she'd started talking, everything was easy. "I was more into him than he was me, and well, he wasn't interested in small-town Wyoming life, with a wife who runs a bookshop and takes in every stray animal she comes across." She gave him a smile, because she was over Cameron. He couldn't hurt her anymore.

Otis nodded, and someone stepped up to the microphone and said, "Welcome to the Swing Ranch Show!"

The crowd cheered, interrupting them. Georgia put her hands together too, smiling up to the man on stage. He went over the dinner menu and how the buffet line would go. As the back tables started to get to their feet, their waiter appeared with two plates of food ready to go.

He set them down, along with an extra bottle of barbecue sauce, and said, "I'll be back to check on y'all in a few minutes."

Georgia looked at Otis's food. He had barbecue chicken, scalloped potatoes, baked beans, and two rolls perched on his plate. "This is great," she said, dropping her gaze to her food.

She sucked in a breath. She didn't have the same fare that he did. Nor did she have what the man had announced was on the menu for the buffet and everyone else.

She had steak and eggs.

"Otis," she said.

He grinned at her, and she found him to be an absolute prince. Her cowboy magician prince, who could make a phone call and work magic at the Swing Ranch Show.

He picked up his fork and pointed it at her plate. "I just want to say that the small-town Wyoming life with a wife who runs a bookstore and rescues every stray she comes across sounds about...perfect."

Then he scooped up a bite of baked beans and put them in his mouth.

Georgia fell in love with him—just a tiny little bit—in that moment. How he knew exactly what to say and do to erase all of the doubts she had she didn't know. She had nothing else to attribute it to besides magic.

Or the Lord, she thought, and that fit better than leaving her future up to the whims of a magic wand. She wanted to rely on God to lead her and guide her, and as she cut into her perfectly cooked over-easy egg and the yolk ran over her steak, she knew God had been leading her carefully to this exact moment in time, where she sat across the table from this beautiful man who'd listened to her, taken what she'd said, and made it into the absolute perfect first date.

"Yes, that's what I'm saying," Georgia said the following day. She loved a lazy Sunday at the bookshop. They closed at three, and she'd just rung out the last customer and locked the door. The weak winter sunlight streamed in the windows, and she allowed the peaceful happiness to infuse into her soul. She'd just told Shane, her brother, that she'd started dating someone new, and he'd been a bit aghast.

"Well, I want to meet this guy soon," her brother said gruffly. "None of this waiting-months thing like the last couple of times."

Georgia rolled her eyes, but she didn't argue with Shane. "He's stopping by this afternoon sometime." She picked up a book someone had laid on a shelf in the wrong place. "I'll start to feel out how he feels about a double date with my married brother."

"Who is it?" Shane asked.

Georgia hesitated. Once she told Shane who had utterly charmed her on their first date last night, he'd want to get together that very evening. Georgia wanted to keep Otis to herself for a little longer.

Not only that, but she hadn't even answered any of Abby's texts about her date with Otis. She'd have to tell her something, because she usually did, and her silence had already told Abby that it had gone well. Georgia liked to keep good things to herself in the beginning, lest they get jinxed by talking about them too much.

"Georgia," Shane warned.

"I'm not ready to say," she said. "It's a drive to you, Shane. We won't just pop in, and making an hours-long drive for dinner with a family member is a big deal for a relationship."

"It shouldn't be," he said. "That's how you'll know if he's worth keeping around."

Oh, Otis was worth keeping around, but Georgia kept that to herself too.

"All right," she said. "Say hi to Marlene for me. Kiss the kids."

"Okay," Shane said with a sigh. "Love you, Georgia. You know that, right? I'm just watching out for you."

"I know," she said. He had a bit of a complex about such things, and Georgia didn't blame him. They both wished they could go back in time and stand watch over the sister they'd lost. Then maybe they wouldn't have lost Lindsey at all.

The call ended, and Georgia put her phone on the nearest shelf. Otis had told her he'd be going to church that morning to meet his brother and get his daughter, then he had to take her up to Dog Valley to her mother. "After that, the whole day is open," he'd said, his eyes round and wide and full of hope.

She'd told him she closed at three on Sundays, and he could come by any time after that. She'd given some very strong hints that she had a Sunday afternoon routine of getting boba tea and taking a leisurely drive to watch the cattle graze in their fields.

She'd just stepped over to the cash register to close it out when her phone rang. She could hear it, but she didn't remember where she'd been when she'd set it down. She found it relatively quickly, but the call went to voicemail before she could answer it.

She hurried to dial Otis back as the wind shook the windows at the front of the shop.

"Otis Young," he said in another of his terrible greetings. "Reporting for duty."

She giggled and shook her head. "Front door or back?"

The wind whistled across his speaker, and he yelled, "Front, but I might be blown to the back if you don't hurry up."

Georgia hurried to the front door, finding him hunched against the glass there, his phone pressed to his ear.

She hastened to unlock the door, and he tumbled inside. She pushed the door closed against the weather and locked it again. She took a moment to lower the blinds before turning to face Otis.

He shook his head, his hair flying left and right before he smoothed it all back. He put his hat back on and grinned at her.

"This is Otis, reporting for duty," she said. "Is *not* how you answer the phone for your girlfriend."

His eyebrows went up and that smile slipped. "Is that what you are?"

She shook her hair over her shoulders too, straightening to her full height. "Yes," she said. "You've played some really great hands the past couple of days."

He prowled closer, his dark eyes practically lit with embers they burned so hot. "I don't know, Georgia. I don't normally call a woman my girlfriend until there's been some…." His eyes dropped to her mouth, and Georgia felt so powerful in that moment. *She* lit that fire within him. He wanted to kiss *her*.

"Kissing?" she provided.

He swallowed, his gaze lifting back to hers. "Yeah. Kissing. *Real* kissing."

Georgia swallowed too, because the man was mouthwatering. He had to know it. "Well, maybe you should keep answering the phone the way you do, then." She gave him a playful look, brushed by him, and added, "I have to finish up the books, and then we can go get tea."

"Tea?" he asked behind her. "Who says we're going to get tea?"

"I told you I had a routine," she said, going around the desk.

"Do you ever break your routines?" he asked as he approached.

"If I did, they wouldn't be routines." She counted money as she looked at him. His smile started out slow but grew in intensity until she had to look back at the cash in her hand.

"I heard of a great new place for hot drinks," he said. "They'll have your tea."

"I like looking at the cows on Sundays," she said. The coins clinked and chinked as she lifted the cash tray out of the register.

Otis was looking at his phone, and he turned it toward her. "Boba tea. Plenty of cows on the way there."

"The tea comes first, Otis."

"Okay." He tucked his phone away. "Do you want to drive, or shall I?"

She cocked her head, wondering if he'd gone insane. "You shall, Mister Young. The princess doesn't drive herself for tea."

He burst out laughing, and Georgia left him in the front of the shop while she went to lock up the money. She didn't think she was high-maintenance, and she could've gone somewhere that didn't have boba tea and been happy.

When she returned to Otis, leafing through a book Joey would probably like, she said, "I don't care what we do, Otis." She linked her arm through his and leaned against his bicep. "Okay? You pick."

He put the book back on the shelf and tilted his head down to look at her. "I did, sweetheart. There's this new place I heard about with great hot drinks. Lots of cows on the way." He offered her a small smile, and Georgia took it and put it in a safe pocket inside her memory.

"What's got you puttin' on a sassy front with me today?" he asked, casually taking her toward the front door.

"I talked to my brother today."

"Oh, honey, I've got eight of 'em. Tell me what he said, and I'll tell you what he meant." He chuckled, and Georgia smiled to herself too. They reached the door, and Otis paused.

"We're going to have to run," he said. "You ready?"

She zipped up her coat and nodded. "Ready."

He waited for her to unlock the door, and then he burst from it. He held it while she fitted the key inside and re-locked it, and then he grabbed her hand and raced with her to his truck. By the time he vaulted into his seat behind the steering wheel, they were both laughing and laughing.

Georgia liked listening to the joy and happiness as it spilled from his mouth, and she leaned her head back against the rest and smiled at him as he finished.

She reached for his hand and squeezed, and he said, "You can be my girlfriend even without the real kissing," in one of his More Serious tones.

"Okay," she said. "And you can take us to watch cows *before* we get tea."

He nodded to the cupholder between them, and said, "I'd hate to mess up your routine."

A to-go cup from Bubble Tea sat there, and Georgia could not believe it. "Otis," she said, releasing his hand to pick up the tea. "You're amazing. Thank you." She took a sip, and he'd gotten everything right. How he did that, she'd never know.

"I'll take amazing," he said. "Now, you better start talking about your brother, or I'm going to talk about mine, and trust me, they're not making me very happy right now."

She couldn't imagine him not happy, but she decided she could tell him about Shane.

"He wants to meet you," she said. "He prides himself on being a good judge of character, and he thinks I wait too long to introduce my boyfriends to him."

Otis glanced over to her. "Is that true?"

"I wait," Georgia said, her voice pitching up slightly. "Yes. Shane can be a lot to take in."

"Do you want him to meet me? Give you an assessment of what he thinks?"

"I don't know," she admitted, looking out her window. Shane had been right about the men she dated. What if he didn't like Otis?

"I'll send you an interview I did with *Country Music*," he said. "Show him that."

"He's in love with you already," she teased. "He loves Country Quad."

"Ah, so he's a smart man." Otis grinned at her, but she must've broadcasted something on her face, because the smile slipped quickly. "I don't care if I meet him or not," Otis said. "Okay, Georgia? So you decide."

She nodded, her throat suddenly so clogged. "I wish you could've met my sister," she said.

"I can't?" He made a turn, and the black dots signifying cows in the snow-tramped fields filled her vision.

She shook her head, the usual peace she stole from the bovines not quite present today. "She died about a decade ago."

Otis squeezed her hand again. "I'm so sorry."

She gave him the best smile she could. "She'd have loved you," she said. "She adored a man who could sing."

"Tex is the singer," Otis said.

"You sing too," she said.

He shook his head, but he wasn't really arguing with her. "Tex and Trace. They're the voices behind Country Quad. I do a few things, but I'm an instrumentalist and a song-writer."

"Lindsey still would've loved you." Georgia shook herself and sat up straight. "Sorry, Otis. How depressing I am today."

"I don't mind." He glanced at her. "Life is hard sometimes."

"Yes." She took a sip of her tea. "But not when there's boba tea and cows."

He chuckled, and she liked that he let her lighten the mood. She liked that he showed up when he said he would. She liked that he was thinking about kissing her, and that he always had everything she liked, right where and when she liked it.

A man as perfect as Otis Young had to slip up at some point, but for today, Georgia let him pull up to the fence so she could sip her tea and watch the cows.

9

Luke Young made the turn into the preschool parking lot, noting only one space remained. He'd recently registered Corrine, as she'd be turning five soon and starting kindergarten. He figured she could probably use a bit of help with letters and reading, and since Mandi, his ex, had no intention of returning to Coral Canyon and Luke took care of his daughter full-time now, he'd gone all-in.

There wasn't much that Luke didn't do all the way, to be honest. Sometimes he liked that about himself, and sometimes it was a curse he had to bear. Today, he took the last spot along the curb and twisted to look at Corrine.

She was a beautiful little girl, with all his dark hair. Her eyes sat somewhere between brown and green, like her mother's, but as she looked back at him, he could see himself in her. She was his, and he had the documentation to prove it.

He'd have loved her no matter what the paternity test had said. He'd always believed she was his, but the unrest in his soul wouldn't quiet until he'd done the test.

"Ready, baby?" he asked.

"Daddy, I don haf my pack." Corrine didn't speak that well, and Luke actually had a meeting with her preschool teacher later in the week. He could understand her, because he was her father, but he'd been translating for others for years.

"It's up here, honey." He picked up the pink backpack with flowers splashed across it. "Unbuckle, and I'll come get you down." He swung out of the truck but left it running. He had errands to do that morning, and then a parenting class of his own to attend. He'd barely make it back to Sunshine Starts in time to pick up Corrine, and the darkness in the sky told him he might be battling the weather that day too.

He went around to the passenger side of the truck and opened the back door. Corrine perched on the edge of the seat, and he drew her right into his arms for a big Papa Bear hug.

"I luff you, Daddy," she said, wrapping her skinny arms around his neck. She was surprisingly strong for a tiny tot of a four-year-old, and Luke choked a little as he laughed.

"I love you too, my baby." He smiled at her, gave her a

kiss on the cheek, and helped her down to the sidewalk. He retrieved her backpack and helped her loop the straps over her shoulders. Then she went half-skipping and half-hopping toward the door.

He followed her, but Miss Jericho opened the door for her and waved to him. She let in a couple of other children, whose moms all stood about where he did, and they all waved to their children. Corrine looked back and blew him a kiss, but he didn't have time to catch it and send anything back to her before she turned and went inside.

He had two and a half hours until he had to be back, and he wasted no time making small talk with the others dropping off their kids. He wasn't blind, though, and he saw one woman eyeing him. She had been since he'd started bringing Corrine to preschool, three weeks ago now.

He didn't nod to her. He didn't tip his cowboy hat. He didn't make eye contact. Doing those things would only encourage her to get closer to him on Thursday, and he wanted to avoid women, not draw them to him.

Behind the wheel of his truck, he put on his blinker to move out into the drive as he muttered, "I have to get out of this town."

Everyone here knew him. Not only had he grown up here, but he and his brothers were country music famous. Anyone who listened to country music knew about Country Quad, and they weren't shy about putting their faces on social media or album covers. *Everyone* looked at him, whether he was putting a loaf of bread in his grocery cart or filling up his truck with gas.

He supposed he was the loudest of the band brothers. He hadn't been shy during interviews, and his personality overshone Trace and Otis for sure. Maybe not Tex, as the man oozed charm. Where he was charming, though, Luke brooded. His bad boy vibes came through in everything he did, even when he was trying to smile.

He got his errands finished and dashed into his parenting class. The community center in Coral Canyon offered a variety of classes, courses, and seminars, and while Luke hadn't yet told anyone in the Young family about his paternity test—or these classes he'd signed up for —he felt the news bubbling in his chest.

Gabe knew, and that was ironic to him. The brother he hadn't spoken to in the longest knew about his true paternity. He'd gotten the child support stopped now that Luke had Corrine with him all the time, and he was currently working on the alimony too. Mandi was living with her parents; dating someone new. She and Luke had been married for fourteen months, and Gabe said he shouldn't have to pay alimony for longer than that.

He already had, and he just wanted to do what was right and fair for everyone.

"Luke, good morning," the teacher said, and he looked up from his thoughts. A man stood at his side, and Luke gave him a smile.

"Morning." He did tip his hat at Gerald Lower, and

the man moved about the room, greeting others. Luke was the only man, and he pushed his cowboy hat lower as Gerald called everyone to order.

The class at this time in the morning only held nine people, and it was specifically for single parents. That meant Luke spent an hour twice a week with eight available women—and they all knew he was single.

He took a seat on the far left side of the room, away from everyone else. He refused to look at the woman coming down the row toward him, and in fact, he folded his arms as if to tell her to *back off*.

She sat two seats away from him, and he caught her tucking her hair in his peripheral vision. He was not interested.

"Today, we're going to talk about establishing routines with your children," Gerald said. "Does anyone have any already?" He gazed around at the class. Luke normally said nothing. He wasn't quite thirty yet, and he'd actually acted as a father for less than a year. He had nothing to offer these people. He was here to learn.

A woman in the front row—Maryann—raised her hand. "My kids have a pretty simple routine, I guess," she said. "Every day after school, they have a chore to do around the house. Then we do homework. Then they can play with friends until dinnertime."

"Excellent," Gerald said.

The woman next to Luke bobbed over one more seat, only leaving one between them. He lowered his head in her direction, a growl starting in this stomach. Didn't she know he was a beast? A caged beast, here in Coral Canyon against his will? If she got too close, he was going to bite.

"Iris," Gerald said, and the woman who'd been leaning toward him jerked to attention. "Why don't you come up here and do this role-play with me?"

The woman sighed, and Luke kept his head low, the brim of his hat concealing her as she got up and left the row. He stood too and moved to the back of the room. He could stand through the class if that meant he didn't have to entertain Iris and her silly ideas about getting to know him.

She did the role play, and Luke actually took a few notes on his phone. When she turned to return to her seat, she froze, her eyes searching the room for him. Their gazes met, and Luke stared at her. Hard. Strong. Unyielding.

The message had to be clear. He didn't know how to make it any clearer for her.

Her shoulders slumped, and she went back to the same row they'd been sitting on. She sat on the very end of it, at least eight chairs away from where she'd been previously.

Yes, she'd gotten the message. Now, if she could communicate that to all the single women in Coral Canyon—in Wyoming—in the world—Luke would be happy.

~

Later that day, he laughed as he carried Corrine on his back. He gave exaggerated bumps as he went up the steps to Mav's front porch, and his brother came out the front door as Luke slid Corrine to the ground.

"You're in a good mood," Mav said, leaning against the doorframe.

"It's cold!" Dani yelled from inside, and Luke gave Corrine a nudge to go inside. She did, and Mav pulled the door closed behind her.

"Headed out to Tex's?" Mav already knew Luke was, so why had he come out onto the porch?

"How's Dani?" Luke asked, tucking his hands in his pockets. "The baby?"

"Good, good." Mav nodded, something lurking beneath the surface. He looked left, then right. "I talked to Gabe today."

Luke stiffened. "It's my business," he said, though if he told anyone first, it would probably be Mav. Or Trace. Perhaps Otis. Definitely Tex. Luke loved his brothers—all of them—and he was getting closer to Morris too.

"I won't say anything," Mav said, pushing away from the house. "But you should."

Luke sighed and looked left too. The wind blew the leafless tree branches, and he felt about as brittle right then. "I know," he said. "I'm not like you, Mav. I don't know how to have a big family dinner and have everyone love me."

He was more the dark horse. The growly bear. The one who threw punches instead of having conversations.

"Everyone loves you," Mav said firmly. "With or without the dinner. It's called texting."

Luke nodded, though he didn't need the lecture. "I'll be back by dinnertime."

Mav smiled and shook his head. "No, you won't. It's fine. I'm grilling hot dogs to go in the mac and cheese tonight. Beth's helping." He lifted his eyebrows. "Do you let Corrine help in the kitchen?"

Luke had just committed that morning to reading with her every day for ten minutes. "Uh, sure. She can help."

If Mav knew how out of his league Luke was, he'd probably file for custody of Corrine. As it was, he nodded again, said, "Have fun out there," and went back inside the house.

Luke loved Mav to the core, but he did not understand him. He often felt like that about his brothers. He wondered how he fit into the Young family. They all seemed so different from him, and he had a hard time relating to them. His capacity to love was endless though, and he had learned from an early age to love someone even if he didn't understand them or agree with them.

Just like the way he went all-in on something, his ability to love others could be a huge curse to him. It certainly hadn't helped him with Mandi.

"That's why you don't need a woman," he reminded

himself as he got back in his truck. "You'll be happier on your own. Love your brothers. Love Corrine."

That would be enough.

It had to be, because Luke didn't want to have his heart shredded and handed back to him again. Oh, no, he did not.

10

Morris Young pulled open the door to the recording studio, his phone pressed to his ear. "That's not in the contract," he said as diplomatically as possible. "The album doesn't have to be finalized until October."

He knew, because he was the one who'd sat in the Nashville office and negotiated the terms. "They're recording today," he said as he looked through the wall of glass separating the entrance of the studio from the recording area beyond it. Tex had designed the barn-studio so that anyone could come inside without interrupting the recording.

They'd be able to see the kids or other guests through the glass, and everyone would be out of the weather until they could converse. Right now, through the glass, Morris found Luke arguing with Trace. He couldn't hear them due to the best recording materials money could buy, but the anger on Luke's face wasn't hard to recognize.

Trace shook his head, utterly nonplussed. He lived a lot of his life like that. Laid back. Casual. Quiet.

However, Morris knew better. Everything on the surface of Trace was exactly that: Surface. He felt things deeply, and he had strong opinions. He had storms brewing and blowing through him. He just didn't let them get out of control.

Luke was the opposite of that, and Trace pointed at something on the sheet music on the stand in front of the two of them. Luke looked at it, his storm blowing out.

"Uncle Morris," a boy said, and Morris turned to find Harry sitting on the couch that had been placed against the far wall. "Uncle Tex wants you."

"Morris?" Roger Alcott asked.

He jolted, remembering he was on the phone with an executive from King Country. "Yes," he said. "It's going well. I haven't spoken with them yet, because we're just getting started this afternoon, but I know Otis said he wanted to hear the first song today, and that they're planning to record."

"I want it in my inbox as soon as you have it." Roger tried to sound tough, but Morris had the inside scoop on him.

"You shall," he said anyway. "I'll talk to you soon." He hung up and turned toward Harry. "You're out here today?" The kids usually congregated inside Tex's farmhouse. Luke took Corrine to Mav's on Tuesdays, Wednesdays, and Thursdays. Bryce, Tex's son was old enough to watch all of the younger kids, but he had basketball practice every day after school, and he taught guitar lessons to a couple of kids around Coral Canyon.

Otis had Joey with him all the time, and Morris hadn't gone through the house to know if she was there or not.

"Yeah," Harry said. "No one else is here today." He looked through the glass, and Morris followed his gaze. Tex had gone back to his guitar, his need for Morris obviously not that urgent. Perhaps he'd seen him on the phone.

Morris took a seat next to Harry. He didn't have any kids of his own, and in a family of eight brothers who did, he felt left out. He sensed the same thing inside this twelve-year-old boy right now. "What's goin' on with you?"

He'd spent time in the NFL, and then coaching boys in bigger bodies than Harry's. He knew emotions and expressions, and while he'd tried to keep things centered on football on the field, when the players came off of it, Morris was there for them. He had been them. He knew them.

"Nothing," Harry muttered. He reached up the exact same way Trace did and smashed his hat lower onto his head.

"Bad day at school?" Morris fished. He didn't look at Harry, because the boys he'd coached in college almost always opened up without the direct scrutiny. He met

Trace's eyes, and his brother immediately grew concerned.

Morris shook his head almost imperceptibly. Surely Trace had seen his son and how upset he was. *Maybe he didn't*, Morris thought next. Trace was an amazing man. A good father. But Morris had learned that he wasn't normal for a male. Most males offered actionable steps for fixing problems. He simply worked more in emotions, and Trace might not have understood that Harry wasn't doing very well right now.

"Not school," Harry said.

He lived with Trace and Harry, and he'd come to know them both better, especially in the past few weeks. Trace had sat his son down and told him, "Your mama's not coming back, buddy. She's got a lot of work to do in Italy, and it's just gonna be me and you for a while."

The boy had cried. Heck, Morris had teared up too. Trace had hugged him hard and told him he loved him, and he was going to be there for him, no matter what.

What about when you have to tour?

The words echoed in Morris's ears. Harry had asked Trace that, and Trace had swallowed several times. *We'll work it out*, he'd said.

"Something with your daddy?" Morris asked next.

"No."

"Someone else at school? That Howard boy at the bus stop?"

"No, Uncle Morris."

"Me?" He looked at Harry then, a smile touching his face. "I've been real quiet at night, I swear."

Harry smiled too, the gesture there then gone. Again, just like Trace. "It's not you."

"Mm." Morris reached over and squeezed Harry's knee. "Must be your momma, then."

Harry shook his head, but he didn't say it wasn't her. Which meant it was.

"Your birthday is in a few weeks," Morris said.

"She's not coming," he muttered. "I mean, Dad said she wouldn't, but I called her anyway." He flipped his phone over on his thigh. "She didn't answer. She *texted* and said it was real late in France—she's in freaking France, Uncle Morris." He looked up then, the disgust radiating from his eyes. "Dad said she was in Italy."

Morris put his arm around Harry and drew him into his chest. "I'm sorry, buddy," he whispered.

"She *texted* me that she couldn't come," he said, his voice breaking. "She couldn't even call me. She hates me."

"No," Morris said, though he didn't know if Val hated her son or not. She certainly hadn't been very motherly toward him. When Trace didn't have him, they'd lived with her parents, and she had been gone a lot.

"She didn't even say happy birthday." He turned and cried into Morris's side, and Morris fought his own battle against his emotions. He used to think they made him soft, weak, so unlike the other tough cowboy brothers he had to live with. They'd always been better than him, even when he grew as tall as Tex, filled out in the gym, and got drafted into the NFL. He still felt weak and less-than.

He'd then gotten injured only a couple of years into his professional football career, and that had only proven to him that his body was too weak to do what it should. Leighann had left about that same time, and Morris knew exactly how Harry felt right now.

Lost. Abandoned. Like everything he'd once known had been taken from him.

He didn't know what to say to his nephew. No one could've said anything to him that would've helped. He let Harry cry, once again shaking off Trace, as well as Tex. Luke tapped his wrist as if Morris could rush compassion and condolences, and he glared him back to the drum set Luke worked from.

The band started to play, because they didn't need Morris to make their music. He liked to sit in on their practices, so he knew what was going on. He acted as the bridge between the band and everyone and everything else, so he *needed* to know what was happening.

But right now, Harry needed him more.

"I know it hurts," he said after another minute. "When I hurt my knee...." He paused, that moment in his life so clear for him. Harry pulled back and looked up at him. "I knew." Morris gave him a shaky smile. "I knew my football career was over. I knew I'd never play professionally again. Still, there's this hope, you know?" He knew Harry knew.

"That's why you called your momma. It's why I went to four doctors."

"But you coached," Harry said.

"And you'll have an amazing birthday," Morris said. He'd personally make sure of it if he had to. He wouldn't have to, because Trace would. "And you'll be thirteen, and you'll get out your guitar and show your daddy how good you've gotten."

Harry brightened. "Do you think I should?"

"I think you better," Morris said. "He should know, Harry. You're as good as him, and you don't play for him."

"No one's as good as my dad." Harry looked toward the glass. "He's like, the best."

"And he's right here," Morris said. "He loves you, and I believe him when he says he's not going to leave you here with anyone. You're his, and he's going to be with you, even if your mom isn't."

Harry wiped his face. "Don't tell him I cried, okay?"

"Oh, I don't know," Morris said. "I can't lie to my brother."

Harry didn't look happy about that, but Morris wouldn't lie to Trace. "You should tell him," he said as he pushed himself to a stand. "How you feel. About your mom. All of it."

"I don't know how," Harry said.

"You just tell him." He turned to see if the band had finished a song so he could enter the studio.

Harry peered at him. "What did you do, Uncle

Morris? When you finally realized you couldn't play football again?"

Morris turned back to Harry. "I prayed," he said. "Day and night." He moved back to Harry and dropped into a crouch in front of him. Their eyes met, and he loved this boy powerfully too. He hoped Harry could feel it.

"I was grieving. I was lost. I didn't know what to do, and I needed help."

"Did God answer you?" Harry seemed so innocent in that moment, and Morris tapped his knee.

"He did, eventually. He told me I better figure out how to mentor others. I had no job. No college education. No skills other than running fast—which I couldn't do anymore. But a job came open at a school, coaching, and it was like light from heaven beaming down, telling me I better figure out how to coach, mentor, and talk to young men."

"And you did."

"I tried," Morris clarified.

"Why'd you come here then?" Harry asked. "To manage the band?"

"Because." Morris straightened, because he couldn't crouch with his hurt knee for long. "They're my brothers, and I needed to forgive them and be with them."

Tex opened the door and poked his head out. "If you've got a sec, Morris," he said, glancing to Harry behind him. "We'd love to talk to you before we do the song again."

Morris extended his hand to Harry. "Yeah, we're coming."

"I'm going in?"

"Yeah," Morris said. "It's time to show your daddy how to make the song better."

Harry wore pure fear on his face, but he put his hand in Morris's and stood up. Tex looked at them both quizzically, but Morris just smiled at him. Harry went inside first, and Morris murmured, "This is going to be great."

"Yeah?" Tex whispered, which for him was almost a shout anyway. The man couldn't seem to keep his voice low. "What is going on right now?"

"You'll see," Morris said, and then he entered the studio too.

11

Trace Young felt like he didn't know his own flesh and blood. His son stood in front of him, adjusting the strap on a guitar that belonged to Otis. He'd asked to use it, and Otis had jumped to get it for him.

He looked over to Morris, who hadn't said a word. In fact, he'd refused to speak, and Trace's patience was dang near out. They hadn't even really started for the afternoon yet, and he'd already endured a rant from Luke, silence from Otis about his new girlfriend, and Tex blathering on and on about how he had all the lyrics memorized already.

He so didn't, and he had to know it. So him saying it annoyed Trace to the point that he simply wanted to take his son and go home.

"You're workin' on *Wishing for Relief*, right?" He

looked to Trace, and then over to Otis. Otis wrote all their music, but during the recording portion of the album-making, a lot got changed. Improved. Improvised. The final songs wouldn't be final until all four of them agreed, and sometimes Otis's original music and lyrics didn't even resemble what they'd eventually end up with.

"Yes," Otis said, a smile crawling across his face. "Have you been listenin' to your dad at home?"

Harry nodded, his fingers moving easily over the strings. Trace had been teaching him the guitar since he was old enough to hold one, and his son's talent always brought a balm to his soul. *Thank you for him, Lord*, he thought as Harry stepped around the music stand, the notes filling this beautiful studio easily.

He'd always loved his son, but Trace had grown to appreciate him too. The boy would lose his head if it wasn't attached to his body, but at least he did his homework before he misplaced it.

"The bridge isn't right," Harry said. "Can you guys play that part?"

Trace expected Luke to argue, because he hated playing out of order. He always wanted to start at the beginning of the song and run through it all, then go over notes and suggestions. This afternoon, he picked up his sticks and beat out a rhythm.

"Where?" Trace asked.

Harry nodded to the stand and started to play the

melody—the part Tex usually did. Trace lifted his guitar and added the harmony, and Otis came in with the fiddle. Tex stood there, his head cocked. Morris had taken up a position in the recliner, the same place he'd been for all of their practice sessions since the studio had been finished.

Harry played the whole bridge, and Trace didn't hear anything. "That's right," he said at the same time Tex did.

"You play it," he said to Tex, and he stepped back. Trace met his brother's eye, and Tex cleared his throat.

Luke rhythm'ed them in again, and the instruments made their music as the band played them. Harry frowned at the music, and then on the riff moving up through the scale, he brightened.

Trace heard it too, and his fingers instantly stopped moving. "Holy cow."

"It's right there," he said, pointing. "That's a B-flat, but Uncle Tex—" Harry cut off and swallowed.

"I'm not playing it right?" Tex squinted at his stand. "It's not a B-flat."

"It should be," Harry said quietly, but Trace barely heard him, which meant the rest of them wouldn't have.

"He's right," Otis said. "It's not a B-flat." He plucked through his notes again.

"It should be," Trace said. "That's the boy's point."

"Make it a B-flat and let's move on," Luke said from the set. Trace didn't even look at him. He had something crawling under his skin today, but Trace didn't know what. He'd find out soon enough, because Luke told him everything.

"You sure?" Tex asked, plucking now too. "I don't know."

Harry removed the guitar strap and rehung the instrument on the wall. He went to sit on the arm of the chair where Morris was. Something huge had happened out in the foyer, and Trace wanted to know what it was. Harry had always been a sober, quiet child. He'd cried a time or two, but not since he was seven or eight years old.

Today, however? He'd sobbed into Morris's chest, and Trace had to fight every paternal instinct in his body not to rush out there to be the one his son needed. He reminded himself that he needed his whole village of brothers to help him with Harry, and his son was obviously comfortable with Morris.

Not him.

That pinched, but Trace couldn't change who he was. He couldn't change Val. He couldn't do more than he'd done for Harry to be comfortable and happy.

"It's a blasted B-flat," Luke yelled, and that brought all the random notes to a halt.

"What is wrong with you?" Tex asked.

"Nothing," Luke growled. "It's—I only have until dinnertime, and we need to record today."

"We just started," Otis said. "I fully expect you to be the one who wants to change *stopped* in the second verse."

"It doesn't rhyme with *wept*," Luke shot back.

"It's not *supposed* to rhyme with *wept*." Otis shook his head. "It's a *slant rhyme*, Luke. And it's the right number of syllables."

"So is swept," Luke said.

"That's the same word!" Otis rolled his eyes and looked at Tex. "Help me out here." When Tex didn't even look at him, Otis silently petitioned Trace.

He'd just had this argument with Luke, so he said nothing.

Tex looked up from his stand. "I think it's a B-flat."

Trace grinned, because that was such classic in-studio Tex. Off in his own head and missing some of the arguments.

"Let's play it that way," Trace said, shooting a look at Luke. The man could play the drums in his sleep, and he did wonder if Luke got bored at band practice sometimes. Trace would rather be here than almost anywhere else, but Luke.... Luke definitely had something going on he hadn't told him about.

They played through the bridge again, and this time, there was no error.

"B-flat," Otis proclaimed, and he picked up his pencil to make the adjustment. "Good ear, Harry." He beamed at him. "You stay right there and tell us what else is wrong."

Trace gave his son a smile too, but he was too busy high-fiving with Morris to see it. Trace once again didn't know how to feel. Of course Morris wasn't trying to replace him. Morris would never do that to Trace. He exuded kindness and compassion, and Trace barely had an ounce of those two things put together. Perhaps that was why Morris could connect with Harry while Trace struggled to do so.

Heck, he struggled to connect to anyone, but he found it easiest with his family.

They worked through the first verse—where Tex forgot the lyrics, of course—and then moved onto the second. Luke, as predicted, came off the drum set to argue for *swept* over *stopped*, but he lost in a vote of three to one, which only lit a fire inside him again.

"All right, all right, all right," Tex yelled over the music after about an hour of playing. They hadn't started recording yet, and Trace's stomach growled for something to eat. Harry looked up from his phone, and Morris from the thick folder he'd opened across his lap.

"Luke," Tex said with a frown. "You have got to get it together."

"Tell us what's goin' on," Trace added. "Then maybe we can record."

Luke's teeth pressed together, and his jaw jumped. He glared at Morris, then Otis, then Tex, and finally Trace.

"Don't you look at me like that," Trace said, some of his own ire boiling out of him. "Anyone with two eyes can see this isn't about the band at all."

Luke deflated, which was about how things with Luke went. He held a lot of pent-up anger or negativity, but as soon as someone called him on it, he could release it. "It's actually a bit of good news," he said. "I just...."

"Don't know how to talk," Trace said, because he'd been afflicted with the same curse. Their daddy wasn't much of a talker either, and both Luke and Trace had inherited that from him.

"I guess," Luke said. He once again joined them down on the floor. "I did a paternity test."

Trace sucked in a breath. *Oh, no,* he thought. *Please, dear Lord, let Corrine be his. She has to be his.*

He'd never really doubted that Luke was Corrine's father—they looked so much alike—but he knew Luke had. Gabe too. Since Trace wasn't one to gossip, he didn't know who else had wondered.

"And?" Tex asked gently.

"She's mine," Luke said, releasing his breath. "She's mine. I mean, she would've been mine anyway, but yeah. She really is mine."

A smile exploded onto Trace's face, and he grabbed onto Luke and hugged him. "I'm so glad, brother." He stepped back and let the others congratulate Luke, all of them offering the same words of joy.

Trace looked at the five of them there, as well as his son. All wearing cowboy hats, blue jeans, and long-sleeved shirts. They dressed like a group even when they didn't have to. They acted as one in public. They were one.

"Why didn't you want to tell us?" Trace asked. "This is good news, Luke."

"Mandi's stayin' in Calgary for...I don't really know how long," he said. He cleared his throat. "I filed for full custody of Corrine and got it. I'm not paying child support anymore, and Gabe is working on the alimony."

"Gabe is?" Morris asked.

Trace suddenly admired Luke more than he had previously. Only a handful of months ago, he'd flown at Gabe, ready to punch his lights out.

"Yeah." Luke cleared his throat again. "I signed up for parenting classes at the community center. I'm doing the best I can."

"Of course you are," Tex said. "No one doubts that."

"I hate it here," Luke blurted out before Tex's last word left his mouth. He looked around wildly. "I can't stand Coral Canyon, okay? There's all these women everywhere, and they're all staring at me all the time." His chest heaved and he sucked at the air. "I'm glad we get to record here, because I know y'all need to be here, but I'm *dying*."

Otis took a step toward Luke, and Trace copied him. Tex did too, and within seconds, they'd crowded around him, even Morris, and wrapped him in all of their arms. Luke never cried. Luke raged. Luke ranted. Luke fought back.

Trace's heart hurt for his brother, and he didn't know how to make it go away. His own heart barely felt operational, and he couldn't even talk to his own son. So he wanted to rage too. He wanted to rant. He wanted to start punching, then run to his truck and drive until the embarrassment and regret brought him back into the arms of his brothers.

"Hey," Tex said, and his voice came out quietly for once. "Hey, it's okay."

Luke started to weep, and he grabbed onto Trace, who held him as tightly as he could. Otis hugged him from behind, and Morris and Tex wrapped them all up together.

Trace never cried either, but he found slow tears crawling down his cheeks too. There was pain here in the studio today, but also a great deal of relief. Of healing. Of comfort.

Luke pulled back, and Trace let Tex take his place. He walked over to his son, wiping his face as he did. He dropped to his knees in front of him and opened his arms. Harry flew into them, and Trace wrapped him up as tightly as he could.

"I love you, boy," he whispered. "I'm sorry your life isn't perfect, and if I could make all your hurt go away, I would." He really would, the way the Savior had taken all the injustices in the world, all the hurt, all the pain, all the terrible things, and paid the price for them. Trace was no savior, but he felt a tiny taste of what he would do for his son if he could. He knew how much he loved his son, and as Harry hugged him back, Trace felt the pure love God had for His children too. He had the ability to make all the pain, hurt, and sorrow go away, and He'd sent his Son to do that.

"I love you," he said, smoothing back Harry's hair. "I love you so much."

"I love you, too, Dad." Harry offered him a watery smile.

"This is about your mom, isn't it?"

Harry nodded, and Trace took him into another fierce hug. He hated that his poor choices had been inflicted onto his child, but he also knew in that moment that God loved Harry too, and that it was good for them to experience disappointment and hard times so they could appreciate and enjoy the happiness and good times when they came.

"All right, what is goin' on out here?" someone asked, and Trace pulled away to see Bryce standing there. "There's no crying in country music."

That broke the tension hanging in the studio, and they all started laughing. Trace stood up and put his arm around his son, and he grinned at his brothers. Luke went back to the drum set. Otis picked up his fiddle. Tex hugged his son. Morris returned to the recliner.

Trace met his eyes, grinned, and said, "Thank you, Morris," before hugging him too.

"Yeah." He pulled away but kept his hands on Trace's shoulders. "I have a secret too."

Trace sobered again. "Oh, boy. Better tell everyone then." He nodded to the group beyond, but Morris shook his head.

"Guys," Trace said, stepping around Morris. "Morris

has something to say too." He looked back at Morris, who probably could've killed him had his eyes been equipped with lasers. Trace let it bounce off of him, because he couldn't handle another cry-fest, and they still had a blasted song to record tonight.

12

Tex Young was ready to head inside and spend time with his wife and son. Abby wouldn't be home from the library yet, and she had to drive the Bookmobile out to Rusk tonight anyway. So he had plenty of time before he'd even see her.

"You better say it," Tex said, his voice maybe a little harsher than he'd like.

Morris kept glaring at Trace as he said, "Fine, but I do not need any help with this."

Trying to get the Youngs to mind their own business was like trying to put the sun out with a tissue. Tex kept that to himself, because if he could help Morris with whatever he was about to say, he would. He wouldn't even think twice about it.

Morris cleared his throat, his anger with Trace fading. Morris never really got angry anyway. He withdrew like a champion, but he didn't argue, fight, or cause contention. He simply...disappeared.

Tex didn't want him to do that again, so he shifted his feet toward him to listen better.

"I think Leighann might be back in town." He cleared his throat. "I swear I saw her at the Christmas Eve tree lighting at the lodge." He met Otis's eye. "Remember we went to that?"

Tex's gaze flew to Otis, because he trusted Otis with his life. "Yes," he said slowly.

"I didn't see her there," Trace said, his eyebrows drawn down into a deep V. "You saw her?"

Morris shook his head. "I think so? I don't know."

Tex hadn't gone to anything at Whiskey Mountain Lodge over Christmas, because he and Abby had just been married and they'd been on their honeymoon. He felt whiplashed around as he tried to observe Trace, Morris, and Otis at the same time.

They'd all told him about the tree-lighting ceremony and the stockings on the wall with excitement. Trace had said something to the effect of, "We need a tradition like that, Tex. It was incredible."

Tex didn't know how to start a family tradition that would unite his brothers. He wanted to, but Gabe wouldn't even come home for longer than a couple of hours, and Luke had just said he hated this town and wanted to leave. They had some traditions—ham on Easter morning, and they'd all send cheesy love songs to each other on Valentine's Day. That had started out as a joke among the band, and with a start, Tex realized that he didn't send anything like that to Gabe, Blaze, or Jem.

So it wasn't a full family tradition.

Sadness punched him in the gut, because he knew Blaze probably wasn't going to continue with the rodeo for another year. He'd almost quit last Christmas too, and guilt cut through Tex that he hadn't asked Blaze about retiring yet.

He quickly added it to his mental list of things to do, and then he listened as Morris said, "I guess I need to find out if it was her or not."

"Why?" Luke demanded from his seat behind the drums. "Why do you care if she's back in town?"

"Luke," Trace said, and Luke looked at him.

Even Tex knew that answer. Morris loved Leighann, and he always had. They'd been divorced for three or four years now, but he hadn't stopped loving her. Tex found a smile spreading his lips.

"So find out," he said.

"You can't be serious." Luke got up once again, and Tex sincerely hoped he didn't work out in the morning for how much he'd been up and down this afternoon. "You still love her? How can you *possibly* still love her?"

Morris squared his shoulders as Luke approached, and Tex gave him bravery points for that. Trace darted in front of Morris, and Otis nearly threw his fiddle to try to grab Luke from behind.

"I'm not going to hit him," Luke said, shrugging off Otis's hand. "My word, you guys."

"You were comin' at him fast," Trace said.

"This isn't any of your business," Morris said.

"You falling back in love with your ex-wife and leaving us high and dry is one-hundred percent my business," Luke yelled.

Tex closed his eyes in a long blink, and he knew: They would not be recording today. "Let's all calm down."

Luke's dark gaze flew to him, and Tex didn't wither at all underneath it. He puffed out his chest instead. "Let's get something clear, Luke. Mav did not leave us high and dry." He held up one finger, then a second. "Things are changing right now. We're doing this album, because it's on our contract, but the truth is, that might be it for us."

"No." Luke shook his head, his jaw so tight. "No, Tex. Don't say that."

"I'm married now," he said simply. "Otis is seein' Georgia, and judging by his good mood the past week or so, I think it's going well."

"Hey, leave me out of this," Otis said. "And it hasn't even been a week, and I haven't even kissed her."

"You haven't kissed her?" Bryce asked. "Dad, why is Abby always talking about that kiss between Otis and Georgia, then?"

Tex drew in a deep breath as everyone's eyes flew to Otis. This was so out of control. "That's not common knowledge, son," he said out of the corner of his mouth.

"Why are you out here anyway? Don't you have a girl to text or something?" He was only half-kidding, his irritation at all these distractions getting the better of him.

Bryce looked half sheepish and half like he'd pour cold water in Tex's bed that night. "I came out to tell you Grandma called and invited us for dinner." He turned to leave. "Sorry I said anything, Otis."

"Bryce," Tex said, regret laced in his son's name.

"It's fine, Dad." He opened the door to leave but turned back. "Harry, you want to come in with me? I did have a girl give me ice cream at school today." He smiled, and Tex rolled his eyes. Yes, he'd apologize later, but he hadn't been off-target.

The kids left, and Tex looked at each of his brothers. Trace stood between Morris and Luke, with Otis off to the side. "My news is my adult son is going to be the death of me."

Otis laughed, as did the others, and that broke down some of the tension between them.

Tex looked at Luke again. "I'm sorry, brother. I really don't think I'll be doing another album."

Luke nodded, as he'd surely known that already.

"If Morris wants to find out if his ex-wife is back in town, he should." Tex removed the guitar strap from around his neck. "Otis can take as long as he wants to kiss Georgia. Heaven knows he shouldn't be in a rush."

"Hey," Otis said again, but then he hung his head. "Yeah, you're right."

"Trace can...well, Trace has things he's dealing with too." Tex minded his tongue, because Trace told him things in confidence, and he didn't want to betray him.

"What are you dealing with?" Luke asked.

"Hey, I already bawled my eyes out because of you," Trace said, thumping Luke on the chest. "That's enough for one day."

"It's just...." Luke let the words hang there, but Tex knew how to finish the sentence.

"It's just that we're all broken a little bit," he said. "We all have something going on that's hard for us. You're not the only one, Luke. You just like to think you are, and you like to separate yourself from us."

"I wish you wouldn't do that," Morris said, his voice barely more than a whisper.

"Same," Trace said.

"There's a reason we're all back in Coral Canyon." Otis moved right into Luke's side and slung his arm around his shoulder. Tex thought that was pretty brave too, but Luke had mostly blown himself out.

"Yeah? What's that reason?"

"When you have to get out of here," Trace said. "I'll take Corrine for you."

"When you're going crazy," Morris said. "You load up and go. I'll handle everything for you."

"When you need someone to vent to," Tex said. "You come on out here any old time. Bryce is fixin' to get a bunch of horses, and they'll sync their heartbeats to yours and make you feel better."

"You're really not going to do another album?" Luke asked, his voice pitching up.

Tex shook his head. "I doubt it, brother. I'm sorry."

He looked at Morris. "You're really still in love with Leighann?"

"I don't know," Morris admitted.

"Bryce is getting horses?" Trace asked, and the spotlight roared back to Tex. "No college?"

Tex sighed and let his chin hang down to his chest. "You guys, I honestly don't know. The boy is...indecisive at best." He grinned around at his brothers, some of whom were only slightly older than his son. His gaze landed on Otis. "Things are going well with Georgia, aren't they?"

"Yeah," Otis admitted, his smile quick and full of light. He looked at Luke. "You really hate Coral Canyon?"

"Only ninety percent of the time," he said dryly. They laughed together, and Tex moved into the huddle of brothers again.

"All right," he said. "Now that everything is out, can we get back to this song? I have *all* the lyrics memorized, and I know we can record it tonight."

Everyone jeered at him that he'd already butchered the lyrics in the first verse, and Tex dodged away from Trace's playful swat.

"Butchered?" he yelled. "I missed a couple of words."

"A couple of *stanzas*," Otis said, his fiddle already back in his hand and his smile as wide as the sea.

Tex laughed, because he knew he was the worst with the lyrics. He loved teasing his brothers that he was the most prepared when his brain simply took longer to grow the memory roots it needed.

They played, and his soul got soothed, and Tex thanked the Lord above for family, friendship, and most of all—forgiveness. He needed to give it whenever possible.

He needed it from others, especially when he entered the farmhouse long after dark and found the kitchen clean and empty, the evidence of the dinner he missed wrapped in aluminum foil on the counter.

He took the plate with him into the bedroom, where Abby sat up, reading a book. "I'm sorry," he said, holding up the plate. "Thank you for this."

She lowered her book and smiled at him. "Bryce said things got a little intense out there tonight."

Tex sighed as he sank onto the bed. "I have to talk to him too. I maybe snapped at him about girls."

"He told me." She reached over and ran her hand down the side of his face. "Three of them came to the house tonight," she whispered. "He got asked to Sweethearts by three girls in one night." Her eyes burned into Tex's. "You will not leave me alone to deal with that again. I have no idea what I'm doing."

She smiled then, but Tex recognized the veiled seriousness in her voice. He twisted and put the plate on the nightstand beside the bed. "I won't," he said, taking her into his arms. "But I'm sure you handled it perfectly." He kissed her, this good woman he loved, and who loved him. She loved Bryce too, and he had no doubt she'd done and said the right thing for him that night.

"I'll talk to him in the morning."

"Yes, you will," Abby said, drawing him down for another kiss. "Because I missed you tonight, and you've been out in that studio for hours."

"Mm." He kissed her again, letting the irritation, frustration, and things he couldn't change in his brothers' lives melt away as he made love to his wife.

13

Otis smiled at his parents as they entered the roller rink. He jumped to his feet and waved, then strode toward Mama and Daddy. As he approached, he said, "You made it," and threw his arms around both of them.

Daddy stood as tall as him, though he'd lost an inch or two due to his age. His dark hair was salted with gray, and he'd started growing a beard. Otis didn't hate it, and he grinned at his father as he stepped back. "Going mountain man, Daddy?" He ran his fingers down the side of his father's face.

Daddy grinned at him. "Just trying to keep up with you boys."

Otis laughed with him, for he hadn't shaved for a few weeks now. It was too dang cold, and the beard did help against the wind.

His mother handed him a gift, and he beamed at her. "Thanks, Mama."

"I can't believe you didn't let me bake her a cake," she fretted, and Otis was so glad Joey's birthday had finally arrived. He'd been fielding Mama's worries for a solid week, since he'd told her he'd ordered a birthday cake for his daughter and didn't need her to make one.

"You're having us for dinner on Sunday," he said. "You're doing a birthday cake for her then." As if Joey needed two birthday cakes or celebrations. But Mama had insisted, and Otis had learned long ago not to argue with her. Not if he valued functioning kidneys, at least.

She'd raised nine boys, and she'd had them all in thirteen years. Oh, no. Mama was not to be trifled with, and as her sons had gotten bigger and stronger than her, she'd learned quickly that a swift jab to the kidney could bring a man to his knees.

He grinned at her and gestured them to come join him at the table. She hadn't started to gray at all, and she tucked her smaller hand into Daddy's and went with him. "When are you moving, dear?" she asked.

"Couple more weeks," Otis said, his impatience driving through him. "I've already got it on the calendar for all the brothers." He looked over to them. "You can just show up at the end for doughnuts and hot apple cider."

"Psh." Mama shook her head. "We can help. You'll need help putting Joey's room together."

He'd done it himself at the rental house where they

lived now, but he said nothing. If they wanted to come, he wasn't going to tell them no. "Maybe you could make ebelskivers at the house while we move," he said. "With apples, and that brandy syrup you used to feed us on Christmas morning."

Mama's face lit up, and she said, "Now, that's the best idea I've heard in a while, Otis."

He chuckled and pointed to the table. Only Trace, Morris, and Harry had arrived, but Joey skated with Harry out in the rink. Otis moved over to the wall and whistled. Joey turned toward him, and he gestured at her to come on back.

The party was about to start, and she should be there to greet everyone properly.

"Is Georgia coming?" Mama asked.

Otis turned back to her, his heartbeat thumping strangely for a reason he couldn't name. Other than he hadn't exactly told Mama about Georgia yet. "Yes," he said slowly. "Who told you about her?"

"No one needs to *tell* me," Mama said, disgust dripping from her voice. "I go to church in this town, young man."

Otis blinked at her, his mind catching up to and cataloguing what she'd said. People were talking about him and Georgia in Coral Canyon? Why?

He looked over to Trace, and his confusion must've been evident, because Trace said, "Bro, you're a celebrity. Of course everyone knows you're dating her."

"*Are* you dating her?" Mama asked, her eyes suddenly hawk-like. Otis felt whiplashed around, trying to make sense of things and keep up with the conversation. Georgia herself called him her boyfriend, so Otis supposed he didn't need to keep Mama in suspense.

"Yes," he said simply as Joey stepped off the rink. She walked awkwardly over to them in her skates, her face flushed with excitement.

"Gramma," she said, throwing herself into Mama's arms. Mama softened like melting butter, and clutched Joey like she was the most precious person in the world.

"Oh, my baby girl," she said. She placed a kiss on Joey's cheek. "You're eight years old today. Can you believe it?"

Joey giggled, and Daddy passed Mama their gift from where Otis had laid it on the table. He'd reserved the entire roller rink for his family. No one else would be there for the next three hours, and he'd ordered enough pizza to kill a couple of elephants. Or feed his brothers, and he suddenly worried there might not be enough food.

"Mama, we're doin' presents later," Otis said, but Mama just looked at him and extended the gift to Joey.

She stepped over to Daddy first and hugged him right around his middle. He grinned and looked down at her, holding her tightly too. Otis loved his parents for how much they loved Joey. They loved all their grandchildren, of course, but watching all of their sons get married and divorced, become single fathers, and struggle with the task, hadn't been easy for them.

"Can I open it, Daddy?" Joey asked.

Otis sighed. "I suppose, Roo."

"She'll want it," Mama said, shaking the box.

Joey took it, her face practically glowing. Harry took a turn hugging his grandparents, and Daddy sat down at the table and started talking to him about a new guitar book he'd found in an old box that had come from the attic out at the farmhouse. Harry was a brilliant guitarist already, and he suddenly lit up the way Joey did.

She ripped off the purple and white paper, sending glitter down to the floor as she did. It concealed a shoe box, and she looked up in anticipation. "What is it?" she asked Mama, but she zipped her lips.

Joey broke the tape keeping the box shut—Mama taped closed every box, as if the wrapping paper alone couldn't keep the lid on—and immediately screamed. "It's the razzle dazzle sweatshirt!" She flung the box and lifted the garment out in the same, swift movement. "With the unicorn on the front! Daddy, look!"

She spun back to him and held up the bright purple, blue, and pink sweatshirt. The tie dye was impressive, as was the glittery, giant unicorn on the front. The lights from the roller rink in front of her played on the white part, and it seemed almost holographic.

"Wow," he said, laughing. "You better say thank you."

Joey whipped back to Mama and launched herself at

her again. Mama grunted as she caught her, and Joey said, "Thank you, thank you, thank you! I've wanted this for my whole life!"

"Her whole life," Otis said, grinning at Trace. He laughed and shook his head too, and the resumed watching Joey. She hugged Daddy again, and then she said, "I'm going to change."

She didn't ask; she simply marched off toward the bathroom, and Otis watched her go. He sat down at the table beside Mama without putting his legs under, same as her. "You know, it took me twenty minutes to get her to wear that for today's party. So thanks for that waste of time."

Mama laughed and patted his knee. "You're welcome."

"Hey-yo," Tex said as he arrived, and Otis jumped up to hug him too. Abby came with him, and Otis swept a quick kiss along her cheek.

"Thanks for coming." He moved over to Bryce, who stood with a girl about a foot shorter than him. She seemed nervous, if the wide, toothy grin meant that, but Bryce laughed as he hugged Otis fiercely. "You didn't have to come."

"Of course I did," Bryce said. "Joey's my favorite cousin." He glanced over to where Harry sat. "Besides Harry, of course."

The twelve-year-old got up at the sound of his name and came toward Bryce. They did a cousin handshake thing that Otis was far too old to understand, and then Harry said, "I didn't know I could bring a date."

Otis yelped in surprised, but Bryce just chuckled again. "Yeah, you should've asked, bro." He took the girl's hand in his and added, "Val, this is my Uncle Otis. My cousin Harry." He nodded past Otis. "My grandparents are over there. Another uncle. That's Trace."

"They're all in the band," she said, her voice filled with awe.

"I have some uncles who aren't," Bryce said. "They're just not here yet." He looked at her, and she looked at him. She was clearly shell-shocked, and Otis knew the size of his family alone could do that to a person, country music band or not.

His nerves fired at him about inviting Georgia to this party. But they'd been dating for about three weeks now, and he couldn't just tell her, "You can't come, because my family is crazy. Like cray-zy."

She'd find out sooner or later, and it might as well be sooner.

"I told you there were a lot of us," Bryce said, and Otis sure did like that he'd said "us," and not "them."

"The party can start!" Mav yelled, and Otis shot a look at Harry with his eyebrows raised before he moved to greet Mav, Dani, Boston, and Beth.

"This is so great, Uncle Otis," Beth said when he picked her up. She giggled at him and clutched his face in her hands. "My momma never lets me go roller skating."

She was quite proper, like Mav's ex-wife, and Otis grinned at her.

"Well, let's make sure you don't get hurt today, okay?" He set her down and pointed Mav toward the counter. In a louder voice, he said, "Skates are over there, guys. Anyone who wants to skate, can. It's all paid for."

Bryce went that way, and that meant everyone would. He was the oldest grandchild in the family, and everyone looked up to him.

People started arriving in droves, and Otis did his best to greet them all and take a moment with them. Luke and Corrine both got skates, and he held her hand as the went around the rink slowly. Oh, so slowly.

He at least looked like he was having fun, and all of the growly beastliness he sometimes exhibited had been put away today.

Joey's friends showed up, and they all freaked out about her sweatshirt.

Morris got there a bit late, but he managed to walk in right when the pizza came out of the kitchen. So he honestly had perfect timing. Gabe tapped Otis on the shoulder about five minutes after that, and such surprise and love shot through his whole body.

"Gabe," he said, spinning and hugging him hard, despite the fact that he carried his little girl in his arms. Liesl was a tiny two-year-old, but Gabe had full custody of her, and he was an excellent father.

He wore a suit, complete with a tie and shiny shoes, and said, "Sorry we're late."

"Not late," Otis said. He stepped away and pointed to the counter. "Skates for everyone over there."

"I want her," Mama said, taking Liesl from Gabe's arms without asking. "Hello, my son." She hugged him and kissed his cheek before taking Liesl over to get some tiny skates.

"She can barely walk," Gabe called after her, but Mama didn't even indicate that she'd heard him.

Gabe sighed and looked at Otis. He started to loosen his tie, his eyes now roaming the three picnic tables where the Youngs had spread out.

"I know this isn't your favorite thing to do," Otis said.

Gabe gave him a sharp look. "I'm here, aren't I?"

"And I'm tryin' to let you know I appreciate it."

Gabe softened as quickly as he'd gone cold. "I'm sorry. Thank you."

"There's pizza and garlic bread," Otis said, indicating the tables. Most of the kids hadn't come in yet, so only the adults had started eating. "And I ordered these dessert cookie pizzas, so save room." He said the last sentence louder and stayed out of the way as Gabe entered the fray.

He got a couple of pieces of pizza and sat at a table with Morris and Trace, which Otis would agree was the safest spot for him. He could've sat with Tex too, or Mav, or Otis himself. The only distance Gabe had between his brothers was what he'd created, and Otis had wanted to tell him that for years.

He never had. Mav did a good job of keeping the family united and talking, and now that Luke was actually working with Gabe on some legal issues, Otis had hope that they'd be stronger than ever moving forward.

He cast a look behind him to the glass doors. It had started to get dark, which meant Georgia should be closing the shop soon. She should be coming, and he found he wanted her there right now. He didn't want to sit with everyone without her. He hadn't gotten any food yet, because he didn't want her to have to eat alone.

After another glance at the party, which was doing just fine, he walked away and to the doors. He peered out into the parking lot, and then he went outside though he wasn't wearing his jacket.

Georgia had just gotten out of her car, and she currently bobbled her purse and two wrapped presents. Otis hurried toward her to help, calling, "Hey, you look lost."

She turned toward him and dropped one of the presents. She gave a quick smile that was filled with frustration, and then bent to pick it up. He arrived, and she shoved the present against his chest. "I look lost?" She shook her head. "That's not what you say to someone in a dark parking lot when they don't know you're there."

Otis burst out laughing and sandwiched the present

between them as he hugged her. "It's so great to see you," he whispered in her ear. "Better?"

She pulled back a little. "Slightly. Now you're smashing your daughter's carefully curated gift."

Otis reached behind her and set the package on top of the SUV. He wanted to be close to Georgia. He wanted her to know how much she meant to him. He'd seen her yesterday—and every day since she'd come out to Tex's with that raspberry white chocolate cake.

"I've missed you," he said, smiling at her. "Better?"

"Getting there." She wrapped her arms around him too.

"You're gorgeous." He ducked his head and placed a kiss on her right cheek. "I like your hair all curled like that." He kissed the other cheek, noting that she pressed into that touch. "How about those?"

"Nice," she whispered. Her fingers slid across the back of his neck, and he shivered. "You're not wearing a coat."

"I was too excited to grab it when I saw you." He smiled at her, and she smiled back. His gaze dropped to her mouth, and she'd taken some time to paint her lips pink. Her makeup was flawless, and she smelled like powder, roses, and sunshine. "You smell great. You look great. I couldn't resist."

Her smile flattened. "You couldn't smell me from inside the roller rink."

"Mm, how do you know?" He put his cheek against hers, dislodging his cowboy hat. He let it drop to the ground, something he wouldn't have done for just anyone. "There's a lot of people in there."

Georgia said nothing, and Otis wasn't sure if she understood what he'd just said. His pulse thundered through his body the way Luke's drums did when they played their encore piece. "I want to kiss you," he whispered. "For real. Before we go in. Can't do that with everyone watching."

"Who says they're not watching right now?"

Otis pulled back and looked into her eyes. So blue and so green at the same time. "Can I?" he asked. Last time they'd kissed, she'd grabbed his collar and laid one on him. He wanted that explosivity again, but he also wanted to go slow and take his time. He wanted her to know there was more to this than how attracted to her he was physically.

"I can't stop thinking about you," he said next. "Why aren't you saying anything?"

"You talk too much," she whispered, and then her eyes drifted closed.

Otis took that for a, *Kiss me, cowboy*, and he slid one hand up the side of her throat at the same time he met her mouth with his.

Instant fire warmed him from the inside out. So much, he was sure his skin was steaming out in the Wyoming winter. He did kiss her slowly, experiencing the smoothness of her lips and the taste of her tangy lip gloss.

He liked the way her hair slid through his fingers, and the way she ran hers down the side of his face. He slipped one hand under her jacket to the small of her back and kept her close, close, as he continued to kiss her, and kiss her, and kiss her.

Otis honestly had no idea where he even was when he pulled away or how long they'd stood there kissing. They breathed in together, but Otis kept his eyes closed. "Better?" he murmured.

"You better greet me like that every time from now on," she said back, her voice throaty and hoarse. Then she kissed him again.

14

Georgia had thought she'd already had the most amazing kiss of her life.

She'd been wrong.

The one in her office from months ago had nothing on this one in the roller rink parking lot. Then, she'd kissed a talented, handsome, kind man. Someone she didn't know, just to get out of a bad situation.

This time, she was kissing a talent, handsome, kind man who she really liked. Who was a good father and son and brother. Who seemed to be as affected by her as she was him. Whose family she was about to meet as his official girlfriend.

As the kiss deepened and accelerated, Georgia let Otis set the pace. He was an exceptional kisser, and she wanted to know how he'd become such. She hadn't asked him about any of his previous relationships besides the one with his ex-wife, but the man had to have kissed a lot of women to be so dang good at it.

He broke the kiss again, leaving her breathless and weak. She realized she was leaning against the side of her car, and she definitely hadn't been when he'd kissed her the first time.

"We better go in," he said, his voice low and sexy. "Everyone will wonder where I went." He gave her a smile, kept her hand in his as he stooped to grab his fallen cowboy hat, and then reached for the present he'd put on top of the car. "What'd you get her? I told you she was gonna have a ton of presents."

"One does not show up to a birthday party without a gift," she said.

"You have two," he pointed out.

She looked at the one poking out of the top of her purse. She honestly couldn't even remember putting it in there. "It's your daughter's birthday," she said. "I'm the new girlfriend. She loves books. I own a bookshop. *Of course* I have two presents."

Otis burst out laughing, his hand in hers tightening. As they approached the doors, he slowed. "Are you trying to impress her or me?"

"All of the above." Georgia's stomach turned over. She hadn't eaten since breakfast, but if she told Otis that, he'd be upset. She hadn't passed out, so she was fine. Her legs felt a bit shaky, but that could've as easily as been from the kissing as the not eating. Or the cologne Otis wore. Or the sexy way his jeans hung off his hips. That blue and black and yellow striped shirt. Any of those could make a woman go weak in the knees, and he had them all.

"You don't need to impress me," he said. "I'm already impressed. In fact, you're way out of my league." He reached to open the door, but Georgia tugged on his hand. He looked back at her, his dark eyes full of questions.

"What does that mean?" she asked.

"Which—what?"

"I'm not out of your league."

He smiled. "You didn't like that?"

"No, I didn't like it." She squinted at him. "You realize you're a country music star, right? If there's anyone out of their league, it's me."

He laughed, and Georgia thought he really found her funny. He wasn't joking. He wasn't kidding. There were no flirtatious vibes coming from him. "Come on," he said, and he opened the door.

She went inside with him, relieved to be out of the cold, but her mind still niggling at her. Why would Otis Young, seriously the best-looking, most talented man in Country Quad, think *he* was out of *her* league?

She didn't have a moment to ask, because they were inside now. Otis got mobbed by Joey and the rest of his nieces and nephews to go skate, and Abby raised her eyebrows at Georgia, the question clear.

Where have you two been?

"In a minute," Otis said, laughing. "Okay, guys? Give

me five minutes. I have to introduce Georgia around." He moved back to her side and gave her a look filled with apprehension. Again, she didn't understand that. This was his family, and while she knew families had challenges, he'd never mentioned that he didn't get along with everyone in the Young clan.

"Mama," he called, and he led her past all the tables with all the staring people to the rink. "She'll kill me if she doesn't get to meet you first." Otis gave her a sexy smile, all of his nerves now concealed somewhere.

Georgia wished she could do that, but she felt sure her smile looked as panicked as she felt.

His mother skated over, a dark-haired little girl in her arms. Her eyes fixated on Georgia, and she passed the darling child to Otis. "You must be—"

"Mama," he cut off. "Let me." He adjusted the girl on his hip, and while Georgia had seen him interact with his own daughter, watching him be so easy and so comfortable with a smaller child warmed her heart.

"Mama," he said again. "This is Georgia Beck, my girlfriend." He smiled at her, only a hint of something in his eyes flashing in time with the red, blue, and white lights out on the rink. "Georgia, this is my mama, Cecily."

"You are a pretty woman," Mama said, and Georgia hadn't been expecting that.

"Thank you," she said. "It's great to meet you." She shook Cecily's hand and looked at Otis again. "And who are you?" She tapped the little girl's knee, put a big smile on her face, and watched the little girl stare at her.

"This here is Liesl," Otis said. "She's my brother, Gabe's, daughter. She's only two."

"She's beautiful," Georgia said. She knew all of Otis's family's names. He'd come over for dinner last night after band practice, and she'd made him quiz her. None of them were married, besides Tex, and they all had kids—except Morris.

She turned as Cecily came off the rink. "Let's go eat with your daddy, Lisel." She led the way, but Otis carried the little girl. At the table, Otis started introducing her around, and the twins shook her hand almost disinterestedly, as Otis had said they would.

Tex engulfed her in a hug, which he also warned her about. Bryce shook her hand. Luke regarded her coolly, but said hello. Trace smiled wide and hugged her. Mav did the same, as did his wife, Dani, who Georgia actually knew and had been to lunch with. She sat next to Abby, and Abby slid over to make room for Georgia there too.

She met his father last, and he seemed calm, quiet, and cool. She looked back and forth between him, his wife, and Otis, and she saw the perfect mix of the both of them inside her boyfriend.

"Pizza," Otis said, putting a plate in front of her and taking a seat at her side. "You're hungry, right?"

"Yes, sir," she said.

"Oh, don't call him sir," Abby said. "He already has a big head."

"I do not," Otis argued back. "Tex, why am I getting picked on? It's my daughter's birthday party." He lifted a slice of pizza as his older brother chuckled. "I paid for your dinner."

"He has a point," Tex said.

"I heard him and Trace talking," Abby said, and Georgia looked between her and Otis like it was a fascinating game of tennis. "He thinks his songs are perfect as-is."

"They are," Otis said. "It's your husband messing up the lyrics."

"What about that B-flat?" Luke asked, and Georgia looked over to him. The man exuded confidence and good-looks, but also a very strong *do-not-even-think-about-talking-to-me* vibe. Georgia ate while Otis went after him with, "The B-flat? The single note in the past four albums that wasn't right? Did any of *you* hear it?"

They all laughed, even Otis, and Georgia finally relaxed. She...belonged here. Right here, next to her best friend and her boyfriend—who was rapidly becoming one of her best friends. She liked the way they talked to each other, and the way the children went around to anyone in the family for help. And anyone would give it.

People moved onto the rink and off it, and after a while, Georgia stood up and put her hand on Otis's shoulder. "I'm going to skate," she said. "Do you want to come?"

"Sure," he said. "But cake is coming out in fifteen minutes, and then we're opening presents."

"I haven't done much more than feed animals and stock shelves in years," she teased. "So I think fifteen minutes is my maximum skating time."

He chuckled and went with her to get skates. By the time they had them on, and Georgia took the plunge and stepped onto the rink, they had maybe ten minutes left before cake. She reached for his hand, and their eyes met. She was suddenly transported back in time about two decades to this same roller rink. She wasn't the prettiest or most popular girl in high school, but Otis was the cream of the crop. Every girl in the world wanted to go out with him, but he'd chosen her.

She hadn't actually known Otis in high school; it was just the feeling that flooded her from head to toe. She didn't want anything to disrupt this magical feeling, but she also wanted to know why Otis felt like she was out of his league.

Before she could ask, he said, "Georgia," in one of his More Serious tones.

"Hmm." Her feet felt stable as they rounded the corner, and she supposed roller skating was like riding a bike.

"Do you like kids?"

"Yes," she said, surprised by the question. He hadn't specifically introduced her to Joey yet, as the little girl hadn't come off the rink to eat.

"Do you want kids?"

"Yes." She glanced over to him. "Do you want more kids?"

"Yeah," he said. "I think I'm doing okay with Joey. Not great or anything."

"Otis," she said.

"What?"

"Your...why don't you think very highly of yourself?" She watched him, and a struggle moved across his face. He shuttered it off, and Georgia didn't like that. She wanted a man who could be himself. Someone who would confide in her—not his brothers.

She suddenly felt at a disadvantage. He'd been with his brothers for decades. Some of them he worked with for hours every afternoon. They'd toured together. They'd lived together. They knew him in a way she didn't—and might never be able to know him.

Her chest stormed, especially when Otis said nothing in his defense. She gently pulled her hand out of his. "It's okay," she said, though she didn't feel like it was okay. "They're bringing out the cake, and this is your party."

"Georgia," he said as she put on a burst of speed to move away from him.

She spun around and skated backward, liking that his eyebrows shot up at her amazing trick. "It's fine, Otis," she said. "You'll tell me when you're ready." She turned around again and skated off the rink with him close behind her. All she could do now was hope and pray he'd get ready to talk to her quickly.

What if he never does? she wondered, but she curtained those doubts behind a smile and plenty of applause as Joey blew out her candles. The Young brothers could make a person feel like a million bucks, and Georgia wanted all of them to come to every one of her parties and gatherings from now on.

The whooping, the hollering, the grins. She'd have thought this birthday party was for a queen, not an eight-year-old little girl.

The presents had been piled onto a fourth table, and Joey sat at it like a princess, her clothes brightly colored and glittering. She wore a smile that Georgia hoped never got erased from her soul by a cowboy who didn't want to confide in her, and she opened present after present.

She got books from some of her cousins. She got a pair of shoes from this uncle, and then a new hammock for her new house from that one. They all had thoughtful gifts that weren't over-the-top, and Georgia once again felt like she fit in with them.

To be honest, she hadn't been expecting that. She'd told herself not to talk about Tex or his brothers with Abby, because she didn't want anything her best friend said to color her relationship with Otis. She didn't need to go into situations or dates with preconceived notions. Otis had planned marvelous dates for the two of them, and he always had her favorites, from food to places to activities.

He really was one of the better boyfriends she'd ever had—*the best*, her mind amended for her—and she didn't want to lose him over something like him needing more time to tell her something.

She caught his eye several times during the gift-giving, and she eventually moved as close to him as she dared to get and still be acceptable in public. He held her hand, so he wasn't shy about having her there, and Georgia leaned into his bicep when Joey picked up her first present.

"I'm so nervous," she admitted.

"She's eight," Otis said. "You'll be fine."

Joey pulled back on the paper and then stopped. "Wait. Who is this from?" She had straight, almost white, hair that fell halfway down her back. Today, it had been pulled into a ponytail, and plenty of wisps came off the front from all her skating.

"That's from Georgia," Otis said, leaning forward. "So you be real kind about it."

Joey met Georgia's eyes, and she nodded at her. She wished everyone else would go back to focusing on the child, but plenty of them lingered on her. What? Couldn't she bring a gift to her boyfriend's daughter on her birthday?

Two was probably overkill, she thought, but she couldn't lunge toward the table and remove the second present now.

"I bet it's a book," Joey said, but Georgia only smiled. She'd guessed with the girl's love of reading that she'd get plenty of books on her birthday. She'd been right too, and she had deliberately *not* bought her a book.

Joey peeled off the paper and opened the box. She studied it for a moment and looked up. Her eyes had widened like plates. "Daddy, it's a reading light."

"Is that right?" Otis grinned at her.

Georgia stepped away from him and scooted onto the bench beside Joey. She knew every single person in the roller rink had just zeroed in on her. She ran events at the shop. She dealt with angry customers. She owned and operated her own business and had for years.

"So, you see," she said. "When your daddy says it's time for bed, but you're in the middle of a really great chapter, you clip it on your book like this." She took the light out of the box and reached for one of the paperbacks her uncle Morris had given her.

She fitted the light right over the pages and clicked the button. "*Violà.* You say good-night, snuggle under the covers, and finish your chapter." Georgia looked down at Joey, and the little girl looked up at her with pure wonder in her expression.

"This is amazing," she said. "I think this might be better than this unicorn sweatshirt."

Georgia laughed and shook her head, because Otis had told her over pizza that his mother had purchased the sweatshirt. "Not even close, honey." She gave her a squeeze and stood back up.

She looked at Abby, who shone like the sun. Tex

looked like he'd been hit with a two-by-four, and every other man's face Georgia scanned looked about the same. It was like they'd never seen a reading light before.

Otis wore the same shock, but it melted away quickly, his smile blinding her. He took her into his arms and pressed a kiss to her forehead. "You are brilliant."

"It's a *reading light*," she said, turning in his arms. She stood in front of him, every eye on the pair of them now. Otis let his hands settle on her waist, and Georgia wasn't sure she liked how intimate they were being in front of everyone. She shuffled forward an inch or two and felt better, but no one else even seemed to be breathing.

"There's one more," Bryce said loudly, and Georgia knew that was from her too. He snapped his fingers in front of his father's face and added, "Give that to Joey, Dad. Why is everyone staring? Does Uncle Otis never date or something?"

Several voices sounded at once, most of them too loud and somewhat nervous, and Georgia laughed, so she didn't hear what everyone said. Otis leaned his head closer and said, "I've dated before, for the record."

"Mm," she said. "I'm very interested in hearing more about that."

Joey took the present from Tex, and Georgia said, "That's from me too, sweetie."

The girl smiled and said, "Wow, Georgia. Two presents? Thank you." She flicked a look at her father, and Otis pulled her right back against his body. Georgia decided she was comfortable there, and the warmth from his skin and body seeped into hers.

Joey peeled off the paper from the tube, and Georgia held her breath. She knew a little bit about Joey from talking to her father, and she'd interacted with the girl at the shop a couple of weeks ago.

"This isn't a book," she said, her voice growing excited. The brown cardboard tube came into view, and she struggled with the white cap on the end.

"Bryce," Otis said, and Joey's cousin bent down to help Joey with the end cap. He got the first one off, and Joey dipped her little hand into the tube.

"I'm so excited," she said, her voice shaking.

Georgia tilted to look at Otis. "Is she really?"

"She loves surprises," he said in a low voice. "And your first gift was so awesome, she thinks this is going to be amazing."

"She's going to be upset," Georgia said.

Joey pulled the huge poster out of the tube and lifted up onto her feet to spread it across the table. Bryce helped her do that too, and even Luke held down a corner while everyone looked at it.

Georgia waited for someone to know what they were looking at, but as more and more of them looked at her, she cleared her throat. "Joey, it's a paint by number poster. You have to back up a little."

She stepped over to Otis's parents and said, "Maybe someone could hold you."

"Come here, Roo," his father said.

Joey got off the bench and her grandfather picked her up. Georgia stood right next to her. "See the whole picture. Don't look at the individual numbers or boxes. See the whole thing."

Joey concentrated, her eyes narrowing. "Oh," she said. "Georgia, I see it."

"What is it, Roo?" Otis asked, coming to Georgia's side. His hand slid along her waist.

"It's a dragon, Daddy. A *huge* fire-breathing dragon!" She squirmed to get down, and Jerry set her on her feet. She scampered back to the table and started showing everyone where the curve of the back was, and where the fire came out of his mouth.

"You are my favorite person," Otis murmured into her ear. "Thank you."

Georgia put her hand over his on her hip and patted it. "Thank you for inviting me."

Abby came toward her. "You're never invited to birthday parties again," she said.

"What?" Georgia blinked a couple of times. "Why?"

"Because we all feel stupid about our gifts now."

"Oh, come on. It's a poster she has to paint."

"Of a fire-breathing dragon." Abby turned and looked at Joey, who was still talking to Corrine, Beth, and Boston. "That girl loves dragon, unicorns, and anything mythical."

"Then you should *want* me to come to your child's

birthday party, so they get an amazing gift." She lifted her nose into the air, and Abby giggled with her.

"I have to say, Georgia," Dani said as she handed her a plate with a slice of cake on it. "I expected a book from you, what with you owning a bookstore and all."

"Yes, well, the gift chooses the recipient, and she got a bunch of amazing books already."

"Well, you're amazing." Dani smiled at her and put one hand on her baby belly. "Ooh, he's kicking."

Georgia grinned, her hand already up. "Can I?"

"Of course."

She and Abby put their hands on Dani's belly, and sure enough, her baby kicked at them. The little thump against her palm made Georgia sigh in wonder and love. "I can't wait to meet him," she said. "Did you guys decide on a name?"

"Not yet, despite having two family parties."

"Well, there's your problem," Otis said. "Trying to get all of us to agree on something is like trying to make the sun become the moon." He squeezed Georgia's hip and stepped away from her.

"We have twenty minutes left, everyone. Get your last skate on. Eat all this cake. We have to start cleaning up soon." He turned and looked at Georgia, the heat between them scorching hot. Georgia ducked her head, because she didn't need to put everything between them on public display.

"Oh, girl," Abby hissed from her side. "You kissed him and didn't tell me."

Dani's eyes buzzed with interest, and Georgia saw no reason to deny it. "Just today," she said. "And I'm not giving any details, so don't you dare hound me."

"Lunch," Abby said instantly. "Us and Cheryl. Send me your schedules."

"Any day," Dani said, but Georgia would have to actually check her calendar. She told Abby that, and then she started to clean up. Wrapping paper, empty used plates, half-full cups. She kept looking for Otis, and every time she found him, she marveled that she had caught his attention.

She did want to know what haunted him, and she told herself she didn't have to discover everything today. They had more time together, and she'd keep getting to know him better and better over time.

He sidled up to her as she threw a stack of cups into the trash can. "Me and you. Dinner tomorrow. Seven?"

"Yes," she said without thinking about it.

"Can't wait," he said, and then he was gone, off to pick up something else, hug a brother good-bye, or yell at Joey to come off the rink for the fourth time.

"I can't either," Georgia said to herself, and what she really couldn't wait for was another one of his very real, very good kisses.

15

Otis stayed in bed late the next day. He could, because Joey didn't have school. They'd been up late at the roller rink, and then at home as she went over and over her presents again. She'd had him help her put the reading light on the Animal Hunters book she was currently reading, and Otis told her not to stay up too late.

He'd told himself the same thing, and then he'd called Georgia to tease her about all the fights he was going to have with his daughter. They'd been on the phone until almost midnight, and when Otis had gone to check on Joey, she'd been asleep, the book open on her chest, and the clipped-on reading light still going strong.

After putting it away and tucking her in, he'd finally gone to bed. He was used to late nights from his time touring with Country Quad, and he'd never really had to get up too early the next morning. Sometimes for a flight or a fan event, but rarely. Mav had been really good about making sure the wake-up calls didn't come until at least eleven.

Today, Otis lifted his head as his bedroom door swung in, and Joey padded into the room. "Daddy?"

"Hmm?" He flung open his blanket, which invited his daughter to come lay by him. She did, her book back in her hand. "Reading already this morning?"

"Yeah." She snugged into the pillow beside him, and Otis smiled over to her.

"Does it feel different to be eight instead of seven?"

She giggled and nodded. "Of course."

"Of course," he repeated, glad he'd gotten a daughter with her head in the clouds. He loved Beth too, but she was so practical already, even at only six years old. Joey had always loved fantastical stories, talking cats, mythical creatures, and far-off lands. Otis had never minded her imagination, and he actually loved her more for it.

"What should we do today?" he asked.

She looked at him, a touch of irritation in her eyes. "I'm reading."

"All day?"

"Yes." She went back to her book and turned the page.

Otis let her do that for a while, his eyes closed and his mind wandering. He liked having another breathing human at his side, and the next time he woke, he startled. "Roo?"

"Right here, Daddy." She reached over and put her hand on his chest. "Mama called."

Otis rolled toward her, still feeling sleepy. "She did?"

"Yeah, she called my phone."

"What did she want?"

"She said she's feeling good today, and she wants me to come up there for a movie this afternoon."

"Okay," Otis said, because now he didn't have to find a babysitter for Joey for his date that night. "I can take you." He let his eyes drift closed again.

"It starts at two," she said. "Or three."

"Is it two or three?"

"I don't know," Joey said.

"What movie is it?" He could probably look it up on his phone. Dog Valley had a single movie theater, and Lauren would probably have her mother with her.

"I don't know."

"What do you know?" he asked, smiling at his daughter. He looked at her, and she looked back at him.

"Mama called," she said with a smile.

"You were still thinkin' about your cats," he said.

"No." She giggled as he started to tickle her. "I wasn't. This book is about dogs."

Otis pulled the book from her hands and kept tickling her. "That's not true. All these Animal Hunters books are about cats."

She laughed and laughed, and when she said, "Stop, Daddy, I can't breathe right," he stopped. They lay beside one another, both of them laughing and trying to catch their breath. Otis loved the soft, slow moments like this with Joey, and he was supremely glad he was here, in Coral Canyon, to have them.

"I love you, Roo," he said.

She stroked her hand over his beard. "I love you too, Daddy." She sobered, and Otis waited. He'd seen this look on Joey's face before, and she had a question for him.

"What's in your head?" he asked.

"I heard Harry say you were dating Miss Georgia." She looked down at his chin. "Your beard is real long, Daddy."

"Yeah," he said, his pulse suddenly lodged somewhere in the back of his throat. "About Georgia...."

Joey looked back into his eyes, hers so open and innocent.

"I am dating her," he said. "Do you know what that means?"

"It means you're her girlfriend," she said. "Oops, no, she's your girlfriend."

Otis grinned at her. "Yeah, that's what it means."

"So you like her, Daddy?"

"Yeah," Otis said, his chest squeezing tightly. "I like her." He could easily admit it to Joey and even his brothers. He wasn't sure he wanted to let himself slide too much, too fast, because he always did that. Then he got his heart in trouble, and it was getting smaller and smaller with every woman who shaved part of it off and wouldn't give it back.

"I like her too," Joey said. "She's nice."

"She is nice," Otis said.

"Can we go to the bookstore before we go to Mama's?"

Otis smiled at her and shook his head. "No, Roo. You got like five new books yesterday."

"I need a new bookmark." Her eyes grew wider, sadder, and she had to be part puppy with that look. "Please?"

"Oh, don't beg, Roo," he said, rolling away from her. "It's not princess-like." He stood and stretched both arms above his head. "I'm gonna shower, and we're gonna talk about breakfast, and then maybe we'll see what time your movie is."

"It's at four," Joey said, and Otis turned around to do his next stretch so he could see his daughter. She already had her nose buried in her book, and he doubted she had listened to her mother at all. Which meant Otis would have to call Lauren. He didn't mind so much, and if he was Mav, he'd have told Lauren about Georgia last week, and she would've met her before Otis let Joey in the same room as her.

He wasn't Mav, and he doubted Lauren cared at all about who he dated. He'd had a few other girlfriends since their marriage had ended, and he hadn't felt any need to tell her about them.

He picked up his phone on the way into the bathroom

and saw a text from Georgia. *Harley said she'd run the shop this afternoon, all the way through close. What are your plans? Fancy picking me up a little early?*

A smile burst onto his face, and he hurried to thumb out his answer. *Absolutely.* He worried that he was coming on too strong. Revealing too much. Moving too fast.

"Go slow," he told himself, pausing in the doorway. He also heard what Abby had told him about Georgia, as much as he wished he didn't.

She falls really hard and really fast, Otis. You have to be careful with her.

He thought the same thing about himself, and he really didn't want to get his heart broken again. So he erased the message and typed out a different one. *Let me figure things out with my ex, and I'll let you know.*

That was non-committal. Casual. He wanted to, obviously, but he wasn't going to go to great lengths. He wasn't sure why he didn't want to reveal his whole hand to Georgia—he'd kissed her last night. A lot—only that he didn't.

As he showered, the answer came into his mind, but he didn't like it.

He didn't want to fall in love first. He simply couldn't. Not again. And that meant he had to slow things down with Georgia, because he felt like she'd already claimed a piece of his heart—and that was a piece he'd never get back if things went south between them.

A FEW HOURS LATER, WITH JOEY READING ONE OF HER birthday books, a brand-new bookmark tucked between the pages, he pulled up to Lauren's house. Her car sat in the driveway, as did her mother's. Otis looked up to the house, which didn't seem any different than any other time he'd come here.

The siding was gray, the shutters white. Her front door she'd painted black last summer sometime, while Otis had been on tour. When he'd brought Joey back for school in the fall, they'd had a brief conversation about it. Otis tried to keep everything between him and Lauren easy and light, so while he didn't understand painting a door black, he'd agreed with Lauren and said it looked nice with her autumnal wreath.

"Let's go, Roo," he said as she hadn't looked up from her book. She did now, and Otis twisted to grab her overnight bag from the backseat. She was staying here tonight, and Otis would come get her tomorrow night so he could get her to school on time on Monday morning.

He got out, the chill of winter stinging his lungs. Joey opened her door as he came around, and he helped her down. "Careful," he said. "It's a little icy right there."

She avoided the slippery section, and Otis took her up to the front door. She didn't knock, because she'd lived here for a long time. Otis hung back, because he rarely went inside Lauren's house. Sometimes he simply sent Joey up the sidewalk while he stayed in the truck.

Lauren came around the corner and bent down to hug Joey, who was already showing her the new book, with the reading light attached, of course. Otis took a step into the house, because he wanted to see how Lauren looked.

She straightened and looked at Otis. "Lauren," he said, reaching to tip his hat. She wore a pair of jeans that seemed to hang off of her frame, which meant she'd lost some weight. She'd paired those with a sweater that looked two sizes too big, and she wore a pair of fuzzy slippers on her feet.

She reached out and put her hand on the wall as she walked toward him. She moved slowly, but her face had some color today, and her hair shone as if she'd just showered and then dried it. "Otis," she said. "Thanks for bringing her."

"Of course." He hated being thanked for taking care of his own daughter. Lauren had spent most of Joey's life as her primary caregiver. "How are you?" He met her in only a couple of steps and swept a kiss along her cheek.

"I'm okay," she said. She twisted to look at Joey. "Joelle, go see Grandma Echo in the kitchen. She was pulling some bread out of the oven a minute ago."

Otis could suddenly smell it, and he watched as Joey skipped around the corner and into the kitchen. Lauren faced him. "Otis," she said. "I've got some news."

He swallowed, because now that he stood a little

closer, he could see some swelling in her face. "You've lost weight," he said.

She nodded. "A little."

"A lot," he argued.

"I'm still dealing with the fatigue and headaches and pain in my joints."

Otis simply watched her, ready for this to be done with. Once he knew, then he could do something.

"It's lupus." She blinked and reached up to run her hands through her hair. Some of it came out on her fingers. "There's hair loss too." She flung the strands away, watching them fall to the ground. "The good news is, people live with lupus for a lot of years."

Otis didn't know anything about lupus. He knew Lauren had faded into a shell of the woman she'd once been. She no longer seemed to be a person in color, but a bunch of bones in too-big clothes, with dull hair and gray skin. He folded her into a hug and held her as tightly as he dared. He certainly didn't want to cause her any extra pain.

"I'm so sorry," he said.

"I have good health insurance," she said, pulling away. "I'm starting on some medications on Monday, and my doctors think I'm going to see some really big improvements."

"That's great," he said. He tucked his hands in his pockets. "I'll call you Monday before I head into the recording studio. I want to know how it goes and if you need anything."

"My mom is around, so." She shifted her feet. "I'm going to be okay, Otis."

"I'm so glad," Otis said, though he didn't think she was out of the woods yet. "I'm still going to call you and keep in touch."

"I appreciate it." She turned and started toward the kitchen. "Any time tomorrow after seven would be best. My sister is coming for dinner at my mom's."

"All right," he said. He watched her go into the kitchen, and then he turned to leave. He wasn't sure how he felt. He wasn't disappointed. Or excited. Or relieved. "Help me, Lord," he prayed, the words as natural as breathing. "If she needs help, I can do it."

He'd learn more about lupus, and a new thought struck him. "I want to keep Joey." He didn't want Lauren to be ill, and he sincerely hoped the medications and treatments would work. His fingers tightened on the wheel, his life suddenly a whole more complicated.

He wanted Lauren to be well. He wanted to keep Joey with him. Mixed-up feelings soared through him, and he only kept driving because he'd been doing it for so long and he didn't have to think about it.

He ended up at Georgia's house, and she sat on the top step and watched a few dogs romp through the snow in her front yard. She wore a bright red coat and a cream-colored, puffy hat on her head. She lifted a coffee cup to her lips and smiled at him as he pulled into her driveway.

Otis looked at her and put the truck in park. He got out and sauntered toward her. One of the dogs caught sight of him and started yapping. All four of them came sprinting toward him, and Georgia whistled through her teeth to call them off.

"They're nice," she said.

"Sure," Otis said, bending down to pat the biggest one, who'd already reached him. His tail wagged in a circle, and that made Otis chuckle. He loved Tex's dog, and when he finally moved into his own house, he'd like to get a canine of his own.

The idea wasn't practical, because he spent long hours in the studio, and he'd have to tour once the album came out next year. Still, he could probably get Mav to tend to the dog when the tour finally started.

All of the canines saw the good pat Otis was giving to the black lab, and they wanted some love too. He chuckled as he tried to scrub them all at the same time, but he only had two hands.

"All right," he said to them. "Go find your mama." He straightened and looked at Georgia. She scooted over, clearly making space for him on the top step. He went to take it, groaning as he eased down. The dogs went back to the snow, one of them barking and barking and barking. None of the other dogs answered it, and Otis nodded to it.

"What's with him?"

"He likes to listen to his own voice," Georgia said, passing him her coffee cup. "There's a little left."

Otis took it and drained the last of her caffeine. "How'd you get him?"

"His owners couldn't handle the barking."

"He kind of sounds like a train horn," Otis said, laughing.

Georgia giggled and nudged his knee with hers. "Be nice."

"He's a dog," Otis said, handing back her empty coffee cup.

"I like him," Georgia said. "He has personality."

"He thrives with you." Otis gave her a smile, and she returned it. The moment quieted, and Otis leaned down. Georgia met him halfway, and he kissed her right there on her front porch. She took his face in one of her palms, and he really liked the way that simple touch claimed him.

She broke the kiss gently, and asked, "Otis, why don't you like yourself?"

He opened his eyes, the sunlight really bright as it glinted off the snow. That dog kept yelling in his train-horn voice, and it echoed in Otis's head until it was all he could hear.

"I like myself," he said.

"Mm, I told you about my weakness with animals. You can tell me about your weakness with self-love."

Otis blinked, trying to figure out what to say. He didn't

want to give away too much, but he also wanted to open this door to his heart.

Should I? he asked himself. Then he asked God.

For Georgia, he thought, and though their relationship still felt new, Otis decided to embrace himself and how fast he fell for women. He took a breath and opened his mouth.

16

Georgia linked her arm through Otis's and hugged his bicep. She leaned her cheek against it, enjoying the small-town silence though she wished Otis would break it.

"I know I'm talented in some ways," he said. "And I appreciate those."

She snuggled deeper into his side and waited.

"I know I'm a good songwriter. I know I can pick up any instrument and play it decently well in about ten minutes. I know I'm not as hotheaded as some of my brothers, and I know most of them can come to me if they need something."

Georgia let a beat of silence go by, and then she said, "All good things."

He dropped his head, and because Georgia had cuddled into him, the brim of his cowboy hat created a semi-private space for the two of them. "I've not had the greatest of luck with women," he said. "I fall too fast, and too hard, and honestly, I'm tryin' real hard not to do that here."

She sat up and away from him, turning to look at him. "A weakness in the mighty Otis Young."

A smile touched his mouth, but it didn't stay. "I have plenty of 'em, Gerogia."

"Yeah? Name another one."

"I don't know how to be a dad," he said, his hands clasping as they hung between his knees. "Notes and measures, I get. How to relate to my little girl, I don't. I'm doing my best, but I know I'm not enough for her."

"I've seen you with her. You're a great dad."

He drew in a breath, held it, and pushed it out. "I'm trying, and I think that's what you see. I know nothing. What I do know is she needs a mother. There's a reason everyone stared at you at the party, and it's because you have this soft, feminine, motherly touch, and it radiated from you."

Hope soared through Georgia, but it only lasted a moment. Immediately afterward, disbelief tore through her. "I don't think that's true."

"It's true."

Georgia appreciated how real he'd been with her. She could feel the vulnerability pouring from him, and she hoped she could make him more comfortable. "I love kids," she said. "I love watching them when they come into the shop and get the books they love." She gave a smile to the dogs still romping through the snow. "I do want kids."

"A lot of kids or one or two?"

Georgia indicated the dogs. "Do I look like a person who puts limits on things?"

Otis chuckled and took her hand in his. "So whatever you get."

"Whatever I get," she said, a swoop in her stomach. "I've been dating a lot lately."

"Yeah? Why's that?"

Georgia took a moment to find the right words in the right order. "I spent a few years building Beck's Books. It's going well. I have all these fun dogs and cats. A bird." She twisted to look behind her, though Sammy wasn't chirping right now. "And I don't know. I still feel like there's something missing in my life."

"And you think that's a cowboy who writes songs for his family band and travels on tour for half the year?"

"I don't know," Georgia said, her voice pitching up. "But I'm dating to find out who it is."

"Why do you like me?" he asked.

Georgia met his gaze, her own heart thundering through her chest. She'd started this conversation to get him to talk, not to start her own confession session. "Really?"

"Yes," he said, not a hint of teasing or flirting in sight. He wore a Very Serious face, and Georgia realized he truly wanted to know.

"You're handsome," she said, looking back toward the dogs. The littlest one, Charlie, sat at the bottom of the steps, gazing up at her. "Come on, Charles. You can come up here." The little bichon Frise came trotting up the steps to her side. She smiled at him and stroked his side. "He always waits to be invited."

"How polite," Otis said dryly. A beat went by before he added, "That's all I get? Handsome? There are a million handsome men."

"In your family," she quipped.

Otis grinned and shook his head. "If you say so."

"You're funny," she said. "Thoughtful. You listen to me. You're a great dad." The train got rolling in Georgia's mouth, and she tried to apply the brakes but couldn't. "You show up on time. You look amazing in a leather jacket. You helped me when I needed it. You can kiss like a professional."

Her voice finally muted, and complete humiliation filled her as her memory recalled all the things she'd just said. Horror struck her behind her tongue as one sentence reverberated through her whole body.

You can kiss like a professional.

She pressed her eyes closed and took comfort from Charlie. She shot to her feet in the next moment, needing to get away from her own idiocy. "Come on, guys," she yelled to the dogs still out in the snow. "Let's go in."

"We're going in?" Otis asked.

Georgia could barely look at him. His eyes landed like

bombs on her face, which felt super-heated past comfortable.

He stood too. "What's wrong?"

"I just said a lot of embarrassing things," she said, turning away from him. Ruby had started to run toward her, and as the pack leader, she'd get the other dogs into the house for Georgia.

"You did not," Otis said.

Georgia gave him a withering look as dog paws hit the porch and they got joined by three more canines. "Then let's add 'you're kind' to the list of reasons I like you." She poked him in the chest, and he reacted in such an exaggerated way by actually falling back a step. "What about you? Do you want to list all the reasons you like me?" She stepped by him and opened the door to let the dog parade enter before her.

"Sure," he said behind her. "You're beautiful. You're smart. You're confident and strong and amazing with kids."

She noted that there was nothing about her own kissing ability in there, as Otis was far more eloquent than her. She indicated he should enter the house too, but he stood his ground a few feet away.

"I've been thinking about you since you kissed me last summer," he said. "I used to find any reason to come by the shop to see you." He swallowed. "You're sexy, and I started to fall too fast, and it scared me."

"Why would it scare you?" she asked.

Otis sighed and ducked his head again. "Let's go inside, and you can make me some real coffee that's hot, and then I'll tell you." He went past her then, and Georgia liked the presence of him in her life, in her house. She followed him and set about making another pot of coffee while he wiped down the dogs with the stack of towels she'd laid out on the counter for that purpose.

She didn't even have to ask him to do that, and she added that to the list of things she liked about him. She liked that he had fears too, as it made him more human. He seemed so...*big*. Larger than life. Like he could hold out his hand and the world would just fall right into it.

He finally settled at the kitchen counter, and Georgia opened her fridge to find something to serve him while the coffee continued to brew. Her mother had taught her to always offer something, and she'd never be able to take Otis home to meet her if she couldn't say she'd given him cookies or something.

To her mother's credit, Georgia had a box of macaroons in her fridge. "I forgot I had these," she said. She pulled the white pastry box out of the fridge and turned toward Otis. "Cookies?"

"You have cookies you've forgotten about in your fridge?" Otis quirked a smile at her. "That would never happen at my house."

"Your house, or your mama's house?" She slid the box across the counter to him.

"Both." He caught the box and took the gold elastic string off the top. "These are beautiful."

"One of my best patrons brought them to me a day or two ago," she said, smiling at him. Things felt better between them, and Georgia regretted not being able to sleep last night. She was a tosser and turner, a worrier, and she hadn't slept well at all. "She brings in her special-needs daughter every Thursday, and she brought me these from a new shop over by the health center."

Otis bit into a dark green one, with pale green cream in the middle. His eyes rolled back in his head, and he moaned. "I'm getting some of these on my way home."

"Tonight?" she asked, leaning her hip into the counter. "I thought we were going to dinner."

"Shoot." He lifted his phone and checked the time. "What time do they close?"

Georgia laughed at his boyishness, and he joined her. The moment lengthened, and she turned to get out a mug for him. As she poured the coffee, the house quieted. She waited for him to say something among all the dogs still panting. At least they'd all laid down somewhere and weren't begging him for a cookie snack.

She placed his mug in front of him, then turned to grab the sugar and get out the cream. Otis seemed to be a sugar hound, and as he spooned in sugar, she slid onto the barstool next to him.

Georgia said, "Let's see..." and slid the macaroons away from him. "I like the sour ones." She selected a yellow macaroon, smelled the lemon zest on it, and took a bite. Obsidian, her grouchy cat who dared leave the top of the fridge, jumped up onto the counter. "Hey," she said, swatting at him. "Get down."

He gave her a look of pure evil, but she returned his attitude in force. "Go on," she said.

He walked as slowly as he could, stared at Otis as he went by, and then leapt lightly to the floor.

"That cat is going to murder me one day," Otis said. He turned to look at Georgia, and they laughed together again. He leaned over and kissed her cheek, and Georgia pressed into the touch.

When he straightened, he picked up the other half of his cookie and ate it in one bite. He lifted his mug to his lips and took a sip of coffee. "Oh, that's good," he said with a sigh. "I might as well start talkin', right?"

"If you want," she said. "I think I'll be able to sleep tonight, at least."

His gaze came back to her. "You couldn't sleep last night?"

Heat migrated up her throat to her face. "I mean...I was worried you might be hiding something big from me."

"Like what?" he asked. "You know I've been married and divorced. I have a daughter. What could be bigger than that?"

Georgia shrugged, though her stomach stung at her. Her mind screamed for her to tell him the truth. Wasn't that what she wanted from him?

"I had this boyfriend once," she said. "Who was really private. It wasn't that he kept big things from me. It was that he didn't want to talk to me about much of anything." She reached for another cookie, this time selecting the pale brown one, as it would be salted caramel. "He worked through things on his own. He didn't want to share with me. I wanted—and still do—a man who's willing to open up and tell me everything. Because that's what I want to do." She broke the cookie in half and offered him a piece.

He took his, but his dark-as-night eyes didn't leave hers.

"I want a best friend cowboy husband," she said with a smile. "Who'll listen to me complain about the shop, though he knows I love it. Who wants to tell me about a terrible day in the studio, though I know he loves his brothers and wants to go back the next."

Otis ducked his head then, and Georgia once again feared that she'd said too much. "Or whoever I end up with. Maybe it'll be that really sexy new mayor."

He whipped his head up again. "Who now?"

She grinned at him. "Oh, someone didn't like that, did they?" She giggled, but Otis stayed Quite Serious.

"I don't like thinking about you datin' someone else, no," he finally said. He popped his half of the macaroon into his mouth. "I don't like that at all."

"I just don't want you to think I'm ready to marry you or anything. That's not what this conversation is. It was hypothetical."

He grunted and stirred his coffee.

"Oh, come on," she said with another laugh. "I'm not interested in the mayor."

"You just said he was sexy."

"He is," Georgia said. "And he knows it." She gave him a punctuated look with raised eyebrows. "Ain't no woman wants a man who knows how awesome and good-looking he is, trust me."

Otis took another drink of his coffee. His eyelashes batted and his mouth curved up as he said, "Maybe that's why I'm not taken."

She burst out laughing and nudged him hard with her elbow. He gave an overexaggerated lean away from her, then came at her and put his arm around her waist. He pulled her—and the barstool—right into his personal space and held on.

"I'm having a hard time believing you like me right now," he said. "Because the last woman I dated ghosted me."

Georgia turned Quite Serious too, smiling in one breath and gaping at him in the next. "What? That can't be true."

"Oh, it be true," he said, reaching for another cookie. "This woman in Florida I dated last year. We met on an app. I'd been down to see her plenty of times. We were dating for like, eight months. We had a lunch date scheduled before I was flyin' home for the summer, and...she just wasn't there. I called her. I texted. I couldn't miss my flight, so I came home. Never heard from her again."

"You have got to be kidding." Georgia didn't know women still did that to men. "Really?"

"Cross my heart," he said soberly. He stared into the depths of his coffee, like perhaps it could tell him where he'd gone wrong in his previous relationship. "My confidence has taken a bit of a beating. My ego too." He took a sip of his coffee. "I got a good album out of it, though." He gave her a smile then, but Georgia didn't know how to return it.

She moved toward him and kissed him, glad when he made a slight noise of surprise and then took to the task of kissing her back. She pulled away a little roughly and said, "She is a really stupid woman," and kissed him again.

She'd practically climbed into his lap before Otis broke the kiss the second time. "Yeah," he said in his low cowboy voice. "Because I kiss like a professional, right?"

Georgia's embarrassment returned in full force. She giggled and ducked her head to hide it against his chest. "I can't believe I said that," she muttered to his shirt pocket. Otis chuckled, so she knew he was teasing. She hadn't been.

If she could keep Otis around long enough to keep getting to know him—and keep falling in love with him—she wanted to. She wanted him in her house every single day. She wanted to go to his. She wanted to keep making a connection with Joey.

And then...well, then, she supposed she'd do what she'd always done. She'd see where God directed her, and she'd make the best of whatever that situation was.

She could pray that was with Otis, couldn't she?

As a very loud cat fight started down the hall, causing Georgia to jump to her feet and run that way, she did exactly that. *Don't let these stupid cats be what drives this handsome, kind, caring cowboy from my life.*

She certainly wasn't going to ghost him—the very thought was incomprehensible. But her arrogant pair of cat brothers beating up on one of her rescues? That could definitely send the cowboy packing.

17

Otis opened his front door to sunshine and blue sky. Tex and Bryce stood there too, a trailer attached to Tex's truck, and Bryce's backed into the driveway as it was. "Morning," he said, stepping back. "I think this only counts as half a favor."

"What?" Tex demanded. "No. This is the whole favor."

"It's at least thirty degrees warmer today than it was when I helped you put on that siding." Otis grinned at Bryce as he walked by. "And you said it would be a few hours, and we were there all day."

"He's right, Dad."

"I don't need your opinion," Tex snapped at him. "I brought me and Bryce. That's two of us. I rented the trailer. We're here first." He came inside and closed the door behind him. "This is the whole favor."

Otis followed him into the kitchen, where the whole island held packed and ready-to-go boxes. "Fine," he said. "You win."

"Can I have a doughnut?" Bryce asked, the box already open in front of him. He looked at Otis with questions in his eyes.

"Yeah, sure," he said.

"Daddy," Joey said from her place at the dining room table. "You wouldn't let me have a doughnut."

"Bryce probably ate breakfast already." Otis's attention slid from his daughter to his nephew. He begged Bryce silently to corroborate his story.

"Oh, uh...."

"We had coffee on the way over," Tex said as he selected a doughnut. "That counts, right?"

"Daddy won't let me drink coffee," Joey said.

"You're eight," he shot back at her.

She came around the table, leaving her book behind, so this was serious.

"And coffee isn't a meal," Otis added. "They're older than you, Roo."

"You can have half of mine," Bryce said. Otis knew he was just trying to be nice, and Joey took the half-doughnut from him. Otis turned away from the scene, because he already had to put up with everyone in his family in his personal space for the next few hours. He couldn't go into it irritated, though he was already irritated.

He'd chosen to move on a Wednesday morning. One,

it was the first of the month and he could. Two, his brothers didn't work in the studio until afternoon. Their kids would be in school, and they could all come and help without making other arrangements—if they could set their alarm clocks for early enough.

Tex had kept Bryce home from school, and Otis had kept Joey, obviously. But the next knock on the door brought Mav, Luke, and Morris, all of them without children. Mama and Daddy arrived next, and finally Trace showed up with another box of doughnuts.

After they'd all stood around and eaten too much sugar and had each drunk another cup of coffee, Otis whistled through his teeth. He got up on a chair and raised both arms as high as he could. He could touch the ceiling from here, so he couldn't get them up all the way. "All right, y'all," he said, reverting to the Texas twang he'd picked up while touring the state. "Let's get this move started. Most everything is packed. We'll take out the bigger stuff first. Everything belongs to me and Joey except the furniture here in the living room." He indicated the couch and love seat, the TV stand, and the barstools, which he'd clumped together on the carpet in front of the fireplace.

"Bigger items in the bedrooms," he said. "No one let Daddy pick up anything heavier than a mouse."

"I can help," Daddy said, but all the brothers overrode him, much to Otis's delight. He gave Daddy a sweet smile and got off the chair. He'd had a great month with Georgia, and he couldn't believe he was moving into a house he owned. A nice house, with a heated driveway, and everything he and Joey could ever want.

He had gone through the house more extensively since seeing it the first time, and he could see himself writing music there, fixing dinner for Joey, and kissing Georgia on that gorgeous back deck, the summer sun sinking in the west.

He wanted that reality so badly, and while they'd hit a little speed bump just after Joey's party, it had been smooth sailing since then.

"Get down and help," Tex said, and Otis blinked his way back to reality. And that reality was chaotic, with men moving everywhere and boxes going out before boxed springs.

"Bigger items first," he yelled again.

"We're just emptying everything," Luke told him as he went by with two boxes Otis had labeled *kitchen*. "We'll sort it out outside."

"Why?" Otis said. "Why not take out the bigger items first?"

Luke ignored him as he went outside, and Otis looked at Tex helplessly.

"It's easier to go with the current than fight it," Tex said with a smile. "Come help me with your bed."

Otis couldn't believe they hadn't started with his bed, and another flash of irritation worked through him. He reminded himself that he was grateful they'd all come to help him that day. When he found Morris and Trace laughing over something on Morris's phone, he told himself he loved his brothers. They were all good men, and they put up with plenty of his flaws and issues.

He and Tex got the bed outside, where everything he owned had been piled unceremoniously on the driveway. He said nothing, but went back inside to get Joey's bed.

He held his tongue while Mav told Mama and Daddy to go wait in their truck or over at Otis's new place. They were just in the way here, unable to do a lot until the boxes got taken across town.

He held his tongue when Luke went by with four hangers carrying suit coats, his phone pressed to his ear.

Finally, it was Tex who said, "Hey, Luke, he said no furniture in the living room." He went that way, and Otis picked up a lamp he did own. "Who are you on the phone with?"

"No one," Luke said. He glared at Tex and lowered his phone as he lowered the couch. "None of your business."

"You've been on the phone forever," Tex pressed.

"On hold." Luke walked away, went down the hall, and disappeared. Tex turned to look at Otis, his eyebrows high.

"I don't know," Otis said. "He's a mystery."

Tex frowned in the direction Luke had gone, but he came to help Otis with the boxes on the table. Then Trace and Morris could carry that out too.

Once that was done, Mav and Luke had started to

pack the trucks and trailers, and Otis couldn't believe how much stuff he had. "There's always more than you think," he said to Mav as he handed him another box.

"You should've seen how much stuff Dani had." He smiled, and he'd be the only brother who could do that after spending so long with Luke at his side. Otis gave his younger brother another cursory glance, but Luke still swirled storms from his face, and Otis didn't want to get burned today.

He'd come clean up tonight, as Georgia had said she'd bring dinner and help him and Joey with the task of getting the rental spotless. He wasn't a total slob, but he wasn't a clean freak either, and who cleaned under their bed regularly anyway? No one he knew.

They drove over to the new house, and the driveway was three trucks across instead of two, and the unloading commenced. The house was twice as big, and Otis worked to get his bedroom set up, as well as Joey's. Anything else they didn't get done that day would be fine. They could eat out and have somewhere to sleep, the two most important things.

Mama, of course, started in the kitchen, so Otis could cook here tonight should he wish to. He *could* cook, but it wasn't his favorite thing to do. Not when he could just as easily pick up his phone and order a deep dish pepperoni pizza with lots of black olives. Or a tower of onion rings and the barbecue dipping sauce to go with them. Or a

Philly steak sandwich with some of the best provolone cheese sauce he'd ever tasted.

His stomach growled, because doughnuts were empty calories, and he was a good father not to let his daughter eat one for breakfast. He came out of Joey's room to find her once again sitting at the dining room table, her book in front of her.

Bryce sat beside her on his phone, and Mama bustled around the kitchen, the scent of garlic and onions filling the front of the house. "What's goin' on out here?" he asked.

"Grandma is making that sausage orzo soup I like," Joey said.

Otis's eyebrows went up. He swept a kiss along Joey's hairline and went into the kitchen. It took twice as many steps as it had in his previous house, but he managed to make it to Mama's side. "The sausage orzo soup? That's Echo Renwald's recipe."

"Yes." Mama looked at him with her defenses already in place. "I called her to get it."

"When?"

"Just now."

"Clearly not," Otis said, grinning at his mother. "You're such a liar.

"I am not." She pushed her unused wooden spoon against his chest, but he didn't budge. "Maybe it was yesterday."

"Yeah, maybe," Otis said dryly. "Because you magically have all the ingredients for said soup."

"Yes, well, you didn't tell me Lauren has lupus."

Otis pulled in a breath and looked over to Joey. "Mom," he said. "Shh."

"She doesn't know?"

"Not yet," Otis said. "Lauren's known for a couple of weeks, but she wants to wait and see how the medicine and treatments do before we sit down together and talk to Joey." Otis gave his mother his fiercest look. "Us, Mama. Me and her. Not you."

She raised her chin. "I won't say a word."

"Why did Echo tell you?"

"She's concerned too." She turned and put a dollop of tomato paste in the pan with the sauteed onions and garlic.

"Lauren and I are adults," Otis reminded her. He'd never had a problem with Lauren's mother, though he suspected her as the voice behind Lauren's decision to file for divorce.

"Daddy," Joey said, and Otis spun that way.

"Yeah, Roo?" He walked toward her as something crashed down the hall. It sounded dangerously like the mirror that went on the brand-new dresser set he'd bought for Joey when she'd moved in with him over New Year's.

"Otis!" someone yelled.

"We need a broom," Tex called.

Otis paused, weariness filling him from top to bottom, and it was barely lunchtime. He turned and found Daddy already picking up the broom and dustpan from the corner of the kitchen. "It got it, son," he said.

Otis let him go deal with his sons, and Otis sank into the chair across from Joey. "What, Roo?"

"Look what I drew for Georgia." She tugged a paper from her book and glanced at Bryce. "I mean, look what Bryce drew for Georgia. Then I colored it."

Otis took the half-sheet of paper from his daughter. In black pen, Bryce had outlined Main Street, with just a hint of Bam Bam's on the north, and the post office on the south. Right in the middle, the star of the picture, was Beck's Books.

Everything looked exactly right, from the fun window displays with hearts in the left one, and a whole rain forest in the other. He looked up at both of them. "This is incredible. When did you do this?"

Bryce shrugged. "I don't know."

Teenagers could be so maddening. Bryce was a smart person; he knew exactly when he'd drawn this. He just didn't want to say for some reason.

"Joey?" Otis asked.

"I asked him to draw something I could give to her," Joey said, looking at her cousin. "Wednesday? While you guys played in the barn." She made the very serious album Otis was recording with his famous country band sound like a bunch of naughty boys wasting time in a barn.

He grinned at her. "It's fantastic. She's going to love it."

"When are you seeing her again?" Bryce asked, his eyes a little bit too interested.

"Tonight," Otis said anyway. He handed the art back to Joey. "She's going to come help Joey and me clean the old house."

"I don't want to clean tonight," Joey complained. "Uncle Tex said we could go to a movie."

"Uncle Tex is not your father," Otis said. He got to his feet. "He doesn't get to decide."

"The movie is at five-thirty," Bryce said. "She could be back by eight, I bet."

"Georgia is coming over right after the shop closes," Otis said, nodding to the drawing. "Don't you want to give her that?"

Bryce stood too. "I'll tell my dad you don't actually want to have a quiet night of cleaning to yourself." He gave Otis a meaningful look, and he realized that Tex was trying to help him. He'd offered to take Joey to a movie so Otis could be alone with Georgia that night.

He told himself that she needed to spend more time with his daughter. They had a bond to form just as much as he did with Georgia. If they were going to be a family, they had to all get along. They had to trust one another. He didn't want to surprise Joey with anything, and his feelings for Georgia were only getting deeper.

Bryce lifted his eyebrows. "Should I tell him?"

"No," Otis said. "You can go, Joey. I'll tell him thanks." Otis faced the hall, squared his shoulders, and strode in the direction of Tex and the rest of his brothers. It was always better for him to face things head-on than to let them fester beneath the surface.

Nothing to fester anyway. Tex was being kind, and he thought of how Georgia had said he was kind too. When he'd asked her later to expound on that, she'd said she'd never had anyone bring her the exact flavor of boba tea she liked, then sit with her for thirty minutes while she stared at cows in a field.

"Kindness," she'd said at the end of the short story. "That was pure kindness."

Otis had wanted her to be happy. He'd wanted her to be impressed by him. He'd wanted her to want to keep going out with him. Deep down, though, he supposed that him wanting to keep her in his life and make her happy could've stemmed from some desire to be kind to her.

In Joey's room, three of his brothers worked to clean up the broken glass. "It's not my fault," Luke said from behind the dresser. He grunted as he twisted a screwdriver. "Mav didn't tell me it wasn't secure on the other side.

"He's right," Mav said, straightening with a large shard of glass in his hand. "It's my fault. I'll replace the mirror."

"It's okay," Otis said, because accidents happened. He cleared his throat, and everyone looked at him. "Thank you." He tried to smile, but his emotions made it wobble, so he simply cleared it from his face. "Thank you for coming this morning to do this."

"Of course," Tex said first, because Tex led in all things. "We're happy to do it, right fellas?"

"Completely overjoyed," Trace said with a teasing smile.

"Yes," Morris said simply. Luke nodded, and Mav said, "I wouldn't be anywhere else. This is why I came back to Coral Canyon. To be close to family." He smiled at all of them, and Otis once again got the impression none of them were better than Mav.

"Well, I appreciate it, and I want you to know it. Mama is making soup for lunch, just so you know."

"No band practice today either," Tex said, his eyes locked onto Otis's. "I decided to take my son to movie."

"Harry and I want to go," Trace said. "What time?" He bent to pick up the dustpan full of glass debris.

"Corrine and I would be in," Luke said.

"I'll talk to Dani," Mav said.

"I'll go if I don't need a date or a child." Morris smiled at everyone, but Otis sensed some sadness behind it.

"It's at five-thirty," Tex said. "Anyone is invited. I didn't buy tickets yet."

"Can Joey go?" he asked Tex. "We were going to meet Georgia for dinner at the old house tonight. Cleaning date. She'd probably like a movie better."

"Sure, she can go," Tex said easily, and Otis moved over to him and gave him a hug.

"Thank you, Tex," he whispered, and he hoped his brother knew it was for more than showing up to help him move. He felt confident he did, and then Otis started cleaning up glass too.

"WHERE'S JOEY?" GEORGIA ASKED THE MOMENT SHE entered the nearly empty house. She carried a huge aluminum tray that Otis recognized. A plastic bag with plates and silverware hung from her arm.

"She went to a movie with Tex," Otis said. "I probably should've texted you."

"Yes, you should've." She hurried the last few steps to the counter and slid the food onto it. She put the bag down too and faced him. "I spent fifteen minutes in line at Brewsters just for her." She frowned, and Otis's regret tripped through his whole body.

"I'm sorry." He moved toward her. "It was kind of last minute. I thought she'd have more fun doing that, we'd work faster without her, and we'd be...alone." His blood burned for this woman, and he took the last couple of steps into her personal space very slowly.

She let him bring her flush against his body. As he kissed her, Otis felt Georgia melt into his embrace. She couldn't be that upset, could she?

"Did you get me anything at Brewsters?" he murmured, his lips catching on hers as he hadn't pulled away very far. He gave her another kiss, this one chaste and quick. "I love that—"

"Honey Mama," they said together, and Georgia smiled. "I think *I'm* your honey mama," she said. "Bringing you dinner and fancy coffees. Volunteering to clean your house. Letting you kiss me before we even get any work done."

Otis chuckled and drew her back into his arms. They swayed as if light, lilting music played and they both wore their best clothes for a private dance. He began to hum an old song he'd written for Country Quad about a decade ago, and on the chorus, Georgia sang the words.

He pulled back and looked at her, surprised. "You know that song?"

"Everyone knows that song, Otis." She smiled prettily up at him. "Isn't it your bestseller?"

Otis blinked. "I suppose," he said. "Trace would know that. He pays closer attention to data facts."

"You write the songs," she said. "You don't know which ones are the best?"

"They're all the best," he said.

She grinned at him, clearly teasing him now. "Otis."

"What?"

"Some are better than others. Surely you know that."

"It doesn't influence future writing," he said. "That comes from the heart." His broken heart, but he decided to keep that to himself. Sudden fear gripped his lungs. What if he and Georgia fell blissfully in love, got married, and started having babies? Would he ever be able to write another country song?

He hadn't been able to last spring—until Isabella had ghosted him. What if that happened again, and he was completely blocked because he was so dang happy?

Don't I deserve to be happy too? he wondered. *Lord, don't I? Surely I can write songs and be in love with a good woman.*

He looked at Georgia as if she'd have the answers from on-high. She smiled at him, kissed him again, and said, "I brought barbecue, so let's get eating. This house isn't going to clean itself."

18

Abby Young went out the back door of the beautiful farmhouse where she now lived. She took a deep breath of the newly February air, and everything in the world seemed absolutely right. She'd dreamed of a life like this, and if she was completely honest with herself, the man she left here to go to lunch with her friends had always been Tex Young.

She still needed to pinch herself that those dreams were now her reality. She went down the steps as she looked next door to the house where she'd grown up. She still went out and helped Wade feed the horses most mornings. Tex and Bryce came too, and all four of them got the job done quickly.

Cheryl, Wade's new wife, couldn't be seen. Abby would start her SUV and check her work email, as she'd taken today off completely to go to lunch with her sister-in-law, her best friend, and another sister-in-law, friend, and co-worker at the library.

Abby loved Cheryl, Georgia, and Dani as sisters-she-never-had, and she'd just reached her car with its frozen windshield when Tex called, "Hon?"

She turned back to the house and the sound of his voice. He stood on the small landing outside the back door, wearing a pair of gym shorts and a blue T-shirt. No shoes. The man didn't seem to feel winter at all. "Yeah?"

"Bryce says he'll die without Cocoa Pebbles."

Abby giggled and nodded. "I'll get Cocoa Pebbles."

Tex waved to her and hopped back inside. By the time she got back from lunch, he'd be in the barn, working on his music with his brothers. Her house would be full of Young kids, and she loved every moment of it.

She'd once thought she wasn't very maternal, but when she got home from the library to find Harry, Corrine, Joey, and sometimes Mav's kids in the basement, all of them watching TV with various snacks around them, her heart swelled with love upon love. She adored Bryce with the same feelings, and it only proved that the human heart could love someone beyond a blood relation.

Bryce was often gone in the early afternoons and evenings, as he played basketball at the high school. Practices took up mid-week afternoons, games on Friday, and the boy had more girls burning up the roads on this more remote, Eastern side of Coral Canyon than ever before.

She got behind the wheel of her SUV, reminding herself that, "Bryce is an adult now, Abby."

And yet, he still wanted her to buy him a box of Cocoa Pebbles. She smiled at the youthfulness of him and looked next door again. Cheryl was almost upon her, and she hadn't even started the vehicle yet. She got that job done just as Cheryl opened the passenger door.

"Hey," she said a bit breathless. "Sorry I'm a minute late."

"I hadn't even started the car." Abby gave her a warm smile, which disappeared quickly at the tension on Cheryl's face. "What's wrong?" She instantly looked back to the house, expecting to see...something bad. Maybe Wade bleeding. The house burning down. Something awful.

"Nothing." Cheryl twisted to buckle her seatbelt, but Abby was no fool.

"Cheryl." She used her best librarian warning voice, and it had never failed her yet.

Cheryl wiped her eyes quickly. "It's nothing. I'm not talking about it." She took a deep breath and put a plastic smile on her face. "It's not bad news. Please, let's just go."

Abby didn't want to invade Cheryl's privacy, though she loved her and would help her no matter what. Her chest stormed as she did what Cheryl said, the words, *It's not bad news* rumbling through her mind.

So they'll tell you when they're ready, she thought. *Maybe she's pregnant.*

She knew Cheryl and Wade wanted to start their family right away. She and Tex did too, but they'd only been married for six weeks. They'd had one opportunity for her to get pregnant, and she hadn't.

She didn't know what to say, so she said nothing. Retreating was Abby's superpower, though she'd tried very hard not to employ it in recent months. She told herself she didn't want distance between her and Tex, her and Bryce, her and Cheryl and Wade, her and anyone important to her.

"You'll tell me when you're ready," she finally said.

"Yes," Cheryl confirmed.

Satisfied, Abby continued toward The Woods Café, their chosen restaurant for today's lunch. She saw Georgia getting out of her car with Dani as she pulled in, but they didn't look around. They went into the café first, and Abby and Cheryl followed them.

Cheryl had composed herself completely, and she hugged Dani and then Georgia as if they were old friends. Their history didn't go back as far as Abby's did, but she was glad they all got along.

They got a table right in the middle of the café, and Abby simply looked at her menu while Georgia and Dani chatted about a new series of books the library had just gotten in. "I've sold a lot of copies of those," Georgia said.

"Our wait list is four months long already."

"I can donate another couple of copies," Georgia said.

"No." Abby looked up from her menu. "No, Georgia."

She looked over to Dani. "If we need more copies, we'll buy them. You should be able to sell your stock too."

"I'm just saying—"

"I know what you're saying." Abby gave her a stern look. "Your heart is too big." That was why Georgia had taken in a miniature pony only two nights ago. When she'd told Abby, Abby had been dumbfounded.

"Do you even know how to take care of a miniature horse?" she'd asked.

Georgia's answer? "I'll figure it out."

Yeah, and that entailed calling Bryce to come help her, which he'd gladly done. The boy loved horses on a deep level, and it would be interesting to see what he did with his life. He'd told Tex and Abby he felt the music calling him. And the horse rescue ranch. And the college in Montana.

He'd made zero commitments as of Abby looking up to order her seltzer water with a hefty wedge of lime. They put in their orders too, and Abby focused on Georgia, the topic of today's lunch. "So," she said casually.

Georgia actually rolled her eyes. If there was anyone more stubborn and set in her ways, Abby hadn't met her yet. "Otis Young is a good boyfriend," she said before Abby could ask any questions. "That's all you're getting out of me."

"A good boyfriend?" Abby's eyebrows went up, and she looked across the table at Dani, who was also married to a Young. "Did you hear that?"

"Otis has always been particularly nice to me," Dani said, smiling. "When I first met the band, he and Tex were super-friendly."

"Luke wasn't?" Georgia asked, feigning shock. "I'm stunned by that."

"I'm surprised Trace wasn't," Abby said truthfully. "He's a great guy."

"He's quiet," Dani said.

"The quiet ones will get you good," Cheryl said with a grin. "I should know. Wade is a quiet man." She looked up as their drinks arrived, and Abby couldn't help the pure joy moving through her. Such contentment and happiness filled her, and she pressed her eyes closed for only a brief moment and thought, *Thank you, Lord.*

She believed God heard prayers no matter how short or how quiet, and when she opened her eyes again, she smiled at Cheryl across from her and Dani seated next to her.

"I feel dumb here suddenly," Georgia said.

"Why?" Abby asked, her eyes tracking a woman who looked so familiar. She'd grown up here in Coral Canyon, and she worked at the public library. She drove the Bookmobile three nights a week to surrounding communities. She met a lot of people, and a lot of people knew her.

Still, she was good with a face, and that woman...she'd seen her recently, but not in person.

"You're all married," Georgia said. "I'm not. I just feel a little like an ugly duckling all of a sudden."

"Don't be ridiculous," Dani said, which was almost identical to the chastisement Georgia got from Cheryl.

Abby said nothing, because the woman with dark brown hair in tight curls that fell to her shoulder had turned fully toward her. She stared openly, forgetting her wits and her manners. The woman caught her eye, noticed the gaping fish-mouth staring, and raised her eyebrows.

Flushing, Abby ducked her head and looked at Georgia. "Don't feel out-of-place because of that," she said. "You belong here."

The woman went by, and Georgia asked in a low voice, "Who was that?"

Abby shook her head, her lips pressed together. She hurried to pull out her phone and text her husband. *I think I just saw Morris's ex-wife at The Woods Café. Will you send me her picture?*

They'd spent last weekend laughing and flipping through a stack of old family photo albums Tex had gotten from his parents. He'd groaned at all of his wedding pictures from two decades ago, and then they'd had a good time poking fun at the fashions and mustaches of his brothers and all of their first weddings.

"Morris?" Georgia asked, peering at Abby's phone. She turned around to find the woman again, but she'd disappeared into the kitchen. "What's her name?"

"Leighann," Abby said, and she quickly filled in the other two women at the table.

"I'll check her name tag," Dani said, her eyes filled with concern.

"I don't get it. So what if it's his ex-wife?" Cheryl asked.

Abby looked at Dani. She didn't know what Mav had told her. She didn't know what was confidential. In a big family, she certainly didn't want to start a gossip chain or be responsible for putting a wedge between her, Tex, and Bryce and everyone else.

"I think...." she started.

Dani picked up where she left off. "Mav told me that Morris would like to be reunited with his ex-wife," she said, quickly clearing her throat. "That can't leave this table."

Good. So Mav had told her too. He hadn't been in the studio when Morris had told Tex and the other band members that, but Abby wasn't surprised everyone in the Young family knew.

"No," Abby said. "It can't."

"Here she comes," Cheryl hissed, and Abby picked up her phone and hurried to swipe it on. She showed it to Georgia, who picked up the game Abby was playing easily.

"Franny is the cutest dog in the world."

"When she's not soaking wet," Abby said, and she turned the phone to Cheryl first so Dani could scope out the name tag of the woman walking by their table.

"You got a text from Tex," Cheryl said, and Abby

pulled her phone back to her own eyes. He'd sent a picture, and she tapped to open it. Her heart pulsed against her chest, suddenly feeling too big for the space she had for it.

She gave the phone to Georgia and tried to see where the woman had gone. She stood with her back to Abby's table as she chatted with the guests there.

"It's her," Dani said, and Abby's phone got passed to Cheryl. "Younger there, but not much."

"Five years," Abby said, taking her phone from Cheryl. "It's her, right?"

"He wants a picture of her," Georgia said.

"How am I supposed to do that?" Abby asked.

"Give me the phone." Georgia held out her hand.

Abby slitted her eyes and glared at her, then slapped her device in her best friend's palm.

"You two scootch together," she said, her voice falsely bright and loud. "I want a picture."

Abby suddenly knew what she was doing. Dani and Cheryl played right into the charade, and Abby hissed, "Hold there. She's not turning."

It seemed to take forever, but the woman finally turned away from her table. Georgia snapped and clicked and snapped some more. "Okay," she said when the woman was still several paces away. "Take one of us." She handed the phone to Dani, and she crowded in close to Abby. She smiled for all she was worth, and she refused to let herself look at Leighann as she walked by.

Once she was gone, Abby cropped in the picture, sent it to Tex, and then their food arrived. She'd ordered a hot turkey sandwich with brown gravy and cranberry sauce, and her mouth watered at the sight and smell of it. She picked up her fork as her phone lit up.

That's her, Tex confirmed.

Abby flipped her phone over, not sure what to do now. She looked at Georgia, who said, "Nothing, Abby."

"You don't think I should tell Morris?"

"I don't know," Georgia said. "I don't know Morris that well."

"Yes, I know," Abby said, shaking her hair over her shoulders and digging into her open-faced sandwich. Some bread, turkey, gravy, potatoes, and those delicious cranberries. "Otis keeps you sequestered away from the family, doesn't he?" She gave Georgia a pointed look, then cast one to Dani before putting her bite into her mouth.

"He does not," Georgia said.

"You two didn't come to Sunday dinner at his parents' this past weekend," Dani said, driving home Abby's point.

"Exactly," she said.

"Exactly what?" Georgia said. "I was at the store until three-thirty, and we didn't want to show up halfway through."

"He dropped off Joey and said you *might* be back," Dani said. "You two never showed."

"Kissing," Abby said underneath a fake cough.

"No," Georgia said, but her face had started to turn a

shade of pink that said yes. She picked up the saltshaker and started abusing it over her French fries. "I like to watch the cows on Sunday afternoons."

"Can you do that while he kisses you?" Abby asked, teasing.

Georgia rolled her eyes, and she looked over to Cheryl. "So, Cheryl, how are things looking at the marketplace right now? I heard you guys are thinking of planning Farmer's Markets this summer."

Cheryl's face brightened, and Abby was actually glad Georgia had moved the conversation away from Leighann and her relationship with Otis. They both still bubbled in the back of her mind, but she shelved them for now so she could enjoy lunch. She'd talk to Tex later and figure out what, if anything, she should do.

19

Georgia shouldered her purse and stood from the table, surprised her back had tolerated a three-hour stint on that hard chair at the café. The food had been phenomenal, and she wanted to come here with Otis. He adored steak, and she'd seen a steak sandwich go by that looked like heaven for him.

Cheryl had ordered a margarita pizza that had tickled Georgia's fancy, though her chicken fried steak had been the best thing she'd eaten in a while. They'd stayed long enough to have coffee and then a chocolate strawberry cheesecake that had changed her mind about fruit and chocolate pairings.

Someone bumped into her, and she turned. "I'm sorry," she said, coming face-to-face with Leighann. Her eyes dropped to the name tag, and the letters stared her straight in the face.

"My fault," the beautiful brunette said. She glanced to Abby, her eyes turning afraid. Then Dani, and she swallowed. "Enjoy your day." She scampered off, and Georgia led the way out.

"She knows who you are," she hissed once they gained the exit.

"She can't," Abby said. "How could she?"

"She has to be new to town," Dani said. "I've never seen her before."

"We eat out all the time," Georgia said. "I've never seen her."

"She still might know you," Cheryl said. "You two are married to two members of *Country Quad*." The way she said the band's name really drove home the point. They were married to celebrities. They'd both been married here, and certainly the whole town knew about those unions, and their new members.

Cheryl rolled her eyes and pushed past them all. "They're normal to you, because you see them behind closed doors. To the rest of us, they're gods." She went toward Abby's car, leaving Georgia to look at Dani and Abby.

"She's right," Georgia said. "Tell me you don't see people staring at you in the grocery store."

"That's because I'm about to pop," Dani said. "Especially after that cake."

They laughed together, and Georgia linked her arm through Abby's and then Dani's too.

Abby surveyed them. "Maybe our cowboys are celebrities. Maybe she knew who we were. I don't know. I'm not going to do anything to drive her away in case she gets back together with Morris, I know that."

"You might have already," Georgia said dryly. "What with that staring."

"You took the picture," Abby said. "So once you marry Otis, and if Morris and Leighann get back together, you're going to have to confess that."

Georgia snorted. "Abby, please. I'm so far from marrying Otis, it's not even funny." She actually laughed, though a piece of her—a piece way, down deep—had started thinking about her future with the cowboy celebrity.

Otis featured very well in Georgia's fantasies, with his cream-colored cowboy hat, his blonde little girl, and that beautiful house on the opposite side of town from Abby and Tex. She'd fallen in love with his house the moment she'd pulled into the driveway, but that might've been because Otis had been waiting for her on the tire swing. He'd literally shoveled a path through the snow to it so Joey could have a swing, and he'd beckoned for her to come to him too.

She'd sat on his lap and laughed as he'd pushed them back and forth.

"Georgia." Abby waved in front of her face. "What's going on in there?"

"Nothing," she said. "I just have to get back to Harley."

"Sure," Abby said, fixing her purse on her shoulder. "I love you. Thanks for coming. If you feel like telling me something about Otis, or the shop, or how you're getting along with Joey, or your mama, or anything at all, you know my number."

Georgia grinned and hugged her best friend. "I love you too," she said. Of course she knew Abby's number. She wouldn't say much about anything Abby had listed, but she knew she could if she needed to.

She hugged Cheryl goodbye too, and then she got in the car with Dani. After all the talking and music in the café, the silence in the car actually made her ears hurt. Dani didn't have to talk just to hear her voice, and Georgia drove her back to her house.

"Thanks for picking me up," she said as they crunched down the dirt road to her driveway. "Mav's truck isn't here." She peered up to the house, and then over to Georgia, obviously surprised.

"Do you want me to wait?"

"I wasn't expecting him to be gone," she said. "Oh, wait. What time is it?" She checked her phone. "My goodness, he's doing the school pick-up." She giggled and released her seatbelt. "He's never going to let me go to lunch with you guys again."

Georgia smiled. "Yes, he will. That man worships the ground you walk on."

Dani giggled, and she didn't deny it. "I think the same of Otis and you," she said. Somehow when she teased Georgia about her relationship with Otis, it was different than when Abby did it.

Georgia only smiled. "We'll see," she said. "We're getting along really well, but it's been a month, Dani."

"How long do you need to know?" she asked.

Georgia looked out the windshield, trying to frame an answer. "I don't know," she said. "How long until you knew you loved Mav?"

"Oh, Mav and I didn't have a traditional love story," Dani said, smiling to herself. "You know it, don't you?"

"Pieces," Georgia said, her heart expanding for this woman. "You went on tour with him for the summer."

"Right," she said. "So we were basically together twenty-four-seven for a couple of months. It takes most couples much longer to get to where we got in only a summer."

"Tex and Abby didn't take long," Georgia said quietly. "They got back together at the end of May and were married before Christmas."

"Not everyone has to do things quickly," she said. "Mav and I were engaged for longer than we really dated, and that worked for us." She gave her head a shake. "I don't think Otis is one who plays games with women, and you two seem really...cute together."

Georgia thought about what Otis had said about his

first wife. "There has to be more than that for a relationship to work," she said.

"Of course," Dani said. "You're a smart woman, Georgia. You'll know if it's right with him before too much longer."

Georgia wanted to ask her how she knew, but a truck came up behind them, and she was parked in the way. Mav couldn't get in the garage, so Dani quickly said goodbye, and Georgia backed out of the driveway. She waved to Mav as she trundled by, and then she went back to the shop, because she really did have to make sure Harley was okay to close up that night.

She did that, went home and took care of the animals, and then looked out her front window, wondering what to do with all this spare time. If it was after school got out, Otis had likely just picked up Joey, and they were on their way out to Tex's. That, or they'd already arrived. No matter what, he'd be in the studio soon enough, and Georgia would lose access to him for the next several hours.

She quickly sent him a text. *Hope you have a good afternoon*, and then she decided to do something she rarely got to do but that which had led her toward opening a bookstore in the first place.

She changed into her pajamas and got in bed, a book and a cup of tea as her only companions. Fine, that was a huge lie. Three of the dogs jumped up on the bed with her, and the fourth whined for her to pick him up too. She only had one non-agoraphobic cat, and Bird joined her on the pile of pillows on the side of the bed where Georgia didn't sleep.

She scooped Charlie onto the bed with her, and she settled in to read. Her mind wandered to Otis every other sentence, until finally she simply sipped her tea and watched the branches beyond the window sway in the wind while she painted glorious pictures of her and Otis, Joey and the other children they'd have, and their pets. Everything was coated in perfection and cowboy hats, and Georgia sighed every so often, praying her dreams could come as true as Abby's, Dani's, and Cheryl's had.

A few nights later, Otis pulled up to a brightly lit house with balloons drifting along the porch railing in the evening wind. "This is a cute house," she said.

"Trace will love to know that." Otis grinned at her, and she giggled with him.

"It is," she insisted. The red brick, single story dwelling sat in a neighborhood north of Main Street. In the spring, every tree on the lane would be blooming, and all the grass would come in green. This house had a porch that ran the width of it, and a charming chimney on top. And a two-car garage, which was rare on these older homes.

"He got lucky with this house," she said. "I'd have

bought it if I knew it was for sale. My house only has one garage."

Otis lifted her hand to his lips, his kiss burning along her wrist. "You ready to go in?"

"Yes," she said, though his reluctance to do so made her nerves shake. "You don't want to?" She thought of what Dani had said—Otis kept her to himself.

"I do," he said. "It's just going to be loud."

"Joey's already inside, so we better go."

Otis had dropped her off with Trace after school, because he'd taken all the cousins to the Build-a-Bison shop to get new toys. Otis had gotten picture after picture—most of them blurry—from his eight-year-old.

Georgia looked at Otis just as her phone rang. He turned his attention from the silent house to her. "It's Shane," she said. She tugged her hand free and swiped on her brother's call. "You're on the phone with me and Otis," she said. "So don't say anything embarrassing."

Shane paused for a blip of time. "Okay," he said. "The whole reason I called is out then."

Georgia laughed, and Shane did too. When he quieted, he said, "Howdy, Otis."

"Howdy, Shane." Otis smiled at the phone as Georgia turned it toward him.

"I was calling to see when you were going to bring him to meet us," Shane said. "And you said his name, which means I now have to Google every Otis within a hundred mile radius."

Georgia shook her head, her smile still in place. "You don't need to Google him, Shane."

"I don't?"

Georgia looked at Otis, who raised his eyebrows. "It's Otis Young. I'm pretty sure you know who he is already."

Shane made a strangled sound, and Georgia rolled her eyes. "Are you telling me I just said 'howdy' to Otis Young, the country music sensation?"

"No," Otis said, laughing. "That would be my brother, Tex. I barely sing."

"You write all the music," Shane said. "You're the talent behind Country Quad."

Georgia raised her eyebrows at him as if to say, *I told you so*. Otis simply kept laughing and shaking his head.

"He doesn't like being called a celebrity," Georgia said, looking back out the front windshield. "He's a pretty normal guy, most of the time."

"Most of the time?" Otis asked. "What does that mean?"

"What about next weekend?" Shane asked. "Marlene said our calendar is clear."

Georgia waved off Otis's question. She'd been joking. He was normal all of the time, except when he disappeared into that studio. He never broke protocol and texted her during their band practices. Sometimes, he was out at Tex's until nine or ten o'clock at night, and it took him hours to come out of the recording fog. She wouldn't hear from him until the following afternoon, and sometimes she got frustrated with his schedule, which was quite opposite of hers.

"I have to close Saturday," she said. "It would be late, or you could come to Coral Canyon." She watched Otis for confirmation. "Or we could do Sunday afternoon, or early evening for dinner, though Otis got in trouble last week for not showing up."

"I did not," he said.

Shane laughed. "Marlene says she wants to come to Coral Canyon. Can we eat at your place, Georgia?"

"Come to mine," Otis said. "I'll feed everyone." He smiled at Georgia. "I don't want Georgia to have to run the shop all day, and then stress about cooking."

Silence filled the truck, and Otis cocked an eyebrow. Georgia's vocal cords thawed, and she said, "See? He's normal. We can eat at six-thirty on Saturday."

"Sure," Shane said, his voice a bit froggy. "We'll bring the kids into the shop when we get there too."

"Great." The call ended, and Georgia leaned her head back against the seat. "They're nice; Shane and Marlene. They have two kids, a boy and a girl."

"I can't wait to meet them," he said as he unbuckled. He got out of the truck and came around to open Georgia's door for her. They went down the sidewalk and up the steps and right through the front door.

Music played in the house, and it was clear a separation existed at this party. Harry stood in the living room with four or five other kids his age. Teenage boys and girls.

All the Young brothers and younger children sat or stood in the back of the house, in the kitchen and dining room area. "There he is!" Trace yelled, and that was the first time Georgia had ever heard him speak louder than normal. "And he brought Georgia."

"I told you they think you've been hiding me," she said to him.

He just rolled his eyes and went past Harry and his friends and toward his brothers, Georgia in tow. They'd just finished saying hello to everyone—Cecily and Jerry both embraced her and wore the hugest smiles on their faces—when the doorbell rang.

"That's the food," Trace said. "Harry?"

"I'm gettin' it," the boy said. He did open the door and start passing boxes to his friends. Georgia saw the way he kept looking at a pretty blonde, and she hid her smile.

Trace said, "He's gonna get a piece of my mind if he keeps up this attitude."

Georgia patted his hand and said, "Leave him to me."

"To you?" Trace said.

She gave him a reassuring smile and stepped away from all the other adults. "Take those into the kitchen," she told the kids. "All of it. We'll sort it out in there." Every box had a bright label on top saying it had come from the Coral Canyon Sandwich Company, and Georgia wasn't upset about that. CCSC had some of the best sandwiches in the world. And their mint chocolate chip brownies? To die for.

One by one, the teens did what she said, leaving only her and Harry at the door. He said nothing to the delivery driver as he handed back the receipt. "Thank you," Georgia prompted, and Harry turned to look at her.

"Yeah, thanks," he said, but the driver was already walking away. He started to close the door, and Georgia knew she only had moments.

"Your family is not an embarrassment," she said. "Your dad has done everything he can to make this birthday what you want, and you better be kind and grateful." She raised her eyebrows as the thirteen-year-old faced her again, his eyes the size of dinner plates. "Otis says so many good things about you. I'd hate for him to be wrong."

Harry looked past her to the kitchen, and she had no idea what he saw there. He met her eyes again and said, "You're right, Georgia. I'll apologize."

She nodded and hooked her arm through his. "Now. Come introduce me to your friends. I'm new to the family too, and they make me mega-nervous."

"You want to meet my friends?"

"Especially that blonde girl," Georgia said, sliding him a look out of the corner of her eye. "She's pretty."

Harry turned red, but he escorted her into the kitchen, where he properly introduced his friends around to not only her, but everyone in the family.

An hour later, just as the presents started to get unwrapped, Trace grabbed her as she put her plate in the sink. "Listen," he said, his voice gruff. He dropped his chin to his chest. "Thanks for whatever you said to Harry. I'm just doin' my best with him."

"That's all any of us do," she said. "I hope I didn't overstep."

He looked up, his smile brilliant and his eyes shone with more gray than brown. He was a handsome man too, and Georgia found she wanted all of these cowboys' stories. They'd make fabulous books, and then she could say they were based on true-to-life experiences.

"If that was overstepping, I hope you'll do it all the time," he said. "I suggested he introduce his friends to us, and he rolled his eyes and turned his back on me."

"Yes, well, he likes one of those girls, and he's trying to be cool." She watched Harry, who sat right next to Sarah. He must be so excited. "And you know what? It's hard to be cool when your dad is a famous celebrity. And all of your uncles. And your cousin is the hottest boy in high school. He's doing his best too."

Trace blinked a couple of times, his eyes on his son and his friends at the table too. The uncles and family members stood around, and everyone cheered as Harry lifted up a pair of new cowboy boots.

"Which girl does he like?"

"You can't tell?"

"Obviously not."

"Sarah," she said. "The blonde next to him." In that moment, Harry beamed at her, and she ducked her head and tucked her hair as she smiled. "Oh, and look. She likes him too." She glanced at Trace. "That's gonna be dangerous. I'd watch out for that."

"This one's from us," Otis said. "Me and Georgia." He gestured for her to come to his side, and she left Trace to go stand by her boyfriend.

Harry opened the plain white envelope and pulled out a stack of cardstock. Coupons. He peered at them, the anticipation in the room growing. Then he jumped to his feet and spun around, his face full of joy and light.

"Line dancing lessons," he said. "Thank you, Uncle Otis." He threw himself into Otis's arms, and Georgia let him take the credit for the gift.

"No way," another boy said. "I want to do that."

A new studio had just opened in town, and the woman who ran it had come by the bookshop a week or two ago. She wanted to leave flyers on the check-out desk, and Georgia had said yes. Everly Avery had a kind face to go with her petite, dancer's body, and Georgia had liked her instantly.

Coupled with the fact that Otis had said Harry had told the band they needed to learn some new dance moves for their concerts, she'd picked up that he would probably like to learn to dance.

"Georgia thought of it," Otis said as Harry stepped back. "You should be thanking her." He smiled at her in a way that made her wish they were alone, and then Harry stepped awkwardly into her.

"Thank you, Georgia," he said. "I've wanted to take dancing lessons for a while."

"How did you know that?" Abby asked, and Georgia hugged the teen and then looked at her best friend. She didn't look super happy. "Making us all look bad again."

"Hey," she said. "Those cowboy boots looked awesome."

"Those were from his father," Abby said.

"Well, what did you get him?"

Tex pointed as Harry sat back down and opened the next gift—a card in a bright blue envelope. Cash fell out of it, and Harry grinned at that too. "Thanks, Uncle Tex," he said, getting up to hug him too.

"That's a good gift," Georgia said. "I'd take that much cash anytime you want to give it to me."

Abby scoffed and hugged Harry too, holding his face in her hands for a beat of time before releasing him back to the table. She looked at Georgia and said, "You're the gift-giving queen."

"We can't all have the same superpowers," she said, but Abby only rolled her eyes. Georgia retreated to Otis's side, glad to have somewhere to feel safe. Somewhere to belong. Someone to belong to.

The party continued to unfold around her, and she basked in the energy this family had. Some of them were really loud—Tex and Luke. Some of them could scare the lights out of a person with a single look—Luke, and even sometimes Trace. Some of them kept to themselves—Morris and Trace.

But they were all kind, and they were all good, and Georgia sure did like being included with them.

"Where are your parents?" he asked as the party started to die down. "Should I be expecting them next weekend?"

Georgia turned toward him, her smile and comfort fleeing the premises. "Uh, they live here in town," she said. "Sort of. On a little farm off the Southern highway."

"Mm, I sense a story," he said.

"There are several," Georgia admitted.

"You don't talk to them?"

"I do," she said, and then she exhaled heavily. "They just...it's hard. Since Lindsey died, things are...strained between us."

"Where does Shane live?"

"Star Valley," she said. "It's almost two hours from there to here."

He nodded again. "Well, I can't wait to meet them," he said, and he went to help Trace take out the trash. Georgia stayed against the wall for another few moments, just trying to get her heartbeat to settle down. The reason she loved the Youngs so much was because she didn't have super-close relationships with her parents. She spoke to Shane often, but the distance between them made it hard to get together.

Otis saw his brothers every single day. They spent

loads of time together, and they included their parents in everything. It was just so *different* than what she knew, and she didn't want to lose him because her family was so dysfunctional.

She sent up a prayer for all of them, the way she did every morning and every night. That was all she could do, and then she had to trust that God would make up anything they lacked.

20

Morris straightened his tie in his truck at Whiskey Mountain Lodge. He reached for the folder with the contracts that had already been negotiated, as well as a couple of proposals he hadn't brought up yet. His stomach tightened, but Morris had petitioned the Lord again on the drive up the canyon, and he truly felt like he should pitch himself to Beau and Graham Whittaker.

He would. If he could get out of the truck.

Morris looked toward the lodge, and only a few cars sat in the lot that afternoon. Check-in hadn't started yet, as Graham had said that was the best time for him to meet with people at the lodge. He also ran an energy company here in town—Springside Energy—and all of his brothers had some role in both that family company and the workings at the lodge.

He thought of himself breaking tackles and running for touchdowns, and that memory got him out of the truck and walking toward the entrance of the lodge. He didn't knock, because it was a place of business today, not a family lodge before a Christmas party.

A man looked up from the podium just inside the door, his smile coming quickly. "Mister Young," he said. "They're waiting for you."

"Thank you, Mason," Morris said.

Mason led the way through the living room and into the hall. Instead of going right to the huge kitchen and dining area, he went left and down the hall. The first door on the right was Graham's office, and he indicated Morris should enter.

He'd been here before; he could've come himself. He nodded to Mason and ducked into the room to find Graham seated behind the big desk, his hands behind his head as he leaned back. Beau had just said something funny, and that caused Graham and Eli—another brother—to start laughing.

Morris smiled at them, and they all jumped to attention when they saw him.

"Morris, hey," Graham said, arriving first. He pumped Morris's hand, and then passed him to Beau and finally Eli. "Sit," he added once the hellos had ended.

Morris sat. He put the folder on the table and said, "The contracts for the concert are ready." He smiled at Beau, because his wife was the lead singer for The Everett

Sisters. They'd sung with Country Quad at Mav's wedding, and they'd done an impromptu concert in the park last summer.

This year, Morris wanted everyone to get paid. He wanted a gig to put together. He wanted to *work.* He'd incorrectly envisioned what it was that the band did most of the time, as it wasn't jet-setting, luxurious meals in five-star hotels, and spa treatments on the weekly.

They...lived quiet lives and practiced out of barn, for crying out loud. Morris was bored out of his mind, with a personality that needed to stay busy. He attended the band practices, but there wasn't much for him to actually *do*.

He needed more to *do*.

"Great," Graham said, reaching for the folder.

Morris picked it up and extracted the pages Graham hadn't seen yet. He then handed it to him for his signature. They'd be hosting the concert here at the lodge this year, and there would be ticket sales through all three websites: The Everett Sisters, Country Quad, and the Whiskey Mountain Lodge.

"I also wanted to talk to you about a couple of other ideas." He cleared his throat and waited for Graham to add his signature to the band contracts. That done, Graham handed the folder to Beau, a lawyer, who would look it all over. It wouldn't matter. He already had, and Morris had done all of the negotiating with him, via email or phone.

"What other ideas?" Eli asked.

Morris glanced at him, and he was more closed off and more refined than his brothers. Eli reminded Morris of Gabe, and the thought of his twin boosted his confidence. Part of this had been Gabe's idea.

"I'm a professional football player," he said. "Or I was. Four years in the NFL before I tore my ACL. I coached collegiate football in the most competitive district in Florida. We turned out pro players year after year."

Eli smiled and folded his arms. "Go on."

"I'm already partnering with Liam Murphy at the clinic." He put down one of the papers. "In conjunction with Ames Hammond and his therapy dogs-in-training, I'll be going to the children's wing every Monday morning to do therapeutic visits."

He drew in a deep breath. "I put together a proposal for some activities here at the lodge. You said eighty-four percent of your guests come with children. I'm experienced in working with younger people, adolescents, youth, and kids. It was part of the public relations training we got through the NFL, as well as the college where I worked."

He handed Graham the pages he'd held back. "I could come a few days a week and do football camps. Or weekends. I could run games. Whatever you think would fit your clientele here at the lodge."

Graham held the papers, but he didn't look at them. "Football. Here at the lodge?" He looked at his brothers, both of whom didn't move or say anything in return. "We do hiking and horseback riding," he said. "It's more... western than football."

Morris nodded, prepared for this argument. "It wouldn't be the only option for that day, of course. Simply another one. A way to enhance what you already do." He pulled his phone from his inside jacket pocket and tapped to get it unlocked. "I looked at the photos on your website, and you have a sand volleyball court." He turned the phone and showed the picture of people playing volleyball, which he'd taken from the Whiskey Mountain Lodge site.

"That's not an organized activity," Beau said.

"But it could be," Morris said. "That's exactly what I'm saying. I could be your sports coordinator—part-time, of course. I'm managing Country Quad, and I need afternoons and evenings for that. But everyone loves playing football in the morning—there's a Turkey Trot on Thanksgiving Day morning for a reason. Start your day off with exercise, a new skill or two for your kids while you sip hot coffee and relax in the sunshine...." He let his voice trail off, the picture now painted.

Graham looked at the pages, passing each one to Beau when he finished it. Beau would then give it to Eli, and since Morris's strong suit was a verbal pitch and himself personally, he'd kept everything to two and a half pages.

When Graham finished, he smiled. "Well, I'm in."

Morris's heart soared, and he smiled, barely containing

the "Really?" that tried to spill from his throat. He couldn't act like he hadn't been expecting a yes.

Eli waved off the last half page. "I am too. We do horse care camps. Why not a football camp? He's right; the parents would probably really like it."

"You said you get quite a few men coming as groups," Morris said too. "Brothers' trips. Father and son outings. Football would be perfect for them."

Beau gathered the pages back together and extended them toward Morris. "You keep them," he said. "In case you need a refresher. I can draw up an employment contract if you'd like. Let you look at it." He'd already started, but again, he didn't need to lay down those cards.

"I think you should," Graham said.

"Sir," Mason said behind them. "I'm sorry, but your next appointment is here."

They all stood, and Morris shook their hands again. His feet barely touched the floor he was floating so high, and he grinned at Mason like a fool as he left the office.

He barely saw the woman standing in the hallway, waiting her turn to enter the office and have some of Graham Whittaker's time.

Everything came crashing down the moment his mind registered what his eyes had seen. That curly hair. That heart-shaped face. Those bright red lips.

He spun around, his feet feeling every particle of flooring now. "Leighann?" he asked.

The woman still looked at him, her body turned so he

could get by her in the hall, but her gaze riveted on him. She swallowed, the anxiety in her expression multiplying.

His own nerves pounced and danced, making his throat tight. She was so beautiful, and everything he'd told his brothers in the barn-studio weeks ago came flying forward in his memory.

You're still in love with her.

She hitched her purse up higher on her shoulder. "Hello, Morris."

"I didn't know you were back in town," he said. He stepped closer to her, then closer. His brain screamed at him that they weren't married anymore. He couldn't just take her into his arms and kiss her. Especially not with her eyes as wide as they were. What was she so scared of?

"Leighann," Graham said, not realizing what he was interrupting.

"Can I get your number?" Morris blurted out.

Leighann's face turned as crimson as her lips, and she shook her head. She turned then and walked silently past Mason and Graham and into the office, her long black skirt swishing by them as she did. She'd been wearing a pale green sweater with the skirt, and Morris's vision suddenly registered the leafy patterns on it.

He blinked, and that went away, leaving only Mason looking at him with compassion, and Graham wearing an expression that said, *Better luck next time, my friend.*

Morris shook himself, pure humiliation pouring through him. "Excuse me," he said, and he spun away from their sympathy and judgment. He didn't need either of those. He fueled his long strides with his embarrassment, and he made it back to his truck in quick fashion.

Part of him wanted to sit right there and wait for Leighann to exit the lodge too. He needed to find out why she had a meeting with Graham, where she lived, and why she didn't want to give him her number.

The other part of his mind told him not to be a stalker. Leighann had said no. He didn't have to like it, but he should accept it. He warred with himself, trying to decide what to do. He didn't want her going out with another man. Ever. He didn't want anyone else to be able to kiss her or hold her hand or touch her anywhere.

His ears roared with white noise, and he looked wildly back toward the door. She didn't exit, and Morris had no idea what to do next.

21

Leighann Drummond smoothed her shaking hands over her skirt, everything around her dark and blurred. Why in the world had Morris Young been here? Why did he have to be the one in the office ahead of her? Why couldn't the Lord just let her live her life?

She'd seen him on Christmas Eve too, and she'd quickly disappeared with Celia Zuckerman. He'd left before she'd had to come out of the pantry, thankfully. That seasonal work had helped her pay her mortgage for another month.

She'd kept working at The Woods Café, and she'd seen the women in the Young family a couple of weeks ago. Abby Young, who'd married Tex, the oldest brother. Leighann hadn't known Tex very well, as quite a large age difference sat between him and Morris, and he'd been off touring with the band for most of their short, two-year marriage.

You were young, she reminded herself. Both her and Morris had been young when they'd gotten married. She'd barely started college, and he'd never finished despite going for a couple of years. He'd been recruited into the NFL, and since she'd fallen head-over-heels for him, they'd gotten married so she could go to Florida with him.

But she'd never really been with him. He was *always* gone—to practice, to games, to different cities all over the country.

She'd seen Cheryl Ingalls at the diner with Abby, which made sense, as Cheryl had married Abby's brother. Dani Young had been there, and she'd married Maverik, the middle Young brother. He'd always been kind to Leighann, and she'd been a complete fool to think she could return to Coral Canyon and not run into a Young.

Even if she did live on the outskirts of Dog Valley and not in Coral Canyon itself. She still had to go to that town for almost everything—but not church. That alone had saved her from running into Morris's parents.

The other woman from a couple of weeks ago at the diner had been Georgia Beck. Leighann hadn't known her then, but she wasn't hard to track down. Leighann's neighbor was a stay-at-home-gossip-monger, and she knew everyone and everything that happened in the whole valley. If a family in Rusk bought a new car, Bridgette knew about it.

So she'd known that Abby's best friend was Georgia, and she'd described the woman with eerie accuracy. Leighann had looked her up online, and she owned a bookstore in town—and she was dating Otis Young.

"Miss Drummond?"

She looked up at the sound of her name. A concerned cowboy sat across the desk from her. "Are you all right?"

"Yes," she said crisply. She blinked herself back to reality and looked to the other two men seated at Graham Whittaker's side. "I'm sorry. I got lost for a moment." She gave a nervous chuckle and reminded herself that she needed this job. Desperately.

The Woods Café wouldn't give her more than twenty hours a week, and she needed more than that to support herself and pay her bills.

"Celia said I should apply to be the full-time cook here," she said. "I worked with her over the holidays, and she was quite impressed with my skills." She'd asked the current cook for a letter of recommendation, and she'd given that folder to Mason. "I had my résumé somewhere."

Graham held up the folder. "Mason handed it to me."

"Oh, good." She exhaled, trying to find her center. It felt wobbly and encased in liquid. It she poked too hard at it, it would gush out everywhere, and she'd be left drifting without an anchor.

This was an important interview, but Leighann had lost her confidence and her train of thought with a single look at Morris Young. The sound of his voice. The shape of his jaw. He hadn't lost a single ounce of charm or good-looks since their divorce, and she'd gotten lost in those deep, dark-chocolate eyes the moment he'd looked at her.

Can I have your number?

She shook his question from her mind and tried to focus. She couldn't, not really. She gave half-answers to Graham's questions, and she stuttered through an old family recipe she'd had memorized for twenty years.

The interview finally concluded, and she knew it had not gone well. She wanted to apologize, but she didn't know how to do that either. There were so many people who needed to hear, "I'm sorry," from her, and she hadn't quite yet figured out how to say the words.

No one waited for her in the hall, and her legs felt numb as she moved. She went into the kitchen, marveling at the size of it. She couldn't even imagine being able to cook here; it would be a dream come true—and the salary would literally save her and her family. Denzel and Eric. They were why she'd come here today.

"Have a good day," Mason said from the podium, and Leighann gave him a strained smile. Everything inside her felt wound tight as she pulled open the door to the lodge and left.

She didn't know what Morris drove, but the huge silver truck she'd seen when she'd arrived was no longer in the parking lot. The rest of the cars were, so she had to assume the truck had been his.

Once safely in her car, she pulled out her phone and

texted her brother. *Done with the interview. Headed to town. I don't see a grocery list for you.*

He'd said he'd send her one, but he'd also had a terrible headache when she'd left that morning for her shift at the café. She'd barely gotten off in time to make it to this interview, and tears came to her eyes as the realization that she'd flubbed it completely sunk into her brain.

"Why?" she asked as she looked up at the ceiling in the car. "Why did *he* have to be here?"

She knew why, though. She had unsaid things to say to Morris Young, and she'd simply never been brave enough to say them. Standing in the hallway of a lodge, with two onlookers, had not been the right time.

But Leighann lived in the valley now, and she couldn't avoid him forever. Unless she locked down her family and went into isolation, he'd find out why she'd come back.

It's time to tell him, ran through her mind, and she'd been having more and more thoughts like that since Christmastime. Before then, when she'd first come back to Coral Canyon last fall. Denzel had needed her after his accident, and Leighann wasn't heartless, no matter what her mother said.

She hadn't spoken to Morris in almost four years, and it was a hard thing to start a conversation with someone after that long, even if they had once been so intimately connected. She'd managed to say hello, but her voice and courage had failed her in every other way.

Denzel didn't text his grocery list, and Leighann

sighed as she put her car in reverse and backed out of the stall. She knew what he liked anyway, but she was tired of not getting the right cereal. So she'd get them all. Put it on the credit card.

The weight on her shoulders intensified as she pulled out of the parking lot. She drove down the canyon nearly by memory, and it wasn't until she'd passed the first road that branched off the main highway up the canyon that she realized she'd barely been paying attention.

She gripped the wheel and looked in her rearview mirror as a big, silver truck pulled out behind her, coming from the road that led to luxurious lake homes at the mouth of the canyon.

Her heartbeat thundered like drums through her whole body. Her vision fuzzed. She went past the next lane and came to a stop at the sign. No one was coming in either direction. She needed to go right and head into town to the grocery store.

She couldn't move.

The truck came to a stop behind her, and she clearly saw Morris Young's face in her side mirror. Had he waited for her? Did he live down that lane and just happen to be leaving his house at the exact moment she'd driven by? Why in the *world* was he getting out of his truck?

Panic struck Leighann like snake strikes, and yet, she rolled down her window as the tall, dark, sexy, ex-football player-now-turned-cowboy approached. Morris did everything with extreme confidence, though she knew he had a softer, more vulnerable side beneath the rugged jaw, black cowboy hat, and designer suit.

"Hey," he said, leaning into her window.

"Hello," she said again.

"I don't want to be a bother," he said. "I really don't. You didn't want to give me your number, and I—it's fine. I mean, it's not fine. But, well, it is what it is." He swallowed, and Leighann remembered kissing his neck when he'd done that in the past.

Her body warmed, and she really couldn't be having these thoughts about this man who wasn't in her life anymore. Except, he was. He stood at her window. He was clearly nervous, and Leighann's anxiety had left the chart an hour ago when she'd first heard his voice, before he'd even exited the office.

"I guess I was just wondering what you were doing up at the lodge?"

Leighann swallowed, pushing down the fear and all the horrible things she needed to tell him. "Their full-time cook is leaving," she said. "I applied for the job."

He nodded, his smile dazzling ad perfect. "I hope you get it." He knocked on the side of her car and straightened. "It really is amazing to see you, Leighann. I swear I won't follow you home." He gave a nervous laugh and retreated to his truck. He clearly had all of his wits and faculties about him, as Leighann did not, because he eased his truck around her sedan and made the right turn ahead of her, leaving her sitting at the stop sign.

Her phone chimed, startling her so badly she jumped. She hurried to pick it up, and she found Denzel's shopping list.

Sorry, her brother had said. *I've been asleep for hours. My head is killing me. I need to get back to the chiropractor, but I called, and they don't have any appointments before mine next week.*

I'm so sorry, she sent to him. See? She could apologize for things that weren't her fault. For things she didn't bear any responsibility in causing.

She looked right, but Morris's truck was long-gone. "I'm sorry, Morris," she said. And she was. She was sorry for their marriage, as good and as rocky as it had been. She was sorry she'd filed for divorce. She was sorry she hadn't been there during his accident recovery.

That alone would've triggered her return to Coral Canyon, and it was the main reason she'd come when Denzel needed her. She'd never be able to live with herself if she'd let another human being go through such an arduous and terrible recovery alone...the way she had Morris.

Regret lanced through her, and she tried to tell herself that he hadn't seemed upset with her. "Because he doesn't know everything." She finally made the right turn to continue toward the grocery store. "Once he does...." He would be livid.

Oh yes, Morris would be absolutely, decisively, and unconditionally angry with her once he knew everything.

22

Blaze Young tipped his cowboy hat to the hostess as he went past her stand. Her face blushed, but such an action that usually would've brought some fleeting sense of satisfaction to his heart didn't this time. He didn't want to make the young woman blush. He was just going to meet his brother for dinner.

Jem sat at a booth in the corner—the same one they'd shared in this steakhouse for the past couple of years. Maybe three or four. Blaze's stomach lurched, and he dang near turned around and walked right back out. The coward inside him would text Jem and say he wasn't feeling well. Mama wouldn't even be able to get after him for lying.

Blaze missed his mama, and she was just one more reason he needed to have this conversation with Jem. It was February already, and both Jem and Blaze should've been in Texas to train by now.

The fact that neither of them had gone yet made Blaze's teeth vibrate with nerves. Why hadn't Jem made the trip? They had an apartment down there they rented every year. One of them should've been there by now.

A screech came from the booth just as it came into Blaze's sight, and surprise darted through him at the sight of Jem...with his two kids. Pieces started falling into place, and they all made Blaze frown.

"Hey," he said as he slid into the open side of the booth. He put his rodeo star grin on his face, though he felt like ripping off his own lips and throwing them as far as he could when he used it. "You have Rosie and Cole." He reached across the table to his almost-three-year-old niece, the one who'd made the terrible banshee sound.

She giggled and climbed right up onto the table. Blaze reached for her, grinned, and settled her on his lap. When he looked at Jem again, all he saw was exhaustion.

"Yeah," he said. "Chanel is out of town again."

Blaze wasn't sure how to respond to that. "For work?" His brother had just gotten divorced about eight months ago, maybe seven. It was very recent, Blaze knew that, and Jem was still trying to figure out how to have his kids with him on weekends, especially when he had to compete or travel.

Most of the rodeo guys who had families either

brought them along, and they lived in trailers or hotels, or they had nannies come. Or nannies at home.

Jem had a house in Vegas, and he could've employed a nanny. Instead, he'd worked out a schedule with Chanel where she had the kids while he worked, and he took them while she did. She'd been traveling a lot more lately, and Jem nodded in response to Blaze's question.

"I can take them tonight," he said. Blaze bounced Rosie, who giggled again. "They love me."

"You'll feed them sugary cereal and let them stay up all night," Jem said with plenty of accusation in his voice. "They're better off with me."

"Like you don't let them eat what they want."

A waitress arrived, and she put down a plate of chocolate chip pancakes. Blaze's point: made. He quirked his eyebrows at the pancakes, and Jem speared him with a look that said, *Don't say anything*.

"Your pancakes are here, Rosie-Row," he said.

She started back across the table, and Jem barely had time to pluck the syrup bottle out of her path before she could disrupt it. With her back on his side of the table, he started cutting her pancakes. The waitress put a plate of chicken fingers in front of Cole, and as the boy had just turned six, he didn't need a whole lot of help to get eating.

"Something for you two now?" she asked.

"Yeah," Blaze said, his rodeo-fake smile back in place. "I need a huge glass of Diet Coke, lots of ice. Bring two of 'em, actually. Right up front. And then I want the ribeye—medium-rare—with mashed potatoes, not baked, white gravy, not brown, and the smothered vegetables."

She stared at him and then got scribbling on her pad. He looked over to Jem, who gave him a smile that said he was being a diva. Blaze didn't care. He wanted what he wanted, and he was willing to pay for it.

The moment her pen stopped scratching, Jem said, "I want the bacon-wrapped scallops, with the white wine sauce and double the asparagus."

"You got it," she said, and she didn't have to take menus, because they didn't have any.

After her departure, the two of them looked at one another. Without a drink or a straw wrapper to occupy his hands, Blaze felt naked. Jem poured syrup over Rosie's pancakes, but his gaze came right back to Blaze's.

"Why aren't you in Texas?" he asked. "The kids?"

Jem shrugged. "I can't go until next week. Even then, Chanel is busting my chops about going at all. She doesn't understand why I can't train here."

Blaze only blinked. "The best trainers are in Texas," he said. "That's why."

"Believe me, I've had this conversation with her." He had a drink, and he picked it up and took a draw. "What about you?" He offered no reason why Blaze hadn't packed and gone.

Fiona, his ex-wife, lived in Southwestern Utah, only a couple hours' drive for Blaze to see his son, Cash. Guilt tore through him. "I think I've got to go see Cash first," he said.

"Don't lie to me," Jem said, folding his arms. "I think it's funny you think you can."

Blaze *really* needed a drink—and not just a soda. He ducked his head instead, because alcohol didn't make a nice Blaze, and he wasn't going back to that man. It also provided a barrier between him and Jem.

"You're not goin' back at all," Jem said, his voice much quieter now.

"I haven't decided yet," Blaze said, and truer words couldn't have been spoken. "I thought maybe we could talk it through." He looked up, hope in his soul now.

"All right," Jem said, putting away his folded arms. "Tell me what's in your head."

"I'm old," Blaze said.

Jem scoffed, but he didn't get it. He was six years younger than Blaze, and six more years on bucking bulls and broncs was a lifetime.

Blaze shook his head, annoyed that Jem hadn't taken him seriously. "I am, Jem. I'm almost thirty-seven. My back hurts all the time. I need surgery. I shouldn't be on a horse or a bull ever again."

If he didn't stay on for another season, Jem wouldn't have a partner in the team roping event. *He can find another partner*, Blaze told himself. And Jem could. No one needed Blaze. They hadn't for a long, long time.

His heart felt like a shriveled piece of charcoal. Burnt

out and worthless. He could literally get in his truck and drive for days, and no one would know or care. Only one person at the training facility had called to find out why he hadn't shown up yet, and that was Tammy Wong. She'd only called, because she was lonely at night, and she knew Blaze would keep her company.

He wasn't interested in kissing her, though he had before. He wasn't interested in staying over, though he had before. He simply wasn't interested in his own life anymore, and he knew he needed a huge change.

"Everyone's in Coral Canyon," he said next. "I gotta admit, I feel left out. I see their pictures on the brothers' text, and I want to be there. I want to be at Harry's birthday with him. I don't even know the boy." He sighed and reached to take off his cowboy hat. He hung it on a hook on the wall and met Jem's gaze again. "Heck, I don't even know most of my brothers anymore. I don't talk to Mama and Daddy. I'm like this...this island out here. By myself. Floating around in a mass of people, day in and day out."

He forced himself to stop talking, because he'd started revealing too much. He knew why he'd separated himself from the family, and it had been a good reason.

He was different than all of them. They loved the country, and he was a city boy—well, except for Luke. That man didn't like small towns about as much as Blaze. They loved huge family gatherings, and they gave Blaze a headache. They honored their wives and mother, and

Blaze had struggled to have a meaningful relationship with any woman, ever. Even his wife. He'd never loved her, not really, and they'd gotten pregnant before the wedding.

None of his other brothers had done that, and Blaze just didn't...fit with the Youngs. He was wild at heart; they could be tamed. He had abandoned the idea of God and religion; they prayed constantly and relied on the Lord to lead them where they should go. He loved a good party; they thought a party was sandwiches and balloons on a Friday night for a thirteen-year-old's birthday.

And yet, Blaze had wanted to be there. He'd *yearned* to be there.

Something inside him had changed, and it had shifted violently.

"And?" Jem asked.

Blaze lifted his chin, glad he had a moment as the waitress arrived with his two huge sodas. He immediately reached for one and the straw she tossed on the table. He took a long drink while Cole said something to Jem about his fries, and then their eyes met again.

"And I don't want to do the rodeo anymore," Blaze said.

Jem gave him a smile full of understanding. "There's your best argument yet," he said. "That one is the one I was waiting for."

"The others are valid," Blaze argued.

"Sure, they are," Jem said. "But really, it's about what you want."

"In this case, it's what I don't want."

"Then you go visit Fiona and you figure out your life. Maybe you can take Cash up to Coral Canyon with you. Her parents would probably like that."

In that moment, Blaze saw Fiona as an island too. She had no blood relatives in her corner of Utah. She lived there alone, with their son, and taught sixth grade. She could do that anywhere, and she'd chosen St. George. *Why?* he wondered. He hadn't cared enough to ask. It was close to him, and he'd made an effort to see his son as often as possible.

It wasn't enough, Blaze knew that. He hadn't won much this past year either. Enough to keep himself putting in special orders and driving a nice truck, live in a nice house and travel when he wanted. But he had no medals or belts. Not this year.

"I'm tired," he said next, the words barely audible to his own ears. He ran his hands down his face, his vision blurred when he looked at Jem again. "I'm tired, and I want to go home."

Jem's sympathy streamed across the table. "Then go, Blaze."

"I don't want to leave you here alone," he said. "You need help with the kids now."

"I'm a grown man," Jem said. "I can handle my business."

Blaze nodded, looking toward the plates of food as they arrived. The waitress read off the order, and she'd gotten his right. Miracle of miracles. "Thank you," he told her.

"Say, are you boys in the rodeo?" she asked.

"Yes, ma'am," Jem said. "I'm Jem Young. He's Blaze."

She hooted, and Blaze wanted her to go. "My son is going to go nuts," she said. "He's got you on his wall."

To his surprise, she was looking at Blaze, and he put his fork down. He had to please the fans. "Want a picture?" he asked.

"Do I ever?" she asked. She took one with the two of them, and one of just him, and then one with him and Jem together, smiling as they leaned forward over Rosie's plate of pancakes. Jem wouldn't let her take pictures of his kids, and she didn't ask anyway. She left, and Jem looked at Blaze.

"I'm tired of that," he muttered, his grouchy face back in place. No, his real face. The man he really was. He cut a bite of his steak, and it was medium-rare. Another star for the restaurant. "So, what should I do?"

"I can't tell you that," Jem said with a chuckle. "You wouldn't listen even if I did." He helped Rosie with her orange juice. "You'll have to decide that yourself, Blaze."

"Yeah, yeah." Blaze glared at Jem, but he wasn't wrong. He did have to decide for himself. He just didn't know how.

Three days later, he pulled up to a house with a zero-scaped yard in St. George, Utah, the red roof tiles shining like gold in the sunshine. He got out of the truck as the front door opened. "Dad!" Cash ran toward him, and Blaze grinned from ear to ear. A real grin. Nothing fake in sight.

"Cash." He caught his boy and lifted him right up into the air. "Your momma let you stay home from school?"

"She said you were coming," Cash said. "And here you are."

He was almost ten years old, and while he was one of the skinniest nine-year-olds on the planet, he wasn't light. Blaze's back protested violently, and it spasmed. He had to put the boy down, and he did quickly. So quickly, he stumbled. Cash slipped from his arms, both of them grunting as they went down.

"Sorry," Blaze said. He found himself down on one knee. Pain smarted through it, but Cash hadn't fallen. "You okay?"

"Yeah, fine." His own eyes looked back at him. "What happened?"

"My back gave out," he said, not bothering to hide it. That alone could've answered this question in his soul. He couldn't physically keep doing the rodeo circuit. His body was tapping out on him. "Go get your mom. I need some help getting up."

Pure foolishness filled him as Cash ran toward the door, yelling, "Mom! Dad fell, and he needs help!"

He didn't have to shout it to the whole neighborhood. Fiona came outside with Cash only a couple of seconds later, but Blaze hadn't moved. He hadn't dared. He looked up at Fi, found the concern written on her face, and extended his hand toward her. "Sorry," he said. "I picked him up, and something twinged."

"Something twinged?" She dashed toward him, took his hand, and steadied him. "Blaze, you're twice as big as me." She sounded scared, and Blaze hated that he'd done that too.

"Just give me something to hold onto," he said, sincerely hoping they didn't both topple to the ground. She held steady and strong, and he got to his feet just fine. "Okay, thanks." He breathed out, trying to find his swagger and confidence again. "Sorry."

"It's fine," she said, brushing off the knee of his pants. "Come inside. I have coffee and doughnuts."

No wonder Cash was bouncing all over the place, yelling for the world to hear. Blaze followed her without comment. Lord knew he wasn't the world's best dad, and he had no room nor right to judge Fiona.

Inside, he took a seat on the sofa and let her serve him coffee and an apple fritter. She sat in the recliner while Cash went to find the new video game he'd gotten last week. The silence in the house drove Blaze bonkers.

"So," he said.

"So," Fiona said.

More silence.

"Just spit it out, Blaze. I know you're not here to see him."

"I am too," he said, irritation flashing through him. "In fact, Fiona, I want to take him. Home. I want to take him home to Coral Canyon, and I want to know what that means for you."

She blinked at him, her eyes filled with shock. She lifted her cup and took a drink, then erased everything from her face as Cash came dashing back into the room. He sat on the armrest beside Blaze and babbled on and on about the game.

Blaze didn't mind one bit. He loved his son's enthusiasm, and he asked him questions about the game. After a little while, he said, "Son, I have to talk to your momma for a few minutes, okay?"

"Why don't you ride down to Leo's and see if he can play?" Fiona asked.

Cash whooped, tossed his video game wherever it landed, and headed for the garage to get his bike. Fiona smiled him out of the house, and then turned back to Blaze. "Leo is homeschooled. He'll probably be a while."

Blaze nodded, his jaw tight. His whole body tight. Nothing tighter than his heart. "Fi," he said again.

"If you want to take him back to Wyoming, I wouldn't object," she said. She got up and left him in the living room as she took her coffee mug back into the kitchen. She didn't turn to look at him again, but he watched her. She was tight too. "I'm not going, though, Blaze. I like it here, and more importantly, it's not there."

"Why don't you want to go back to Rusk?"

"I left everything in Rusk," she said. "It has to stay there. It's a door I'm not willing to open."

He didn't know what that meant. She'd taken Cash to visit her parents once or twice. *In ten years,* he thought. Once or twice in *ten years*. That was nothing. Their boy didn't know either set of his grandparents, and he'd only met his uncles a handful of times.

Blaze's mind fired over and over again. "You'll let me take him?" He stood and went into the kitchen. She washed the dishes almost angrily. She'd always gone into Mad-Merry-Maids when they talked about something she didn't want to talk about.

She faced him, and he was just glad he didn't have to ask her to look at him while she talked. He liked to see a person's face when he spoke to them; then he could determine intent and emotion.

"I've had him for a decade," she said, her voice breaking. "I know you love him, Blaze. I know you do. But you have no idea what it's like to be a full-time single parent. If you want that—if you *really* want to take him to Coral Canyon—then I'm not going to say no."

What she was saying was that he'd be back in less than a week, with Cash and an apology that he was such a terrible father. After all, Blaze had done such a thing before.

Why am I so broken? he wondered, and it wasn't for the first time. He'd been thinking it a lot recently, and over the years, he'd tried to push away his self-doubts and inadequacies by training harder, riding faster, winning more.

"I want to take him," Blaze said. Perhaps when he stepped up to the plate this time, he wouldn't strike out. Despite his record, maybe this time would be the time he'd stick to something, learn something, and grow and change.

"So you're going to quit the rodeo?" Her eyebrows went up.

"I'm thinking about it." He took a deep breath, unsure why he couldn't make this decision. "This is a crucial part of the decision," he said. "If I couldn't have him, what's the point?"

Fiona came toward him, her dark eyes blazing with the fire he'd once found so desirable. Right now, he felt nothing for her. He hadn't felt anything for anyone—besides Cash and Jem, and maybe Jem's kids—in a long, long time. He'd enjoyed seeing his brothers last year for Mav's wedding, and again for Tex's. But he'd spoken true with Jem. He didn't know them, not the way a brother would be friends with his siblings.

"The point, Blaze," she said, getting right in his face. He didn't dare look away for fear she might grab a knife or something. *She's not going to grab a knife*, he told himself. Fiona wasn't a violent person. Still, something about her made him look right at her and maintain that eye contact.

"Is that you're doing what you're meant to do. I think

you know you need to go back home, but you don't want to do it."

"I *do* want—"

"If you did, you'd already be gone," she said. "You do what you want, when you want. You always have." She offered him a sincere smile and cupped his face in her hand. "You feel like you should go, and you're trying to find every reason in the book *not* to go. I'm not going to give you one." She dropped her hand and stepped back. She turned, and the intensity in the room leaked away.

"I'll miss him terribly," she said. "But he's your son too, and if you're ready to be his dad...I'm not going to say no."

Fiona retreated to the sink and started rinsing the dishes again, this time in a much calmer manner.

Blaze didn't know what to say or do. His chest stormed like someone had shoved an active beehive beneath his ribs. Insects flew up his throat, choking him.

I'm ready to be his dad.

The thought entered his mind and spurred his feet to moving. "I've got to make a phone call," he said. "When Cash gets back, I'm gonna take him to lunch, okay? I'll wait for him outside."

"Okay," Fiona said, and then Blaze was gone. Out of the house, down the steps, back to his truck. He had a whole lot more than one phone call to make, but he started with the easiest one.

"Blaze," Tex said only a few rings later. "What's up, brother?" He sounded genuinely happy to hear from him, and Blaze exhaled. The last of the horrible tightness that had been plaguing him for days, weeks, months eased.

"Tex," Blaze said. "All I need is a yes or no answer."

"Oh, boy." Tex chuckled. "I'll do my best."

Blaze drew a deep breath. He needed someone—anyone—to tell him what the heck to do. *Please*, he thought, and that was as close to a prayer as Blaze got.

"Should I retire from the rodeo this year?"

23

Otis swung Joey up into the air, both of them laughing. He caught her in both arms on the way down and held her against his chest. "All right, Roo, you have to be good for your grandma and papa tonight."

"She'll be fine," Mama said.

Otis ignored her. Of course Joey was going to be fine. She wasn't the only one staying with his parents that night. They'd arranged a grandkids sleepover, and Joey had been talking about it for a week. It happened to coincide with Otis's dinner date with Georgia and her brother and his family, so he'd been more than happy to agree to the date and time.

Harry and Corrine had already arrived, and they were in the kitchen with Daddy, getting their hands dirty with some pizza dough. As Otis bent to put Joey on the ground, the front door behind him opened and Mav and Dani entered.

Beth and Boston shouted hello, and Otis got out of the way before he got steamrolled by children eight years old and under, his own daughter included. She adored Beth and Boston, and Otis didn't even have a chance to remind her to be polite before she ran off with them.

He sighed and looked at Mama. He handed her Joey's backpack. "She's been havin' a hard time goin' to sleep at night," he said. "She'll probably be fine here, but I thought I'd mention it."

Mama took the backpack and put it on the couch beside Corrine's cartoony one. "Why's that?"

"I think it's the new house." He glanced at Mav as his younger brother slung his arm around his shoulders. He could use the strength, actually, and he appreciated Mav so much. "She's been sleeping with me every night since we moved in."

"That's not good." Mama frowned. "I'll see if I can work it into a conversation tonight."

"It's okay, Mama." Otis didn't need her causing more problems.

"I'll be discreet." She turned to hug Dani, and Otis twisted into his brother's embrace too.

"You look tired," Mav said.

"It's not been going well in the studio," Otis said. He didn't need to explain more. Mav had spent plenty of time in the recording studio with Country Quad over the years.

"Luke?"

"It's the music." Otis could admit that too. "There's something...this album has been a beast, that's all."

"And it's Luke." Mav gave him a smile. "Though he does seem to be calming down some."

"He's going to be gone every day next week," Otis said. "Vacation."

"I know," Mav said. "We're taking Corrine for him." New worry entered his expression. "He wouldn't tell me why he had to get out of town, without his daughter—or anyone else."

If Otis didn't have Joey and Georgia counting on him, he'd have gone with Luke. "I think Morris is going to go," he said. "He won't be alone."

"That's not what he told me this morning." Mav's eyebrows drew down, but Otis didn't have time to discuss it further. He'd seen and heard Morris and Luke making their plans right in front of him. He supposed things could've changed, and he didn't know about it.

"I have to go," he said. "I'm picking up dinner in fifteen minutes, and then I have to do a crash-course in cleaning before Georgia's brother shows up."

"Good luck tonight," Mav said.

Otis nodded, waved to his father, and left his parents' townhome. They'd moved off the family ranch over a decade ago, when the land had gotten to be too much for Daddy to handle on his own. The twins were nearly finished with high school, and neither of them had stuck around Coral Canyon for long.

He and Mama lived in a fifty-five-plus community, which meant they didn't have to shovel snow, mow grass, or repair the exterior of their home. They had three bedrooms and a great big living area, all on one level, and it was enough to house all the grandchildren for a night or two.

Otis very nearly plowed into Bryce as he left the house, and Otis chuckled as he put both hands against his nephew's chest. He looked straight into Bryce's eyes. "I can't believe you're here."

"It's grandkid sleepover night," Bryce said, like, *Duh, Uncle Otis, where else would I be?* The boy was eighteen years old now, five older than Harry. He was a man, but Otis supposed he'd always be a grandchild too.

"I know," he said. "I thought maybe you'd have a date or something."

Bryce shook his head and adjusted the duffle bag on his shoulder. His dark eyes shone with secrets he wasn't spilling. "It's actually nice to have a night off."

Otis burst out laughing. "If only we could all say that."

Bryce tipped his cowboy hat—something he'd been wearing more and more lately—and went in the house while Otis continued toward his truck. He got the food without issue and made it back to his new house.

He and Joey had only been there for ten or eleven days now, and since he hadn't amassed a bunch of stuff over the years, he had all the boxes unpacked and everything put away. Parts of the house felt a little sparse, but Otis liked the clean lines and clear counters.

He loaded the hot food into the oven and set the temperature as low as it would go, as instructed. The cold items he piled into the fridge. He hurried to wipe down the door handles and countertops, then the guest bathroom. He'd just flushed the toilet when the doorbell rang.

"Come in," he yelled, shoving the bucket of cleaning supplies into the tub and yanking the curtain closed. He could put it away later.

No one came in, and he strode down the hall and around the corner. His piano glinted in the lights coming in the window from the front of the house, and when he tried to open the door, it was locked. He wrestled with the handle and the deadbolt for a moment before getting it open.

Georgia stood there, her blonde hair spilling over her shoulders in waves. She took his breath away, and he scanned her in jeans, a pair of ankle boots, and a rust-colored coat that hid her shirt underneath it.

"Hoo boy," he said, reaching for her. "I haven't seen you in forever."

"It was Thursday night," she said dryly.

"More than twenty-four hours," he murmured, leaning closer to her.

"My brother just pulled in," she warned.

"So I can't kiss you?"

"Not right here." She moved even closer to him and entered the house. "They'll probably be a minute unloading their kids."

Otis tapped the door closed with the toe of his cowboy boot and pressed Georgia into it. She giggled, but Otis silenced that when he kissed her hello. It felt like a moment had passed before the doorbell rang again, not a minute, and he pulled away with reluctance.

"You've smeared my makeup," Georgia said in a low voice.

He took another look at her. "Pure perfection," he said, though she may have a tiny bit of a pink streak moving from her lip and toward her cheek.

"I'm going to go check." She hurried away from him, and Otis watched her go. She'd been over to his house before, but not a lot as he worked in the evenings. How badly things were going in the studio had prevented him from seeing her last night, and another round of weariness tugged through him.

He shelved it all as the doorbell rang again. This was just like being on stage. He could plaster a smile on his face and charm her brother and his family all night long. He'd done it plenty of times for the fans of Country Quad, once when he'd had walking pneumonia for two weeks.

Otis opened the door, that country star smile already stuck in place. "You must be Shane," he practically yelled. If he'd been the Big Bad Wolf, he'd probably have blown his own house down.

Shane stood at the back of the porch, and Otis dropped his eyes to the two kids closest to him. "Oh, my mistake. I'm seein' a boy named...Johnny, and a little girl named...Diana." He chuckled as their eyes widened.

He stepped back out of the way. "C'mon in. Dinner's heating up." The kids entered, certainly not shy, leaving Otis to meet the more important people. He knew Shane's opinion of him mattered a great deal, and Otis stuck his hand out as the man approached. "I've heard a lot about you, brother."

Shane wore a glow about him, and the moment he put his hand into Otis's, he pulled him into a man hug, slapping him on the back a couple of times. "It's great to meet you." He turned to his wife. "Marlene. Welcome to my house."

She had chin-length auburn hair that hung as straight as straight could be. Her bright eyes had to be hazel, but it wasn't terribly bright here. Otis flipped on the light in the hallway leading back into the house as Shane and Marlene entered.

"It's great to be here," Shane said. "Georgia never introduces us to her boyfriend this early."

"You said I had to," Georgia said, appearing at the corner down the hall.

Otis closed the door and turned. He found Shane and Georgia hugging, and he took Marlene's coat for her. He deposited it on the piano bench and squeezed past her to get Shane's.

"This place is gorgeous," Marlene gushed.

Otis took Shane's coat, noting that Georgia wiped her eyes as she turned away from him. He knew she'd seen her brother at Christmastime—or so she'd said—so he wasn't sure what that was about. His heart thumped at him, and the moment he'd gotten rid of Shane's coat and returned to her side, he leaned in close and whispered, "You okay?

She nodded at him, and their eyes met. Otis didn't care that her brother and his wife had their eyes trained on him and Georgia. His eyebrows went up, and she smiled. "I'm fine, Otis. I could use a drink, though."

He got the hint, and he looked at Shane and Marlene. They both wore stars in their eyes, and Otis had interacted with people like this before. Fans. Shane had barely said hello to him, and they stared at him like he had gold skin, eyes, and teeth.

He'd have to carry the conversation until they settled down, and he said, "I don't drink, so I didn't get any alcohol. Georgia said y'all wouldn't care." Maybe he threw in a little country accent. The way Georgia rolled her eyes told him he definitely had. "I have sparkling cider, Diet Coke, this amazing raspberry seltzer, and water. Or milk. Orange juice. My daughter loves orange juice. And the restaurant sent a gallon of sweet tea."

"I want that," Georgia said. "Please."

"You got it, sweetheart." His eyebrows went up at Shane and Marlene. "Anything?"

"I'll take sweet tea too." Marlene linked her arm through Shane's, who simply stared. "Shane," she barked.

He startled and said, "Yes, sweet tea is fine."

Otis moved behind Georgia while she slapped at her brother's chest and told him to stop acting like a schoolgirl with a crush.

"I'm not," Shane hissed at her. Otis kept going, because he didn't need to contribute to this conversation. Her brother was acting weird, but Otis wasn't going to call him on it. Georgia had more than enough skill to do that.

He got down glasses and poured tea. The kids climbed up on the barstools, and he got them sodas.

"Oh, no, no, no," Marlene said at the first crack of a soda pop can. "Johnny, you can't have that."

Otis turned from the oven. "Sorry, Marlene. He asked for it, and I didn't know."

"He knows," she said, arriving at the counter. Her son tried to lift the soda can to his lips, but she grabbed it from him before he could get a drink. The brown cola slopped down the back of her hand and splashed on the counter.

"Mom," he whined.

"No," she said. "You can't have it this late at night."

Otis reached for the kitchen washcloth and went to help them clean up. "You can take one home with you, buddy," he said. "Then you can ask your mama when you can have it. It's not now or never."

Marlene looked at him, wonder in her eyes. "Yes," she said. "Good idea, Otis."

He wiped the counter and handed her the washrag. As she wiped her hand, she said, "Sorry he opened that one."

"It's fine." Otis picked up the can and took a long, healthy drink, the carbonation burning every inch of his throat. He gave a long, "Ahhh!" as he lowered the can. "It won't go to waste."

The kids giggled and laughed, and Otis went back around the island and into the kitchen. He knew everyone was staring at him. In Country Quad, most of the attention landed on Tex. He stood in the middle of the stage. He had the brightest spotlights. He carried them during a performance.

Otis didn't like the extra weight of all of that, and after he'd gotten out the food, he drained the last of the cola. New jitters would be in his bloodstream before long, but he faced Georgia and her family all the same. His smile came back into position, and he asked, "You want to eat first, right?"

"What's second?" Johnny asked.

"Well, I think your daddy is going to grill me tonight," Otis said, turning his attention back to the boy.

"Grill you?" Diana asked. "Like a hamburgerler?"

Otis laughed, because he did like these kids. "It's a ham*burger*," he said. "But not really like that. He's going to ask me a million questions to make sure I'm good enough for your aunt Georgia."

"He is not," Georgia said, though she'd told him Shane would do exactly that. "Are you, Shane?"

Otis looked at him, and there was some level of competition there. He clearly loved Georgia and wanted to protect her.

"Aunt Georgia always goes out with weirdos," Johnny said. Marlene gasped, and Shane lurched forward.

He grabbed his son off the barstool and said, "That's enough out of you. Come sit down so we can eat." He whisked the boy away, but Otis saw the way his face turned a shade of red he hadn't seen in a while.

He looked at Georgia, whose face had turned more the color of milk. He went to her and took both of her hands in his, blocking her view of her brother and sister-in-law as they dealt with their children in hushed, harried voices. "Hey," he said. "Look right here at me."

Those pretty blue-green eyes met his. He smiled at her. "I might be a weirdo, but I'm okay with it." He lifted both of her hands to his mouth, kissing one after the other. "Life would be boring if one of us wasn't a little weird, right?"

"I'm so sorry," Shane said, and Otis turned around. He kept one of Georgia's hands in his.

"It's fine for me," Otis said, his voice even and as mellow as he could make it. "It's Georgia who seems to be having a hard time with it."

"I'm fine," she said.

"Oh, ho ho." Otis chuckled as he looked at Shane. He kept his eyes on his sister. "We both said 'fine,' but brother, we both know a woman's version of fine is not the same as a man's." He released Georgia's hand and headed back into the kitchen. "Marlene, do you want to help me with the plates and stuff?"

"Yes, sir," she said, and she and Otis started setting the table. He glanced over to Georgia and Shane. They had their heads bent together, and Georgia had...retreated. She'd disappeared inside herself, and that upset Otis.

He put down a plate, and Marlene sidled up to him with a knife and fork. "She'll set him right," she murmured. "She always does."

"He seems to be the one cowing her right now," Otis said back as equally as quietly.

"They have a unique relationship." Marlene paused to watch them too. "It's complicated."

"Why's that?"

"Because they lost Lindsey," she said simply. She moved around him though he hadn't set any more plates. He didn't get it. He knew they'd lost their sister, but he didn't know how that made their relationship more or less complicated.

As he watched, Georgia came back to herself. Her eyes grew angry and full of fire, and she started into Shane with that girl-boss tongue of hers. It made him smile, because he knew in that moment that Georgia would never simply let him get away with something she didn't like. She wouldn't let him drift away the way Lauren had.

She wouldn't take any garbage from him, and he'd never have to guess how she felt.

He may have fallen a little more in love with her in the ten seconds she took to set her brother straight. Then she lifted her shoulders, exhaled mightily, and came over to the table. "Can I help, Otis?"

"Sure," he said as if nothing had happened, and nothing had been said. "Food's on the stovetop. Let's get it over here." He was actually glad her family wasn't perfect, because with eight brothers and all of their kids, nothing in the Young family ever happened without a lot of noise, some hurt feelings, and plenty of forgiveness.

He continued around the table, finally putting down the last plate in front of a chair where Shane stood. "I apologize, Otis."

"Nothing to apologize for," he said easily. "I have eight brothers, Shane. Eight. Trust me, there's nothing you can say or do to upset me." He looked over to Georgia. She stirred the scalloped potatoes in one aluminum tray while Marlene mixed the salad dressing into the leafy greens. He didn't need to say that Shane better be nice to Georgia, so he just patted the man on the shoulder and went to help get the food on the table faster.

"Otis," Shane said, and he turned back to him. "I'm sorry for acting like a schoolgirl with a crush. It's just that you're...*Otis Young*."

He chuckled and shook his head. "Yeah, and I'm just a man who wants to impress his girlfriend's brother." He tipped his hat the way Bryce had earlier and added, "If you want me to sign anything before you go, I'm happy to do it. But it's Tex's signature that earns the big money."

"Are you serious?" Shane asked.

"Oh, yeah," Otis said, deciding the women could bring the food over. He returned to where Shane stood. "If you can get all four of us to sign something, that's worth some money. Otherwise, it's Tex."

"No, I mean, you'll sign something for me?" He wore the look of a little boy on Christmas morning.

Otis couldn't believe it. Sure, he and Trace and Luke had a few hardcore superfans who came to see them. Everyone was happy to meet the band as a whole. But it really was Tex most people loved—especially the women.

"Yeah, sure," he said casually.

Shane whooped and said, "I'll be right back." He jogged toward the front door, and Otis turned back to the kitchen.

"Where are you going?" Marlene called after him.

"To get the records I brought. I told you he'd let me get them signed."

"Oh, my word," Marlene said, pure horror in her voice. Her gaze flew to Otis's. "Otis, I tried to get him to leave them home. I *begged* him."

Georgia put the bowl of salad on the table, and Otis looked at her. She wore a resigned expression on her face. The front door slammed closed. Otis wasn't sure if he should laugh or keep trying to understand how Shane saw him. It wasn't how he saw himself at all. Not even a little bit.

Georgia stepped up to him and patted his chest. "Just sign them, and then maybe he'll calm down."

Otis caught up to the situation then and grinned at her. "He's a nice guy."

"He's over-eager," Marlene griped. "He *promised* me he wouldn't act like this." She practically slammed the tray of barbecue meatloaf. "I'm going to rip those albums to shreds. You should've *heard* him this week. It was *Country Quad this* and *Country Quad that*. He even said he might ask you to play *Down the Tree-lined Lane*." She shook her head, her stick-straight hair flying. "I can't believe him."

"Hey, whoa." Otis moved over to her, his smile genuine and full of compassion now. "Marlene." He took her by the shoulders and looked right into her eyes. She wore an expression of fear and pure humiliation. "I don't care. I wouldn't have offered to sign the albums if I didn't want to. It's fine."

"We're just supposed to be having dinner," she said meekly.

"And we will," he said, drawing her into a hug too. She clung to him, and Otis didn't know how else to reassure her that he was fine. Everything was okay. "*Down the Tree-lined Lane* is one of my favorite songs. I'll play it. I don't care." He pulled away. "Okay? This is nothing to me. I don't care."

"He doesn't mean it's nothing," Georgia said quickly.

"He just means Shane asking him to play and sign isn't a big deal. That that's what means nothing." She gave him a quirked-eyebrow look, and Otis nodded.

"Yeah, what she said."

Marlene wiped her eyes and sniffled. "Okay. If you're sure."

"I'm sure," Otis said as the front door slammed closed again.

"All right," Shane said, his voice more labored now. Otis turned, and then lurched forward to help Georgia's brother. He carried no less than two dozen records—actual records—and CDs, all with a bulging folder on top.

"My word," Otis said, taking the top half of the items. "What is all this stuff?" He looked at the folder as it flipped open with the air current lifting it. His heart boomed in his chest. "Holy cow, this is an exclusive poster from our first album." He quickly set down the stack of CDs he'd grabbed and lifted the poster. It was in mint condition, protected inside a plastic sleeve.

He looked at Shane in wonder. "I haven't seen one of these in a decade."

"You probably have a ton of those," Shane said.

"No." Otis shook his head. "They only printed twenty-five hundred, and they're a huge collector's item now. None of us have one."

"Otis," Georgia said, her voice carrying a bite he didn't like. "Should I put this food back in the oven?"

"No, ma'am," he said. He put the poster back in the

folder. He wanted to take a picture of that for his brothers. In fact, he wanted to offer to buy it from Shane. But all of that could wait until after dinner. "We're ready to eat. We can do this later."

He gave Shane a pointed look, and the man put his records down on the table in the living room too. They joined the women in the dining room, and Otis took Georgia's hand in his. "Do you want to say grace?"

"Yes," she said. As she did, Otis kept his eyes closed and his mind right in the moment. After all, once Shane settled down, Otis felt certain there would be plenty of grilling happening—and not the kind with a hamburger.

24

Georgia tapped her brother's name on her phone and read his text again. *We really like him, Georgia. He's by far the best man you've dated in years.*

Shane had gushed over Otis, actually. They'd been talking about him and the dinner at his house for five days now, and Georgia sighed. She didn't need her brother's approval of Otis, or his assessment, to know he was the best man she'd dated in years. She sure wished she could get him to text her back in the evenings. Or call as he drove from Tex's back to his place. It was a fifteen-minute drive, and she'd even suggested to him that he could drive and call her at the same time. Kill two birds with one stone type of thing.

He hadn't done it. He claimed to have so much on his mind after band practice that he couldn't think about anything else. Georgia knew things with Country Quad were strained at best at the moment, but she felt…a tad neglected in the evenings.

She didn't want to text Shane for the fifth evening in a row, so she flipped over her phone and got up from the couch to make the cats' breakfast. They were so spoiled that she made them a variation of overnight oats every evening, and she hadn't done it yet.

All she thought about was Otis. He dominated everything she did during the day too, from what she ate for lunch, and when, to when she could help customers and when she couldn't.

She started putting together the duck pate and cream mixture only to have Harley come into the kitchen and say, "I did that already."

Georgia looked up from the bowl. "You did?"

"I texted you." Harley opened the fridge and pulled out the plastic container. "It's right here."

Georgia looked down at the concoction she'd started. "I'll just make this for the next day." She frowned as she measured the cream. "I even opened the fridge to get this out." She hadn't seen the cats' breakfast, and irritation sang through her.

"That's because you're wrapped up in Otis," Harley said in a sing-songy voice.

Georgia wanted to deny it, but she couldn't. In fact, she only got more frustrated. She slopped gross, duck-infused milk over the side of the bowl, and Harley jumped back. "I didn't mean anything by it," she said.

"I'm not upset with you."

"So you're upset with him."

"No."

"With yourself?"

Georgia once again said nothing. She mixed everything together while Harley set a couple of pieces of bread in the toaster. "Hey, I got another appointment for another apartment tomorrow," she said. "It just went up tonight. I'm hoping no one else will go look at it on Valentine's Day."

"That's great," Georgia said. "I hope you get it, but you can stay here as long as you want."

"Yeah, I know," she said. "I'm still okay to have my galentines over tomorrow night? You'll be at Otis's right?"

"Yeah, it's fine." Part of Georgia wanted to stick around here for Harley's Galentine's Party. She always put on a good time, and Georgia had attended a couple of shindigs in the past. Otis had wanted to take her somewhere fancy and exclusive for Valentine's Day.

She'd said no. She wanted to get together with him and Joey at their house. He'd kept Joey behind him for weeks now, and the last time Georgia had truly interacted with her had been her birthday party, almost a month ago.

She wanted to get to know the little girl. She wanted Joey to be comfortable with her. In her mind, if she and Otis got married, she wanted a lot of the groundwork it took to be in someone's life laid and done. Solid and strong. She couldn't do that if Otis dropped his daughter off with Mav, his parents, or Luke all the time.

So she'd put her foot down and said she could attend Harley's Galentine's party or she could come to his place for dinner and a movie with him and Joey. His choice. She'd even bring dinner. They'd compromised, and he was providing dinner and Georgia was bringing the movie. Joey would be with them the entire time, and Georgia couldn't wait until tomorrow night.

She couldn't just show up with a movie, of course. She'd been gathering little sweets all week to take to both Otis and Joey, because that was what Georgia did. She had a bag of popcorn that she'd bought from a friend who knew how to do a tiny injection into the bag to make the buttery oily stuff pink. So when she poured it out of the bag, they'd have pink Valentine's Day popcorn for their movie.

Joey would *love* that, and Georgia couldn't wait to see her face when she saw the pink popcorn spilling from the bag. She'd gotten a box of beetroot mints for Otis, as he'd said he liked to have something to suck on during band practice. She'd bought these chewy caramels too, because he'd admitted to loving all things caramel.

For his popcorn for movie night, she'd braved a windy afternoon yesterday and walked down the street to the kitchen store. A couple of local caterers sold bottles of salad dressing and other long-shelf-life items in the store, and she knew Tina Hensley made the most divine buttermilk caramel for popcorn. So she'd be popping Otis his own bag of the stuff, then pouring that all over it until it was nice and ooey-gooey-sticky-scrumptious.

Her smile came as she thought about surprising the two of them tomorrow night. She didn't care if Otis didn't get her anything at all. He would, though, because he was the man who'd taken her to the Swing Ranch Show and booked a private table with a special meal. He'd known her favorite boba tea, and he'd sat with her while she watched the cows. He'd definitely have something up his sleeve for Valentine's Day.

"He has that unicorn again," Harley said, and Georgia spun away from the cats' breakfast.

"Obsidian," she warned, advancing on the gray cat. "That's not for you." She'd bought the unicorn for Joey, of course. Otis said she had plenty, but Georgia didn't think an eight-year-old girl could ever have too many unicorns.

Maybe if one of them was covered in cat spit, they could. Instead of trying to get him to drop it, she returned to the bowl and pinched off a chunk of the pate she hadn't mixed in with the cream yet. "I want it." She held out the pate, and Obsidian dropped the tiny unicorn.

Harley swooped in to get it, and Georgia gave her naughty cat a treat. Of course. A reward for doing something bad. No wonder the cat kept trying to get into things he shouldn't.

"I'll make sure the laundry room door is closed. I swear it was."

"I swear he can open it," Georgia said as her friend went down the hall. She glared at her cat, but he just jumped up onto the counter and stalked closer to the bowl of cream and duck pate.

"Nope," she said. "Nope, nope, nope. This stuff isn't free, and you already got an extra bite." She elbowed him back and finished mixing everything together. She did let him lick the bowl, and Onyx descended from the fridge to assist with that. All the dogs sat on the line marking the entrance to the kitchen, and Georgia got out a package of pepperoni to treat them. She couldn't help herself. If she couldn't see Otis tonight, she might as well enjoy herself.

The following evening, Georgia pulled up to Otis's dark house about ten minutes after she was supposed to be there. Her heart fell to the soles of her shoes. He wasn't here either. Country Quad had called practice early, but they hadn't canceled it completely. If he was still at Tex's....

She plucked her phone from her purse to call him. It rang on the way up, and his name sat there. Satisfied, she answered with a, "Hey, where are you?"

"There was a slight mix-up at the restaurant," he said. "Joey and I are still here, waiting for the food."

"Oh, okay."

"I'm probably thirty minutes away," he said. "I see you in the driveway, so you should just go in."

She looked left and right. "You can see me in the driveway?"

"I got the security system activated," he said, a hint of pride in his voice.

Boys and their toys, Georgia thought, smiling to herself.

"I get a notification when there's movement in the cameras. I should've texted you, but I'm helping Joey with her math facts, and I didn't realize how late it had gotten until I got the notification."

"All right," she said. "How do I get in your house if there's an active security system?"

"Give me a minute, and I'll turn it off and open the garage door for you."

"You can do that?"

"State of the art, sweetheart." He chuckled, and Georgia joined her giggle to his. Not even a minute later, the garage door rumbled up. Georgia got out, collected the laundry basket of items she'd put together for her evening with Joey and Otis, and lifted it toward the camera. She grinned and then went inside, because it was mid-February and still plenty cold in Wyoming.

She'd barely put the basket on the kitchen island when Otis called again.

"What in the world did you bring?" he asked.

"Movies," she said. She rummaged through a few of the gifts, finally lifting them out. "A couple of miscellaneous gifts for you and Joey. Nothing huge."

"It clearly shows a laundry basket," Otis teased. "And it was full."

"I didn't spend much," she said.

"Was there a limit?" he asked. "On the spend? If so, I did not get that memo."

Georgia ducked her head though he wasn't there to see her. "No limit."

"Phew."

"But you better not have spent much," she said. "I wanted a quiet evening with you and your daughter. That's priceless."

"Hmm, well, we'll be there in a few minutes."

"Can't wait." Georgia let him end the call, and she finished setting up their gifts. Joey had four, and Otis had three, as she'd found a giant bag of shelled pistachios at the market today that screamed his name. He kept a bag in the console of his truck, and Georgia had ridden with him enough to know it was getting empty.

Once that was done, she moved the laundry basket to the dining room table and laid out their movie choices. Otis only had the nicest, newest technology, so she'd brought several blu-ray discs. All eight-year-old-friendly and which she could stand to watch. She'd consulted with Abby on the movies, as she'd rented most of them from the library.

Abby and Tex had left town for the night. He'd rented some swanky cabin in the woods for the weekend, and the two of them had escaped without Bryce, Franny, or any obligations. Georgia sighed as she looked at the row of kids movies, family films, and a couple of animal documentaries.

She wanted her handsome cowboy husband to anticipate her needs, and then meet them. She told herself Otis had done that a few times in the several short weeks they'd been dating, and she had nothing to complain about.

Georgia sank onto the couch with nothing left to do but wait. By the time Otis and Joey came through the garage door, Georgia's stomach felt like it might claw a hole in itself just to get to her other organs.

"Put it on the stove, baby," he said to Joey. To her, he said, "I am so sorry, Georgia. They messed everything up at Mimi's, and I had to wait behind all these other couples."

"I got my homework done," Joey said.

"The stove, Roo," he said, clearly not happy with her. "Put that stuff on the stove. You're going to drop it."

Georgia joined them in the kitchen, and she took the plastic bag swinging from the girl's arm before she dropped it. She gave her a smile and then looked at Otis. Flustered as he was, he didn't meet her eye. She started helping him to unpack the food, and then he said, "Shoot. I left the ice cream in the truck. Be right back." He ducked out of the kitchen, leaving Georgia with Joey.

She looked at her, and Georgia looked on back. "He's a little all over the place."

"He was yellin' in the truck on the way home." Joey got up on the barstool, her eyes landing on the gifts. Her face lit up, but she didn't reach for hers, obvious as they were.

"What was he saying?" Georgia asked.

"Something about how he hasn't seen you in forever, and now he's lost all this time, and this food better be worth it." She smiled, not worried at all about tattling on Otis.

Georgia giggled with her and pointed to the gifts. "I got you guys a couple of things for Valentine's Day."

Joey wore pure delight on her face. "I got all this candy at school too. Daddy says I can't eat it all in one day."

"He's probably right about that."

"I didn't know you gave gifts on Valentine's Day." Joey got up on her knees. "I usually just get cards and candy." She looked up from the unicorn, her eyebrows up.

"Well, I like to give little things for everything," Georgia said. "My momma used to always give us something huge at Easter. We'd have an egg hunt, of course, but we got one amazing gift for our Easter baskets too."

"What did you get?" Joey asked.

"So many things," Georgia said. "One year, I got this amazing foam topper for my bed. It made my mattress so soft and so much better." She smiled at Joey. "We didn't have a lot of money, so it was a huge thing to get those gifts." She glanced over to the door, expecting to see Otis. How long did it take to get ice cream from a truck in the garage, four steps away?

"You didn't wrap them," Joey said.

"I don't wrap non-birthday or non-Christmas presents," she said. "It's like...a fairy brought them. The tooth fairy doesn't wrap anything, right?" She beamed at Joey, who of course still believed in the tooth fairy.

Georgia pointed to the tiny unicorn. "My cat wanted that, and he got it out of the laundry room a couple of times. I tried to get all the cat saliva off."

Joey looked at her with wide eyes. Georgia smiled warmly at her. "Next to it is a keychain kit. You can make the unicorn into a keychain for your backpack."

"Are you kidding?" Joey leaned forward and picked up both items. "That is so cool."

If only Georgia could be amazed by something so simple. She said, "I can help you after dinner, but I know your daddy wanted to watch a movie, so we'll have to see what he says."

"Okay," Joey said.

"That's popcorn for the movie," Georgia said, keeping the pink part of the surprise to herself. "And a little bird told me you like bubble gum, so I got you my favorite kind." She tapped the bag. "You have to ask your daddy before you chew this too, okay? I don't want to get in trouble."

"He doesn't let me have gum very often," Joey said,

reaching for it. "He thinks sugar is bad for my teeth." She shook her head and frowned. "He eats so much candy at night. You should see him."

Georgia giggled at the girl's tone and the way she'd just ratted out her dad. He still hadn't come back in, and Georgia turned toward the garage door. "Maybe I better check on him." He had been quite late, and she still had to go through his gifts. They had to eat. Make a keychain. Pop popcorn.

She opened the door. "Otis?" The garage was dark. The door closed. Otis was not there, but his truck was. Frowning, she reached to flip on the light. "Otis?" He definitely wasn't there, and her heartbeat tripped up her throat.

She turned around, and Joey still knelt at the counter, now examining the contents of the keychain kit. "Where would your daddy—?" she started. She cut off when Otis came around the corner from the front door, the biggest bouquet of deep, blood-red roses in his arms. So many, he had to hold them with both hands. The blooms billowed up all the way to his chin and expanded out past his arms.

He wore the biggest smile Georgia had ever seen, and any foothold she'd had hanging on to keep herself from falling all the way in love with him disappeared.

25

Ah, so Georgia liked roses. Otis could see it in her face. In the way her eyes softened, and she settled her weight onto one hip. In the way her shoulders went down as she sighed. She walked toward him, glancing over to Joey as she went past her.

She'd insisted on spending the evening together with his daughter, and Otis sincerely hoped she regretted it. He laughed internally, because he didn't. Not really. He just wanted Georgia to himself, to kiss, to hold, to maybe kiss some more during the movie. He couldn't do any of that with his daughter around.

"Are you trying to make me fall in love with you?" she whispered as she paused a couple of feet in front of him.

"Would this do it?" he asked.

She joined him, wrapping her hands around the

dozens and dozens of stems and leaning down to smell the flowers. "I love roses with everything inside me."

"I figured," he said.

"How?" Her eyes came up to his, and he'd been wrong about a lot of things in his life. He sincerely hoped he wasn't wrong about the desire and love he saw swimming in her gaze.

"You have all those bushes in front of your house," he said. "And you have about a dozen vases in your office. You said you put your roses in them as they bloom throughout the summer." He shrugged, but he really couldn't do that much without being in danger of dropping the flowers. "I figured."

"These must've cost a fortune," she whispered, her fingers dancing delicately over the velvety petals.

"You said there was no cost cap."

"Well, my mints are going to be a really lame gift now." She pulled her hands back. "And where in the world are you going to put those?"

"You're the one who brought a laundry basket," he teased. "I thought we'd put them in there, and then I can come by the shop tomorrow and set them up in your vases for you." They'd probably fill all twelve vases, and they'd cost a small fortune, not a whole one.

The look on Georgia's face was worth every penny. He walked the roses over to the laundry basket, checked on Joey, who was busy with something Georgia had given her, and went back to his girlfriend. "I got one more thing," he said, taking her hand in his. "Come with me."

He took her around the corner and down the hall to his front office. He picked up the little brown bag from the top of his grand piano and handed it to her. She eyed it and then him, asking, "What is this?"

"Open it and see."

"I think someone is going to usurp me as the best gift-giver," she said, but she wasn't upset about it. She pulled out the earrings and gasped. "Otis." Her eyes drank in the jewelry, which was a pair of books. Not just any book. Her favorite book—The Velveteen Rabbit.

"Where did you get these?" She looked up at him, and Otis fell in love with her. He'd already been almost all the way there, but seeing her joy at something that had cost him fifty dollars and taken a phone call told him how appreciative she was.

"You sell things like this in your shop," he said. He cleared the emotion from his throat. "I checked out the back of a pair, got the name and number of the woman, and called her." He shrugged like this was no big deal. That anyone would've done this for Georgia.

Tears filled her eyes, and she flung her arms around his neck. "Thank you." He held her within the circle of his arms, letting his eyes drift closed as he took a long breath of her. She smelled like peaches and cream and old paper and fresh laundry. "Thank you so much, Otis." She stepped back and busied herself with the books. "Help me put them on."

"You don't have to put them on."

She gave him a *really?* look, and he did what she said. He liked touching her hair, and the side of her neck, and he let his hands go where they didn't need to go so he could do both. He brought her face to his and kissed her, the union slow and sweet and sensual.

She'd said nothing about Shane's opinion of him, other than he and Marlene had liked Otis a lot. He honestly didn't care what her brother thought of him. As long as Georgia liked him, he was good. Judging by the way she kissed him, she sure did like him.

Otis put the brakes on his arrogant thoughts. He'd been kissed like this before, and those relationships hadn't worked out. He didn't think Georgia had a ingenuine bone in her body, but he'd been surprised by women before.

"You know how to do Valentine's Day," she whispered, his face in both of her hands. "I shouldn't be surprised, but I kind of am."

"Ouch," he said before kissing her again.

"The food," she whispered. She didn't try to step back or put any distance between them. "Your daughter."

"They can wait," he murmured, and he touched his lips to hers one more time.

An hour or ninety minutes later, he applauded while Georgia poured pink popcorn out of the bag. Joey shrieked with joy and dashed over to Georgia. "I can't believe it," she gushed. "How did you do that? I've never seen anything like it!"

Georgia shook salt all over the princess popcorn and handed the bowl to Joey. She came bounding toward him like a baby deer. "Daddy, look at this popcorn!"

"I see it, Roo," he said, chuckling. "It's incredible." They'd eaten. He'd loved his gifts from Georgia, and they'd helped Joey make her unicorn keychain. She'd selected a movie, and they'd paused it about thirty minutes in for a "popcorn break."

His bag finished popping, and he pulled it out of the microwave. "Is mine going to be blue?" he teased.

"No," she said, snatching the bag from him the moment he retrieved it from the microwave. "You guys go sit down. If we don't keep watching the movie, I'll have to leave before it's over."

"Go on, Joey," he said.

"You too," Georgia said. "I'll bring this over."

Otis cocked his eyebrows at her. "What are you going to do to it?"

"Nothing." Her voice went all high and squeaky.

"You're a bad liar," he said, chuckling.

"It's all restaurant-grade." She pushed against his chest. "Hurry up, or it'll be cold."

The movie started blaring again, and Otis sank onto his

couch though every cell in his body wanted to turn around and see what Georgia was doing. The microwave ran again, and he thought maybe some sort of specialty butter. They'd spent a lot of their mealtimes together eating out, but she'd said she could handle herself in the kitchen.

The scent of caramel met his nose only half a beat before Georgia lowered the bowl of popcorn in front of his face. "Happy Valentine's Day," she said.

He took the bowl of hot, creamy, caramel popcorn, everything inside him dancing and happy. "Ho-ly wow," he said, grinning and grinning and grinning. "You are the best girlfriend I've ever had."

She laughed as she stepped by him and sat next to him. He lifted his arm so she could sink into his side, which she did. "Don't get it in my hair, okay?"

"No, sir," he said. It wasn't the easiest thing to eat one-handed, but Otis managed it for several minutes. "You don't want any?"

"No, I'm stuffed from all that pasta," she said. The movie wore on, and Otis put his bowl on the coffee table in front of him. He turned and stretched his legs out on the couch, noticing that Joey had curled up in the recliner and had fallen asleep.

He nodded over to her, and Georgia looked, giving her the warmest, most maternal smile Otis could imagine. Joey needed someone like her in her life, and Otis wanted so badly for her to have a full-time mother.

Georgia turned back to him and lay in his arms, the two of them smashed onto the couch together. "Thanks for letting me have some time with her, Otis."

"I see now that you both need it," he said.

"Yeah." She lifted her head and kissed him, and Otis wasn't going to argue with that. There was something magical about February fourteenth, or maybe it was Georgia Beck herself who brought all the goodness into his life. He wasn't sure. He just knew he better not mess up and lose this woman. His heart would break, and Joey would never forgive him.

A WEEK PASSED. THEN TWO. OTIS COULDN'T GET OUT of the studio before ten o'clock to save his life. Joey was asleep on Tex's couch every time he went to get her, and then they had to drive home and do their whole bedtime routine again.

He didn't talk to Georgia in the evenings, and as spring arrived in Wyoming, people started coming out of hibernation. The shop got busier. She started her weekend activities for kids, and Otis went to help her every Saturday. Joey loved going to the bookshop, even if the weekend activity was something she didn't like.

She simply didn't do it. She'd wander around, find a book, and sink into one of the bean bags Georgia kept in the front corner, right where the best light came in from outside.

February became March, and Otis had just finished helping her clean up after a pot of gold activity that had been overbooked. Both Harley and Georgia seemed about to split at the seams, and he was looking forward to an afternoon nap as he'd taken Joey up to Lauren's last night.

Her treatments were going okay. Not as good as the doctor would've liked, and they'd fallen back into some more testing. They hadn't said anything to Joey yet, and she was such an agreeable child that she didn't mind reading while her mom napped, or helping her grandmother with fabric while Echo sewed for clients.

Otis had just gone back into the front of the shop after putting away the tables, the cordless vacuum in his hand for all the glitter, when he heard angry voices from the front of the store. He immediately looked to the check-out desk, but Harley stood there with a customer.

Anxiety poured from her eyes, and she said, "Georgia's mother came in."

Otis hadn't met her parents yet, either of them. He couldn't make out the words, but they didn't sound happy or harmonizing. He hurried around the bookshelf, because he didn't think Georgia would make a scene in her own shop.

Sure enough, she stood silently while the woman in front of her spoke in a loud voice. He scanned the shop, and several parents and patrons remained. Georgia would be humiliated and mortified.

"Hey," he said as he arrived. Her mother cut off mid-sentence and stared at him. "You must be Georgia's mother." He put his celebrity smile on his face. "I've been so excited to meet you."

"Otis," Georgia said under her breath. Her voice unnerved him. It held nothing. No emotion. No inflection. Nothing. Unshed tears sat in her eyes, and Otis had to take a leap of faith.

He handed her the vacuum. "Georgia said she had something for you in her car. Come with me, and I'll get it for you." He linked his arm through her mother's, giving her no choice but to go with him. "It's Janet, right? I'm Otis Young, her boyfriend. She's been spinning tale after tale about her childhood, let me tell you." He walked her through the bookstore and down the back hallway. He had no idea if he could get back in the building if he went outside, and right now, he didn't care.

"Her boyfriend?" Janet asked in disbelief. "She hasn't mentioned a word about you, young man."

"Oh, I know," he said, though it did sting a little that she hadn't even mentioned him to her folks yet. "That Georgia, she's a real expert at keeping secrets." He smiled like this was a good thing. It was true, but he wasn't sure how proud she should be of it.

He pushed the door open and took Janet outside. It was definitely warmer than it had been, but there was still a ways to go before one could go outside without a jacket. He currently didn't wear one, and the way the door thunked closed behind him told him he would not be able to get back in that way.

He also couldn't open Georgia's car. "Oh, I didn't grab the key," he said, slipping his hand out of her mother's arm. "Shoot. I'm gonna have to call her." He patted his pockets and didn't find his phone. "Blast. I plugged in my phone in Georgia's office. See, my cord doesn't work, and I didn't know it until this morning, when I got up and my phone was almost dead though it had been plugged in all night."

Janet narrowed her eyes at him. She'd said only a few words to him, and she certainly wasn't star-struck the way Shane had been. "What did you say your name was?"

"Otis," he said with a smile.

"Where do you live?"

"Right here in Coral Canyon," he said. "You're down on the south highway, right?"

She didn't confirm. "How long have you and Georgia been dating?"

"Couple of months," he said. It felt like longer than that, but he didn't say so. Technically, their first kiss, which had sparked her to life inside his mind, was eight months ago now. He didn't mention that either.

"You're not married, are you?" Janet wore several lines around her eyes, and when she squinted, she looked somewhat mean. She had the same blue-green eyes as Georgia, but her hair had gone gray and white.

"No, ma'am." He rocked back onto his heels, hoping he could pass this inspection. "I was once, but not anymore."

"She dated a married man once," Janet said. "A real scandal, that was."

Otis chuckled. "Really? I haven't heard that story yet."

"Georgia won't tell you," she said. "You have to know to ask. That's how Georgia is. Always keeping things to herself. If you don't ask the right questions, you don't know anything." She glared at him and then the back door of the shop. "It's always been about her. She's just as selfish now as she was when my younger daughter died."

Otis swallowed. He wasn't sure if it was his place to say something or not. His chest pinched, and he sent prayer after prayer toward heaven. "I don't think Georgia is selfish at all," he finally said, his voice barely loud enough to be heard over the breeze in this back alley behind the shop. "She's kind to my daughter. She listens to her and spends time with her. She's great with kids. She has a real talent for running this shop. She's the best gift-giver my family has ever seen."

Janet seemed to morph into a worse version of herself with every word he spoke. "She has you hoodwinked, boy."

"I'm thirty-four years old, ma'am," he said, louder now. "I'm not a boy. And your daughter is one of the hardest working women I've ever met. She's a good woman, with plenty to offer to me or anyone else in this town. You have no right to come to her shop and yell at her in front of her patrons and friends. *You're* the selfish one today."

Janet fell back a step, her eyes wide.

"Otis," Georgia said from behind him, and he spun toward her. His heart thundered through his chest, and he stepped over to her.

"I'm sorry," he said. "I was just trying to help."

"Momma," Georgia said. "Daddy's coming around to pick you up."

Silence descended on them then, and a few moments later, the *chug-a-chug* of an engine filled the single-lane alley. A truck appeared, and Janet went to get in the passenger seat. She didn't say goodbye. She didn't look back.

Otis took Georgia's hand in his and squeezed tightly. Even when the truck drove by them, Janet didn't look at either of them. Her daddy did, and Otis dipped his hat. He did the same, and then they were gone.

"You can go," Georgia said as she turned back to the door.

"No, I'm not going to go," Otis said, darting in front of her. "What in the world was that?" He searched her face, trying to find any inkling of emotion. Any hint as to what had happened in the five minutes he'd been in the back putting away tables.

Georgia had disappeared on him again. Just gone.

"Georgia," he said, maybe a little bit too loud.

She dissolved into tears, and Otis caught her and hauled her tightly against his chest as she sobbed. "Okay," he said. "It's okay. Shh." He ran his hand over her hair and soothed her, all the while thanking the Lord that he'd been there today.

Help me help her, he kept thinking. For a woman like Georgia, providing help was difficult. She was so capable and so headstrong, and he absolutely didn't want her to retreat to a place where she couldn't be those things. *Please, just help me help her.*

26

Georgia couldn't settle on any one thought. So much had happened in the past fifteen minutes, and she couldn't fathom the idea of going back into her own bookshop. At least not for a while. Maybe once everyone who'd been there when Momma had shown up and started yelling had left. Maybe then.

Otis held her within the safety of his arms, and she clung to him the way she would if she were in the middle of the ocean, drowning. His voice hummed in her ears, words she couldn't make sense of. It didn't matter what he said. He was there, and he'd diffused the situation easily. Almost effortlessly. Momma had gone with him, which spoke a great deal about him, not her.

Georgia finally found a thread to hold onto, and she gripped it as she quieted and calmed. Otis didn't give her an inch of space, even when she tried to pull away. Irritation sparked within her, and he seemed to know it. He did let go then, and Georgia stepped out of his arms.

"Sorry," she said.

"I don't think it's you who needs to apologize," he said.

He certainly didn't, and Georgia wiped her eyes on her sleeve as she looked to her left, in the direction Daddy had driven away with Momma.

"She's...not well," she finally said. Otis's fingers brushed hers, drawing her back to him. She went, laying her cheek against his chest. "She just came in mad as a hornet. She gets this way sometimes. Daddy says she's refusing to take her meds again, and she's convinced today is the day Lindsey died."

"But it's not," Otis said.

"No," Georgia said. "It's not for a few more weeks." She hadn't told him. She didn't want to make a big deal out of it. She'd mourn in the way she always did. She'd call Shane, put him on video, and they'd go see their sister's headstone.

There's no reason Otis can't go with you, she thought. If they were meant to have a long-term relationship, he'd want to be there. He should go. It would be something she did every year, just like she had for the past ten.

"She was upset I didn't come for breakfast like I usually do. I tried to tell her it wasn't today, but when she's off the rails like that, there is no calming her down."

"I'm so sorry," Otis said.

"She's so...cruel." Georgia took a breath, her lungs still

hitching from the crying. "I know she doesn't mean it, not really. But it's like she knows all the things I doubt about myself, and she throws them at me like bombs." She shook her head as she stepped away from him again. "It's embarrassing to have her show up in the shop in front of everyone."

"They understand," Otis said.

Just then, the back door opened, and Harley came out. "Oh," she said when she saw them standing right there. "I was just coming to check on you." She wore simultaneous apprehension and relief in her expression. "Only Mrs. Valencia is here, and she wants to ask you about that space opera book you told her son about." She hooked her thumb over her shoulder. "I told her you'd call her, but—"

"It's okay," Georgia said. She knew Theodora Valencia didn't care about the space opera. She wanted to make sure Georgia was okay. "I'll go talk to her." She drew in a deep breath and pushed her hands through her hair. "I look okay?"

"Gorgeous, as always," Otis murmured, his eyes stuck to her.

"Yes," Harley said.

Georgia nodded and went with Harley. Otis brought up the rear, but then he faded away from her as she spoke to Theodora. They hugged, and Georgia assured her she was okay. They did chat about the space opera book for a moment, and then the other woman left the shop.

Several others had come in, and Georgia's energy

started to return. She really didn't need Otis hanging around now that the pot of gold event was done and cleaned up. She couldn't leave Harley on the busy spring Saturday to tend to the shop herself, and after she'd helped a man and his teenage daughter find the vampire book they were looking for, she migrated to Otis's side.

He stood in the children's section, looking at the back of a book she knew Joey had already read. "She's got that one," she said. He looked at her as if he'd forgotten he stood in a bookshop. "Your daughter. She's read that one." Georgia took the book from him and put it back on the shelf where it went. "You don't need to stay, Otis. I'm fine."

"I'll get lunch and bring it back."

She nodded, because that was what he'd have done without the shouting episode from her mother. Or her complete emotional breakdown. Tears pricked her eyes again, but Georgia blinked them back and kept straightening the shelves. "I'd love something really rich. Pasta and cake. Something like that."

He chuckled, his touch along her hip welcome and warm. "They have that cannoli cake at Fire-Roasted Grill. That?"

"Yes, please," she said. "They have an amazing cheese-stuffed chicken there too, and you can get a side of ziti with marinara."

"That's what you want?" He broadcast playful vibes toward her, and she nodded.

"Yes, sir," she said, turning into him fully. She looped one finger through the belt loops at his sides and pulled him into her. "Please, Otis. If you don't mind. It'll be a wait."

"I don't mind at all." He wrapped his arms around her and gazed down at her. "I want you to be okay for real. None of this shuttering yourself off in zombie mode." He studied her, and she wanted to hide from him.

Her pulse bumped harder, but she maintained eye contact. "I'm trying," she said. "I'll be okay, really. I just need some really good food." She smiled at him, and he returned it. He kissed her quickly and stepped back, taking all the comfort in the world with him.

"Otis?" she asked as he started to turn to leave.

He looked at her again.

"I usually go over to my parents' a couple of days after a thing like this. Would you...would you go with me this time?"

Without a moment of hesitation, he said, "Absolutely. Tell me when, and I'll be there."

She nodded, already starting to retreat back into the shouting episode and what she'd have to do to smooth it over. In reality, Momma should have to do something, but she wouldn't. Georgia would either go address it and apologize so she could have her momma in her life, or she'd ignore it and everyone would pretend like it hadn't happened.

She hated the second option, because then her feelings

festered inside her. She didn't like allowing her mother to fill her with negativity and harsh words that haunted her. So she'd go see her parents in a few days, and perhaps with Otis at her side, it wouldn't be terrible.

He left, and she got back to work. Her attention divided itself between customers, shop needs, her mother, and Otis. Always Otis. She thought she could weather any storm with him at her side, and she prayed her parents wouldn't scare him off.

Before Otis returned, Abby walked into the shop. Surprise lifted Georgia's heart, and she hurried toward her best friend and hugged her. "What are you doing here?"

Abby gripped her with a strength only she had. "I heard your mother came into the shop." She didn't have to say anything else, and Georgia's emotions tightened and spiraled again. She clenched her eyes closed and simply hung on to Abby.

Several moments later, she finally let go. Abby watched her, of course. The woman was relentless about some things. Being there for Georgia was one of them. "I heard Otis was here."

"He was," she said. "He went to get lunch."

"You're okay?"

"Getting there." Georgia gave Abby a smile, noticing something was different. "Abigail Ingalls." She reached out and touched her friend's hair. "You cut your hair." She grinned and grinned. "It's so cute."

Abby flipped the far shorter ends of it over one shoulder and then the next. "Thank you. I was just down the street. Nellie came in and said your mom had been here. I knew I had to come, but my hair was soaking wet. And you know Kellie-Jean. She is not fast with the styling."

Georgia giggled with Abby. "But you don't want her to be," she said. "You want her to go over everything, step by step, so you can do your hair the way she does." She touched it again. "It's so much shorter."

"Too short?" Abby's expression held a hint of worry now. "I didn't tell Tex I was cutting it either. He thinks I had to service the Bookmobile today."

"You lied to your husband?" Georgia pressed one hand to her chest in mock horror.

"No," Abby said. "I did drop off the Bookmobile. I just don't service it. I mean, *I'm* not a mechanic."

"Did he really think you'd be under the hood?" Georgia laughed with Abby.

"I have no idea what he thinks," Abby said among all the giggles.

"Howdy, Abs," Otis said as he returned. He glanced at Georgia and then back to Abby. "Your hair is nice. Did you want to stay for lunch?" He lifted the enormous brown paper sack he carried. "I'm fairly certain there's enough for fifteen people in here."

"Yes," Abby said. "You Youngs don't know how to make small meals."

Otis chuckled and started for the office. "Come on back when you can, then."

Abby linked her arm through Georgia's. "He's a smart man, giving me a minute with you alone."

"Is he?"

They sauntered through the store, and Georgia nodded to Harley that she'd be in the back. Her assistant nodded and kept putting out the new bookmarks they'd gotten in.

"Yep," Abby said. "How are things going with him? You said Shane liked him."

"Shane is *obsessed* with him," Georgia said dryly. "Things are good, Abs. Really. I'm going to take him to meet Momma and Daddy for real in a few days. Once she gets back on her meds. Then...I don't know." She paused at the mouth of the hallway and looked down it. She could distinctly remember coming out of her office and seeing him right there in the hall for the first time. She'd pulled him into her office, demanding that he kiss her.

"I sure do like him," she murmured.

"He sure does like you too," Abby whispered back, her smile wide and contagious.

Georgia looked at her, her fear getting the best of her. "What if it's too good to be true?" she asked, her voice almost reverting to a child's.

"It's not," Abby said firmly. "Otis is a great man. A good father. He'll take really good care of you and all of your pets." She nodded like she'd seen the future and knew all. "Now come on. I have to text Tex and tell him I'm eating here with you two. He'll probably want me to bring him some leftovers."

Georgia went with her into the office, and Otis had already gotten out another chair for Abby. He really was practically perfect in every way—except for his long afternoon and evening silences, and maybe the way he treated her like she might shatter at any moment. And fine, sometimes he still greeted her with weird and wacky things.

But she did like being with him, and she didn't want to think about *not* being with him. So she simply wouldn't.

A WHOLE WEEK LATER, GEORGIA WOUND HER HANDS together as she said, "It's the one on the right up there. The blue house."

Otis kept driving until the appointed address, then he pulled up to the curb. Almost all of the snow was gone down in the valley now, though the weather forecast kept threatening to bring more. Morris reported that Whiskey Mountain Lodge still had a lot of snow, but they were up in the canyon above town. He'd gotten a job up there doing football camps for their guests. He hadn't really started yet, but he went almost every morning to plan, talk to guests, and get preliminary details done.

With the truck stopped, Georgia simply looked at the house. Nothing seemed amiss here, but she knew better.

The walls of this rambler held so many memories. So many conversations. So many good times, bad times, terrible things, amazing happenings.

"Did you grow up here?" he asked.

"Yes." She wasn't sure how long she sat there before she sighed and turned toward him. "It'll be easier to just get it over with."

"I'm game," he said, giving her a kind smile.

She unbuckled and slid to the sidewalk. Otis joined her, took her hand in his, and squeezed. He'd taken Joey to Dog Valley and her mother's again last night, just so he could be available for Georgia today. He'd said if Lauren couldn't take her, he'd have called Mav, Luke, Trace, or Tex. Of course. He had plenty of family available and willing to help.

With Shane so far away, Georgia often felt completely alone. Truth be told, that was why she took in every stray she heard about. She herself felt like a discarded dog, and she just needed someone to care for her and love her, even as straggly and sick as she might be.

She went up to the front door and rang the doorbell. Otis shifted at her side. "You don't just go in?"

"It upsets Momma," she said. "The door will be locked, besides."

Otis reached out and tried to turn the knob. No dice. "Huh," he said. "I didn't know people in Coral Canyon locked their doors."

The door opened before she could respond, and

Daddy stood there. "Princess." He grinned at her and drew her into a warm hug. "It's great to see you. Come in, come in." He stepped back into the house, gesturing for her to hurry up and follow him.

She did, and Otis said, "Howdy, sir. I don't think we've truly met."

"Daddy, this is Otis Young." Georgia watched as they shook hands. "Otis, my daddy, Clive."

"Wonderful to meet you," Otis said. "Thanks for having us over for breakfast. It smells amazing in here."

Georgia's nose kicked into operation, and she did smell bacon and maple syrup. "Yes," she agreed. "It does."

Daddy would've done the cooking, and since their house was almost eighty years old, it didn't have the open concept the way homes did today. She led the way past the living room, a half-bath, and a bedroom before walking into the kitchen and dining room combo area.

Momma sat at the table, and when she looked up, Georgia could see she'd been crying. "Momma," she said, hurrying to her side. "Are you okay?" She dropped into a crouch and looked up at her mother.

"Janet," Daddy said before she could answer Georgia. "Georgia brought her boyfriend for breakfast, remember?"

Momma's eyes cleared instantly. "Yes," she said, smiling. "Hello, dear."

Georgia found the life in her mother's eyes. "Hey, Momma." She leaned up to hug her, and then she got back to her feet. "Do you remember meeting Otis last weekend?" She extended her hand toward him, and he came straight to her side.

Momma stood too, and her eyebrows bunched together. "A little," she said as she drank in the tall man at Georgia's side. "I wasn't very nice to you."

"Oh, you were perfectly nice to me," he said. "It was—"

"Otis," Georgia said. He closed his mouth and put a smile there instead. "Momma, do you remember coming to the shop?"

She wore distress in her expression now. "Daddy says I wasn't very nice." She looked at him, and he nodded in Georgia's peripheral vision.

"No," she said. "You weren't."

"I'm taking the meds now."

"I can see that." Georgia drew in a long breath, counting up to four as she did. She blew it all out slowly too. "I love you, Momma, but you can't come in my store and scream at me."

"I'm so sorry," she said, sinking back into her chair. "I just get upset sometimes, you know?"

"We all do, Momma." Georgia pulled out the chair beside her and sat down. "It's my *bookshop*, Momma. There were customers there."

She nodded, a fierceness coming into her face now. "I know. Daddy told me."

Georgia covered her momma's hands with hers. "Okay, I forgive you." She smiled as Daddy put a huge pan of scrambled eggs on the table.

"Sit down, Otis," he said. "There's plenty of food, and Georgia tells me you have an appetite that requires it."

"Oh-ho," he said, chuckling. "Is that what she said?" He gave her a look that said they'd talk about that later and sat beside her. Daddy kept bringing over food—bacon, waffles, syrup, butter, and a tray of roasted potatoes and onions—before he sat down too.

"Georgia," he said. "Tell us how you met Otis and how long you've been seein' him." He nudged the spoon for the eggs. "And someone start eating. I've been cooking for a long time, and this ain't goin' to waste."

Georgia got busy putting food on her plate, her heart happier than it had been in a while. She wasn't sure what this morning would've looked like had she come alone. Probably not this. But she hadn't come alone, and she glanced at Otis, who'd covered his plate with waffles and then layered bacon on top of them.

"Well, I met Otis last fall," she said. "Maybe late summer. He was standing in the hall when I needed help with something, and he helped me."

He lifted his eyes to hers, that intense buzzing between them instant and hot. "Yeah." He cleared his throat. "But I guess I wasn't so good at...the helping, because she never called me. Started seein' someone else. We didn't reconnect until the beginning of January."

Georgia's pulse galloped through her body. "It wasn't that you weren't good at it," she said. Quite the opposite.

"It was just...." She didn't know what to say, and the longer she sat there, the higher Otis's eyebrows got. *It was just what?* he kept silently asking her.

"What'd he help you with?" Daddy asked just before putting a big bite of eggs in his mouth.

Otis started to laugh, and heat filled Georgia from top to bottom. "Nothing," she mumbled.

"Oh," Momma said. "Shane says he's going to be in town for Lindsey's tribute." She beamed around at everyone as if they hadn't been talking about something else entirely. Georgia met her father's eyes across the table, and he nodded slightly. Yes, the medication dose was still being adjusted.

"That's great," Georgia said. She could use the distraction anyway. "Why don't you tell Otis what we usually do, and he'll see if he can make it?"

"Why wouldn't he be able to make it?" Momma demanded.

"Momma, he's a country music star," Georgia said, deliberately not making her voice sound patronizing. "He's really busy, and he has a trip to Nashville coming up." She looked at Otis and kept buttering her waffle. "Plus, he's got a daughter, and his ex-wife up in Dog Valley has some health problems. I'm just saying, he might not be able to make it."

"Tell me about it," he said. "And when it is, and I'll see."

"How old is your daughter?" Momma asked instead.

Otis didn't bat an eye. "Eight, ma'am."

"That's nice. So we go to the cemetery every year...."

Georgia let Momma talk and talk, because it always helped her. She barely ate anything she talked so much, but Georgia knew it didn't matter to Otis. He finished eating and took her hand in his, a silent reassurance that he was right there with her, and he wasn't going anywhere.

It was a simple, beautiful thing, and Georgia thanked the Lord that he'd been standing in that hallway all those months ago when she'd needed him. And here he was now, right where she needed him, when she needed him there.

Simple. Beautiful. And something she hoped she could have in her life for a long time to come.

27

Maverik Young heard his wife gasp behind him as they went up the stairs. They'd been in the basement with the kids, watching movies and putting together a puzzle for the evening. The kids had fallen asleep an hour ago, and Mav and Dani had finished their movie in comfortable and companionable silence before deciding to go to bed.

"Mav," Dani said, her voice full of pain and air.

He hurried up the last three steps and turned to find her frozen about halfway down. She was nine months pregnant now, and she had one hand on her baby belly and one gripping the railing. She was looking down at herself, and when she looked up at him, he saw the pure urgency in her eyes.

"I think my water broke."

He zipped down the steps to her, not sure what to do.

Portia, his first wife, had gone into labor while Mav had been in South Carolina. He'd gotten on a plane and made it to Jackson before Beth had been born, but he didn't know this part of it. He hadn't been there.

He reminded himself that this was exactly why he'd quit managing his brothers' band. He *wanted* to be here for this part of it.

"We have to go to the hospital," he said. *Right?* echoed loudly in his head, but he didn't say it out loud.

"The kids," she said.

"I'll call Morris." That was the arrangement Mav had made. Morris lived with Trace and Harry, but he didn't have any children. His obligations were the easiest to get out of. He could come day or night. "Let's get you upstairs to the couch."

She managed to keep walking, and Mav didn't let go of her arm once. When she rested safely on the couch, he hurried to call his brother.

"We don't have a name for him," Dani said, her voice pitching up. "Two family naming parties, and we've got nothing."

"He's going to have a name," Mav said. "We'll know it when we see him."

Morris's line rang and rang, and Mav glanced over to the clock in the kitchen. It was after eleven, but Morris was in his mid-twenties. Didn't they stay up all night long? Mav frowned when the call went to voicemail.

He kept his back turned to Dani and tried Morris

again. His mind raced. If he couldn't get Morris this time, he'd try Trace. He hardly ever slept, and he could go wake up Morris and tell him to get over here. With Beth and Boston asleep, surely they could stay here for a few minutes alone.

Dani wouldn't like that, but she sucked in another sharp breath while Morris's line rang and rang.

Mav turned back to her, noting how pale she'd gotten. "He's not answering. I'm trying Trace." He hung up without waiting for the voicemail to pick up. He dialed Trace, and his brother answered on the second ring.

"Howdy, Mav," he said like it was completely normal to be calling at this hour. Band members did live a different life sometimes. On tour, they slept most of the day and were up most of the night. Dinner was breakfast. Dawn meant bedtime.

"Trace," he said. "Dani's going into labor, and Morris isn't answering his phone."

"I'll get 'im," Trace said, his voice far more serious now. "He had a headache and went to bed early."

"Do you think he can still come?"

"If he can't, I will," Trace said. "He can get Harry to school in the morning." Scuffling and movement came through the call, and it felt like forever before Trace said, "Morris. It's Mav. They're havin' the baby."

He'd clearly pulled his phone away from his mouth, because his words came through muffled. Morris said something Mav couldn't hear, and in front of him, Dani relaxed. She tapped her phone, and Mav watched the time start to count up.

It didn't matter how far apart the contractions were. Her water had broken, and that meant she had to get to the hospital. They'd driven the route already. All right, Mav had. He'd done it alone when he'd gone to pick the kids up from school. He knew the best route, and that it took eight minutes to get there.

She's not going to have the baby in the next eight minutes, he told himself. He paced anyway, and then Morris said, "I'll be there in twenty minutes, Mav."

"Okay, thanks," he said. "You know the garage code?"

"I know it."

"The front door has a code too," he said.

"Yes," Morris said. "You gave it all to me. I'm fine. I can get in."

"Do you think we should go before you get here?"

"I have no idea," Morris said.

"I'm fine," Dani said. "We can wait for him."

"Okay," Mav said, but he wasn't sure who he was talking to. "See you soon." He hung up and strode behind the couch. "I'll get your bag, okay, sweetheart?"

"Thank you," she said. How she could be so calm, he wasn't sure. Of course, she'd done this before, and she hadn't run into the room ten minutes before the baby had been born. His heartbeat roared at him, though, and Mav couldn't make it stop.

He grabbed the bag from inside their walk-in closet,

then got himself a pair of shoes and socks. Dani would need those too, and he gathered everything and went back into the living room. She hadn't moved, and Mav hurried to get his socks and sneakers on.

"Shoes, my love," he said, but Dani had closed her eyes. She breathed in and out slowly, one hand resting protectively on their baby.

Mav got down on the floor and put her socks and shoes on for her, and when he straightened and knelt in front of her, she smiled at him. "Thank you."

"I love you," he said, returning her smile.

"I love you too."

"Did you have another contraction?"

She shook her head, and they both looked at the timer. It was going on seven minutes now. Mav was no expert, but he thought they should be closer together. "We're still going," he said. "Your water broke." He'd wanted to take the birthing and parenting classes with this pregnancy, and Dani had gone along with him, though she'd had a baby before.

Boston was almost seven, so it had been a fair few years, and they'd become familiar with the hospital here in Coral Canyon, as well as more current products in the baby market. They had it all, as Dani was due in only two days. The stroller sat in the back of their SUV, as did the car seat. Dani had packed it all last week. Diapers, clothes, special baby shampoos—they'd been collecting things for nine months.

Mav got to his feet and looked at his wife. Things seemed too calm. "Should I get you to the car? We can wait for Morris there?" He'd heard horror stories of women having babies on the side of the road, then others about a flurry of activity as their wife went into labor so fast.

This was the opposite of that, and Mav itched to *go*. He'd been waiting for this moment for what felt like a lifetime, and he couldn't just stand here and do nothing. Dani reached out her hand, and Mav helped her stand.

The moment she did, she gasped and froze. Mav moved right into her side, shoring her up. "It's all right," he said, though he had no idea what tore through her body. "Lean into me, love."

She did, and Mav gladly bore it. He'd do anything he could for Dani, and he thanked the Lord for her every morning when he woke up and every evening before he went to bed. Her phone ticked on the couch, and Mav watched it, mentally calculating the seconds until she relaxed.

"Seventeen seconds," he said. "Is that a long contraction?"

"I don't know," she said. "Let's go." She took ginger steps toward the garage, and Mav left everything but her. He could get her in the SUV, and then come back for the bag, a bottle of water, and his wallet. Hopefully Morris would be here soon.

Dani didn't move fast these days, and tonight was

even more snail-like. He eventually closed the door behind her, and she started reclining the passenger seat. He dashed back inside to collect the baby bag she'd packed. She'd gone over all the items with him, as she had an outfit she wanted their son to wear to meet the family.

Mav remembered he was supposed to call her mother, and he swiped her phone from the couch. Susan, Dani's mother, could've come to sit with the kids tonight too, but Mav anticipated needing her after school, so he and Dani had devised a two-pronged approach. Morris and Susan.

With the bag, water, wallet, and her phone, he hit the button to open the garage door. It started to lift, and then it went back down. Mav frowned and tapped it with his elbow again.

The door rose to reveal Morris standing there. "Hey," he said. "I guess I was trying to get in while you were trying to get out."

Relief filled Mav. "Thanks so much for coming." He glanced at Dani, but she hadn't moved. She looked as if she were sleeping, and Mav's heartbeat danced through him. He just wanted to be at the hospital. Nothing bad could happen there.

"Kids are asleep," he said ot Morris. "I wrote out a schedule a week ago, and it's on the fridge."

"No school tomorrow," Morris said as he entered the garage. "Beth's here?"

"Yes," Mav said. "Dani's mom's number is on the

fridge. You know how to get in touch with Mama. Uh... what else?"

"Go," Morris said. "I know how to keep a child alive for a few hours." He grinned at Mav and went into the house. Easy peasy.

Mav opened the back door of the SUV and threw everything inside. "Okay?"

"Fine," Dani murmured. She'd been so tired, and Mav wished her water had broken as she'd gotten out of bed in the morning. Because it was going to be a long night.

Twelve hours later, Dani still hadn't had the baby. Her water had broken, so she'd been admitted to the maternity ward. But she'd made no progress. Mav sat in the hard chair beside her bed, playing the same game on his phone he'd been playing for hours now.

He was so ready for this to be over. He closed the game in frustration and exhaustion—Dani had dozed a little bit overnight and continued to do so now. He hadn't. He'd been so worried she'd be in pain or need him that he hadn't been able to fall asleep. He'd closed his eyes, but they still felt like someone had rubbed glass in them.

The door opened, and their doctor entered. "Miss Dani Young," he said as if he'd been waiting all day to see her. "Still no baby." He looked down at her chart and handed it to the nurse. “Let’s see if we can’t get you moving a little, should we?”

“Yes,” Dani said, and to Mav it sounded like a choir of angels.

“We’re going to give you Pitocin,” he said. “It’s what we give moms to induce then. Your water broke a while ago, and we need that baby to come out.”

Mav was on board for that, and he watched the nurse poke the needle into Dani’s IV. Whatever that magic substance was, he hoped it got things moving fast. Everyone in his family had known they’d gone to the hospital by morning, and he’d spent an hour texting with his brothers and parents. Then Dani’s mom. Then back to Otis or Tex or whoever had asked if Dani had made any progress.

Dani groaned, and Dr. Darwood grinned. “That’s what we want to hear.”

“We do?” Mav asked.

“Oh, yes,” the doctor said. “A quiet mom is a mom not in labor.” He signed something on her chart and gave it back to the nurse. “I’m going to call Dr. Thompson. You’re doing an epidural, yes?”

“Yes,” she said, trying to push herself up further. Mav jumped up to help her, but that didn’t seem to make her feel better. Her eyes looked a little wild, and he didn’t like that either.

The drug helped a lot though, and things definitely picked up. Dani progressed faster, and she got the epidural. Soon enough, Mav stood behind her and braced her body as the doctor told her to push.

"This baby is a stubborn thing," he said after several tries with no infant. He didn't remember Beth taking quite so long to be born. Of course, he'd been a different man then, and he couldn't quite recall.

"He's a Young," Dani said, panting. "What did you expect?"

Mav grinned, because that was about as mean as Dani got.

"One more time," Dr. Darwood said. "Come on, baby. It's time to be born." He nodded to Dani, and she pushed. Mav felt like he was helping in some small way as he kept her upright, and then a terribly terrific cry filled the air.

Dani sagged back against him as Dr. Darwood boomed, "Here he is. Nice a round and perfect." He lifted the baby up, and Mav could only stare at him.

His son.

Joy and love filled him over and over again. He stayed with Dani while the nurses whisked away the child. They brought him back and gave him to Mav while the doctor finished up with Dani, and he turned him so she could see his face.

"He's so beautiful," he said to her, wonder in his voice. "He doesn't have dark hair." He'd been expecting the boy to look exactly like him, which made no sense when he truly thought about it. "He looks like you, baby."

"I'm ready for him," she said, her arms up and open

and waiting for Mav to pass her their son. He did, and the love streaming from Dani made his heart sing.

"He doesn't look like me," she said, stroking one finger along the top of his head, where a definite blond fuzz grew. "He's a Young."

"He has some big lungs," the nurse said. "Cried and cried when we bathed him." She smiled at the baby and looked at Mav and then Dani. "I just need a name for him."

Mav met Dani's eyes. "He maybe looks like...." He didn't look like Mav, who had the softer rounder features in the Young family. Tex and Luke and Blaze all had sharper, more square features, like their father.

"Blaze," he said. "He looks like Blaze and Luke." He wanted to name the boy Lars, but he'd wait to see what Dani said.

"So definitely a Young," Dani said. She smiled at the baby, bouncing him slightly. "I think Lars, Mav."

"I was thinkin' the same thing." A smile burst onto his face.

"Lars," the nurse wrote. "Middle name?"

"Mav?" Dani guessed, but Mav shook his head.

He didn't want the baby named after him. "What about John? We could call him LJ or just Lars that way." Dani did like initials for a name, and Mav had resisted it when they'd first started talking about names. This way, there could be a compromise.

"Lars John Young," she said. "Yeah, that's nice."

The nurse wrote it down, and Dani said, "Get his meeting clothes, Mav. I'm sure there's someone here to see him."

"There are a few people in the waiting room asking about you," she said. "You can't go, but he could take the baby out." She nodded at Mav. "For a moment. We want him to get fed soon too."

He nodded and after she'd gone, he asked Dani, "Who's here? I didn't even keep anyone updated on the progress."

"If I know Abby, she's been here since dawn." Dani wasn't kidding either. She quickly unbundled the baby and put him in the cute blue romper. His tiny chicken legs didn't look quite human, and then she wrapped him up again, practically covering the entire outfit.

Mav took the baby and pressed a kiss to his forehead. "All right, buddy. Let's go see who came to see you." He left the room, and the same nurse who'd just taken Lars's name said, "We're moving her to room four-fifteen. She'll be there when you get back."

"Thanks," he said. Down the hall and out of the maternity ward he went, and a waiting room opened up. It was full of people, and Mav's steps slowed. It had been such a long night, it took him a moment to realize all of the people in the room—every single one—belonged to him.

"Wow," he said under his breath. "Look, bud. Everyone came to meet you." He took another couple of steps, and his movement caught the attention of Luke, who shot to his feet.

"He's here," he yelled.

Mav couldn't believe Luke was here, but he was. And he smiled and cooed at the baby. Tex and Abby and Bryce had come. Mama and Daddy, of course. Mav held up the baby and said, "We named him Lars," before passing the infant to his mother. She sighed, already in love with him, and started rocking him in his arms.

"He looks like Blaze," Mav said to Tex. "A little like you. I can't decide which he looks more like. Maybe Luke too."

"We'll do a line-up," Tex said, and he grabbed Luke by the arm. "Where's Blaze?"

Mav's heart stuttered. "Blaze is here?"

"Him and Jem," Tex said. "Trace called 'em last night, and they got on a plane."

Trace and Morris and Otis moved, and sure enough, there stood Blaze and Jem. Mav started to laugh, and they came toward him doing the same. The three of them embraced, and then Blaze stood next to Tex, who stood beside Luke, and with Luke looking like he could commit a murder in the next ten seconds, and Tex grinning like a fool, and Blaze trying not to do either, Mav studied them.

"I think Blaze," he said. "Where's the baby?"

Mama had given him to Abby, and she brought him over and held him next to Blaze. They had the same jaw and slope of their nose. "Definitely Blaze," Tex said. He then took the little boy and kissed him, and Mav's love and appreciation for his family expanded and grew.

"Thanks for coming," he said to everyone. His voice cracked, but there was so much commotion and noise, he didn't think anyone heard it. They each hugged him, and everyone asked about Dani. The other kids wanted to meet their new cousin, and it was a rowdy Young family party...until the nurses came out and said, "Mister Young, your wife is asking if you and the baby are still alive."

He chuckled, collected his son, and quickly went back to Dani's side. "They love him," he whispered as he handed Lars to her. "I love him. I love you." He pressed a kiss to her forehead, and she smiled up at him.

"I love him and you too."

28

Otis entered the recording studio on a day when he wanted to take everything outside and let it feel the rush of the spring air. The weather had finally started to warm up in Wyoming, and there were flowers pushing through the ground at his house. Joey wanted to go around every morning before school and take pictures of what was growing in their yard. Otis let her, because he didn't have the same wonder as an eight-year-old, and he fed off of hers.

Luke and Trace were the only ones in the studio, but they were both looking at a packet of papers. "What's that?" Otis asked.

"Our itinerary for Nashville," Trace said. "Morris made you a copy."

"Next week?" Otis itched to just sit and play his guitar. He'd spent a couple of hours on the piano bench that morning, something seething inside him he couldn't name.

"We leave on Thursday," Luke said. Just like that. Like it was no big deal that they had to be on a plane in two days.

Panic reared inside Otis. "What?" he asked. "Since when?" He picked up his packet, and right at the top, it read *NEW TRAVEL DATES. IF YOU NEED HELP MAKING ARRANGEMENTS, PLEASE SEE MORRIS ASAP*.

Otis needed help, because he was supposed to be at the cemetery with Georgia and her family on Saturday. He couldn't miss it.

Joey would need someone to look after her too, and he frowned as he saw the additional meetings with their record producers on Friday and Saturday.

"Why are we meetin' with Martin on a Saturday?"

"Because he's going to Mexico next week," Morris said from behind him, and Otis turned. He wanted to fling the packet at his brother, though it wasn't his fault things had changed.

"I gotta be honest," he said "I don't know if I can go."

"You have to go," Luke said.

"It's your album," Morris said, his eyes flying wide.

"No," Otis said, always uncomfortable when anyone called the album his. He'd never wanted that glory. "It's *our* album." He sighed. "Guys, Georgia's family has this thing this weekend. It's important."

"What thing?" Trace asked.

Otis only shook his head, all the answer he was going to give right now. "I—Lauren can't just take Joey. She has a treatment in Casper on Friday." He knew that, because she shared her calendar with him. "I thought we were going next week."

He studied the itinerary again. The meeting on Friday was specifically about the songwriting. He'd have to defend some things, and he'd make concessions on others, and the whole meeting would be to rip apart the music and lyrics he'd written, and then put them all back together again. Most of the time, the whole band started the meeting, but only Otis finished it.

Perhaps he could fly back after that and still make it to the cemetery on Saturday morning. He'd go without sleep if he had to.

But no, the meeting on Saturday was with their big producer, and if he didn't okay the album, they'd be starting over from scratch. Otis and the rest of Country Quad had spent the past four months in the studio, and none of them could fathom starting over now.

A sigh pulled from the top of his head to the bottom of his feet. "I'll figure something out with Joey."

"I'm sorry," Morris said. "I didn't know, but if we don't go this weekend, then we're three more weeks before Martin gets back."

"Can he video in?" Trace asked.

Otis appreciated the suggestion, because it meant

Trace was trying to make this work for him. "It's fine," he said. "I'll talk to Mav and Lauren. Maybe Mama can help with Joey while I'm gone." He had no idea what to say to Georgia. "Oh, and Blaze is coming this weekend."

Blaze had come to see Mav's baby, but he'd left soon after. He'd said he'd be back for a few days this weekend too, and now Otis wouldn't get to see him. No, he wasn't going to ask his brother to tend his child while he came for a visit. Mama could do it, or Lauren maybe, or Mav. Otis didn't want to ask at all, and everything had gotten so complicated with Lauren's illness and Otis's relationship with Georgia.

He had no idea what life held for him anymore, when before, he'd known. He couldn't fathom touring with a wife and family, and doubts started to stream from one side of his mind to the other.

He shoved the itinerary behind his music and turned to pick up his guitar. He just needed to play. He could think about hard things later.

Tex took forever to come into the studio, and by the time he did, Otis was ready to leave.

"Finally," Luke said. "I was just about to come up there and get you."

"Sorry," Tex said, but he didn't elaborate. He looked at the packet, said nothing, and reached for his guitar.

Must be so nice, Otis thought. To have someone in his life there to pick up all the pieces when he needed them to.

He schooled his thoughts and his emotions. It wasn't fair to Tex to think such things. His brother had sacrificed a lot over the years for Country Quad. Otis had too, and he hated that everything fell on the same day.

He prayed during the practice session that day. He let anyone change anything they wanted, to which Luke finally threw a drum stick and said, "Otis! Where are you, bro?" before stalking out of the studio.

Otis blinked at his back, then looked at Tex.

"You're really not here," Tex said, unlooping his guitar strap from around his neck. "I'm calling it."

"You can't *call* it," Trace bickered back at him. "We leave in two days. This isn't ready to play for the execs!" He was yelling by the time he finished, because Tex had just walked out too.

He and Otis looked at one another. "What just happened?" Trace asked.

"I maybe checked out," Otis said. He hadn't meant for everyone to get bent out of shape.

"We've all done that before," Trace said. "Luke would've been back in two minutes." He watched the door, but neither Luke nor Tex returned.

"I guess we're done." Otis took off his guitar and set it in the stand. "I have to go talk to Georgia anyway."

"I'm sorry this conflicts with that," Trace said. He didn't move fast, and Otis decided he had a few minutes to spend with his older brother. Along with Blaze, he'd once done a lot with Trace. He still did.

Right now, Trace seemed...lost.

"Hey," Otis said. "Are you okay?"

"Yeah, fine," he said. Trace sighed as he left the studio. He didn't leave the barn though, and instead, he sank into the couch out in the lobby area. Otis went with him, and the two of them sat there for a moment.

"I've been thinkin' about dating a little," Trace said. "But it makes me sick to my stomach."

Otis only nodded. He couldn't pretend to understand Trace's situation. Lauren wasn't as present as she'd once been, but she only lived fifteen minutes away. His ex-wife lived in Europe. Harry never saw her. They didn't talk to her that Otis knew of.

"Why is that?" Otis asked. "Because of Harry? Because of the band? Travel? Touring?"

"All of the above," Trace said.

"You don't want to quit Country Quad."

"Do you?"

Otis said nothing, but the answer was no. He finally shook his head. Trace did too. "Yeah," his brother said.

"It's a hard place to be in," he said. "What are we gonna do? Be Country Trio?" He looked at Trace. "Because you heard Tex. He's done." Otis swung his hand in front of him. "After this album and tour, he's done, Trace."

"I heard him."

Otis felt like he'd spent a long time climbing an arduous trail. The view at the top had been spectacular, but now someone was trying to convince him to jump off without a safety net.

"Maybe you should date a little," Otis said. "Then you'll know if that's just nerves or if it's something else."

"I don't know," Trace said. "I'm not like you, Otis. I don't laugh and talk to women. I barely talk to you guys."

"You got a supermodel to fall in love with you, bro." Otis laughed. "There's something about you someone is gonna love."

Trace gave him a small smile. "We'll see. I don't know. Harry says I can't date anyone in town. That it would be too embarrassing for him."

"Yeah, well, he's thirteen," Otis said, as if he knew how thirteen-year-old boys thought. He'd been one once, but that had been a long, long time ago. "Remember what we thought of Daddy when we were thirteen?"

"Mortified," Trace said dryly.

Otis chuckled, and they sat together for a few more minutes. He finally stood. "Okay, well, if I have to make all kinds of arrangements in two days, I best be goin'."

"Me too."

They left the studio together, and Otis collected Joey from the farmhouse. She'd just finished eating, and Otis waved away Abby's offer to make him a plate. "I'll eat later," he said.

With Joey loaded up, he told her, "I have to go to Nashville on Thursday, Roo. I'm gonna call your momma and see if she can take you while I'm gone."

"Okay," Joey said. "How long will you be gone, Daddy?"

He'd shoved the itinerary in his music folder. "I think until next Thursday," he said. "A week." It was a long time. "Maybe I'll have Uncle Mav come pick you up on Sunday night."

His brother's baby was a week old now, and they were all at home, doing well. Otis frowned to himself. He didn't want to ask Mav to watch another child. Who was Luke going to rely on? Or Trace? Who would take Harry for him?

He called his mother instead of Lauren, and she answered with, "Hello, son."

"Mama," he said. "I need help."

"I know. Y'all are goin' to Nashville on Thursday."

Otis sighed. "So you're taking Harry and Corrine?"

"Yes," she said. "I'm happy to have Joey too."

"I was gonna call Lauren, but it's a long time for her to have Joey." Joey looked at him, something in her eyes. "I'll call you back." He hung up with his mother and glanced at his daughter. "What?"

"I'd rather go to Grandma's," she said. "Mama doesn't have very much to eat."

"What?" Otis dang near drove off the road. "What do you mean? She has food to eat."

"She doesn't cook," Joey said. "Last time, I had to make my own mac and cheese, and I spilled on the stove, and she got really mad." Her bottom lip shook.

"Joey," he said. "Really mad like I tell you to get permission before you use the stove, or really mad like really mad?"

"Really mad," Joey whispered. "Then she called Grandma Echo, and I stayed there the rest of the weekend."

Otis had no idea. "Why didn't you tell me?"

"Mama said not to. That she was just tired, and she didn't mean it."

"I'm sure she didn't." Otis sighed.

"What about Georgia?" Joey asked. "Maybe she'd let me stay with her." She wore hope in her eyes, but Otis was already shaking his head. "Why not, Daddy? I like Georgia. She's nice."

"She is nice," he said. That wasn't the issue. "She's not...I mean, we're not married, Roo. She's just my girlfriend."

"We could at least *ask* her," Joey pressed.

"I think you should go with Corrine and Harry," Otis said, already reaching to call his mom again. Joey folded her arms in one of her going-on-sixteen moves, but Otis ignored her. That handled, he said, "Let's swing by her house right now. I need to talk to her anyway."

"Fine."

"Fine."

A few minutes later, Otis pulled up to Georgia's house. Darkness had started to fall, so he didn't see her or any dogs out in the yard. He and Joey walked up to the front steps, and he knocked on her door.

Harley opened it a few seconds later with, "Oh."

"Is Georgia here?" Otis asked. He tucked his hands in his front pockets.

"Is that a poodle?" Joey entered the house without being invited in, but Otis was too tired to call her back.

"Georgia," Harley called. "Otis is here."

"Otis?" She came out of the hall, a tiny black kitten in her hands. Joey went nuts, and Georgia took a few moments with her before she handed the kitten to Harley. With Joey properly occupied by Georgia's many pets, Otis wandered back outside. Georgia joined him, pulling the front door closed behind her.

"What are you doing here?" she asked. She'd grabbed a jacket, and she zipped it up to her throat. "Is everything all right?"

He shook his head, unable to even look at her. "I have to go to Nashville."

"Yeah," she said. "I know. Next week."

"*This* week," he said. "Thursday, Georgia. I'm going on Thursday, and I won't be back for a week."

"Oh." She didn't say it was okay, but Otis desperately wanted her to.

"Joey wanted me to ask if she could stay with you, but I told her no."

"She can," Georgia said. "I can work it out with Harley for school and stuff."

"She's staying with my mom."

"Oh."

Otis could feel her retreating, and the thing was, he did the same thing. "Georgia," he said. "I don't—didn't know about this. I want to come on Saturday. You know I do."

"I know," she said.

He faced her now, the storm about to whip into gear. "This is how my life is. It's unpredictable. Things change all the time. When I tour, it'll be just like this."

She nodded, her eyes cast downward onto her hands. "It's just one more album."

"Maybe," Otis said.

She looked up. "It's not? Abby said there was just this last one."

"For Tex," he said.

"And you've said a hundred times that Tex is Country Quad." Georgia blinked at him, but Otis didn't have an answer for her. She shuttered everything off, the exact way he disliked. "I'll tell my parents you can't come this Saturday."

"Georgia," he said. "Don't shut down on me."

"What am I supposed to do?" she asked. "Cry you won't be there? Yeah, I'm upset you won't be there. But you can't be there. So...I'm not going to cry over it. It is what it is." She turned to go back inside. Otis followed her slowly, pushing the door closed with his foot.

Joey sat on the floor, no less than five dogs surrounding

her. She held the kitten, and blast it all, the gray cat who usually perched on the fridge and looked like he was calculating guest's deaths sat at her side.

Of course.

"Roo," he said. "We have to go."

"Look at these dogs, Daddy!" She wore pure delight in her eyes, and Otis knew he wouldn't be getting her out of there any time soon. He looked at Georgia helplessly, and her glare could've sliced a hole through his entire torso.

She bent down and took the black kitten from Joey. "Baby," she said. "Your daddy has a lot to do tonight and everything. You better go with him. The dogs aren't going anywhere."

"Can I come see them soon?" She patted one of the bigger ones, and he looked like he'd died and gone to doggy heaven.

"Yes," Georgia said with a smile. "Now, come on. It's time for you to go." She stood and put the kitten in a box on the kitchen counter. The gray cat jumped back up on top of the fridge and gave Otis a look that said, *Adios, cowboy*. The dogs came toward him as Georgia and Joey did, and he chuckled and patted them all.

"Go get in the truck now," he said to Joey.

Georgia opened the door, and dogs and the little girl spilled outside. He glanced behind him, but he didn't know where Harley had gone.

"She left," Georgia said. "She got an apartment of her own."

Otis nodded, and he ran his fingers along Georgia's hip. She didn't lean into him, and she didn't take his hand in hers. "I'm sorry, Georgia."

"I know you are." She still didn't say it was okay, and Otis didn't know what else to say or do. He waited a moment, desperate for divine help from above. Nothing came.

Maybe he was supposed to do nothing. Maybe he'd overthought this, and sure, she was disappointed. But they were okay.

"I'll call you tomorrow," he said.

"Mm."

He went down her front steps and got behind the wheel of his truck. She wasn't waiting on the front porch when he looked back to it, and another mighty sigh slipped from his lips. "Come on, Roo," he said. "Let's get home and get some laundry in." They were both gonna need it.

As he drove away from Georgia's, he couldn't help feeling like he'd just made a terrible mistake.

29

Georgia met her mother's eyes and quickly looked away. She knew what Momma was thinking. *Where's Otis?*

Nashville, Georgia wanted to scream. She hadn't texted, because her emotions were already high today. She got out of her SUV to go sit in her parents' truck. Shane hadn't arrived yet, and she might as well talk to them.

"Morning," she said, hauling the bouquet of assorted flowers she'd gotten at the grocery store into the back seat with her.

"Where's Otis?" Momma asked.

"He had to go to Nashville with the band," she said, and Georgia had a vision of herself saying that numerous times in the coming months. If it wasn't Nashville, it would be another city somewhere, where he and his brothers were putting on concerts.

She looked out the window, glad the sun was shining today. "It's a pretty day," she said. Lindsey would've liked a day like today. She'd have been outside biking, trail running, or hiking. All the things Georgia hated. She and her sister had always joked that all of those genes had skipped her completely, and since Lindsey came after her, she'd gotten them all.

She smiled sadly to her partial reflection in the glass, her thoughts on her sister. She had been outside on a day exactly like today, doing what she loved. The sun had been shining just like this a decade ago. The sky had been blue, with those puffy clouds Georgia could see today.

Lindsey had been hiking and climbing alone, something she'd done many times before this fateful date. Her boyfriend at the time was supposed to meet her, but he hadn't, and she'd gone alone. Georgia sometimes wondered what her sister had been thinking that afternoon.

She didn't like thinking that she'd been afraid, alone, worried. She must've been, and Georgia knew all of those feelings keenly. When Lindsey didn't return, Georgia had called Will. He'd told her he hadn't made it out of the office.

Things escalated from there, including the police, search and rescue, and a whole slew of volunteers. Georgia shut down the thoughts, because she didn't like reliving those few days where she didn't know where her sister was or if she was alive.

"There's Shane," Daddy said, and Georgia turned to look left as she hadn't seen her brother pull up on the right. "He's alone too."

Georgia's heart took courage.

"Marlene didn't come?" Momma sounded squeaky, and Georgia watched the side of her face. She wasn't happy, but Georgia didn't know why. This was their core family. Shane had driven for over two hours to be here.

He got out of his car and lifted his hand in a wave. Georgia collected her flowers and went to join him. She hugged him hard and said, "It's good to see you again."

"No Otis?" he asked as he embraced her back.

"He had to go to Nashville," she said. "Where's Marlene and the kids?" The truck doors slammed closed behind her, but Georgia didn't turn. She met Shane's eyes as she pulled back. "Is it a big deal that he's not here?"

"I don't know," Shane said, his attention diverting to over her shoulder. "Hey, Daddy." He went to hug their parents, and Georgia started a new circle of thinking. She hadn't spoken to Otis since Tuesday night, when he'd stopped by her house to tell her he wouldn't be here this weekend.

He'd texted that Joey would be at his parents, and she was welcome to text his mother and see if Joey wanted to do something after school or over the weekend. She hadn't answered.

He'd texted on Thursday morning before dawn to let her know he was on the move and heading for the airport.

He'd let her know when he got to Nashville. She hadn't answered.

He hadn't texted again, and she supposed her silence had said more than any return response could've.

Guilt pulled through her now. Otis had once told her that she shuttered things off, and he was right. She did it to protect herself. She needed time to sort through all the confusing pieces and make them line up the right way.

"Georgia," Momma called, and she turned away from Shane's car. She'd been staring at it for some reason. She joined her mom, dad, and brother, and they started down the path that led out to Lindsey's headstone.

She would start the reminiscing, because she always did. She was the oldest, and Shane followed her lead. Momma would be crying before they got there, and Daddy would be straight-faced and stalwart, as he was in most things.

"Remember when she made her prom dress out of duct tape?" Georgia broke the silence with her voice, though it didn't come out loud.

"You came home from college to encourage her," Momma said.

Georgia smiled and nodded. "Yes, I did."

"She was always the life of the party," Shane said, and Lindsey was. Those genes had somehow skipped Georgia too. She loved reading and stationery and living with a lot of animals. She loved her life, but it was far quieter than Lindsey's had been.

"She always knew when I needed her to call me," Georgia said. She missed that so much about her sister. Abby had sort of stepped into the role, and she did seem to have that same sixth sense that Lindsey had possessed.

"She made really good coffee," Daddy said.

"She was a good cook all around," Georgia said, looking at him. "You taught her everything, and she actually liked it."

A smile twitched against his mouth. "You weren't so bad."

Georgia didn't respond. The headstone neared, and she let Momma and Daddy go ahead. She and Shane always hung back to give them a moment alone. She wasn't sure why. Lindsey had been in her life as long as she'd been in Momma and Daddy's. They'd been the best of friends for Georgia's whole life—until the day Lindsey had died.

She waited for the familiar guilt and shame to overcome her. Usually, here at the cemetery, she had thoughts like, *You should've told her not to go.*

When she texted that Will hadn't shown up, you should've told her to go home.

Why did you let her go climbing alone?

Today, none of that came. Lindsey had died ten years ago now, and Georgia couldn't have prevented it. The sun shone a bit brighter in that moment, and Georgia felt like the Lord had reached into her heart and plucked out the dark, dead parts.

It was okay.

She was okay.

Lindsey was okay.

Tears pricked her eyes, and Georgia linked her arm through Shane's and leaned her head against his bicep. "Where's Marlene and the kids today?"

"Johnny has a soccer game," Shane said.

His family had missed coming to the cemetery for a *soccer game*. Otis had gone to Nashville for *his job*.

Why had she been so upset? Was she still upset?

Yes, she wanted him here. She needed his support.

She was in love with him.

She pulled in a breath sharp enough to make Shane look at her. "What?"

Georgia shook her head, because Daddy had just turned around. "Nothing. Come on." She walked over to the headstone and knelt down in front of it. She brushed off the dirt and debris that had collected over the winter and early spring. She placed her flowers on the stone and smiled at her sister's name. "Love you, Linds."

She stood and moved back, overcome with emotion. Different emotion than things she'd felt here at the cemetery before. She itched to call Otis and apologize. Perhaps she hadn't closed him out too much yet.

She prayed she hadn't.

Momma stayed and stayed at the headstone, and Georgia couldn't take it for another second. She turned and started walking back to the parking lot, her phone already out. She called Otis, but his phone just rang and rang and rang.

"Otis," she said when his voicemail picked up. "It's Georgia. Can you call me when you get a chance?" She didn't know what else to say, so she ended the call with that. Frustration filled her, because Otis wasn't great at responding to messages.

He's in meetings, she told herself. *He'll call you back when he can.*

Apparently Otis couldn't call her back that afternoon or evening. Or at all the next day. Georgia was sure he wasn't working at the record studio all day on Sunday, and her frustration turned to irritation and then anger.

She sent him a quick text, hoping it was light and casual and easy. *Hey, I just wanted to find out how your meetings went. I hope you're doing well.*

It sounded like something she'd send to a colleague, not her boyfriend, and Georgia wanted to delete it the moment she sent it.

She couldn't, so she put her phone away and started making the cats' breakfast for the following morning.

Monday came and went without any texts or calls from Otis. Georgia sat at her desk on Tuesday morning, staring at her device. Willing it to ring or chime. Something. She knew it worked, because Abby had texted a few times last night, and so had Harley.

"Maybe something's wrong," she said to herself. The clock told her she had another half-hour until she opened the bookshop, so she quickly tapped to call Abby.

"Georgia, hey," her friend said after the first ring. "I'm headed into a meeting."

"I'll be fast," she said. "You've heard from Tex, right? They didn't die in a fiery plane crash on the way to Nashville?" She hadn't checked the headlines or anything, but she felt certain the mood at church a couple of days ago would've been completely different if five of the Young brothers had met their demise.

"Yeah, I just talked to him a few minutes ago," Abby said. "Why?"

"I've texted and called Otis, and he's not responding."

Abby didn't say anything, and Georgia wasn't sure if she preferred the gabby Abby or this silent one. Silent usually meant she was thinking, and Georgia typically didn't need her thinking too hard about anything Georgia-related.

"What?" she asked. "Just tell me, Abby."

"Honey," Abby said, her voice on the edge of delicate. "I think Otis thinks you guys broke up...." She blew out her breath. "I was going to call you, but Tex said I should let the two of you work out your own problems."

"I...." Georgia scoffed. "I've called and texted him since Saturday."

"Maybe he hasn't gotten the messages."

"Tex's phone works in Nashville," Georgia pointed out. "He wouldn't just ghost me, would he?" His previous girlfriend had done that to him, and it had affected his self-image for months. Maybe it still did; Georgia wasn't sure. What she knew was she didn't think Otis would do that to her, to anyone. He knew how it felt.

"No, of course not," Abby said. "Like I said, I think he thinks you won't be calling or texting. Maybe he's not looking for them."

"They come to your phone whether you want them or not," Georgia said. She shook her head, this conversation going in circles. "Thanks, Abby. I was just checking to make sure he was still alive, and it sounds like he is."

"Georgia," Abby said.

"It's okay," she said. "Sorry to keep you from your meeting."

"I'll bring dinner tonight. Bryce has a date, and Franny would love to play with your dogs."

"Sure, okay." Georgia wasn't going to say no to free food. "See you then." She hung up and stared at her phone. Should she try him one more time? She just couldn't believe he'd ghost her. He also wouldn't just turn off his phone and bury it somewhere in his hotel room. He had an eight-year-old daughter who probably texted and called him every single day.

Georgia took a breath and gathered all of her bravery close. Then she tapped to call Otis...just one more time.

30

Otis truly felt free with a guitar in his hands, his fingers moving easily over the strings. The music sounded good today, and he grinned at Trace as his brother stepped up to the mic to sing his part. Otis joined in a measure later, and by the end of the song, he knew they had another number one single. In fact, he'd be shocked if Martin didn't release *Going Home* first, before the whole album dropped.

The last of the sound faded, and Tex stepped away from his mic. Otis fell back too, and they all looked at the row of executives about ten yards from them. On the other side of the glass, they wouldn't be able to hear them, but when the clapping and whooping started, silent as it was, Otis started to laugh.

"Finally," Luke yelled, and Tex turned to Trace and gave him a big hug.

They'd been working tirelessly in Nashville for the past few days. The first two days had been meeting upon meeting. Otis had barely had time to eat, breathe, go to the bathroom, and sleep before someone else wanted to see the band, talk to the band, catch up with the band.

He realized now that yes, they were blessed to be working out of a barn-studio in Coral Canyon, but that it did make this part of the process harder. The label was used to having access to them every single day, and now they didn't. So the questions and concerns had piled up to nearly destruction mode.

Someone had to answer for them, and more often than not, that was Otis. Tex sang and played what Otis put in front of him. Trace worked with his lyrics a lot, and the two of them had refined everything over the past few months. Luke had opinions that were mostly made of wind, but some of them made it into the work.

Morris had been in meetings while the band had been here working on songs, and he'd agreed to two calls per week to keep everyone in Nashville up to date with the work going on in Wyoming.

That would mean more for him to do, but Morris was constantly looking for more work. He'd picked up volunteering at the hospital and teaching football camps at Whiskey Mountain Lodge to stay busy. A couple of calls every week was probably like handing candy to a baby.

The door opened, and a man named Benjamin stuck his head in. "Let's take a break, boys. That was great."

"Did we get it recorded?" Luke asked.

"Yep. We'll get it mastered and sent to Martin to see what he thinks." Ben put his arm around Tex's shoulders and went with him. Of course. Tex was the true celebrity of the band, and everyone at the label treated him like the mastermind behind everything.

Except for the people who knew. Coleman met Otis at the door and said, "Otis, that song...." He grinned and shook his head. "Amazing." He glanced over to Trace. "Did you both work on it? Should we credit the two of you?"

"Yes," Otis said at the same time Trace said, "No."

"Yes," Otis said again. "Trace sat down with me on this one for sure." He gave his older brother a look that said, *don't argue.*

Trace didn't, and Coleman grinned at them both. "Great, great, I'll make sure our copywriters get that right. Now, talk to me about *When She Say No.* Do we want that to be the first song on the album? Thoughts?"

Otis's thoughts revolved around getting a drink and then calling his mother. Joey had dropped and broken her phone on Thursday morning, so Otis hadn't paid much attention to his device since then. It tended to overwhelm him even on good days, and since Georgia had ignored all of his messages since last Tuesday—*a week ago now*, his heart sobbed—he saw no point in being glued to the stupid phone.

He did want to be accessible to his mother should she

need something, but every time he'd called, she'd said things were going great. Joey was happy with Corrine and Harry, and they were all doin' just fine.

Otis wished he was. He played the part, talked to Ben until his throat hurt, despite the water he kept guzzling, and went back into the studio.

By the time he and his brothers left King Country, the sun was nearly gone from the sky. "This is why we need to be in Nashville," Luke said.

"So your mother can watch your daughter full-time?" Trace shot back. "I like being in Coral Canyon. My son needs a stable school and life in one place."

Otis said nothing, though the could've amen'ed Trace's sentence. Tex did said, "Amen, brother," and that only made Luke boil hotter.

"We had a great day in the studio," Otis said, watching Luke as he turned redder and redder. "Let's not ruin it tonight, okay?" He sighed and pushed his cowboy hat back to wipe his hand through his hair. "I'm starving. Who wants to go out with me?"

"I have to help Harry with his math," Trace said. "Bring me something back?"

Otis looked to Tex. "Tex?"

"Yeah, I'm in," he said.

"Luke?"

"Yep, fine." He'd go, but he wouldn't be happy about it. That, or he'd gnaw and gnaw at the topic until Otis wanted to scream at him. He hoped neither, but only the Good Lord above could help Luke at this point.

Trace got a car back to the hotel while the others got a ride to one of their favorite places in Nashville: Kentucky Hot Style. Everything here had plenty of spice and heat, and Otis's mouth watered before they'd even sat at a table.

He checked his phone and found nothing there. Displeasure that his mother hadn't updated him on Joey and disappointment that Georgia still hadn't responded to him at all mixed together into a dangerous cocktail. He wasn't the happy one tonight.

Tex said, "I'm so glad they found something they liked," and looked at Otis.

He grunted, because his thoughts weren't here in Nashville. Maybe he could get his flight changed to tomorrow morning. Even as he thought it, he knew he couldn't. Morris would kill him. They had one more full day at King Country, and every time there was a question or issue, Otis had the answer. Not Tex. Sometimes Trace, and Luke had a keen ear and mind too. He generally didn't say much to the music execs, but he'd buzz and buzz and *buzz* in Otis's ear.

"I thought you were really happy with today's session," Luke said as the waitress put down glasses of water.

"You boys want anything to drink?" She spoke in a candied voice. None of them looked at her. At least not directly.

"I'll take a lot of Diet Coke," he said. "Tons of ice."

"You're Country Quad," the woman said.

That brought Tex's head up. He put on his winning smile and said, "Yes, ma'am. I'll have sweet tea with all the lemon you've got."

"Just water for me," Luke said, still not looking at her. Otis wasn't interested in her either, but he could make eye contact. Irritation at Luke sparked through him, but he swallowed the words.

She left without making too big of a fuss over them, thankfully, and all eyes came back to Otis. "What?" he asked.

"Why are you all grumpy?" Luke asked. "I'm the one who usually acts like this, even on a good day in the studio." He actually smiled, and all of Otis's annoyance with him flew away.

"It's nothing," he said. That was what he got. Nothing. Nothing from his mother. Nothing from Joey now that her phone had been broken. Nothing from Georgia. He hated feeling like he was worth nothing, and he reverted to the man he'd been in Florida, standing on a woman's doorstep who had never contacted him again.

Would Georgia do that? Could he text her and find out if she was in the shop or if Harley could check him out? He'd definitely still have to buy books for Joey.

"Hello," Luke said, nudging Otis. "What is with you?"

Otis blinked and looked at him. "I don't know. I

just...." He looked to Tex, but his oldest brother simply looked back.

"You can tell us," he said after a couple of seconds of silence in their booth.

"I don't know," Otis said again. "I miss my daughter. I like being here, but I like being in Coral Canyon with her. I feel torn. Mama isn't texting me. Georgia won't talk to me." He gave his phone a little push, but it didn't go far on the table. The plastic case stuck and didn't slide. Otis's frustration reared. "Trace doesn't want credit for the songs. Luke is gearing up to tell me something about one of them he doesn't like, and Tex gets all the attention."

He glared at his brothers, and then broke into a smile. "Does that about sum it all up?"

Tex started to laugh, though only some of what Otis had said was actually funny. "I feel you, brother."

"Do you?" Otis asked.

"Keenly." He looked at Luke. "This one's always tellin' me something he doesn't like." He grinned at Luke and then the waitress as she set down their drinks. They ordered, and Luke went right back to the conversation they'd been having.

"I don't tell you half of what I don't like," he said.

"Heaven help us," Tex said. "There's more?" He kept grinning as he unwrapped his straw and plunked it in his drink. He zeroed in on Otis again. "Why won't Georgia talk to you?"

"Her sister died ten years ago," Otis said.

Luke whipped his gaze to Otis's too. "What does that have to do with you?"

"The anniversary was on Saturday," Otis said. He thumped the back of his phone. "I told her I'd come to the cemetery with her and her family, and then the trip got changed, and I couldn't go. She wasn't very happy about it. She hasn't talked to me since Tuesday. Last Tuesday. A week ago now." He shook his head, his lungs feeling like someone had punctured them with hot pokers. "I think... Well, I think that's probably it for us."

"Because you couldn't go to the cemetery?" Luke's eyes went wide. "Otis, you're going to travel all over for a tour within the year."

"I know." He sounded absolutely miserable about it too. "Which is why I think it's over. I mean, she hasn't responded to my texts. I only sent a couple, but I expected some sort of response. And she won't like it when I have to come here or tour or any of it."

He swept his gaze past Tex and Luke and picked up his cola. "It's probably better this way anyway. Then I won't be lettin' anyone down when I have to work."

"I'm confused," Tex said, his eyebrows drawing down. "Abby said she's called and texted you." He turned his phone toward Otis, and he started to read their texts.

I talked to her this morning, Abby's read. *She's responded to his texts and called him a couple of times. He won't talk to her.*

That's not what he's saying right now, Tex had sent.

Weird, Abby had responded. *That's what she said. I don't know all the specifics as to when or if she left a message.*

Tex hadn't said anything else.

Otis looked up and into his brother's eyes. For some reason, he liked that Georgia hadn't given many specifics. She never had gossiped about their relationship with her BFFs, and he really liked that. "Why wouldn't I get her texts or calls?"

Luke tapped and lifted his phone. Both Otis and Tex watched him. "It's ringing," he said.

Otis switched his gaze to his phone. It was not ringing. He picked it up, and it sat there, the screen blank as usual. "I'm so confused."

"Restart it," Luke said, ending the call. Otis pressed the power button and held it until the phone sang and it started to restart.

"I wonder how much I've missed," Otis said. "Maybe Mama's been trying to get in touch with me."

Tex started tapping on his phone. "I'll text her."

"Trace just texted to say he needs to know where we are so we can order for him," Luke said. He looked up, his eyes wide. "He said he tried to call Otis, but it went to voicemail."

"He did not call," Otis said. "You guys have been with me the whole time."

"Something's going on with your device," Tex said. "When did it stop working?"

"I don't know," Otis said. "I talked to Mama over the weekend. I called her on Sunday."

"Yeah, but when did she last text or call *you*?" Tex's eyebrows went up, and Otis watched him tap on his phone, right on "Brother Otis." The call started, and Tex tapped the speakerphone icon. It rang once, then again.

Otis's phone sat dormant. Fear ran through him. "What if Georgia really did call? She's gonna be so mad."

"She'll understand a broken phone," Luke said. "She's rational."

Otis would like to think so. At the same time, Georgia had to retreat inside herself sometimes. That was what he'd thought she'd done. She did come around, though, and when she hadn't...well, Otis had assumed that was it for them.

"Can I borrow your phone?" he asked Tex. "I can call her from it, right?"

"Sure."

Otis grabbed the phone and slid out of the booth. His heartbeat sprinted through his chest. Tex had Georgia programmed into his phone, as she was his wife's best friend. He tapped to call her as he strode toward the exit of the restaurant. Her line rang once, then twice.

She answered with, "Hello, Tex," in one of the coolest voices Otis had heard her use. A smile zipped onto his face.

"Georgia," he said. "It's Otis." He wasn't expecting screaming or shrieking or a gasp or anything. Some reaction would've been nice, though. He looked at the phone. Maybe he had some seriously bad energy that could affect digital devices, and he'd just ruined Tex's too. The call was still connected. "Hello?" he asked.

"You have some nerve," she said. "I've called you and called you. I texted. Everything. Who do you think you are? Some mighty country music star?" She scoffed, and Otis's mind went blank.

"No," he managed to say.

"I don't think we should see each other anymore," she said.

"Georgia," he said, desperation in the syllables. "My phone's not working. We just figured it out, and I borrowed Tex's phone to call you."

More silence, and Otis could just see her standing in the bookshop with her mother, letting Janet rail on her and rail on her. He didn't want to do that. She'd retreated. He wasn't there to snap her out of it.

"Georgia," he tried again. "Don't shut down on me, okay?"

"I have to go," she said. "You called right at closing, and I still have a customer in the shop."

"Call me back," he said quickly. "On Tex's phone. Or Luke's. Mine isn't working all that great."

"Sure," she said, so much sarcasm in her tone that Otis knew she didn't believe him. Why wouldn't she believe him? "Goodbye, Otis." The call ended, and he stared at the screen as the timer stopped ticking up and he lost her.

Disbelief tore through him. "Lord," he said as he looked up into the nearly dark sky. "What am I supposed to do now?"

He got no answer from above, so he turned and went back inside the restaurant. He practically threw the phone back to Tex. "She broke up with me."

"No," Luke said, shocked.

Tex looked as equally as stunned. Their food had come, and he paused with a French fry halfway to his mouth. "She did?"

"Guess she's not rational after all." Otis had seen her in her irrational moments, and she always came out of them. Maybe he could wait an hour or two and try calling her again. He didn't think she'd be calling him.

31

Georgia woke on Wednesday morning with a salt-encrusted face. Confusion sprang through her mind. A dog shifted down by her feet. Then she remembered crying as she closed up the shop last night. As she drove home. As she fed her cats and dogs and a rabbit she'd picked up at the animal shelter late last week. She'd managed to adopt out the kittens, but she'd sobbed through making the creamy duck pate for Onyx and Obsidian. Her canines had crowded in around her last night, the only things keeping her somewhat grounded.

What a lie. She wasn't grounded in any sense of the word. Harley was opening this morning, and Georgia didn't have to be at the shop until afternoon. She didn't want to spend the day crying over Otis Young, she knew that. She'd texted Abby and told her not to bring dinner, and to her surprise, Abby hadn't.

Her doorbell rang, and Georgia picked up her phone to check the time. Her alarm hadn't gone off yet, so it couldn't even be seven-thirty yet. Nope. Only seven-seventeen. As she held her phone, a text popped up.

It's Abby. I'm coming in.

Georgia did lock her doors at night, but she also had an electronic lock on her front door. It had a four-digit PIN, and Abby knew it. Five seconds later, her voice called, "Georgia?"

All the dogs barked, three of them jumping from the bed in a frenzy. They tore out of the bedroom and down the hall, and Abby's sweet voice cooed to them.

Georgia didn't move. She stayed with Charle in bed, and Abby found her moments later. "Sorry it's so early. I have a meeting at eight-thirty at the library before we open." She wore a pair of black slacks and one of her professional librarian blouses. This one was a creamy yellow with brown horses on it. So Abby and so chic-yet-country at the same time.

She wore concern in her eyes as she came toward Georgia. She climbed right into bed with her and laid her head on Georgia's shoulder. "What happened?"

"He said his phone wasn't working." She shook her head. "What a lame excuse, right? I mean, whose phone just stops working? Like, he didn't go to Mars. He's in freaking Kentucky." Her eyes burned, but Georgia would not cry in front of Abby.

Abby didn't say anything, and Georgia definitely

didn't like it this time. The dogs jumped back up onto the bed, and the biggest one—a huge mutt mix with a precious face—tried to lay right on top of Georgia. That only made her want to cry harder, though she'd sometimes cuddled Teddy and stoked his head until she absolutely had to get out of bed or risk being late to open her own bookshop.

After some shifting and movement, everyone found a place they could be, Georgia included.

"When did you fall in love with him?" Abby asked in a quiet voice.

"I don't know," Georgia whispered. "This hurts, Abby. It hurts so much."

Her friend lifted up onto her elbow and looked at Georgia. "Maybe his phone really isn't working."

"Have you tried calling him?" She reached up to wipe her eyes.

"Yes," Abby said. "He didn't answer, and Tex said he was right there next to him, both of them looking at Otis's phone. Nothing."

Foolishness started to run through her. "Maybe I made a mistake."

Abby smiled at her. "We all do it, Georgia. Remember how miserable I was without Tex?"

"I remember."

"So call Tex and ask for Otis. They're always together. He'll talk to you."

"You think so?" She hadn't told Abby she'd told Otis

she didn't want to see him anymore. Tex obviously had though.

Abby smiled at her. "Yeah, I think he will."

She rolled over and picked up her phone. She dialed Tex back, and his line rang and rang. "He's not answering."

"He's probably in the studio already," she said.

"Hello," Tex said. "Georgia?"

"Yeah," she said, recentering her focus on the call and not Abby. "Tex, is Otis around?"

"Uh, not right now," he said.

Her heart fell to her toes. "Oh, okay."

"He's, uh, fixing something. I could have him call you when he, uh, gets...there."

Georgia squinted. "Gets where?"

"Here," Tex said, clearing his throat. "When he gets back here."

"Is he fixing his phone?"

"I don't know," Tex said.

"What do you mean, you don't know?" She looked at Abby, because her husband wasn't making any sense.

"I have to head into the studio, Georgia. I'm sorry. I'll tell him you called."

"Okay." Georgia had no choice but to let Tex go. "He made no sense."

"I heard him." Abby wore a thoughtful expression as she stared off at the wall. She took a deep breath, which broke her thinking session, and she slid to the edge of the bed. "I hate to leave you like this, but I have to get to my meeting too."

"Yeah." Georgia laid back onto her pillows as Abby left. Not five minutes later, Onyx came into the bedroom, meowing as if he hadn't eaten in decades. Georgia didn't get up right away. She wondered how broken Otis's phone really was. Could he just not get texts and calls? Could he call out to her or his mother or daughter? Could he still see his security system footage when someone pulled up to his house and went up to his porch?

Her mind ran in circles, and Onyx pawed her face, a bit of claw out. "Hey," she said. "No claws. I'm coming." She got up and got busy feeding all of the animals, Onyx included. She did save him for last as a way to tell him he couldn't scratch her to get fed. He glared at her from the fridge, but she gave him his attitude right back.

The idea that had struck her continued to boil and bubble all through her morning chores, her shower, and her primping for the day. She still had a few hours before she needed to be at the shop, and Georgia shouldered her purse, opened her stationery cabinet and selected a few of her favorite things, grabbed her keys, and headed out with a, "See you tonight, everyone. Be good today."

She sometimes ran errands on her Wednesday mornings. Sometimes she went to the gym and did a yoga class. Sometimes she slept late and padded around the house.

Today, she drove to Otis's house on the outskirts of town. She slowed as she neared the house, not quite sure when the cameras on the security system would pick up her arrival. She parked at the curb and picked up her beloved stationery. It was ivory-colored, with roses along the top and bottom. It reminded her of historical movies, when two people could fall in love without ever having touched.

She sighed and started writing.

I'm sorry.

She couldn't fit very much onto a single sheet of paper, and she started another one.

I shuttered you out.

I don't want to break up.

In fact, I'm in love with you.

Please forgive me.

When you get back,

Please let me know.

Stop by the shop.

Something.

Georgia decided that was enough. If the "I'm in love with you" sign didn't work, nothing else would. Her heart crashed like thunder in her chest, but she stacked all the notes and put them in the right order.

"Please," she prayed as she put her SUV in drive and inched down the road toward his house. "Please let him see this on his phone. Please touch his heart with kindness and forgiveness."

She already knew Otis was kind. He lived with eight brothers too. Surely he knew how to forgive.

She pulled into his driveway and looked down at the stack of stationery in her lap. "You can do this," she told herself. She wouldn't even have to talk to him. The signs would do the work, and then...then all she could do was pray.

Pray she did as she got out of the SUV. As she walked up the sidewalk and onto the porch. She didn't bother ringing the doorbell or knocking. She wasn't sure if the cameras picked up sound or just motion.

Georgia tucked her hair behind her ear and looked up into the camera mounted above the front door. She backed up a step to where she thought the best angle for viewing would be.

She held up her stack of stationery, slowly counting to three inside her head until she'd shown all of her signs. After that, well, there wasn't much else she could do.

She nodded at the camera, smiled as if Otis himself was standing there in front of her, and touched her fingers to her lips. She blew the kiss to the camera just as the papers in her other hand started to slip.

She dropped them, and then hurried to pick them up before the breeze could whip them too far from her. She had four or five of them in her hand when the front door opened. Surprise filled her as she looked up.

Otis stood there.

Georgia felt like throwing up. She scrambled to her feet, the stationery now forgotten. "Otis," she said. "I—I didn't know you were here."

He looked like he'd just gotten out of bed, what with the gym shorts and the gray T-shirt and no shoes whatsoever. She'd never really seen him like this before, and she found she could only stare.

He looked up to the camera and back to her. "Did you mean that?"

Bravery like she'd never known filled her. She lifted her chin and stared at him. "Every letter. Every note."

A smile touched his mouth and spread across his whole face. "I haven't showered or brushed my teeth yet. But I think you better come inside."

"Why's that?" she asked.

"So I can kiss you without the neighbors watching." A glint fired in his eye, and he backed up, leaving the doorway wide open for Georgia to enter.

Her pulse whipped through her veins, and she...went inside and closed the door behind her.

Otis hadn't waited in the wide hallway in the front of his house. She peered into his music office, but he wasn't there either.

"I'm just gonna change," he called to her, and she went further into the house. He hadn't said why he was home, or how long he'd been there. She saw no evidence of Joey, though the girl would probably be at school by now.

Trepidation moved through her while she waited, and she kept drumming the tips of her fingers together to try to get the nerves out. They wouldn't truly go—until she heard Otis walking toward her.

He came out of the hallway that led back to the bedrooms, and he now wore his trademark jeans, plaid shirt, cowboy boots and hat, and that sexy smile on his face. "Good morning," he said as he approached.

Pausing just out of arm's reach, he held up his own piece of paper. This one wasn't a fancy piece of ivory stationery, but a plain white paper from a printer or copy machine. It said, *I love you too* in big, bold, blue letters, and Georgia melted on the spot.

She zipped her gaze up to his. "Really?"

"I'm not just sayin' it because you did," he said. "Honest, I'm not. I flew home in the middle of the night, then drove from Salt Lake City, because there were no flights to Jackson yesterday. I've been here since about two-thirty in the morning, and then I spent an hour trying to fall asleep while thinking about how I could get you back today. Should I stop by the shop? Bring you breakfast? Talk to your Momma and Daddy first? What?"

Tears filled her eyes. "I'm sorry, Otis."

"You said that already." He shook his head. "No need to say it again."

"I feel awful." She sniffled, and Otis closed the distance between them. She moved right into his chest and said, "I love it when you hold me. I want you by my side in hard things. I was just disappointed you couldn't be there on Saturday, that was all."

"I know, sweetheart. I was disappointed too."

"I know you have a job." Her tears fell, but she didn't

care. Not with Otis. "I know you'll be on tour. I won't mind, I swear. And when I do, I'll just talk to Abby and Dani and Cheryl, and we'll be okay."

"We will," he said.

She pulled back and looked at him. "I don't mean to shutter you out."

"My SIM card was compromised," he said, his eyes soft and full of love. "I got a new one at the airport in Salt Lake, but it was far too late to call you."

"I know you didn't ghost me."

"I would never do that," he said. "To anyone, but least of all you." He leaned closer, his eyes drifting closed. "I am in love with you, Georgia Beck. I know who you are, and I know you needed a couple of days to come to terms with me bein' gone on your sister's tribute." He pressed his cheek to hers, the softness of his beard like velvet. Her heartbeat kicked into a new gear, because he'd said he was in love with her.

"I really did call and text you," she said. "Starting on Saturday—while I was at the cemetery, in fact."

"I believe you." He moved back and gazed at her. "I will have to tour for this album. I haven't decided if I'm going to stay on with Country Quad or not. Tex is leaving, and everything with it is up in the air." He seemed a little stressed about that, and Georgia wanted to be his safe place too.

"I'm here for it," she whispered. "For you, for Joey, for

anything you want to talk through or out or anything. I love you, Otis."

He grinned, lowered his head, and kissed her. Georgia had been kissed before by other men. None of them had ever compared to Otis Young. And being kissed by him when he'd said "I love you," and she'd said it back?

She'd never, ever felt as cherished, as beautiful, or as worthy as she did in that moment, while he kissed her the way he did.

32

Luke stirred the tomato soup, feeling just a bit like he'd overcommitted in making this dinner. The pasta boiled out of control, and the water splashed over the side of the pot and onto the hot burner. It hissed, and he did along with it.

He reached to flip off the flame under the soup, telling himself he wasn't the problem. This wasn't his house. This stove was insane. He hadn't cooked with gas in a long time.

Behind him at the kitchen counter, Corrine hummed along with the TV show he'd put on her tablet for her, oblivious to his distress at the stove. He adjusted the flame under the boiling pasta and told himself he wasn't distressed.

This was vacation. A nice, spring vacation in the mountains of Utah. Last time he'd escaped Coral Canyon, he'd gone with Morris to the US Virgin Islands. Anything to get out of the cold and darkness and snow.

Now that spring was blooming everywhere, and the band was on a break while Morris and Tex dealt with the execs at King Country, Luke had brought Corrine with him on this mountain adventure. They had plans to rent a four wheeler tomorrow, and the next day, he'd take her on an easy hike to a waterfall.

She gladly went along with whatever he did, and Luke loved spending time with her. He could make chicken nuggets and hot dogs, corndogs and peanut butter and jelly sandwiches. Easy stuff. He drove through places and got her cheeseburgers and fries. He fed her the squeezable applesauce packets and small fruit cups of peaches and pears. In most things, he felt like he was doing a decent job —for someone who had no idea what they were doing.

Tonight, she'd requested tomato soup with noodles, "the way Grandma makes." He'd called his mother and discovered it was just canned soup with pasta, and Luke could boil water and add liquid to a soup concentrate.

Sort of.

The timer went off, and he pulled the pasta. The hot water sent up a plume of steam he leaned away from, and then he set the pot in the sink. "Almost done," he said to Corrine, flashing a smile in her direction.

"Like Grandma makes?" she asked. She'd stayed with Luke's mother for a week while he went to Nashville a few weeks ago. Corrine had been talking about it ever since.

Grandma had pink bubble bath that smelled like rainbows and cotton candy. Grandma laid in bed with her and read her a story before bed. Grandma made French toast in the shape of Mickey Mouse ears.

Luke didn't hold a grudge. He had a lot to learn about being a father, and it hadn't killed him to go into Georgia's shop and get some more books for his daughter. He spent time with her every day until band practice—when she wasn't at preschool and he wasn't doing his parenting classes—and he'd figured out which bubble bath his mom used and bought some.

"Just like Grandma makes," he confirmed as he turned back to the stove. The soup had bubbled a minute ago, which meant it was hot enough to feed to his four-year-old. He scooped some noodles into a bowl and then ladled the soup over it.

He put it in front of Corrine, and she knelt up on her barstool. Her face filled with light, and she looked up at him, her dark eyes sparkling. "It's just like it, Daddy."

He smiled at her. "Yep. Here's a spoon. Be careful. It's hot." He put the utensil on the counter, and she reached for it. Luke loved good food, but he could eat canned tomato soup and pasta too, so he dished himself a bowl and went to sit beside Corrine.

"Should I make a fire tonight, bug?"

"Can we roast marshmallows again?" She had red soup leaking from the corner of her mouth.

Luke ripped off a paper towel and wiped her face.

"Yep." He took a bite of his dinner, glad he and Corrine had made this escape together. Yes, he had her full-time in Coral Canyon now. He'd had her since Christmas—for over four solid months. She'd be five in a few weeks, and he hadn't heard a word from Mandi. He wondered if she'd come back for their daughter's birthday, but something told him she wouldn't.

She'd likely send a gift and a card. Luke had always done at least that. He hadn't spoken to his ex-wife in a while, and he had no need to do so now.

He looked at Corrine. "So you're gonna be five soon."

She looked at him, and he could see her all grown up in the blink of an eye. "Can I have one of those pony cakes?" she asked.

Luke wasn't sure what that was. "A pony cake?"

"They have them at the grow-sheria-store." She took another bite of her soup. He'd put in a lot of pasta, and it was more like a casserole. A tomato soup pasta casserole. "I want a blue one, with the cloud on his back."

"We'll see," Luke said, because that was what he said to anything he wasn't sure about. He could do some research and figure out what she was talking about, and since he couldn't bake, he might as well get her cake at the grocery store. "You'll be goin' to kindergarten next year," he said. "We have to go do those tests when we get done with the hiking and fishing."

"Okay," she said, not concerned about her kindergarten entrance tests. Nor should she be. Luke wasn't, though he suspected she'd need some sort of speech therapy. Her preschool teacher said she was bright and quick, but everyone had a hard time understanding what she said. Sometimes even Luke.

He'd gotten a letter from the elementary school, and he honestly had no idea how they'd known he lived in Coral Canyon. The principal or secretary probably lived nearby. He'd then gone to register Corrine for kindergarten next fall, and that alone made his stomach tighten.

Registering his daughter for school meant he'd be living in Coral Canyon next fall. *Living* there. Not just crashing on someone's couch or renting a hotel room. He hadn't had a permanent residence in so long, and Luke actually had never wanted one.

He looked at his beautiful daughter, and the world shifted. It had been every day since he'd picked her up from her mother's and taken her to his house for the holidays. He was currently renting a basement apartment plenty big enough for him and Corrine. It had come partially furnished, which he'd needed, because he'd been living out of a travel trailer previous to returning to Coral Canyon last spring.

Almost a year ago now.

He couldn't believe it had been that long. At the same time, the time had passed so dang fast.

"I think maybe we should look at finding a house," he said next. The narrowness of his throat didn't lessen despite his attempts to swallow correctly. "A real house. For me and you."

"And Mommy?" Corrine looked up at him.

Luke saw all the innocence in the world in her eyes. He had no idea how to talk to her about her mother. She didn't ask many questions—she was four—but she of course knew her mother. She'd lived with her for the first three and a half years of her life.

"No," Luke said slowly, keeping his voice low. "Mommy won't live with us, bug. It'll just be me and you." He put a smile on his face. "But we could have our own yard, with a big swing set. Maybe a trampoline. You can go to school, and maybe a dance class."

Trace had told him Harry's line dancing lessons were going well, and the studio where he went offered all kinds of things. He'd seen little girls Corrine's age going in wearing leotards and ballet shoes, and she'd probably really like that.

Luke hadn't looked into it yet, because the tasks he had to do every day sometimes overwhelmed him.

"A dance class?" She dropped her spoon into her soup. "Like Merrilee Amelia?" She slid from the stool and started doing some steps up on her toes. Her smile reached clear up into the rafters of the cabin he'd rented, and Luke found himself chuckling.

"Who's Merrilee Amelia?" he asked.

"Daddy," she said, coming back down onto her feet. "She's only my favorite pig."

"Oh, of course," he said. She climbed up next to him, and Luke put his arm around her tiny body. "I love you, Corrine."

"Love you too, Daddy." She didn't get upset by too much. Luke suspected that came from always being passed around. Mandi hadn't exactly been stable, though she had always been in Coral Canyon, and that was only more fuel on the fire for Luke to find a way to offer supreme stability to his daughter.

He wasn't bringing random women into her life. Mandi had a new boyfriend every other week, and he had no idea what Corrine had been exposed to.

He could cook and take care of her. She had nice clothes, and he always got her to preschool on time.

Next, he needed to find a home for them.

His nerves shook at him, the sound of maracas in his ears. But Luke also knew it was time. He was an adult now; he had a child; he could settle down in Coral Canyon.

It felt like a huge step, but Luke also felt absolutely ready to take it. Just because he was nervous about this new development in his life didn't mean he was wrong.

Corrine continued to tell him about the cartoons she loved, and Luke did his best to listen and interact. They finished dinner, and he built a fire in the huge hearth in the living room. She got out the marshmallows, and Luke got down the graham crackers and the chocolate bars.

"What is this?" she asked.

"You've never had a s'more?" he asked. He couldn't believe that. "Really?"

Corrine looked at him with wide eyes.

"I used to have them all the time when I was a boy," he said. "Papa made a fire every time we went camping, and we'd have tin foil dinners and then s'mores."

Corrine sat on the hearth with him while the flames crackled behind them. "Did all the uncles go camping, Daddy?"

He chuckled, his memories flowing fast now. "They sure did, bug. All of 'em." He stuck a marshmallow on a stick for her. "You roast it, just like last night. Stand up now. Don't try to twist."

She'd done that last night, and she'd caught a few marshmallows on fire. He'd eaten them, because he didn't mind the charred black outside of a burnt marshmallow. Corrine didn't like it though, and she did a lot better getting hers more golden if she stood up.

"When it's done," he said. "We'll put it on this." He broke a cracker in half and put a couple of squares of chocolate on it. "Then we put another cracker on top, and it makes a little marshmallow sandwich." He beamed at her. "They're called s'mores."

"This is so essiting," she said.

Luke laughed, because he hadn't been excited about s'mores—at least not the way Corrine was—for a long time. He'd lost a lot of enthusiasm for a lot of things the older he got.

He wanted to find the joy in living again. His heart grew heavy, but he kept his smile on his face for Corrine. He laughed when she got sticky marshmallow all over her face, and the melted chocolate between her fingers. She loved s'mores, and he loved her—and s'mores—and after he'd laid in bed with her and read her a story so she could sleep, he pulled her door almost all the way closed and faced the kitchen and living room where they'd spent their evening.

It was one of the more perfect nights he'd had.

What about the band? The question streamed through his head, causing instant frustration. Luke couldn't answer that question, and that bothered him. His whole identity felt wrapped up in Country Quad, and Tex was leaving.

Anxiety skipped through his bloodstream, and no amount of prayer, meditation, or therapy had helped Luke. He hadn't tried a lot of any of those, but he didn't think they'd help.

He cleaned up the kitchen, then the s'mores, using sure, methodical movements. His bedroom was actually upstairs on the second level, and he'd told Corrine where he'd be. He'd shown her how to get to him. He had no doubt she'd be in his bed before midnight, and he didn't mind. He was a little nervous in a new place too.

"You need a new place," he told himself. "Physically, mentally, emotionally." He left off spiritually, but it sounded in his ears anyway.

He paused and looked out the windows and into

absolute darkness. Not many people lived on the mountain in the winter and spring. It was more a place people came in the summer to escape the heat of Las Vegas or Arizona.

"Lord," he said. "I'm gonna buy a house for me and Corrine in Coral Canyon." It wasn't really a prayer, but God had never let him state something he wanted to do without giving him some sort of impression that it was right or wrong.

Warmth filled him, and he once again knew it was time to provide that solid foundation for Corrine. Above ground. Out of someone else's basement.

"What about the band?" He asked the question aloud this time, but he still had no answer. He wanted to keep Country Quad alive. They had recording facilities in Coral Canyon now. Tex didn't *have* to quit.

For some reason, it always took Luke longer than everyone else to accept the reality of things. Tex had flat-out told him he was done after this album, and yet Luke still hadn't gotten it through his thick skull.

He did get out his phone to text Otis. *Hey, I'd love to get the name of your realtor when you have a sec.*

Oh yeah? Otis texted back. *You're going to buy in Coral Canyon?*

Yes.

Otis called, and Luke rolled his eyes as he answered with, "Hey."

"I'm sort of stunned," Otis said.

Luke trusted his brother, though he didn't understand him sometimes. "You bought a house."

"Yeah, but I like Coral Canyon," Otis said. "I have a very serious girlfriend and an eight-year-old I can't just take on vacation during the school year." That was all Otis-code for, *You don't have any of that, bro. What's in your head?*

Luke barely knew what was in his head most of the time. He acted irrationally sometimes, and that came from his temper, not a calm mind.

"It's time," he said, and that was all the reason he needed.

"Sure," Otis said. "I'll send you his contact info."

"Thank you," Luke said.

"How's the cabin?" Otis asked.

"Amazing," Luke said, glancing around at all the blond wood walls.

"Georgia wants to know if it's required to do outdoor things there."

"Required?" Luke repeated. "Uh, I don't think so."

Otis chuckled. "I'll let her know."

Luke didn't get it, but he didn't need to. "Okay, well, I'm wiped from the drive and then making dinner. Say hi to everyone for me."

"Stay safe, brother," Otis said. "Love you, Luke."

He felt loved in that moment, and he said, "Love you, too, Otis."

Upstairs, he brushed his teeth and looked into his own

eyes. They reminded him of Tex's, of their father's. "It's time," he repeated to himself, and he actually discovered a thread of excitement moving through him at the prospect of becoming a homeowner.

"Daddy," Corrine said in a sleepy voice. "It's too quiet downstairs."

"Come on then," he said, scooping her into his arms. "You can sleep with me, but I'm warning you. I'm gonna snore."

She giggled in his arms and snuggled into his chest, her eyes drifting closed already. She'd be asleep before he even got his phone plugged in. He settled her on the opposite side of the bed, the blankets here nice and fluffy.

He had just plugged in his phone when it vibrated, and he saw a message from Mandi. His pulse fluttered for a moment, and then he frowned. What did she want?

Luke, I know it's late, but I remember you being a night owl. Call me when you get a minute.

He had a minute right now, but he was tired. He didn't want to talk to his ex-wife. "Tomorrow," he muttered to himself, and then he flipped his phone over, switched off the lamp, and snuggled down into the soft, warm bed to fall asleep.

33

Trace kept snapping his fingers as he drove, and he became aware of it as he rounded the corner and saw the house that had been described to him. *It's the cute little white brick one*, Everly had said. *I have a big US flag out front for my brother*.

Said brother served in the US Army, and Everly was proud as punch of him. Trace had enjoyed talking to her via the dating app he'd joined a month ago, and just because he hadn't told anyone—not a single soul—about it didn't mean he was embarrassed to be using it.

He had told both Morris and Harry that he had a date tonight. He wouldn't say who with, as even going on a date was a huge step for Trace. Joining the dating app hadn't been that hard, and he'd messaged with several women. Out of all of them, Everly sparked his interest the most, and he'd quite enjoyed having an adult conversation with someone who wasn't A) male, B) a family member, and C) obsessed with the band.

He and Everly talked about everything under the sun, and he actually felt like a more well-rounded person since he'd been messaging with her. He'd finally gotten up the nerve to ask her out earlier this week, and they'd set up dinner for Friday night.

Harry had not been happy, but Trace hadn't been able to get him to say why. Morris had said he'd try to find out why the idea of Trace dating bothered his son so much, but Trace didn't hold out much hope. The boy had turned thirteen earlier this year, and Trace swore his brain had fallen out of his head and currently resided somewhere under his bed.

Often, Harry had no reason for why he reacted or felt a certain way. His body was changing, and he had hormones from here to the Pacific Ocean. He liked girls now, and it was a dangerous, dangerous combination to have a big crush on a girl and not be able to talk about it.

Harry had never been much of a talker, and Trace figured he simply took after him. He hadn't ever felt the need to fill the world with his voice for no reason. If he thought something needed to be said, he said it. Otherwise, he just kept his mouth shut. Half of the Young brothers could really benefit from his example, but he didn't think there was anything that could get Tex or Luke to stop talking.

He smiled to himself as he pulled into Everly's driveway. He managed to still his fingers and take a deep breath. "It's fine," he told himself as he reached for the bouquet of flowers he'd bought only twenty minutes ago. Dani used to own a flower shop in Louisville, and she'd told him that he could never go wrong with flowers—unless she had an allergy.

So then Trace had asked Everly about her allergies. None. So he was good.

"You've dated before," he told himself. Maybe not for a while. Years. Maybe not someone as normal as Everly, but that should only make things easier. "You've had no problem talking to her."

But he knew texting was far different than face-to-face communication. Wildly different.

He went up the walk and to the door. The doorbell chimed loud enough for him to hear warbles of it outside. His pulse covered up any other sounds.

After what felt like a long time, the door opened. A beautiful—scratch that, gorgeous—woman stood there, and Trace's saliva turned to sand. His tongue got all stuck in it, and he couldn't even say hello.

Everly Avery wore a denim dress with sleeves down to her elbows and the skirt brushing the tops of her knees. She wore cowgirl boots with it, which meant she only showed the tiniest bit of skin along the tops of her shins, her arms, and along her throat.

Trace found her to be absolutely stunning. She couldn't be taller than five-foot-three or weigh more than a hundred pounds, and she'd told him she was petite. So that fit.

"Are you lost?" she teased, and that thawed Trace and brought him out of his staring spell.

He chuckled and held up the flowers. "No, ma'am, I don't reckon I am."

"These are beautiful," she said, taking the blooms. "Come in while I put them in water."

"Sure, okay." He followed her inside, taking in her house. It wasn't large, just like she'd said it wasn't. It was remodeled, just like she'd said it was. Art hung on the walls, and he recognized one of the paintings from a picture she'd sent him via the dating app. "Oh, this is Friday Afternoon."

She glanced over to him from the kitchen, her smile bright. "Yes. I can't believe you remembered that."

"I told you I was impressed you can paint." Trace had no artistic skill with a brush, that was for sure.

Everly put the flowers in water and came toward him. Her long, dark hair cascaded over her shoulders in waves, and Trace's hands started to sweat just thinking about touching it. "You still haven't told me what you do for a living." She stood next to him, and Trace watched her out of the corner of his eyes so as to not be too obvious.

"I haven't?"

"No, sir," she said. "And you know it."

"Is that still a requirement to go out tonight?"

"You bet it is."

"You haven't Googled?" He looked fully at her now, finding her eyelashes long and curled, touched black with mascara. She was a beautiful woman, even if she wasn't the supermodel or princess Trace had dated previously. He didn't need someone like that, despite what his brothers teased him about.

Everly was on the opposite end of the occupation spectrum for Trace. A small-town dance teacher wasn't anything like his ex-wife—a supermodel living in Europe now—or the last woman he'd dated—a legit princess living in New York City.

"No," she said. "Though I think it's quite telling that I can Google you, as if I'll find something online about you."

"You will," he said.

"Most people can't say that," she said.

Well, Trace wasn't most people.

He lifted up his phone and pressed the button to get it on. He had a heart at the top, which meant he'd matched with someone on the dating app. He didn't bother swiping it away. This was his first date with Everly, and she might not even go on it with him.

He'd already pulled up Country Quad, where he featured prominently over Tex's left shoulder, his guitar in his hand and a *don't-mess-with-me* look on his face. He handed the phone to Everly and turned away.

"You've got more art over here." An enormous painting of the ocean sat above her mantle, and Trace went to examine it. He wondered if she'd traveled to this place, or if she'd conjured it out of her mind's eye.

"You're a Rockstar," she said.

He chuckled and shook his head. "No. Country music isn't rock."

"This says your band crosses the line between country and rock." She came to his side again, interest in those dark, deep eyes. "You're famous."

"Only on the Internet," he murmured.

She grinned at him. "Or the stage. Or anywhere South of Nashville." She gave his phone back and picked up her purse. "Did you have a place in mind? Or do you want me to pick?"

"We're going?"

She gave him a smile full of spark. He felt it flow through his blood like lava, and he recognized female interest when he saw it. "Yes," she said. "I think I can stand to go out with the—what was it?"

"Nothing," he said. He shouldn't have shown her an article. He should've just told her who he was. Him and his dang inability to speak to pretty women.

"The best guitarist of our time," she said with a grin. She linked her arm through his as he sighed. Everly ignored him or hadn't heard him. "Will you play for me sometime?"

"Maybe," he said. "It's my job, you know. I'm not askin' you to dance for me."

Her eyes sparkled and everything inside Trace came

to life when she said, "If you ask me to dance for you, Trace Young, I will."

The breath left his body, because this woman.... This woman was unlike anyone he'd ever met before, and he hadn't been living with his whole heart since his divorce. He knew, because it beat now in a way it hadn't in a decade.

"All right," he said. "I'll play for you sometime, then."

"Perfect." She led him toward the front door.

"And I have somewhere in mind," he said. "Devil's Tower? It comes highly recommended from everyone I talk to."

"It's fantastic," she said. "I highly approve."

"Winning already," he joked, and they laughed together. Trace floated to the truck, because what he'd hoped and prayed for—that talking to Everly would be as effortless in person as it had been online—had come true.

The next morning, Harry stomped into the kitchen far earlier than Trace usually saw him on a Saturday morning. "You went out with my line dance instructor?"

Trace turned away from the pressure cooker, where he'd just put a half-dozen eggs to boil. He looked at his son's very upset face, and then the device he held up. He and Everly sat there, on someone's social media.

His mouth went dry. "Uh, yes. Who is that?"

"This is Shawn Edwards," Harry said. "Dad, you can't go out with her."

"Why not? She's not a child." He'd checked, because Trace was nowhere near his twenties.

"Because, Dad." Harry slumped into a chair at the table just as Morris came into the kitchen. "Everyone at school has a crush on her. They all follow her on social media, because they think she's hot, and she teaches these social media dances."

Trace didn't know any of this, and his chest felt like someone had wrapped it in rubber bands. More and more and more of them added to the pressure.

Harry's phone vibrated over and over. "*Everyone* is texting me." He looked up at Trace, pure misery in his eyes. "Do you *know* how embarrassing this is?"

"I didn't know," Trace said. He sat down too. "Honest, son, I didn't." He looked to Morris for help, but he only held up one hand. Trace looked at Harry again. "She was real nice."

"Of course she's nice," Harry said with plenty of exasperation. "That's part of why everyone has this huge crush on her."

"She's thirty-three years old," Trace said. "I think it's weird you all have crushes on her."

"I don't," Harry said. "But Dad, everyone in town follows her. You don't get it, because you don't have social media."

"Yes, I do."

"*Real* social media, Dad." Harry rolled his eyes.

Trace didn't argue the point. He had a publicist who posted for him several times a day, actually. Posts, videos, funny clips. Reposts. He was a public figure, after all, and people wanted to feel connected to their country music starts. Trace as a man couldn't stand social media, so no, he didn't post and he didn't follow anyone.

"Maybe everyone in town follows me," Trace said.

"Dating another celebrity?" Morris asked, totally *not* helping.

Trace gave him a death glare. "No. Shut your mouth."

"Everyone in town follows her," Morris said.

"You can't go out with her again," Harry said, looking up from his phone. His fingers practically smoked from how fast he'd been typing. "Was it a horrible date?"

It was absolutely not. Trace had already asked Everly to go out with him again. She'd already said yes. He looked at the anguish on his son's face. He didn't want to hurt Harry any more than the boy was already hurting.

Everything swirled around Trace, through Trace, beneath and above Trace. And he did something he swore he'd never do: He lied to his son.

"Yeah," he said. "I don't think you need to worry, boy. I'm not going to go out with her again."

His heart broke, but Harry jumped to his feet and grabbed Trace in a hug. "Thank you, Dad. Thank you." He hurried out of the room, leaving Trace with Morris.

"You big fat liar," Morris said.

"I didn't lie," Trace said. "I didn't say the date was bad. I said I wouldn't go out with her again."

Morris cocked his head but didn't say anything. "I have to get up to the lodge."

"Okay."

"Good luck explaining to Everly that you can't go out with her again because all the fourteen-year-olds in this town have a crush on her." Morris quirked his eyebrows, and what he'd said made Trace sigh like he was trying to power a sailboat with just his breath.

Morris left, and the pressure cooker started wheezing steam out the top. Trace stepped over to it and flipped the knob so it would come to pressure instead of boil out of control.

"Yeah," he muttered to himself as he looked down at his phone. How was he going to tell Everly he couldn't see her again?

"Why is this a thing?" he asked. The one woman who'd brought him to life was the one he couldn't have. "Couldn't You have made her horrible, or something?" He looked up toward heaven, but God didn't provide a way for Trace to let Everly down easy.

He looked over his shoulder and considered seeing her anyway. Just keeping everything on the down-low. Harry wouldn't have to know.

No. He shook his head, feeling trapped between his son, whom he loved and wanted to desperately protect, and Everly, whom he wanted to get to know a lot better as they dated, fell in love, and got married.

He had to choose, and he hated decisions like this.

Hey, he typed out to Everly. He had her number now, so he didn't have to message her on the app. *Listen, I don't think it's going to work out. I'm real sorry, and I hope you had fun last night.*

34

Morris pulled up to Whiskey Mountain Lodge, his eyes scanning for Leighann's car. It had become a habit, though he'd only seen it once. He wasn't entirely sure she worked here at the lodge. She'd interviewed months ago, but he hadn't gotten her number, and they weren't in contact.

He'd been coming up to the lodge for several weeks now, developing his camp and planning out how things would go. He ran things by select guests, the Whittakers, and anyone else they brought out to watch him.

He hadn't been up to the lodge in a couple of weeks, because he'd been in Nashville ironing some band details flat. Today, however, he'd run his first football camp with the guests who'd signed up for that morning's class. His nerves blared at him like a horn on a runaway truck, but Morris had been nervous like this before. He'd thrown up before every game during his first season in the NFL, and again as head coach of the football team at the prestigious college in Florida.

This was a football camp. In small-town Wyoming. No one had their eyes on him, and Morris hated that as much as he liked it.

Things with the band had picked up a little bit. He had a standing call every Monday afternoon with Ben and a couple of other music executives now. They wanted more details of what Country Quad was doing in Coral Canyon. The band thought it was for them, so they could keep everyone up-to-date.

King Country had insisted on the calls for them, because they wanted to stay up-to-date. No one wanted more marathon meetings like they'd done several weeks ago, and it was Morris's job to make sure everyone stayed happy.

Most of the time, he wasn't sure if he was advocating for the band or reassuring the music execs. It felt like he was on a very skinny balance beam, and it could fall either way at any time.

He opened the door to the lodge and went inside, the scent of maple syrup greeting him. Warmth flowed out of the lodge, and he thought they should probably get all their windows open and let in the spring air that had arrived. Today was supposed to be the warmest day yet, and Morris hitched his duffle bag higher on his shoulder.

"Mom," a boy said, and Morris looked his way. "It's

Morris Young." He wore wonder in his eyes, and Morris's chest filled with pride. It had been a while since anyone had looked at him with recognition or awe, and he had to admit he liked it.

"Howdy," he said, though he didn't wear a cowboy hat. He did when representing the band, but he was at the lodge today to run a football camp. Not do horseback riding lessons. "Who are you?"

The boy, who was probably twelve or thirteen just like Harry, simply stared at him, open-mouthed.

"This is Ryan," his mother said, nudging him. "He signed up for your camp this morning."

"Perfect," Morris said. "You come with me, young man. We're meeting out on the back field." He grinned at the mother and started for the doorway that led into the back of the lodge. Another short hallway took them outside, and Morris breathed in a lungful of the crisp, morning air.

"I saw your name," Ryan said. "I thought it was you, but I wasn't sure."

"Yeah," Morris said, putting down his bag. "I live here in Coral Canyon now. I grew up here." He gave the boy a smile. "Where are you from?"

"Oklahoma City," he said. "I play running back on my team there."

"Yeah? How fast is your forty yards?" Morris hoped he wasn't coming off as combative. An assistant coach in

Florida had told him once that he couldn't do that even if he tried. Still, he didn't want this boy to feel bad.

"About eleven seconds," he said.

Morris's eyebrows went up. "That's phenomenal." He unzipped his bag and pulled out the football. "You run. I'll throw."

The boy took off without further instructions. He ran a pattern—he really had played football before—and Morris threw the ball to his left. He had to increase his speed and lean to get it, but he did catch it.

"Yeah!" Morris clapped and cheered for the teen as he came trotting back, the biggest smile on his face.

Behind him, the door opened, and someone said, "See? They're right there. You didn't miss it."

He turned to find a woman standing with two more boys.

"Howdy," Morris said, jogging over to them. "Are you signed up for the football camp this morning?"

"Yes, sir," one of them said. He elbowed the other. Morris had seen this behavior before. In fact, he'd participated in it with his brothers. It always happened when they'd been arguing about something. The one who did the elbow jab was telling the other one, *Told you so. I was right.*

"We should have six people," Morris said, looking to the back door. "Tell me your names, please."

Graham had emailed him a list of the people registered for his first camp, and Morris checked them off as they got said. The other three people arrived, and Morris surveyed his first football camp. It had filled up—he'd capped it at six for this first time—and a bolt of happiness filled him with a flash of warmth.

"Welcome," he said to the kids. They had to be twelve to register for the camp, and everyone in the group fell into their teen years. "This isn't a tackle camp, so keep that in mind. We don't need to be throwing anyone to the ground today. The goal is no injuries."

"Yes, sir," someone said.

Morris nodded at them all. "Well, that's the secondary goal. The first goal is to have fun learning something new." He touched the football to his chest. "I'm Morris Young, and I played for four years with the Savannah Scots. I tore my ACL at the end of the fourth season, and I moved into coaching in Florida."

The teens nodded along, and he continued with, "I'm managing my brothers' band now, so I live here, and I'm glad to be here with you this morning." He tossed the ball to the boy on the end, who happened to be Ryan. He was the only kid who'd shown up without anyone else. "You tell me about yourself in a couple of sentences."

One by one, they went around and said a few things. Morris nodded at them encouragingly, and when the ball came back to him, he asked, "What do you think is the most important thing to know about football?"

"The rules?" a boy guessed.

"The plays," the single girl who'd signed up said.

Morris nodded at both of them. "Important, sure." He looked at the other kids. "The most important thing to know about football varies on who you talk to," he said. "Some people swear they have the sport in their blood. Some people can study the game on paper but then can't play it."

He tossed the ball up into the air and caught it again. "The most important thing to know about football is that anyone can play it. If you have the love and the drive, you can learn what you need to learn to be successful at football."

He bent and got out the cones he'd brought. "We're going to start with a drill. This is to get you loose. Get you talking. Laughing. Then, we'll see what we need to learn."

He continued with the camp, everything moving along smoothly, though one of the boys could barely run without tripping over his own feet and the girl forgot that they weren't tackling today and knocked her brother to the ground.

At the end of the hour, Morris couldn't stop smiling and all of the teens helped him get all the balls and cones they'd gotten out over the past sixty minutes. He thanked them all, laughed with them, and looked just as shocked as the rest of them when a woman came outside with a tray of cupcakes.

Not just any woman. Leighann.

Morris's heart fell to his shoes and lurched back into his chest. She wore a pretty blue dress with a white apron over it. Smears of chocolate adorned the apron, and she smiled at the teens like she had a lot of experience with them too.

"Just one each," she said. "They're chocolate with buttercream frosting. I checked with your parents for allergies, and we're good."

The kids all took one, each of them saying, "Thank you, Miss Leighann," before they went inside. Morris marveled at the construction of the cupcakes. The domed frosting was green, just like the grass on a football field, and she'd piped on the white lines to make the yardlines and sidelines.

A perfectly shaped football had been stuck into the frosting at an angle, and he could only imagine how long it had taken to make these.

"I didn't know there were snacks afterward," he said.

"There are." She met his eyes, still some level of apprehension in hers. Or maybe that was the pure electricity Morris felt moving through all of his bones and sinews. Could she still have feelings for him? Even one or two?

He definitely had a whole football team of feelings for her, and she lifted the tray to indicate he should take one. "Is the other for you?" he asked.

"I wasn't sure how many kids there were," she said. "I knew Graham had said an even number, but whether that was six or eight, I couldn't remember." She gave a nervous laugh. "I probably won't eat it."

Morris took one of the cupcakes, almost afraid to take a bite and mess it all up. "What'll you do with it?"

"I'll take it home," she said. "My—" Horror crossed her face, and Leighann clamped her lips closed. "My, uh, brother will probably like it."

"Oh, are you living with Denzel?"

"He lives with me," she clarified, her chin lifting up.

Morris nodded, suddenly self-conscious to eat in front of her. He wanted to ask her for her number again, but he didn't quite know how. He lifted the cupcake instead. "Well, I usually save my sugar consumption for after a real meal, so I'll save mine for home too."

"Are you living in Coral Canyon then?" she asked. "Permanently?"

"I live with Trace right now," Morris said, his head nodding too much. He couldn't get it to stop. "But yeah. I'm here. I manage the band now." He swooped the cupcake around the back field. "And do these camps, obviously."

"Denzel said he saw you at the hospital."

"Yeah, yep." Morris absolutely couldn't eat the sugary cupcake now. The electricity between him and Leighann had infected his bloodstream, and his pulse had picked up speed. The sugar would only amplify that. "I do some volunteer work there on Mondays is all."

"Wow. Three jobs."

"Just two," he said. "The band is all afternoons and evenings, and you know me." He chuckled, which gave him a moment to find some solid ground in his life. "I need to be busy all the time."

She offered him a rare smile, and it felt like heaven had shone its rays down on him. "Yes, I remember that."

Morris sensed her departure, and he practically yelled as he said, "Any chance you might give me your number now?"

Her eyes locked onto his, and Morris kept his smile in place. "I...Well, the truth is Leighann, I've been thinking about you a lot." He reached up to push his cowboy hat down, only to realize he wasn't wearing it.

The door opened and a woman said, "Leighann, that timer is going off, but I can't tell if the pancakes are done."

"I'm coming," she said, already turning and walking away.

Morris sighed as she left. "Strike two," he muttered to himself, once again noting that the woman didn't even look back. She never had. Leighann was a strong woman who made sure decisions. He knew she had doubts—they'd been married for two years—but she stuck to her guns. She had conviction. She worked through her insecurities until she got a place where she was confident in what she'd decided to do.

Morris finished packing up his duffle bag, but he didn't want to go back through the lodge. He might accidentally beg Leighann for her number again, and he wanted to maintain some semblance of self-respect.

Not only that, but the sun had crested the Tetons, and

it warmed his face and brought him happiness. He needed to find a winter sport that would get him outside, because he always felt more like himself when in nature.

He'd just reached his car—and since he'd spoken to Leighann, he knew she was here and so hadn't looked for her sedan—when his phone chimed in a series of sounds. He tossed his duffle bag in the back of his truck and pulled out his device.

Good morning to one and all, Beau Whittaker had sent. *The weekend is off to a great start. We just wanted to take a moment to officially welcome two new people to the Whiskey Mountain Lodge family.*

Morris Young, who you may have seen lurking around in his athletic clothes and tossing footballs. He runs our football camps four days a week.

And Leighann Drummond, who I know we've all gotten to know in the past couple of weeks since she started full-time here at the lodge as the kitchen manager and chef.

Everyone say a rowdy howdy, and welcome them to the family. Be sure to say your name, so they can put your number in their phones should they need anything from anyone here.

Several people already had, including Graham and his brother Eli. They both had roles here at the lodge, and Morris couldn't help feeling like he belonged here.

Family.

That word had a nice ring to it, and he looked back to the lodge. He couldn't help but wonder if the Lord had arranged for him and Leighann to be working at the same place, at the same time, so they could try again at being a family.

She'd gotten pregnant while they were married, but she'd suffered two miscarriages. The family they'd wanted they hadn't been able to have. His sadness started to overshadow the sun, the happiness, and the great camp he'd just run. He only let it for a moment, and then he pushed it away.

All the chimes helped too, and Morris scanned the welcome's and hello's from the others at the lodge. He hadn't answered yet, but his tongue dang near choked him when he saw, *This is Leighann. Thank you all for the warm welcome.*

She'd included a smiley face with her message.

But more importantly, now Morris had her number "should he need anything from her."

35

Gray Hammond laughed as he embraced his brother, Cy. "Look at you all clean-shaven." Gray hardly recognized him, and Cy ducked his head as he pulled back. With his cowboy hat on, hiding his longer hair, and without the beard, he looked a lot younger.

Gray reached up and rubbed his own face, where he held plenty of gray in his beard. Maybe he'd look younger too. Maybe he shouldn't worry about being sixty-one with gray hair. "You look great," he said to Cy.

"Thanks," Cy said. "Patsy said the choir director should look less 'scruffy.'" He glanced over to his wife, but she was busy attending to their youngest, a little boy named Wade who'd turn six by the end of the year. He could be a little devil, just like his father, and Gray couldn't wait to see what he did with his life.

"Where's your wife?" Bree asked, and Gray turned toward his oldest brother's wife.

"Howdy to you too." He laughed as he hugged her, because he knew Bree loved him as much as Elise. Fine, maybe not as much, as they'd been best friends before Gray had met Elise and Wes had met Bree. "She's coming with Hunt, Molly, and Ryder."

Gray did love his grandson with his entire being. Elise did too, which is why she'd ridden with them to help out. He suspected it was so she wouldn't have to make the seven-hour drive with Jane's attitude, Tucker's whining, and Deacon's continual yelling at his handheld video game.

Gray had done all of that, and currently, Jane had found Ava, Ella, and Easton to harumph with. They all lived here in Coral Canyon, though, so they didn't have to leave their friends all summer the way Jane did. Apparently this was "social suicide" for a fourteen-year-old going on thirty, and Gray had made the grave mistake of telling her Hunter had enjoyed their summers in Coral Canyon.

Jane had gone somewhat ballistic, and Gray and Elise had agreed privately not to compare her life to Hunt's again. It wasn't fair to any of them, and Gray looked away from his daughter.

"Where's Wes?" he asked.

"He and Mike are picking up dinner," Bree said. "Come sit, Gray." She had a whole bunch of chairs for him, and he checked for his younger boys—eight-year-old

Deacon and eleven-year-old Tucker—before taking a seat. They'd found Chris and Lars, Ames's twins, and were currently taking popsicles from their aunt Sophia.

Gray jumped to his feet when Colton approached with their father in slow, measured steps. "Just a bit further, Dad," he said, and Gray moved his chair for his daddy.

"Right here, Dad."

"I'm fine," Dad said, but Gray and Colton exchanged a glance. Colton had driven down to Ivory Peaks to get their father, and Gray and Elise had gone home to help Molly and Hunter get their children's equine program closed up for the long holiday weekend.

They usually stayed in Colorado during the summers, but with it being Ryder's first real summer of his life, they'd wanted to come north too. Hunter rarely took so much time off from his busy CEO position at the family company, but he said this was important.

That meant that Molly couldn't be on the farm to run her equine program. They still had several employees there to run the operation, but they'd given everyone but essential animal care personnel the weekend off.

Everyone settled again, and Gray surveyed his family. He loved their Independence Day tradition of gathering here at Liberty Park in Coral Canyon. They brought dinner for their family and visited all evening until the featured band of the year started playing, which happened about dusk.

They'd play for an hour or so as the sky continued to darken, and then the fireworks would light up the sky in a super show of patriotism.

He got back to his feet as Tex Young arrived with his new wife and son. He and Abby Ingalls had gotten married over the holidays, and Gray had heard both Wes and Ames talk a lot about them. Bryce, Tex's son, taught Ames's boys the guitar, and last year, there had been an impromptu country music concert right here on the lawn when the Young brothers from Country Quad had teamed up with the Everett Sisters.

Gray didn't see anyone from the lodge yet, besides Bree and Sophia and Patsy, who had all once worked there. Bree still did from time to time, but Patsy ran the apple orchards and raised four children while Cy continued to build custom motorcycles.

Sophia supported Ames in his endeavors to raise and train police dogs, and they had four kids too. Their youngest was only four, and she'd been the youngest Hammond until Hunter and Molly had had Ryder last summer.

Gray sat back and closed his eyes, letting the cool breeze drift across his face, bringing the scent of cinnamon and sugar with it. The warmth from the July day still radiated through the sky, and he didn't mind it so much here in the Grand Tetons.

"Get another seat," Bree said, and Gray opened his

eyes. “Oh, brother,” she said next. “Gray, he brought Gerty.”

Gray blinked at the three people now walking toward them. One was definitely his brother, Wes. And his son, Michael. He held hands with a pretty blonde teenager—Gerty Whettstein.

Gray was well-versed with Michael and Gerty, as they both worked the farm he technically owned. Gerty lived at the farm every day after school and all day on Saturdays and Sundays. Both her dad and stepmother worked at the farm too, and Gray loved all three of them.

“I don’t see how this is a surprise,” he said.

“It’s not,” Bree murmured as she expanded the circle she’d made to make room for three more chairs. “I’m just—” She sighed. “How did you handle this with Hunter?”

“Everyone knows how I handled it with Hunter,” Gray said as he got up to help and then greet his brother and his nephew. “And look what happened.”

“At least he went to college,” Bree said before she smoothed a smile across her face and turned into her husband. “Hey, baby. How was the drive?”

“Long,” Wes said, his expression full of storms and spitfire. “Michael drove us, and wow, the boy’s afraid of the gas pedal.”

“I am not,” Michael said. “That was a construction zone, Dad.” He rolled his eyes, and though Gray had seen him that morning, he hugged his nephew.

“You tell him, Mikey,” he said. “Howdy, Gerty.”

"Hello, sir," she said, but Gray hugged her too.

He said, "You don't have to call me sir."

"No, sir." She smiled at him, and Michael indicated she should sit in the chair furthest from his parents. He sat between them, the perfect buffer.

He'd barely gone down when he jumped back up. "Wait, there's Bryce. Gerty, you have to meet him." They both got back to their feet and went to talk to Bryce Young. Gray noticed several people loitering near their group now, and at first, he thought them to be Country Quad fans.

Luke and Trace Young had both arrived with their kids, as had Morris. The latter had played professional football, and Gray marveled at the level of talent in that family.

But the people stalling as they walked by weren't old enough to be crushing on band members and pro football players. They were girls about the same age as Gerty and Michael. They were there to talk to Bryce Young. Or catch his eye. Something.

He didn't pay any of them any mind at all, and he whooped as he saw Michael and lifted him right up off the ground in a hug. He met Gerty and politely shook her hand, and Gray noted that Mikey put his hand right back in Gerty's afterward.

"Bryce is popular," he commented to Wes.

"He's a nice kid," Wes said, obviously watching his son and Bryce too. "He's been over a few times. He and Mikey were on the same debate team, project, thing last year. I don't know."

"Looks like Tex brought his guitar," Gray said.

"They're going to do a concert," Bree said. "With the Everly Sisters. They planned it this year." She nodded past the outer ring of people, which included Ames and Cy, who stood talking to Zach Zuckerman and Finn Barber. "Lily's carting her fiddle. That's how you know it's serious."

Sure enough, Gray watched as Lily and Beau Whittaker approached, she carrying her fiddle and a bunch of blankets, a backpack on her back, and Beau lugging a cooler. Their son—they only had one—came with them, carrying all of their chairs. He had to be twenty by now, but Gray wasn't sure when his birthday was.

They waded right into the crowd, and everyone kept picking up and moving, expanding, flowing together as more and more people arrived. All of the Whittakers came, and with them, the Everly Sisters. Their mother and her husband, whom Ames and Cy had been visiting with. Their long-time cook and her husband.

Annie, Colton's wife, had once been a huge part of the Whittaker clan, and that's where the lines blurred between Whittakers and Hammonds. Gray and every one of his brothers had married someone who worked there and claimed to belong to the Whiskey Mountain Lodge family. The Whittaker Family.

From there, the Youngs joined in with such a strong

musical connection to Lily, Vi, and Rose Everett. With the nine brothers, Gray felt a connection to them too.

"Can you imagine having eight brothers?" he asked Colton.

"I think I'd die," Colt said, laughing. "I can barely remember y'all's names now as it is." They watched as more Youngs arrived—Mav and Dani and their three kids. They were the largest family of the Youngs so far. Another couple of brothers Gray hadn't met yet, and being as social as he was, he got to his feet to go see who they were.

The rodeo brothers, he assumed.

"Gray," Tex said, indicating the two of them. One set down his little girl, and she followed her brother over to a blanket Bryce stood beside. She tugged on his shorts, and he lifted her into the air with a huge grin. No wonder all the girls flocked to him. Tall, handsome, and good with kids. He was checking boxes for girls left and right.

"This is Jem," he said, indicating the man still watching his daughter and Bryce. "And Blaze."

"Howdy," Gray said. "It's great to meet you." He recognized Blaze the most. "I've seen you on TV."

"Just once or twice," he said with a smile.

"Have you guys met Wyatt Walker?" Gray asked. "He summers here too." He looked between the two brothers. "Is that what y'all are doin' now? Summering in Coral Canyon?" He wasn't sure why he'd turned into such a cowboy, but Blaze and Jem wore the largest cowboy hats he'd ever seen. Maybe that was why.

"I'm undecided," Jem said.

"Yeah," Blaze said, his smile as wide as wide could be. "Undecided."

"They're here now," Tex said, plenty of hedging in his voice. "And yes, they went to dinner with Wyatt and his family last night." He gestured them toward some chairs, and Gray let them go. By his count, only one Young remained, and he hadn't seen Otis yet.

He retreated back to his chair and accepted the can of pink lemonade from Wes. "I love the Fourth of July," he said.

"It's the best," Wes agreed.

"Daddy," Tucker said, and Gray bent to lift him onto his lap.

"What, bud?"

"When's Mommy gonna be here?" He looked at Gray with such mourning in his eyes. "She has my swim shorts, and they have the sprinklers goin' over there." He pointed to the west, and Gray saw a steady stream of kids in swimming suits heading that way. So he didn't miss his mother. He just needed his trunks.

"Uh, I'm not sure, buddy." He looked at Bree, and she bent to get something out of the ginormous bag beside her chair. "Ask Auntie Bree if she has anything you can use." He honestly didn't care if Tucker stripped off his shirt and went in the black cotton shorts he currently wore. They'd dry. Elise would have more clothes for him.

"I sure do," Bree said. "And I know your momma

would want you to wear sunscreen." She gave Tucker a look, and he didn't argue with her. She got him all ready, and he went off with all of his cousins his age, and that was someone from every family except Colton's.

He looked over to his brother to see if that bothered him, but Colton had his hand in Annie's and his face turned toward their father. He radiated happiness Gray could feel from over here.

Another contented sigh moved through his body. He loved his family. He loved the friends they'd made here in Coral Canyon. They still had two months of summer ahead of them, and Hunt would be here for one of them. All the best fishing in the world in the lake just beyond their front door.

He couldn't wait.

Wes sighed too, and Gray looked over to him. "It'll work out," he said, and Wes nodded though he still looked like he'd swallowed eels and they were flipping their pointed tails against the back of his throat. "What's he thinking after graduation? Gerty's younger than him."

Gray looked over to the teens, who hadn't left Bryce's side. They sat on the blanket now with more little kids, and Gray's heart warmed again. He did note that Michael held one of his cousins in his lap—Ames's youngest—but Gerty did not. She actually seemed sort of uncomfortable.

Wes glanced over to Bree, and she was pretending not to listen. "He's honestly thinking military," Wes said, another sigh accompanying it.

Bree's mouth hardened into a fine line, but she said nothing. Gray didn't know what to say. He looked back over to Michael. "The Lord knows what he needs to do. He's a good kid. He'll get there."

He believed that too, though he knew it was sometimes painful to hear as a parent. It was hard to trust in the Lord like that when it came to one's children. Gray knew, because he'd done it. He'd lived through it—and he still had three more to go. One look at Jane told him he wasn't out of the woods at all. Not with her.

Still, trust in the Lord he would. But first, he accepted a slice of watermelon going around on a plate, and he lifted it in a silent toast to Bree and Wes. They all started to laugh, and as he bit into the cold, juicy fruit, Gray had the feeling that there was no better day to be alive than the Fourth of July, only hours before a fireworks show.

Now, if his wife, son, and grandson would hurry up and get here, he'd be complete.

36

The family site where everyone had gathered for the Fourth of July came into view, and Otis muttered, "Praise the heavens."

Georgia glanced over to him. "What?"

"This picnic basket is no picnic to carry," he said. His muscles strained, as he'd also looped three camp chairs over his shoulder, and he took quick steps so he wouldn't have to have his feet off the ground for too long. She sauntered alongside him, one hand linked in Joey's, and the other holding the leashes for two of her dogs.

"Tex is coming," she said, and Otis looked up from the ground. He was concentrating so hard on just putting one foot in front of the other. Just getting to the spot in the shade his family had picked for their evening picnic before the fireworks.

"Praise the heavens," Otis said again, and he gladly

handed his older brother the basket of food Georgia had graciously put together for this shindig. They'd all gathered here at this park for the Fourth of July last year too, along with the Hammonds, Whittakers, and Everetts.

"I have to go get my guitar still," Otis said. They'd done an impromptu concert last year, but this year, they'd all deliberately planned to bring their instruments and play before the band started at dusk. After that, it would just be rude to play over someone else's gig.

Morris had tried to get Country Quad on the schedule for the Independence Day concert this year, but it had already been booked. Word among band members, though, was that Country Quad would headline this concert and fireworks celebration for the town next year.

This year, they were doing a concert up at Whiskey Mountain Lodge as part of the Harvest Festival. Morris had organized and negotiated everything, and Otis couldn't wait to perform again.

"Give those chairs to Wes, and go get it," Tex said.

Wesley Hammond came toward him, and Otis handed him the camp chairs he had slung over his shoulder. "Thanks," he said, grinning at the man.

"No problem," he said. "Mikey, you wanna go with him and see what else he needs help with?"

"Yes, sir," Michael Hammond said. "Will you tell Gerty?"

Wes didn't roll his eyes, but Otis heard the action in his voice when he said, "She knows, son. She saw you walk away to come help." He turned and headed back toward the group. It had swelled since the last time Otis had looked up, and he nodded at Georgia.

"Better go get us some spots in the shade, sweetheart."

She smiled at him and kept walking. "Okay, baby."

Otis sure had enjoyed the past three or four months with her since his red-eye return to Coral Canyon. His stopover in Salt Lake had literally saved him, though he hadn't known it at the time. He thanked God every day for a cellphone kiosk in that airport that had been compatible with his phone so he could get a new SIM card. Without it, he wouldn't have seen Georgia's security system video make-up, and he'd have probably made a huge fool of himself to win her back.

In the end, neither of them had needed to win the other over for anything. He loved her; she loved him. The only reason he hadn't proposed yet was because she'd said she wouldn't say yes until they'd been dating for six months. She believed in love, marriage, and eternal happiness, but she didn't want to jump the gun.

He'd found her passed out in her office the first week of January. It was now the first week of July.

Six months.

"Otis," another man said, and he turned toward the familiar voice.

"Hunter Hammond," he said, laughing the moment he finished talking. "You're here this summer." Otis embraced the younger man, his roly-poly baby squealing and laughing between them.

"Here," Hunter said. "Go see your cousin." He handed his one-year-old to Michael. "How was your drive?"

"Oh, you know," Michael said. "Hours and hours of my dad sighing. If he wasn't doing that, he was firing questions at me."

Hunter chuckled and reached for his wife's hand. "Hang in there, Mikey. You never know what the future holds for you."

Otis watched them walk away, and then he turned to Michael. "What was your dad sighing about?"

"I brought my girlfriend with me this year," Michael said. "He thinks I'm too young. Haven't dated enough. All that stuff." He bounced the baby on his hip and smiled as the little one did. "I don't know how to tell him that just because I'm young doesn't mean my feelings aren't real."

Otis didn't know what to say either. "Are you going to college?"

"I have one more year of high school," Michael said. "Then, I don't know."

Otis opened the back door of his truck. "Well, I don't know you real well, but you're a nice kid. Bryce has always said good things about you."

"Bryce is the best," Michael said with a grin. *Everyone* who talked about Bryce said that, Otis included.

He pulled out one guitar and handed it to Michael. "I

got married pretty young. A lot of my brothers did too. I'm not sayin' it's like this for everyone, but none of our marriages lasted that long. Some not even a year."

Michael's jaw jumped. "I think my dad wants me to have more life experience."

"It's not a bad thing," Otis said. "But again, I'm not saying one way or the other is better. You just gotta do what you think is right. Listen to your heart, and the Lord. That's what my mama taught us boys." He grinned at Michael. "Some of us do it better than others, of course."

"Yeah." Michael smiled at him, and Otis gathered the other two guitars.

"All right," he said. "This is it." The walk back to the large, shady area was much easier without so much weight around his shoulders and in his arms, and he and Michael chatted easily about school, the weather, Coral Canyon, and music on the way back to the group.

Otis sighed as he set his guitars next to his empty chair. He wasn't sure if he should sit down or go around and greet everyone first. He moved over to Mama and Daddy, leaning down to hug them.

Joey had found a blanket with some of the younger Hammond kids, including the two Bryce gave guitar lessons to. Otis's oldest nephew had just graduated from high school about a month ago. Right now, he'd enrolled at Montana State University, and Otis wondered if a young, blonde, beautiful Bailey McAllister had anything to do with that.

Bryce had denied it vehemently, claiming that he'd been thinking of applying to MSU even when he lived in Boise. Tex had corroborated his story, but Otis knew Tex worried about Bryce.

He should, too. The young man had a ton of talent, and his whole life in front of him. Otis had just spoken true about getting married too young. And Luke had gotten married younger than him. Then Morris and Gabe, both by the time they were twenty-two.

It was *young*, and just because that was their last name didn't mean they had to go saying I-do the first chance they got.

Otis definitely felt more grounded now, and he glanced over to Georgia, who'd turned her chair toward Abby and Dani. They gabbed, and when Cheryl arrived ahead of her husband, everyone got to their feet to go help Wade.

He wasn't anywhere in sight, and Tex asked, "Is he wearing his prosthetics, Cheryl?"

"He wouldn't," she said. "He's getting out his wheelchair." She didn't seem that concerned, but Tex and Trace both left to go help the man.

Otis pulled up a chair beside Lily Everett and Bree Hammond. "Howdy, ladies."

They both smiled at him and said, "Otis," in tandem.

He leaned closer, waving in Rose Everett too. She and her two sisters had all married and used different last names now, but they'd always be the Everett Sisters to him. "Listen, you guys," he said. "I want to ask Georgia to marry me today. Huge group thing? Or I sneak away with her about dusk and get down on both knees?"

Lily cast a glance over to Georgia, who was just now retaking her seat. She looked around for Joey, found her, and then started searching for Otis. "She's lookin'," he said, and they all sat up straight. Otis turned toward Wes, and said, "How's Easton doing in that art program?"

"Good," Wes said, only taking his eyes from Michael and Gerty for two seconds. "He likes it."

"That's great," Otis said as Georgia went back to her friends. He really liked that she had friends in his family, and that she got along so well with everyone.

He leaned back into the ladies, and Bree said, "Otis, she's one you take off on your own."

"I agree," Rose said.

"You brought the ring?" Lily asked.

Otis patted his shirt pocket. "Yes, ma'am." Her eyes shone like stars. All of the women's did. "Good move?" he asked.

"It's the best holiday in the world," Bree said. "Beautiful summer evening. Cold watermelon and lemonade. Great music." She beamed at Otis. "I think it's a very good move."

"It's memorable," Lily said.

"What is?" Elise Hammond sat down in an empty chair and sighed. "That drive is not fun." She stole the attention of the other women, who exclaimed they didn't even realize she'd arrived. She was good friends with all of them, as her history at Whiskey Mountain Lodge and in Coral Canyon predated Otis's by years.

He stood and went to sit by Morris. He sat with Luke, who laughed with Mav and Jem. He hadn't seen Blaze yet, though Otis suspected he was here somewhere already. Jem had little kids the same age as Corrine, which naturally paired him with Luke, and Otis sat with them for a few minutes.

He got up and joined Georgia's parents for a few minutes, and then Blaze leaned over and said, "Boo." He laughed as Otis jumped to his feet to hug him.

He drew Cash into his chest too, and then pointed out where Harry was standing with Bryce, Michael, and Gerty. He was definitely closer to their age than anyone else—or he wanted to be. Cash looked up at Blaze, who nodded once at him.

Otis grinned at him. "You reminded me of Trace just then. He and Harry can have whole conversations with just eyes and chins."

Blaze shook his head and laughed, and Otis shifted some chairs as Wade arrived with his wheelchair. Tex put on quite the show to make sure he was okay, and that was only topped by Bryce whooping and causing a big scene as he jogged toward a very pretty blonde woman who'd just arrived with her parents. Graham and Laney smiled as Bryce lifted Bailey right up off her feet, the two of them laughing.

Then they steered their other two children into the Whittaker fray, but by this point, all the families were mixed up, with connections running all over the place.

The group continued to get bigger and bigger, and Otis loved every minute of it. Eventually, he met Trace's eye, and they reached for their instruments. One by one, they came out, until Lily held a fiddle, and Tex stood in the middle of the group, crooning for all he was worth.

Others gathered around, and as the sun set, Country Quad and The Everett Sisters entertained those within earshot. Otis could've played forever, his fingers plucking the strings and his voice knowing exactly which hole to fill in the harmony. He was never quite as happy as he was when he played the guitar.

Except for maybe with Georgia's hand in his, the guitars and instruments now put away as the contracted band took the stage. Their spot was about two hundred yards from the stage, so they wouldn't be blasted by the music. The fireworks would fill the whole, wide, Wyoming sky above them once true darkness fell.

Joey returned to them and Otis wrapped up her bony frame in a blanket while she laughed.

Dusk fell, and Otis touched his shirt pocket. "Georgia, sweetheart," he said. "Let's take a walk."

She gave him a look. "A walk?"

"Five minutes," he said. He grinned at her. "You can bring the dogs."

They panted at her feet, both of them content to stay right there.

"Otis, is this something weird?"

"Why would it be something weird?"

"I'm not an outdoorsy person," she said. "I don't take walks." She settled into her chair like she'd be going nowhere.

Otis wasn't sure what to do. Torn, he glanced over to Tex. His brother had involved everyone in his proposal to Abby, even complete strangers up in Dog Valley. They'd known Abby, but not him, and yet he'd charmed them into the perfect proposal.

Otis only wanted to do the same—the perfect proposal, not including strangers in it.

Abby met his eye, and she leaned forward. "Did you need me?"

"Yeah," he said, making quick decisions. He stood up and gestured to his daughter. "Will you watch Joey while Georgia and I take a quick walk?"

Abby's eyes flew to Georgia. "A walk?"

"It's at least a thousand degrees," Georgia said, folding her arms and crossing her legs. She was not going.

Otis blew out his breath. "The sun is down. It's cooling off quick."

She simply gave him a look that said if there wasn't chocolate cake at the end of the walk, she wasn't going.

He sat back down. "Fine," he said in a loud voice. "I

guess I'll just have to ask you to marry me right here, in front of everyone and their dog. Literally."

Abby shrieked, which only brought more attention to their little pocket of people. Otis smiled benignly, like he'd said nothing out of the ordinary. "Georgia, go," she said. She got to her feet too. "Go. I'll sit with Joey."

"Oh, it's too late now," Otis said, still putting on a good show. He could if he had to. He retrieved the ring from his pocket. "Georgia Beck."

She got to her feet, mostly because Abby was shoving her out of her seat.

Otis stayed in his seat. He looked over to Lily, who pointed sternly to the ground. He slid to his knees and held up the ring.

"Wait, wait," Tex said. "Guys, he needs some light. There's no way she can see that ring."

"She probably would've had she gone on a walk wth me," Otis boomed.

Georgia said nothing. She barely moved. She'd gone into her self-protection mode, and Otis grinned at her. She was still present, just processing. Hopefully, she'd have enough time to get to "yes," by the time he asked his question.

Flashlights got turned on, and all the phones in the group shone on him and Georgia. Someone whistled and said, "That's a big diamond."

"See? That's the kind of diamond you need to propose with," someone else said, and it sounded like Hunter.

"He is not proposing," Wes said. "He's seventeen years old."

"You're not either," Tex said, but Otis couldn't see him because of all the lights turned his way.

"Can you all be quiet?" he bellowed. "I'm trying to do something here." He took a breath and cleared his throat in an overexaggerated way. "Georgia Beck." He smiled up at her, this gorgeous woman he loved with his whole heart. "I'm in love with you. By my count, you kissed me for the first time almost a year ago. We've been dating-dating, like serious dating for six months. That's not too fast, and I think it's time we made it all official. I want you in my life every single day. You and all the dogs, cats, and gerbils."

She scoffed, her smile growing now. "I don't own any gerbils," she called out to the crowd.

"Yet," Abby yelled, and everyone chuckled and giggled.

Georgia shook her head and looked at him again.

"I love you," he said again. He lifted the diamond a little higher. "Will you marry me?"

She gazed at him, then held out her left hand so he could slide the ring onto her finger. He did while the whole crowd of their friends and family watched in silence. She studied it for a moment, and then said, "Yes, of course I'll marry you."

Their pod of people went wild, and with that many cowboys and kids and women, they made quite the racket.

Georgia fell to her knees in front of Otis, took his face in her hands, and kissed him. He got transported right back to her office, when she'd pulled him in for that first kiss. The flashlights around them shook and shimmied as people waved their phones, but Otis only wanted to kiss his fiancé.

He pulled away, because she'd refused to go on a walk with him, and they were kissing in front of at least fifty people. "I love you," he whispered.

"I love you too, Otis."

They got to their feet, and Georgia held up her left hand, the back of her hand out. She cocked her hip, grinning from ear to ear. She squealed too and danced over to Abby and Dani. The women gathered there, and Otis finally got a true breath as he faced his brothers.

Blaze pounded him heartily on the back, and even Luke said, "Congrats, Otis. I'm really happy for you." He'd purchased a house a couple of months ago, and he'd been working hard to gut it and get it in shape for him and Corrine to live in. They currently still lived in the basement apartment, but Luke claimed the house was almost ready for them to move into.

He hugged Tex, who said, "Married life is the best, Otis. You're going to love it."

Trace put on a brave face, but there was something behind the mask Otis needed to dig at. Not tonight, but he'd come back to it one afternoon when the two of them were alone in the studio.

Jem hugged him, as did Morris, who said, "You're a lucky man, Otis."

"Don't I know it," he said, smiling. "Maybe you next."

Morris laughed and shook his head. "I doubt it. The woman who I want to talk to won't give me her number." He seemed good-natured about it, and Otis had told him to use Leighann's number from the group text at Whiskey Mountain Lodge. Morris, ever the morally-north brother, wouldn't do it.

Mav held him tightly, no words needed. They were close in age, and close in every other way. Gabe hadn't made the trip to Coral Canyon for the fireworks, and Otis couldn't help feeling sad about it. He should be here, with the rest of them. At the very least, his daughter should be here to play with her cousins. They needed that bond.

He quickly pulled out his phone and texted him. *I asked Georgia to marry me tonight. She said yes. I wish you were here.*

Gabe responded quickly, because his phone was like a third hand. *I'm happy for you, Otis. Congratulations.*

Nothing else. No acknowledgement that he was wanted in Coral Canyon. He showed the phone to Mav, who nodded. "That's about how he is," he said. "We'll just keep telling him how much we love him, and maybe someday, he'll believe us."

Otis hugged his mom and dad, and they both congratulated him. Then he and everyone else settled back into the seats and their personal conversations. Georgia came to sit with him, and he wrapped his arms around her and let his hands fall to her lap.

He wasn't the most popular band member, and that didn't matter. He didn't know all the intricate details of all of his brothers' lives. He knew Luke had struggles, and Trace was hiding something. He knew Jem and Blaze should both be on the rodeo circuit and weren't, so something was going on there. He knew Morris desperately wanted to reconnect with Leighann, so he sent up a prayer that the Lord could facilitate that as easily as he'd put Otis in Beck's Books only moments before Georgia had passed out.

If He could do that, He could help Morris and Leighann get back together. He could soothe whatever plagued Trace. He could help Blaze and Jem with their ailments, mental, physical, and emotional. He could put a balm over Luke's angry heart and help it heal.

The Lord could watch over and keep Mav, Dani, and their children safe and protected. He could touch Gabe's heart and let him know how very much the Young family in Coral Canyon missed him and loved him. He could help Tex, Abby, and Bryce with any of their transitions.

With God, all things were possible, and Otis pressed his eyes closed and let the darkness press in around him. Then, he could feel the love of the Lord, the love of his family, and the love of the good woman he'd just proposed to.

The first crack of a firework startled him, and the

crowd park-wide rose up in a giant "ah" that filled all of Coral Canyon. The bright white sparks in the sky made him smile. Joy filled his whole body and soul.

Georgia turned and dipped her head, and Otis rose up to meet her in a kiss. "Sorry I wouldn't go for a walk with you," she murmured against his lips.

"It's okay," he whispered back. "I think it turned out all right."

"I love you so much."

"I love you too." He kissed her again, and he could've done that for the rest of the night. But Joey said, "Daddy! Daddy! Did you see the witch hair?" and he figured he better mind his manners. After all, there was already a show going on, and Otis did love a good fireworks extravaganza.

Read on for a sneak peek at **MORRIS**, featuring Morris Young, the next member of the Young Family who's just discovered...well, you better read the sneak peek chapters below - keep tapping and scrolling to get to them! - to find out what Morris has going on in his life...

Sneak Peek! MORRIS Chapter One:

Morris Young turned away from the kitchen island when he heard footsteps coming toward him.

"Aren't they feeding you at the wedding?" Trace asked. His brother already wore his cowboy hat, and Morris really needed to get into the right Wyoming mindset.

"Yes," he said, lifting another bite of cold cereal to his mouth. "Have you eaten wedding food before?"

Trace chuckled and shook his head. "It's been a while."

"Tex and Abby served real food," Morris said. "I've been to Stone Gate before. It'll be all this frou-frou food without gluten or sugar." He took another bite of his shredded wheat.

Trace gave it a glare. "That's not much better."

"This has frosting," Morris argued. "It's a thousand times better." His brother opened the fridge and peered inside. A sigh accompanied the action, and Morris's heart went out to his older brother.

He loved and appreciated Trace more and more with each passing day. He'd lived with him for the past year now, and Trace had never once suggested in any way—vocally or in action—that he didn't want Morris there. His son, Harry, had become a teenager, and he didn't make things easy for Trace, that was for sure.

He'd joined a dating app a few months ago, and the one woman he'd met and was interested in was the one Harry insisted he not see. That hadn't been easy for Trace either. Last Morris had heard from him, he'd stopped getting on the app altogether.

"You could come with me," he said, trying to keep his voice casual. "There's always a lot of single women at weddings."

Trace turned on the full force of his glare. Morris chuckled and shied away from him. "Yikes. I'm not Luke. I can't withstand that thing." He laughed, and Trace joined him.

He went back around the island and sank onto a barstool. "I guess I could come. Harry's over at Tex's tonight, and he won't be home any time soon."

That he would not. Tex was hosting a cousin's night, and he'd invited all of the younger Young generation for pizza, games, and a sleepover at his farmhouse on the west side of town. As far as Morris knew, everyone but Lars—the newest and youngest Young at only three months old—had gone.

Tex was a saint, that was for sure. Morris loved having his nieces and nephews in his life too. He simply preferred them one on one instead of in a large mob.

"So come," Morris said. "It's Misty Keller. You knew her older brother." When Trace continued to wear a blank expression, Morris added, "Holt."

"Oh, Holt Keller." Trace's frown returned.

"It's not his wedding," Morris said.

"Do you have a plus-one?"

"I didn't respond specifically that I would have a guest," he said. "So you eat now and not then. There'll be a chair for you. Plus, then we can leave early." Morris wasn't even ten years out of high school yet, and being back in Coral Canyon meant some of his friends from his youth were still around.

Just getting married for the first time. He didn't mind attending the weddings and parties. He simply felt...too old for them. He'd lived two lives already—or at least it had felt like it. One in the NFL. One as a collegiate football coach.

He was just now starting his third life as Country Quad's manager, and he couldn't help the way his mind traveled down a road he'd been on before. One with Leighann Drummond. He'd been married to her before, but that had only lasted a couple of years. She'd ended things with him just before his devastating ACL injury, and he hadn't spoken to her since.

Well, until last spring. They now worked at Whiskey Mountain Lodge together, and she brought out a tray of something scrumptious and beautiful after every football camp he did. He'd asked her for her number twice now, and twice she'd either said no or been distracted enough not to give it to him.

He had it through the group texts that came from the lodge, but Morris didn't possess the courage to use her number—which she had *not* given to him—for personal use. Despite what his brothers had suggested, he hadn't done it. He wouldn't.

"All right," Trace said. "Let me go change."

Morris whooped and then drained the milk from his cereal bowl. He washed it out and set it to dry in the rack beside the sink, so he wouldn't leave dishes for his brother. He collected his keys and grabbed the gift he'd gotten for Misty and...well, whoever she was marrying that day. Morris steeled himself to get recognized, especially if Trace was going to be with him.

He'd lived his whole life in the shadow of Youngs older than him. Tex had been like a god at Coral Canyon High, and Trace a prince. All of the Youngs towered over six feet tall, and while Blaze and Jem had excelled at sports, so had Morris. Eventually.

He and his twin, Gabriel, were the youngest brothers,

and everyone had sort of forgotten about them. He said sort of, because the more time he spent with Tex, Otis, Trace, Luke, and Mav, the less he believed that he'd been forgotten.

Overlooked, maybe. Definitely. Luke had graduated when he and Gabe were Freshmen, which meant they lived their last three years of high school with just each other. The other seven brothers were gone out of the house, living their lives. The band had started very soon after that, and Luke had never known a life where he wasn't country music famous.

Morris reminded himself that he'd been drafted into the NFL after his sophomore year of college, and he certainly didn't have room to complain about his life and getting lucky breaks. Of course, then he'd gotten a very unlucky one only a few years later.

"Ready," Trace said, pulling Morris from his memories.

He gave his brother a grin and grabbed his cowboy hat from the hook just inside the front door. He usually took his hat off the moment he arrived home, and only put it on right when he was leaving. "Great, let's go." They went outside and got in Morris's truck. He had two more weddings to attend before this summer ended, and his heart suddenly felt heavy.

"Hey, uh." He glanced over to Trace. "What app are you using for the dating? Or were you using?"

Trace's eyebrows went up. "You want to use a dating app?"

Morris swallowed, because no, he didn't. Trace already knew that. "I—" The truth was, he'd seen Tex and Otis fall in love, and he wanted that feeling back in his life. He missed having a companion, a spouse. Not only that, but he was the only Young without any children, and he hated how that made him the odd man out.

"You miss Leighann," Trace said, real quiet, the way Trace said things that were one-hundred percent true.

"She won't give me her number," Morris said just as quietly.

"Maybe you need to try again."

Morris gave an exasperated sigh. "I don't know what that means. I've told her I want to talk to her."

"Have you asked her out?"

Morris's stomach tightened at the very thought. "I—no."

Trace let a block or two go by in silence. Then he said, "I think you're not usin' the right words, Morris."

He dang near rolled his eyes—and he definitely wanted to drive them off the road. "I don't know what words to use, Trace. I'm not you or Otis or Tex." He stabbed a glare in his brother's direction. "Or Mav."

"Hey, don't lump me in with them," Trace said. He lifted his phone. "I had to use a blasted app, because I don't know how to talk to a woman in person." He seemed genuinely upset, and Morris's irritation blew itself out.

"You talk to women fine," he said. "You had a great time with Everly."

"Don't," Trace said.

Morris wouldn't. "What about that Brynlee woman? You liked her."

"The fact that you called her 'that Brynlee woman' says it all." He looked out his window and refused to meet Morris's eye again.

"Yeah, all right," he said. He wanted to help Trace with Everly, but he didn't know how. The one time he'd tried, he'd gotten the line, "You don't have kids, Morris. It's so much more complicated than you're making it."

He hadn't brought her up again. He just hated seeing Trace so unhappy.

"Maybe we'll both meet someone at this stupid wedding," Morris mumbled as the ivy-covered building came into view. Stone Gate was one of the oldest buildings in the valley, and that meant they could charge thousands to have a wedding there.

The gardens were impeccable, and Morris sipped apple cider while frilly music played from hidden speakers. He and Trace stuck together, and Morris kept flitting from pod to pod of high school friends he didn't care about anymore.

"Trace Young," a woman said, and they both turned toward the brunette.

"Aspen North." He laughed and enveloped her into a

hug that lifted her right up off her feet. "What are you doin' here?"

"My cousin is the groom," she said, giggling as she tucked her hair behind her hear. She looked past Trace to Morris, but she didn't even see him. "Hello, Morris."

"Afternoon, Aspen."

"What are you doing here?" She swatted at Trace's arm, and Morris had never seen such blatant flirting. At least she wasn't wearing a wedding ring. He didn't know her story, as she was about five years older than him. Trace was a dozen years older, so he wouldn't be robbing the cradle if he went out with her.

Before Morris knew it, Trace had linked his arm through Aspen's, and they'd gone to find a seat. "I'll save one for you, brother," he called over his shoulder, but he didn't even wait long enough for Morris to lift his fancy flute of cider in acknowledgement.

And now he was on his own. Standing in some maze of a garden, in the heat, waiting for a wedding to start that he didn't care about anyway. Had people felt like this at his wedding?

Most likely, he thought. He set his empty glass down on a table and started following the crowd.

"Morris," someone said, and he turned toward the male voice. When he came face-to-face with Clancy Powell, he wanted to run in the other direction.

"Look at you, bro," he said, his own chest puffing out.

He'd gained about thirty pounds in the nine years since they'd graduated. "What are you doing here?"

"I live here," Morris said, trying to keep his voice even. Clancy hadn't been a nice guy in high school, and the sneer on his face sure didn't indicate that he'd changed much.

"Couldn't hack it in the NFL?" he asked.

"I got injured," Morris said. "It happens." And it did. To a lot of men. He looked left and right for any escape he could find. His eyes landed on Leighann.

Time froze, and Clancy could've said any number of things. Morris wouldn't have heard them. All he could see and experience was Leighann Drummond in that gorgeous peach-colored dress.

The top was made of lace and dove into a deep V that went almost to her navel. Sheer fabric stretched over flesh-colored material that kept her covered while creating the illusion she wasn't.

At her waist, a silver belt made with gems glittered in the sun, and the soft, flowing fabric melted to the ground in waves of light orange. She made him think of peaches and cream, and his mouth watered for her.

The earth moved again, and Morris swallowed. *Now or never.*

"Excuse me," he said, his eyes locked on hers. Maybe he hadn't used the right words with her. Perhaps Trace was right.

Help me find the words, Lord, he prayed as he approached her. A hedge sat on his right, with an open area on the left, where a fountain babbled. Beyond that, the wedding had been set up, and more and more people were taking their seats.

He arrived right in front of Leighann, and he did what was most natural. He reached out and took her hand in his. "Leighann," he said. "You look amazing." He cleared his throat. "Beautiful."

"Thank you," she murmured.

He gave a nervous chuckle. "If I'd known you'd been invited, we could've come together." He raised his eyebrows at her, but those weren't the right words.

Lord, he thought desperately.

"Listen," he started, his eyes dropping to their joined hands. Hers had always fit in his so precisely. Could she not feel that? Did she not see it? "I want to go out with you." He swallowed. There. He'd said it. Couldn't get plainer than that.

He looked into her eyes. "I want us to try again. I miss you. I want—" He watched her swallow too, but her eyes didn't leave his. "I want to see if we can have a second chance at happiness. At what we could've had before."

She opened her mouth, and he quickly said, "Don't say no. Sit by me today. Dance with me tonight. Then, if you're absolutely sure it's over between us, you can use my number from the Lodge group text and tell me no."

Again.

Please don't let her tell me no for a third time, he thought.

Just looking at her, he knew it wasn't over between them. Maybe it had been for a while. Maybe with all the miles he'd kept between him and Wyoming, it had been.

Now?

With the storming desire in her eyes? The electricity arcing between them? The way her fingers curled and held so tightly to his?

Nothing had ended between them.

Before she could answer or agree, and before he could say, "We better go sit down," someone said in a high-pitched, child-like voice. "Momma?"

To his great surprise, Leighann slipped her hand out of his and turned in the same motion. A little boy with dark hair ran toward her, and she scooped him right up into her arms. "What, baby?"

"I lost you," he said, putting both hands on either side of her face and squishing her cheeks.

She laughed, and Morris heard the nervous energy in it. "I'm right here, baby. You were supposed to stay with Uncle Denzel." She cut a look in Morris's direction, and he found his heart pounding, pounding, pounding like a whole marching band of bass drums.

She had a child?

He had to be about four or five, and that made no sense on the timeline in Morris's head. None. At all.

The little boy turned toward him as she settled him on her hip, and Morris sucked in a breath.

He'd just looked into a pair of eyes that mirrored his own. He had the rounder features of his mother, just like Gabe, Mav, and Otis.

This boy did too.

Morris would bet everything he owned that the boy in Leighann's arms was a Young. And that meant...he was looking at his son.

Sneak Peek! MORRIS Chapter Two:

Leighann Drummond couldn't hold back the tears. She knew the moment Morris put all the pieces together, and it didn't take him long. Seconds. His eyes changed, and he drew in a breath that flared his nostrils.

He wore a pair of black dress shorts—if such a thing existed, and they clearly did—with a short-sleeved white shirt, a blue tie, and a big ole Wyoming cowboy hat that sent her pulse a'fluttering. The man had charmed her from the moment she'd met him over seven years ago now.

"Go find Uncle Denzel," she choked out as she put her boy down. "Go on. Momma needs to talk to…." She didn't finish the sentence, and Eric ran off before she did anyway.

"Leighann," Morris said with plenty of danger in his voice. "Who was that?"

Tears splashed her cheeks, ruining her makeup and her day. No, *she'd* done that almost four years ago when she'd filed for divorce, then found out she was pregnant, then didn't tell the father.

In her defense, she'd lost two babies at that point in her life, and she had no reason to believe she could carry this third pregnancy to term. As the days became weeks and then months, everything in Leighann's life had shifted.

She'd known it was time to tell Morris since the day she'd seen him at the lodge, seven months ago. She'd been praying and begging for the right way to do it. The words in the correct order. Something.

She hadn't gotten them. She wasn't ready. A wedding for a high school friend hardly seemed like the right time.

And yet, here she stood.

She glanced over to another couple as they went by, and there were suddenly too many eyes in the vicinity. She turned away from the festivities and Morris. She walked away, but her ex-husband followed her. He'd let her go a few times now, but not this time.

"Leighann," he insisted.

A few more steps, she prayed. She couldn't see anyone out here in the garden anymore, and when she couldn't stand to take another breath of overheated August air, she spun back to him. Time had run out.

"He's your son," she blurted out.

He stopped as if he'd hit a glass wall, the shock on his face about what Leighann had imagined. "You're joking."

"I'm not," she said.

"You...what? You...what's his name?" Morris spoke in fragments when he was flustered, and boy, did he have something to be flustered about.

"Eric Garfield," she said, and his mouth dropped open. She couldn't stand to look at him, so she turned away again. "You loved Morris the Cat, remember? And well, I always argued that Garfield was better, and when we got married, you said we could have an orange tabby cat." She paced back and forth in rapid steps, her blasted heels pinching her pinky toe on her left foot.

She spun back to him. "We laughed about that, remember?" Tears spilled down her face, but Morris stood there like he'd been hit by a linebacker going sixty miles per hour.

Honestly, he'd probably been less shook when that had happened to him on the football field.

"We said we'd get two of them," she continued, wiping sloppily at her face. Everything felt too hot, and more eyes landed on her. On the two of them. "And you'd name yours Garfield, because you obviously can't name it Morris, but I'd name mine Morris, and then I'd have two of you."

Leighann needed to stop talking. She needed to find a cool patch of shade and something to drink. Anyone with a cold cloth she could hide her face in while she sobbed would be welcome.

"Honey," a woman said. "Are you all right?" The blonde with concern on her face wasn't welcome. Leighann waved at her, but she gave Morris a look like he'd done something terribly wrong to make Leighann cry the way she did.

"I can get you something to drink," the woman said. "Are you with someone...else here at the wedding?"

Morris said nothing, but he didn't turn and leave either.

Leighann sniffled and gathered her hair into her hands. She'd spent an hour curling it for this stupid wedding. And why? She'd barely spoken to Misty since high school.

Deep down, she knew why. Morris lived in Coral Canyon now, and she'd suspected he'd be here. He'd been much better friends with Misty than she had, as they'd grown up together on the east side of town.

"I'm okay," Leighann said. "It's nothing he did, really."

"Are you sure, sweetie?" The woman positioned herself between Leighann and Morris.

"Nancy," a man said. "She said she's okay." He stepped over to Morris and extended his hand. "Howdy, Morris. I loved watching you play on Sunday afternoons."

"Thank you, sir," Morris said, his voice deathly quiet. He glanced at the man, but his eyes came right back to Leighann.

The man reached for his wife and put his hand on her elbow. "Hon, they used to be married. Let them work it out, okay?" He nodded his cowboy-hatted head at Leighann and then Morris, and the couple made their departure.

Morris folded his arms. "How are we going to work this out?"

"If everyone could take their seats, please," someone said into the mic. Morris twisted and looked over his shoulder. He was so kind, and so good, and so respectful, he wouldn't want to miss Misty's wedding or cause a scene.

"Leighann," he said, facing her again. "I want to meet him. I want him to know who I am. I want to be his father." He spoke in sure, strong sentences, and she'd only seen him break down and babble a couple of times. Each time she'd lost their baby. When he'd been drafted into the NFL, and when he'd been told he couldn't play anymore.

She'd already filed for divorce by then, but he'd called her anyway, a big, heaping mess of a man whose whole career had ended with a single wrong second on a field in Denver.

Leighann held a lot of regrets in her hand, and one of the biggest was that she hadn't been there for him in that doctor's appointment. That she hadn't been at his side during his healing and recovery. That she hadn't championed him to his next level of greatness.

Because Morris Young was great. No matter what life

threw at him, no matter what injustices God allowed him to suffer, he always got back up.

Peace filled her heart, confusing her.

He can recover from this, she thought, and the words were not her own.

She nodded, a well of strength appearing inside her she didn't know she possessed. "You can meet him. After the wedding? Tomorrow for breakfast?"

"I work at the hospital on Monday mornings," he said evenly. "Can I come by your place after that?"

"I work at the lodge," she said.

He blew out his breath, his impatience obvious. "Then tonight," he said, looking down at his clothes. Then hers. "You'll have to make all the proper introductions tonight." He said it almost like a threat, and then he turned to face the wedding. "Come on. We better go sit down."

He actually offered her his arm, and though Leighann feared she looked a fright, she linked her hand through his steady elbow and let him lead her over to the chairs which had been set up for the wedding. Everyone stared at them. Positively everyone, and she didn't dare look at Morris's face.

He was Morris Young, hometown hero and heart-throb. Rich football player. The pride and joy of Coral Canyon, even if he hadn't come home until all of his brothers had. Fine, not all of them, but a lot of them.

She spotted Denzel, and he only had one seat next to

him. Morris nodded to the other side of the aisle. "Trace is over there."

"My brother," she whispered.

He paused right in the middle of the aisle and met her eye. "You will not leave without introducing me to him."

She nodded, and they went their separate ways. Leighann had barely sat down when the wedding march started, and her blood felt like hot water streaming through her veins. Misty had been waiting for her and Morris to sit down.

Denzel couldn't stand, but he tracked Leighann's every move. He didn't even watch the bride walk down the aisle with her father. Truth be told, everything Leighann saw existed behind a white film, like a piece of waxed paper had been placed over her eyes.

"What in the world is going on?" Denzel asked. "You walked in with Morris Young like you're part of this wedding party?"

"What?" Leighann asked.

"The wedding party." Denzel made some stabbing motions toward the altar, and sure enough, all the bridesmaids and groomsmen already stood up front. She and Morris had come in *after* them.

A moan started in the back of Leighann's throat. No wonder everyone had been gaping at them. She met her brother's eyes, and she didn't have to say anything. He knew who Eric was. "He knows, doesn't he?"

Seeing as how Eric looked exactly like Morris in every

way, Leighann could only nod. Somehow, she made it through the wedding, and she hadn't taken two steps past Denzel to help him with his walker when Morris appeared in front of her.

"Let me," he said, deftly lifting the apparatus and positioning it in front of her brother. "Howdy, Denzel."

"Morris," he said pleasantly. He shot Leighann a look that told her she should've handled this over coffee, the way he'd advised her to many times.

She looked away, because she'd told him his racecar driving would end up killing him one day. Not quite, but the man could barely walk, and she'd had to come back to the valley to care for him.

"Do you have a way home?" Morris asked, drawing Leighann's attention back to him. "Leighann and I need to talk, and she can take me back to Trace's. Perhaps Trace could take you home." He looked at Denzel and then Leighann. "Whenever you're ready, of course." He put a smile on his face, and how he did that, Leighann would never, ever understand. "Trace has found himself a date."

He hit the T hard and chuckled. Denzel joined in with him, and then said, "I can go with Trace, sure."

"Great," Morris said. "Let me tell him real quick, all right?" He went off to do that, and Denzel and Leighann both watched him. Her fingers ached for how hard she clutched her son's fingers. "Momma," he complained. "You hurt me, Momma."

She released her grip, her tears suddenly filling her

eyes again. "Sorry, baby." She crouched down in front of him, though no one should ever wear heels and crouch. "I want you to stay with me, okay? Don't go wandering off in the gardens."

He nodded, just about the cutest thing in the world. Leighann loved him with her whole soul, and she straightened and looked at Denzel.

"Where are you going?" her brother asked.

She wasn't sure, so she said, "I don't know. My guess is to get something to eat." They wouldn't stay at the wedding. Morris would want a nice, private booth so he could try to connect all the dots. She'd watched the man study in college. She'd watched him train for the NFL. She'd watched him pour over playbooks and charts, and the man had a mind like no one else.

He could handle many things flying at him at once, and he didn't like to be idle for longer than ten seconds.

Morris returned, and Leighann took a deep breath. "Okay," she said. "Well, I'll see you at home, okay?"

"I'm good," Denzel said as Trace approached. He looked at Leighann, nodded, and dropped his gaze to the little boy at her side. She felt no need to hide him, though Trace wore his shock openly. It flowed from him, and he couldn't look away from Eric for anything.

"Trace," Morris barked, and his brother visibly flinched.

"Yeah, yep," he said, clearing his throat. "That is your...." His face turned pink, and he ducked his head, pushing his cowboy hat lower over his eyes. "Yep. Come on, Denzel, I heard if we get over to the buffet fast enough, there's snickerdoodles."

He steadied Denzel on the stone walk, and Leighann's heart expanded for the kindness of the Youngs. She didn't deserve to be part of this family. Was that one reason she hadn't told Morris? Did she not find herself worthy of love, of respect, of a place to belong inside the huge, loud, loving Young family?

Morris had always had some rifts between him and his brothers—one of which was Trace. There didn't seem to be anything troubling between them any longer, and Leighann told herself that so much could change in only a few years.

Looking down at her son told her that in a shout. A scream. A shriek from the inside of her soul.

Morris stepped right in front of Eric and crouched down. "Your momma says your name is Eric," he said. He didn't sugar-coat his voice. He didn't baby-talk to his three-year-old.

The boy looked up at her. She nodded and said, "You can talk to him."

"Yep," Eric said. "What's your name?" He reached out and ran his fingers along the brim of Morris's hat. Morris's face lit up like he'd just met Santa Claus, and Leighann's heart simultaneously healed a little and shrank a little.

"Morris," he said as Eric dropped his chubby fingers to his face.

"Baby," Leighann said. "Don't touch his face, remember?"

Her son pulled his fingers back, and Leighann amended her thoughts. *Their* son. Eric wasn't only hers, not anymore.

Morris looked up at her, and she said, "He's a little boy. He likes to touch everything. At least his hands don't go in his mouth anymore." She tried on a smile, and surprisingly, it fit okay. Morris returned it as he straightened.

"Dinner?" he asked.

She nodded, and he led the way out of the gardens and through the enormous stone building to the parking lot. He went straight to her car, which alarmed her until she remembered he'd seen her driving it before. She helped Eric into the back seat, but Morris leaned in and buckled his safety belt.

Her lungs shivered and shook as she got behind the wheel. She couldn't believe she was about to be trapped in a confined space with her gorgeous, sexy, cowboy ex-husband. She'd felt a current between them since she'd run into him outside of Graham's office. This inexplicable pull that couldn't be denied.

He'd asked her for her number multiple times. He'd said he missed her. That he wanted another chance with her. That he wanted to try again.

Had he said all that before or after he'd seen Eric?

Before, her mind whispered, and she looked over to

him as he bent his tall frame and got in the passenger seat. He had to move it back, which he did with a chuckle. "I haven't been in a sedan for a while," he said.

No, men as important and as rich as Morris drove expensive trucks that cost more than her house. Leighann didn't like the poisonous thoughts, and she once again reminded herself that *she* had chosen not to tell him about his son. Her. She couldn't then blame him for not knowing about his son.

"Where do you want to go?" she asked

"Where's his favorite place?" Morris asked.

Heat filled Leighann from head to toe. Of course he'd just want his son to be happy. She almost wished Morris would be selfish or unkind. Then he wouldn't be quite so perfect.

"We don't really go out to eat," she admitted, the heat flying through her for a new reason now. "I, uh, don't have much money for things like that." She looked away from him, her eyelashes fluttering strangely for some reason. Almost like if she couldn't see him, he wouldn't be able to see her.

"Leighann," he said quietly.

"We're fine," she said, perhaps a bit too harshly. She took a deep breath. "Since I got the job at the lodge, we've been fine." She glanced over to him, not truly looking at him. "Better."

He nodded and said, "Let's go to Devil's Tower. They have kid food there."

The drive didn't take long, and Leighann let Morris lead. He leaned into the hostess podium, and Leighann wasn't surprised when they got seated in a corner of the restaurant where hardly anyone else sat.

Morris sat on one side of the booth, with Leighann and Eric on the other. He looked at her and flicked his eyes to Eric. Again, and then again.

Leighann didn't need to see a menu. She hadn't been back in Coral Canyon for a year yet, but Devil's Tower was a staple. She gently took the crayon from Eric's fingers. "Baby," she said as he looked up at her. She nodded to Morris across the table. "Do you know who that is?"

Eric looked at Morris, and they looked like twins. Like him and Gabe did. Like Eric was a carbon copy of Morris, without any of her DNA in there at all. She knew he had it, because she'd carried him for a full nine months. But he was all Young, from head to toe.

"Yeah," he said. "Morris."

"He's your father, Eric," she said. The words weren't as hard to say as she'd anticipated. "Your daddy. Morris is your daddy."

Eric looked at him again, and Morris reached across the table and tapped his nose. "We have the same face," he said. "Can you see it?"

Eric got up on his feet on the bench, not bothering to get down and go around. He never did. Counters and stools, tables and chairs, were just obstacles for him to climb. He went over the table and sat right in front of Morris.

He chuckled as he took off his cowboy hat and tossed it on the bench beside him. Leighann's heart melted into a pile of goo as she watched them interact. "You have a beard," Eric said as he touched Morris's face.

"Yeah, I do," he said. "You have my eyes." They looked at one another, and Morris leaned down and touched his lips to the boy's forehead. It was so sweet and so pure, tears came to Leighann's eyes again.

"All right," Morris said. "You go sit by your momma again."

She helped him back to the bench, then met Morris's eyes again. "I'm sorry," she said.

"I'm going to call my brother the moment I get home," he said, his smile fading away. He picked up his menu as if he needed to look at it. "He owns a father's rights firm in Jackson, and he'll make sure we work this out the right way."

Fear squeezed Leighann's lungs. "Are you going to take him away from me?"

Morris looked at her from over the top of his menu. "How old is he, Leighann?"

She swallowed, not sure where he was going with this. "He was born in July," she said. "July eighth. He just turned three."

Anger flashed across Morris's face, and that was an emotion Leighann hadn't seen from him very often. It only struck more shame through her, as well as another healthy dose of terror.

"You should've told me in February," he said. "When we bumped into each other at the lodge." His dark eyes burned with fire. "July eighth was less than a month ago. You should've told me, so I didn't miss his birthday for the third time in a row." His voice grew louder with every word, and Leighann didn't know how to absorb all the negativity flowing from him.

He buried himself behind the menu again. "Who takes care of him while you're at the lodge?"

"Denzel," she whispered.

"Mm, he's injured," Morris said. "I'll be picking him up in the morning. What time do you leave for work?"

"You have your volunteer shift at the hospital."

The menu came down again, and Morris quirked his eyebrows at her. "What time? And I need your address."

She swallowed, as he'd given her zero wiggle room. "I have to be up there for breakfast," she said, hating how shaky her voice came out. "I leave at five-thirty."

"I'll be there at five-twenty-five," he said.

"He's not up by then."

He put his menu down on the table. "Are you seriously going to argue with me about this? You'll be lucky if I don't show up with my lawyer brother and a pair of cops and pack up everything he owns and take it and him back to my place."

She shook her head, her tears splashing her face. "Please, Morris."

"Three years you stole from me," he said. He took a deep breath and closed his eyes. When they opened again, dangerous fire burned there. "I'll call my brother tonight. He'll tell me my rights. I want to take care of him while you're at work, so I'll be at your place at five-twenty-five. I don't care if I have to go into his room and carry him out while he sleeps. He's *my* son, and I have rights."

Leighann nodded, her stomach jittery and vibrating. "Yes, you do."

Morris deflated, as the angry bad-cop wasn't really his style. "I'm sorry." He exhaled too. "There's a lot to work out."

She nodded, glancing over to Eric. He colored away on the paper depicting the real Devil's Tower Monument. "He'll be ready for you in the morning." She met Morris's eyes again. "We'll work something out."

"Thank you." He didn't go back to the menu, and his gaze shifted to his son. "Would you have said no?"

"What?"

"After tonight. The dinner. The dancing at the wedding." He looked at her again. "If we'd been able to do that, would you have then told me no, you didn't want to see me again? You didn't want give us another shot?"

Leighann's chest felt like someone had scrubbed it clean with steel wool. She swallowed, her mouth so dry.

No one had brought them anything to drink yet, which she found odd. "No," she said. "I wouldn't have said no."

Morris nodded, and he actually smiled a tiny, shy smile at her. "Okay," he said. "Well, let's see what happens then."

~

Coming soon!

Tex (Book 1): He's back in town after a successful country music career. She owns a bordering farm to the family land he wants to buy...and she outbids him at the auction. Can Tex and Abigail rekindle their old flame, or will the issue of land ownership come between them?

Otis (Book 2): He's finished with his last album and looking for a soft place to fall after a devastating break-up. She runs the small town bookshop in Coral Canyon and needs a new boyfriend to get her old one out of her life for good. Can Georgia convince Otis to take another shot at real love when their first kiss was fake?

Morris (Book 3): Morris Young is just settling into his new life as the manager of Country Quad when he attends a wedding. He sees his ex-wife there—apparently Leighann is back in Coral Canyon—along with a little boy who can't be more or less than five years old... Could he be Morris's? And why is his heart hoping for that, and for a reconciliation with the woman who left him because he traveled too much?

Trace (Book 4): He's been accused of only dating celebrities. She's a simple line dance instructor in small town Coral Canyon, with a soft spot for kids...and cowboys. Trace could use some dance lessons to go along with his love lessons... Can he and Everly fall in love with the beat, or will she dance her way right out of his arms?

Her Cowboy Billionaire Birthday Wish (Book 1): All the maid at Whiskey Mountain Lodge wants for her birthday is a handsome cowboy billionaire. And Colton can make that wish come true—if only he hadn't escaped to Coral Canyon after being left at the altar...

Her Cowboy Billionaire Butler (Book 2): She broke up with him to date another man...who broke her heart. He's a former CEO with nothing to do who can't get her out of his head. Can Wes and Bree find a way toward happily-ever-after at Whiskey Mountain Lodge?

Her Cowboy Billionaire Best Friend's Brother (Book 3): She's best friends with the single dad cowboy's brother and has watched two friends find love with the sexy new cowboys in town. When Gray Hammond comes to Whiskey Mountain Lodge with his son, will Elise finally get her own happily-ever-after with one of the Hammond brothers?

Her Cowboy Billionaire Beast (Book 4): A cowboy billionaire beast, his new manager, and the Christmas traditions that soften his heart and bring them together.

Her Cowboy Billionaire Bad Boy (Book 5): A cowboy billionaire cop who's a stickler for rules, the woman he pulls over when he's not even on duty, and the personal mandates he has to break to keep her in his life...

Books in the Christmas in Coral Canyon Romance series

Her Cowboy Billionaire Best Friend (Book 1): Graham Whittaker returns to Coral Canyon a few days after Christmas—after the death of his father. He takes over the energy company his dad built from the ground up and buys a high-end lodge to live in—only a mile from the home of his once-best friend, Laney McAllister. They were best friends once, but Laney's always entertained feelings for him, and spending so much time with him while they make Christmas memories puts her heart in danger of getting broken again...

Her Cowboy Billionaire Boss (Book 2): Since the death of his wife a few years ago, Eli Whittaker has been running from one job to another, unable to find somewhere for him and his son to settle. Meg Palmer is Stockton's nanny, and she comes with her boss, Eli, to the lodge, her long-time crush on the man no different in Wyoming than it was on the beach. When she confesses her feelings for him and gets nothing in return, she's crushed, embarrassed, and unsure if she can stay in Coral Canyon for Christmas. Then Eli starts to show some feelings for her too...

Her Cowboy Billionaire Boyfriend (Book 3): Andrew Whittaker is the public face for the Whittaker Brothers' family energy company, and with his older brother's robot about to be announced, he needs a press secretary to help him get everything ready and tour the state to make the announcements. When he's hit by a protest sign being carried by the company's biggest opponent, Rebecca Collings, he learns with a few clicks that she has the background they need. He offers her the job of press secretary when she thought she was going to be arrested, and not only because the spark between them in so hot Andrew can't see straight.

Can Becca and Andrew work together and keep their relationship a secret? Or will hearts break in this classic romance retelling reminiscent of *Two Weeks Notice*?

Her Cowboy Billionaire Bodyguard (Book 4): Beau Whittaker has watched his brothers find love one by one, but every attempt he's made has ended in disaster. Lily Everett has been in the spotlight since childhood and has half a dozen platinum records with her two sisters. She's taking a break from the brutal music industry and hiding out in Wyoming while her ex-husband continues to cause trouble for her. When she hears of Beau Whittaker and what he offers his clients, she wants to meet him. Beau is instantly attracted to Lily, but he tried a relationship with his last client that left a scar that still hasn't healed...

Can Lily use the spirit of Christmas to discover what matters most? Will Beau open his heart to the possibility of love with someone so different from him?

Her Cowboy Billionaire Bull Rider (Book 5): Todd Christopherson has just retired from the professional rodeo circuit and returned to his hometown of Coral Canyon. Problem is, he's got no family there anymore, no land, and no job. Not that he needs a job--he's got plenty of money from his illustrious career riding bulls.

Then Todd gets thrown during a routine horseback ride up the canyon, and his only support as he recovers physically is the beautiful Violet Everett. She's no nurse, but she does the best she can for the handsome cowboy. **Will she lose her heart to the billionaire bull rider? Can Todd trust that God led him to Coral Canyon...and Vi?**

Her Cowboy Billionaire Bachelor (Book 6): Rose Everett isn't sure what to do with her life now that her country music career is on hold. After all, with both of her sisters in Coral Canyon, and one about to have a baby, they're not making albums anymore.

Liam Murphy has been working for Doctors Without Borders, but he's back in the US now, and looking to start a new clinic in Coral Canyon, where he spent his summers.

When Rose wins a date with Liam in a bachelor auction, their relationship blooms and grows quickly. **Can Liam and Rose find a solution to their problems that doesn't involve one of them leaving Coral Canyon with a broken heart?**

Her Cowboy Billionaire Blind Date (Book 7): Her sons want her to be happy, but she's too old to be set up on a blind date...isn't she?

Amanda Whittaker has been looking for a second chance at love since the death of her husband several years ago. Finley Barber is a cowboy in every sense of the word. Born and raised on a racehorse farm in Kentucky, he's since moved to Dog Valley and started his own breeding stable for champion horses. He hasn't dated in years, and everything about Amanda makes him nervous.

Will Amanda take the leap of faith required to be with Finn? Or will he become just another boyfriend who doesn't make the cut?

Her Cowboy Billionaire Best Man (Book 8): When Celia Abbott-Armstrong runs into a gorgeous cowboy at her best friend's wedding, she decides she's ready to start dating again.

But the cowboy is Zach Zuckerman, and the Zuckermans and Abbotts have been at war for generations.

Can Zach and Celia find a way to reconcile their family's differences so they can have a future together?

His First Love (Book 1): She broke up with him a decade ago. He's back in town after finishing a degree at MIT, ready to start his job at the family company. Can Hunter and Molly find their way through their pasts to build a future together?

His Second Chance (Book 2): They broke up over twenty years ago. She's lost everything when she shows up at the farm in Ivory Peaks where he works. Can Matt and Gloria heal from their pasts to find a future happily-ever-after with each other?

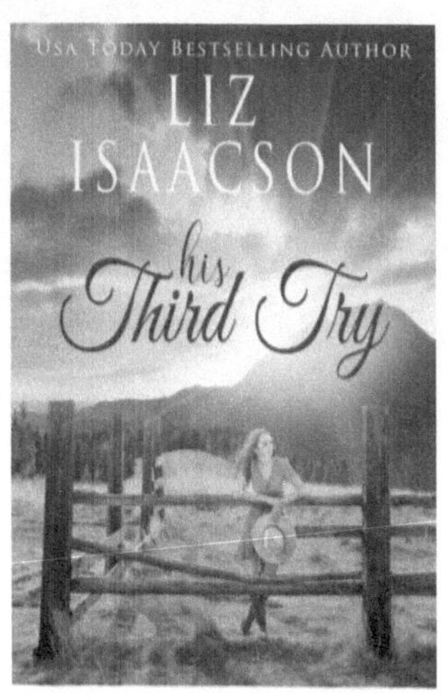

His Third Try (Book 3): He moved to Ivory Peaks with his daughter to start over after a devastating break-up. She's never had a meaningful relationship with a man, especially a cowboy. Can Boone and Cosette help each other heal enough to build a happily-ever-after...and a family?

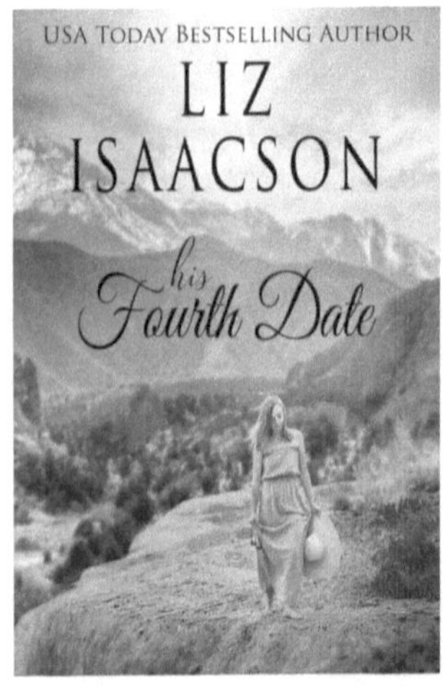

His Fourth Date (Book 4): Their relationship has been nothing but loose goats, a leaking roof, and her complete humiliation after he pays her mortgage so she won't lose her farm. Travis wants to go back in time and start over with Poppy, but he doesn't know how. Can a small town speed-dating event get their second chance off on the right foot?

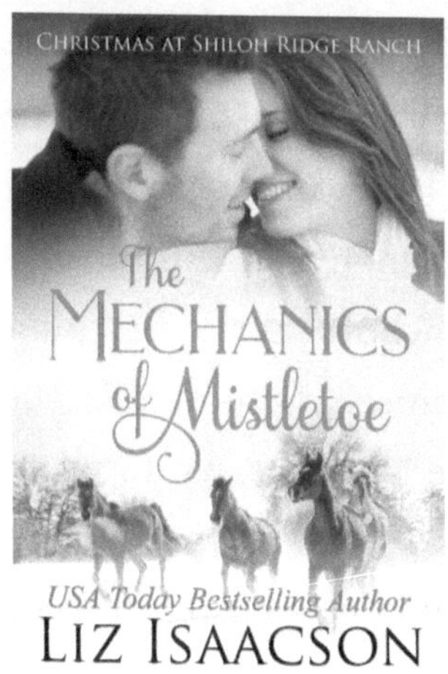

The Mechanics of Mistletoe (Book 1): Bear Glover can be a grizzly or a teddy, and he's always thought he'd be just fine working his generational family ranch and going back to the ancient homestead alone. But his crush on Samantha Benton won't go away. She's a genius with a wrench on Bear's tractors...and his heart. Can he tame his wild side and get the girl, or will he be left broken-hearted this Christmas season?

The Horsepower of the Holiday (Book 2): Ranger Glover has worked at Shiloh Ridge Ranch his entire life. The cowboys do everything from horseback there, but when he goes to town to trade in some trucks, somehow Oakley Hatch persuades him to take some ATVs back to the ranch. (Bear is NOT happy.)

She's a former race car driver who's got Ranger all revved up... Can he remember who he is and get Oakley to slow down enough to fall in love, or will there simply be too much horsepower in the holiday this year for a real relationship?

The Construction of Cheer (Book 3): Bishop Glover is the youngest brother, and he usually keeps his head down and gets the job done. When Montana Martin shows up at Shiloh Ridge Ranch looking for work, he finds himself inventing construction projects that need doing just to keep her coming around. (Again, Bear is NOT happy.) She wants to build her own construction firm, but she ends up carving a place for herself inside Bishop's heart. Can he convince her *he's* all she needs this Christmas season, or will her cheer rest solely on the success of her business?

The Secret of Santa (Book 4): He's a fun-loving cowboy with a heart of gold. She's the woman who keeps putting him on hold. Can Ace and Holly Ann make a relationship work this Christmas?

The Harmony of Holly (Book 5): He's as prickly as his name, but the new woman in town has caught his eye. Can Cactus shelve his temper and shed his cowboy hermit skin fast enough to make a relationship with Willa work?

The Chemistry of Christmas (Book 6): He's the black sheep of the family, and she's a chemist who understands formulas, not emotions. Can Preacher and Charlie take their quirks and turn them into a strong relationship this Christmas?

The Delivery of Decor (Book 7): When he falls, he falls hard and deep. She literally drives away from every relationship she's ever had. Can Ward somehow get Dot to stay this Christmas?

The Blessing of Babies (Book 8): Don't miss out on a single moment of the Glover family saga in this bridge story linking Ward and Judge's love stories!

The Glovers love God, country, dogs, horses, and family. Not necessarily in that order. ;)

Many of them are married now, with babies on the way, and there are lessons to be learned, forgiveness to be had and given, and new names coming to the family tree in southern Three Rivers!

The Networking of the Nativity (Book 9): He's had a crush on her for years. She doesn't want to date until her daughter is out of the house. Will June take a change on Judge when the success of his Christmas light display depends on her networking abilities?

The Wrangling of the Wreath (Book 10): He's been so busy trying to find Miss Right. She's been right in front of him the whole time. This Christmas, can Mister and Libby take their relationship out of the best friend zone?

The Hope of Her Heart (Book 11): She's the only Glover without a significant other. He's been searching for someone who can love him *and* his daughter. Can Etta and August make a meaningful connection this Christmas?

Rhett's Make-Believe Marriage (Book 1): She needs a husband to be credible as a matchmaker. He wants to help a neighbor. Will their fake marriage take them out of the friend zone?

Tripp's Trivial Tie (Book 2): She needs a husband to keep her son. He's wanted to take their relationship to the next level, but she's always pushing him away. Will their trivial tie take them all the way to happily-ever-after?

Liam's Invented I-Do (Book 3): She's desperate to save her ranch. He wants to help her any way he can. Will their invented I-Do open doors that have previously been closed and lead to a happily-ever-after for both of them?

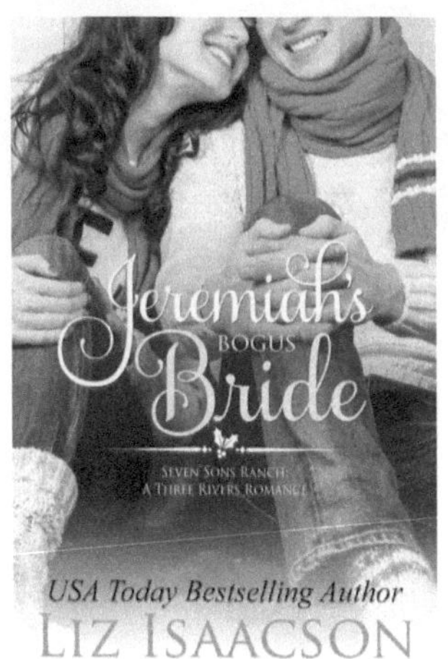

Jeremiah's Bogus Bride (Book 4): He wants to prove to his brothers that he's not broken. She just wants him. Will a fake marriage heal him or push her further away?

Wyatt's Pretend Pledge (Book 5): To get her inheritance, she needs a husband. He's wanted to fly with her for ages. Can their pretend pledge turn into something real?

Skyler's Wanna-Be Wife (Book 6): She needs a new last name to stay in school. He's willing to help a fellow student. Can this wanna-be wife show the playboy that some things should be taken seriously?

Micah's Mock Matrimony (Book 7): They were just actors auditioning for a play. The marriage was just for the audition – until a clerical error results in a legal marriage. Can these two ex-lovers negotiate this new ground between them and achieve new roles in each other's lives?

About Liz

Liz Isaacson writes inspirational romance, usually set in Texas, or Wyoming, or anywhere else horses and cowboys exist. She lives in Utah, where she writes full-time, takes her two dogs to the park everyday, and eats a lot of veggies while writing. Find her on her website at lizisaacson.com.

www.ingramcontent.com/pod-product-compliance
Lightning Source LLC
Chambersburg PA
CBHW050609110726
47899CB00001B/32

9781638761198